By REX DANCER

SIMON & SCHUSTER
New York   London   Toronto
Sydney   Tokyo   Singapore

Postcard from Hell

SIMON & SCHUSTER
Rockefeller Center
1230 Avenue of the Americas
New York, New York 10020

SIMON & SCHUSTER and colophon are registered trademarks
of Simon & Schuster Inc.

Designed by Hyun Joo Kim
Manufactured in the United States of America

10   9   8   7   6   5   4   3   2   1

Library of Congress Cataloging-in-Publication Data

Dancer, Rex, date.
   Postcard from Hell / by Rex Dancer.
      p.   cm.
   I. Title.
PS3554.A514P6   1995
813'.54—dc20   94–40420   CIP

ISBN 0-684-80362-3

For Kelly Cibulas, and Kelly McGillis

Chapter

·1·

It was the slowest, deadest part of night, when time itself was barely moving, and André Derain was wide awake—again.

Two months had passed since he and his *belle amie* Bleusette Lescaut had moved from her place in the French Quarter into his deceased parents' house in the Garden District. Andy—only his relatives used the formal "André"—couldn't recall a decent night's sleep in all that time.

Something was wrong. Wrongest of all, he didn't know what it was.

Maybe it was just the quiet. The Garden District was as purely New Orleans as the Quarter, yet altogether different, and maddeningly quiet. In the Quarter, especially around Bleusette's big house on Burgundy Street, prowling humanity had kept the night hours full of sounds: music, laughter, drunken shouts and curses, the occasional scream, and the recurring punctuation of police sirens—much like New York, another place Andy had called home.

Here in the mouldering, genteel, historic Garden District, nothing ever stirred in the soft, ghostly darkness. Occasionally, a dog might bark or a cat skitter across the roof, or he'd hear the faint rattle of a streetcar moving along St. Charles Avenue. Andy liked it when a storm would roll in across the bayous from the Gulf of Mexico. He'd drift into dreams amidst the comforting sounds of thunder and wind and drumming rain. But then he'd awaken again, to the thick, heavy, dead quiet.

Worse than the quiet was the lack of music. In the Quarter, there was always music—a nearby radio or phonograph, someone playing a sax or a harmonica or a guitar—at any odd hour of the night. In the Garden District, no one played anything. Here the night was for sleeping or the dull babble of some idiot television set.

Sometimes, of course, for better or worse, there was the telephone. It rang now, a sudden, shrill summons.

Andy rolled over and snatched up the receiver, lest another ring awaken the lovely, dark-haired woman slumbering beside him. Bleusette did not appreciate late-night disturbances. She'd had enough of those in her previous career.

"Yes?" he said quietly, into the mouthpiece.

The easy, rumbly, slow-talking voice on the other end belonged to Lieutenant Paul Maljeux of the French Quarter's Vieux Carré District police station. A good friend of Derain's in high school, Maljeux was a better one now—two decades later. There was a slight edge of excitement to his speech, but no real urgency. Never that. Maljeux would doubtless make a long rambling soliloquy out of his call for help if he were drowning.

"Sorry to wake you, Andy boy. I wouldn't do it except that I thought you might be grievous vexed with me if I didn't, considering what's afoot."

"You didn't wake me," said Derain. "I was just lying here listening to the clouds move. What's up?"

"Well, if you haven't hocked all those fancy cameras of yours, I think I got a job of work for you."

Work. When he'd been living in New York, Andy had been one of the most successful fashion and celebrity photographers in the business. He'd had picture spreads in *Vanity Fair* and done covers for *Vogue* and once was even honored with a small solo exhibition at the Whitney Museum. Since coming back home to New Orleans with his mental state and career in tatters, he'd supported himself mostly by shooting parties and weddings and freelancing the occasional crime story. His earnings for the month just ended had come to five hundred and thirty-two dollars and seventy-five cents. He'd convinced himself that he didn't mind, that it was worth it just to be out of New York and the fast lane and back in New Orleans, the natural habitat of the burned-out case, a town known for the slows.

"Kind of a late hour for wedding pictures," he said, "or is someone after a high school graduation portrait?"

"Ain't no nuptials we got on our hands here, Andy," Maljeux said. "You're still selling crime photos to the newspapers, right?"

"On the rare occasion when they're willing to part with a few extra bucks—which isn't often these days."

"Well, I think this is going to be one of those occasions. We got us a real first-class murder. A homicide *très sérieuse*. You know Crayfish Joe Coquin?"

Joseph Coquin was famed as one of New Orleans' great gourmands and one of the biggest mobsters in the city, his amplitude one of fleshly as well as criminal importance.

"Someone whacked Crayfish Joe?" said Andy. "It'd take an awful lot of bullets to fill up that sleazebag."

Maljeux gave one of his friendlier chuckles. "Wasn't Crayfish who just left this life in such a hurry. It was his pretty-boy son Philippe. Down on Tchoupitoulas Street by Audubon Park. Seems the amorous young *gentilhomme* was exploring the wonders of some good-lookin' bimbette in that red Ferrari of his, when an evil person or persons unknown happened upon them. The patrol officer on the scene reports one of the victims was shot up so bad all that's left is the makin's of étouffée."

Derain could hear another voice interjecting some obscene comment in the background, which Maljeux ignored. There was laughter.

"I just now got the call, Andy," the lieutenant continued. "I told the officer on the scene to stay off the radio with this, given the gravity of the situation and Crayfish Joe's tendency to rashness when something riles him, as this will surely do. Joe's got people listening to the police channels all the time. But the regular newsies gonna get wind of this soon enough. If you get on down there *tout de suite*, I'll see to it you get a few snaps of the bodily trauma before the evidence guys move in. But you gotta hurry.

Tchoupitoulas and the park. The car's on the river side of the street. Red Ferrari."

"Got it."

"Don't understand why we didn't get a citizens call on this one. The gunfire should have sounded like Mardi Gras."

"Silencers, maybe?"

"Silencers. That's right. Professionals. This one's probably gonna be a long solve."

"Much obliged, Paul. See you there."

Andy hung up and sat on the edge of the bed. He wasn't obliged at all. He was in no mood for photographic studies of human beings shot into stew. Maybe just lying there listening to the peeping insects and muttering birds for what remained of the night wouldn't be so bad after all.

"Who the fuck was that, Andy?"

Bleusette rolled over on her side to look at him. She sounded very sleepy—and irritated. She had very dark eyes, but they picked up glints of light, like a wild animal's in the woods.

"It was Paul."

"Son of a bitch. Maljeux know I get up at goddamn six o'clock to open my restaurant. It's not like when I was in the life."

"He was tipping me to a shoot. A murder down by the river. Some big-time gangster's son. The pictures ought to be worth some money."

"Fuck pictures. You want to make some money, come help me out in my restaurant. *Mon Dieu,* you could make more on busboy tips than you do with those cameras."

"I didn't come back to New Orleans to be a busboy, darlin'."

"What gangster's son?"

"Crayfish Joe Coquin's. Philippe."

"Philippe? I lose a good night's sleep because of that bastard Philippe Coquin? When you gonna give up this shit, Andy?"

"It's what I do, Bleusette. I'm a photographer. It's all I've ever been."

"You told me you were only going to be an artist now. Take art pictures—maybe a few weddings in your spare time. Not fucking dead gangsters. Who wants to look at those? When you gonna start taking art pictures again?"

Andy stared at the darkness. They'd pursued this line of discourse before—almost every day, lately.

"Go back to sleep, darlin'. I won't be long." He patted her bare thigh.

She turned away from him. "I straightened out my life, Andy. *Tout droit*. When the hell you gonna do that with yours?"

"I thought I did that when I came back to New Orleans."

"You're still a fucked up mess, Andy. *Bien sûr*."

This was his dead mother's bed and the woman in it was not his wife—not yet. Up until a few months before, Bleusette had been a prostitute, fabled in the French Quarter as one of the most beautiful—and most expensive—women ever to have practiced that trade in New Orleans. She'd also been one of the best dressed, cleverest and most careful. No drugs, no diseases, no pimps, no bad boyfriends, except for the occasional besotted saxophone player—and now, occasional burned-out photographer. Only a couple of abortions, long ago, and a continuing penchant for Pernod, straight. A mix of Cajun, Creole, and Irish, with just a touch *"de couleur,"* Bleusette was a child of the bayous who had gone off with her mother to the Caribbean, turning up again as a teenager in New Orleans to practice her mother's trade because that was all she knew—though she'd been taught much. Andy had known her nearly all his adult life, staying in touch with her throughout his years in New York.

Andy's own mother, with her feigned and exaggerated sense of propriety, would have been outraged to find Bleusette not only in her bed but fully installed as chatelaine of what the tour guides working the Garden District liked to point out as "the Derain mansion."

But his late mother had put in a few years herself in Baton Rouge roadhouses and legislators' hotel rooms before latching on to Andy's high-born, philandering, physician/politician father. In New Orleans, you never wanted to dig into things very deep. Not the mouldy façades of the decaying old houses; not the lives of the those who dwelled therein.

The Derains were considered "old New Orleans." The hypocritical snobs who used such terms failed to appreciate that women like Bleusette represented the oldest New Orleans. Some of her ancestors had been strutting the Quarter when the city belonged to Spain.

Andy rose and went into the adjoining bathroom, closing the door gently and then bending down a little to look at himself in the small, old-fashioned round mirror that hung over the basin. Andy was six feet tall and used to bending, as Bleusette was all of five foot four.

Splashing water over his face and brushing down his over-long and lately graying sandy hair didn't improve his sleep-starved appearance much. He was only thirty-seven, but the handsomeness that had helped make him such a glamorous fig-ure in his fashionable New York days had begun to wear away. There were deepening creases alongside his mouth, and his thin lips now seemed to turn habitually downward. His brown eyes looked dull and tired, as though weary from all that they'd seen. He'd begun, he supposed, to resemble his life.

It helped when he smiled—people, especially women, were still charmed by that—but he wasn't up to so amiable an expres-sion at the moment. His "job of work," as Maljeux had called it, wasn't going to be a lot of fun.

Two more murders. All those years of continual police sirens in New York, yet there he'd never seen a single corpse. Since com-ing back to New Orleans, he must have looked upon a good three dozen or more dead people—all up close.

Étouffée.

"If you're not going to be happy, then you should come back to New Orleans," Bleusette had told him on a bleak, despairing night two years before, when he'd called her, half drunk and des-perate, from his expensive Upper East Side Manhattan apart-ment. "Best place in the whole goddamn world to be unhappy, *bien sûr.* You come back home, Andy. It's time."

And so he had, renting what had once been slave quarters in the rear of Bleusette's big Burgundy Street house, installing a photo studio on the ground floor and living quarters on the level above. And that had been fine. Bleusette had long been his friend and proved an amiable landlord as well—and in time, quite something more.

And soon now, maybe, his wife. She'd suggested marriage, and he'd quickly affirmed the idea, though they hadn't gotten much beyond that. In the days before World War I, when the Sto-ryville madams reigned supreme in New Orleans, it was common for crib girls to marry respectable customers. Andy hadn't exactly been a client of Bleusette's, but he'd been happy enough in her company—and that of other prostitutes of the town. In this he followed the example of his idol Ernest Bellocq, the turn-of-the-century photographer who had been to New Orleans' whorehouses what Toulouse-Lautrec had been to Paris's Moulin Rouge.

Andy had taken a lot of photographs of whores for the book of nudes he had hoped to complete but now doubted he ever would since most of the prints he'd collected for it were now microscopic pieces of ash floating around the Louisiana sky somewhere. Bellocq had never done a book; his original prints were in a little archival museum on Royal Street and his plates owned by a collector in New York. Andy's book was to have been a homage. Now they'd both likely be forgotten.

Returning to the bedroom, Andy dressed as quickly and quietly as he could—pulling on a pair of khaki shorts and an old white shirt and slipping his bare feet into a beat-up pair of boating moccasins. It was fall, but the heat still hadn't let go of New Orleans. He wished there was time for a shower.

Bleusette stirred again just as he was about to go out the bedroom door.

"You want to kiss me goodbye, Andy?"

"Sure." He went to the bed, leaned over, and touched his lips to her silky, bare bottom.

"When we get married," she said, "you still gonna do that?"

"Of course," he said, straightening. "I'm a traditional guy, and that's an old New Orleans tradition."

"I know some others lot older than that."

"Some I never heard of, probably."

"Ain't nothin' you never heard of, Andy."

"*À bientôt*, darlin'."

She turned her head away, settling back on the pillow. "By the time you get back, I will be working this very same ass off in the restaurant."

Her recently opened French Quarter café, specializing in tourist favorites, had been her idea, not his. He said nothing more as he closed the door behind him.

There were two other women in the house—his elderly Auntie Claire, who had been living there since Andy was a small child, and the family's longtime maid, Zinnia, who had been there even longer. Both, he was sure, were asleep. He went down the stairs and out the front door with a care not to awaken either of them. He felt enough of an interloper in "the Derain mansion" as it was.

He saw a curtain move in an upstairs window of his next-door neighbor's house. It was never too early or too late for Mrs. Boulanger to be at her prying and spying, though she otherwise refused any dealings with the Derain household. Bleusette had told him how much she had longed for the respectability of the Garden District—until she finally moved into it. Now, in her own words, she was beginning to find the bourgeois life "a *très grand* pain in the ass."

He said his usual prayer as he turned the key in the ignition of his rusty white 1977 Cadillac convertible. This time it was answered. He waited until he was sure all the engine's cylinders were firing, then clunked the overlong, ancient car into reverse and backed down the drive.

He headed toward the river, thinking again of Maljeux's description of the victims—and of another possible reason for his sleeplessness. There were few human beings walking the planet and the French Quarter that he cared for as much as he did Bleusette. He'd no more hurt her than he would his Auntie Claire. But the notion of him and Bleusette as the happy, domesticated married couple was beginning to make him nervous—and maybe a little *un*happy.

Maybe he would have done better praying for the engine not to start.

Chapter
·2·

The murder had attracted a large crowd of police, but no civilians had yet come to gawk at the gore, probably because of the early hour. Maljeux was standing just inside the yellow crime scene tape that had been strung all over the area, talking with some plainclothes detectives. None of them seemed to be doing much of anything.

On duty, Paul almost always wore a neatly pressed uniform, no matter how soggy the heat. This night, the lieutenant was in tan pants, open-collared yellow shirt, and black-and-white checked jacket. Andy guessed he had been summoned from some off-duty retreat—probably his late-night hangout, One-Legged Duffy's, a quiet jazz joint over in Faubourg Marigny. The lieutenant, one of the better amateur musicians in New Orleans, occasionally sat in on trumpet there.

Duffy's was owned by a Creole pianist named Loomis Demarest, who, discreetly, was also Maljeux's lover. Only Andy and a few others knew about this secret liaison. Maljeux's wife was not among the few others. No one, not even among the criminals Maljeux regularly rousted, was of a mind to inform her of this interesting circumstance. The rule in the French Quarter was laissez faire. Everybody had a secret. You left it at that.

"We're just waitin' on the forensics boys, Andy," the lieutenant said, lifting up the tape to admit his friend. "You got a few
minutes, but you'd better make use of 'em."

"Always try to. They find you at Duffy's?"

Maljeux nodded, moving with Andy toward the Ferrari.
"Loomis and I were having us a nightcap or two and tootling
around a little. He got a new Diane Schuur CD, and we were
working up a little of her style on 'Louisiana Sunday Afternoon.'
Hot but sweet. Real nice song."

"How come you caught the case? This is a long way from the
French Quarter."

"Homicide's got the case," Maljeux said. "The chief asked me
to get on the scene as senior officer—in case Crayfish Joe shows
up and needs a little calming down. I guess I know him better
than anyone else in the department. This isn't the most joyous
news he's gonna hear this week. We're waitin' on making the
next-of-kin call till we can get the bodies out of here, but word
moves fast in this town."

"Only thing that does."

The Ferrari and surrounding crime scene had been brilliantly
lit by some portable floodlights, and the shot-up sports car was
like something on display at an auto show—a macabre, surrealis-
tic auto show. A detective was poking around on the other side of
the vehicle, reminding Andy of a street person looking for something useful in a trash basket.

"It's okay with the homicide guys that I take some pictures?"
Andy removed the lens cap from his battered Nikon, pausing to
set the f-stop after estimating the exposure. With all this light, he
could get a good picture with an Instamatic.

"It's okay with them if it's okay with me, and you know I
never mind having you around practicing your art on deceased
citizens. Just don't mess with anything."

Andy could see what looked to be the mostly naked body of a
dark-haired woman bent double over the back of the Ferrari's
front seat. Except for her long, black hair, she was colored as
bright a red as the car's exterior. The gaudy hue hadn't come
from paint. Andy glanced away, taking a couple of deep breaths
before looking back.

"Don't worry. I won't touch a thing."

The girl apparently had attempted to escape into the back—a

pointless act of final desperation. The skirt of her short dress was hiked above her hips and the top pulled down to her waist, though this was likely young Coquin's work, not the killer or killers'. She was wearing neither bra nor panties. This took some looking to notice. The glaze of blood over her body was thick.

Now he could hear sirens. Doubtless more police.

The windshield and passenger side window had been shot out, and he was able to get several clear pictures. He snapped them very quickly. The many bullet holes in the woman's back, buttocks, and legs looked like the pockmarks of some horrible disease. There was nothing in this view that the local papers would want to put on anyone's breakfast table. Andy moved around to the passenger door in hopes of a more seemly shot, finding a decorous angle that showed only her bare shoulder and hair.

He thought of moving closer, then changed his mind. He didn't want to look at the woman's face. It disturbed him that her hair was so much like Bleusette's.

Moving to the driver's side of the Ferrari, he found young Coquin's remains lying facedown on the pavement beside the open door, one foot still in the car, caught and held twisted beneath the seat. Philippe was wearing an expensive-looking and very shiny light gray suit. His pants were down. Coitus interruptus.

Andy aimed his camera so the viewfinder showed only Coquin's back and head and the Ferrari's left rear wheel. He shot a few frames, stepped back, shot a few more, and then felt a hand on his shoulder.

"Didn't think you could make all that much love in a Ferrari," Maljeux said. "That gearshift could cause serious injury."

"They've had their share of that."

"You take notice of what's wrong here, Andy?" Maljeux said. In habit, he smoothed down his thinning blond hair, then removed his gold-framed aviator glasses and wiped them clean with a freshly pressed handkerchief. This often signaled that he had arrived at some conclusion.

Derain stared at the car and bodies, then shrugged. "They're in a No Parking zone?"

"That New York humor, Andy?"

"Something like that."

"Well, what's wrong is that the woman took most of the

rounds—nearly all of them, and from two different directions. Looks like they emptied a couple of automatic-pistol magazines into her. But the late Philippe here, he's got only two bullet wounds. One in the shoulder, and one through the head. They wanted him dead, sure enough, but the lady—her they wanted pureed."

Andy could now see the front part of her head. He turned away. "I think I've got enough."

"What I'm getting at," said Maljeux, "is that I don't figure this to be any kind of mob hit directed at the Coquin family. Nothing to do with business competition, *compris?* Crayfish and the other *grands hommes* in town have been gettin' along just fine lately. No sir, I think this was some kind of a Frankie and Johnny, like we get from time to time in the Quarter. Usually it's just knives or razors. I think this poor lady was doin' somebody double, and he called her play. Philippe just picked the wrong place and time to pitch some woo."

"He sure picked the wrong lady. Who was she?"

"Beats the hell out of me, but we'll find out directly."

The plainclothes detective who'd been poking around the car got down on his knees and stuck his head beneath it.

"I thought you looked under there, Larsen," Maljeux said.

"I did. But this time I see something I didn't before."

The detective dropped to his belly and reached behind the tire. When he got back up again, he was holding a small automatic pistol gingerly by the barrel. He brought it close to his nose.

"I think it's been fired," he said. "But I don't think it belongs to the perps."

"It's gotta be the late Philippe's," Maljeux said. "Maybe he got himself a little last-minute vengeance."

The detective produced a plastic bag and dropped the weapon into it. Andy got a quick picture of him doing it.

"Time to go," Maljeux said.

They started walking back toward the yellow tape. More police cars were arriving, and a TV station news van was pulling up. Andy's shoe ticked against something metallic, sending the small object rolling. Maljeux scurried ahead to stop it, picking it up with his folded handkerchief.

"Brass shell casing," the lieutenant said, displaying it. "You gotta be careful, Andy. That's why we always string these yellow

tapes at crime scenes now—even nickel-dime stickups and bur-
glaries. Keep people from disturbing evidence. Did you know
that in something like ninety percent of the cases that get solved,
it results from a thorough crime-scene investigation?"

"Sorry," Andy said. "I'll be more attentive."

Maljeux squinted at the empty shell casing again, then folded
the handkerchief around it and stuck that in his pocket.

"Nine millimeter," the lieutenant said. "Too big to come from
that dainty little poker-table gun of Philippe's. We'll pick up all
the brass scattered around here and examine it for fingerprints.
You never know. Did I ever tell you we got a conviction once from
a fingerprint left on some chewing gum?"

"I think you spared me that."

Maljeux looked past Andy and up the street.

"Here come the TV boys. I'm gonna give you a little shove
when you go under the tape, like I was throwing you outa here."

"They won't believe it."

"Course they won't, but at least I can say I did it. How's
Bleusette? You two set a date yet?"

Maljeux now routinely asked this question.

"We keep talking about it, *comme toujours*. She still wants a
church wedding, or says she does, but she's not getting anywhere
with the priests. I don't think she likes their terms."

"Hell, she left the life. What do they want?"

"Something to do with religious conviction."

"Bleusette's got as much religion as the holy fathers got a
right to expect, considerin'. More than most—in the Quarter."

Maljeux lifted the tape. Andy ducked quickly under it before
his friend could give him the promised push.

"Don't let me catch you violating police regulations again,
Derain," Maljeux said loudly.

Andy kept walking. A TV reporter snatched at him.

"Hey, Andy. They ID the victim yet?"

"Yeah," said Derain, moving on. "It's some dead guy."

Chapter

·3·

Andy left the area at some speed, his mind still so fixed upon the gruesome scene he'd just photographed that he almost collided with a yellow Mercedes stretch limo that came hurtling out of a side street and swerved rudely toward him. At the last moment, it straightened and sped past him on down toward the river, barely missing Andy's left front fender.

A collision would have been doubly unfortunate. Andy recognized the stretch as Crayfish Joe Coquin's. The car had been full of faces—ghostly, pale, malevolent faces, staring straight ahead except for a man in the back, whose dark eyes peering from between folds of fat had turned with stern annoyance upon Andy's Cadillac. His expression would not help Andy's sleeplessness.

Andy headed directly for the newspaper instead of his Garden District house. He'd converted his basement into a new photographic studio of sorts, to replace the one he'd lost in the fire that had driven him and Bleusette out of the French Quarter, and he usually did his processing work there. But it seemed wiser to forgo that stop and deliver his film to the newspaper photo desk raw. Though the paper wouldn't go to press for many hours and the editors would take their time putting this story together and deciding on pictures, it would still count for something to have his roll in first.

The night photo editor, a friend, was suitably impressed with Andy's alacrity.

"You got Coquin pictures already?" he said, as Andy set the roll on his desk. "We just picked up the call."

"I was in the neighborhood," Andy said. "Exclusive close-ups. Guaranteed front page."

"We sent two photogs. The city editor won't want it to be for nothing."

"They won't be able to get what I got," Andy said, not wanting modesty to get in the way of badly needed money. "But it's a big story, right? You can run all our stuff."

"We'll see. Anyway, I'll print these up for you in either case."

"Thanks."

"Still can't figure out why you'd want to give up all that high-priced magazine work to come back down here and chase sirens—especially for what we pay you."

"It was for my health."

In terms of his mind and spirit, that was the literal truth, but most people here would take the line for a joke. In this city, health was about as big a concern as theology or medieval art. If you were worried enough, you might cut back from doubles to single shots of whiskey. Paris Moran, a movie-actress friend of his, had once said of New Orleans, "If I'd been born here, I'd be dead now."

He pulled up in his driveway just as bits of sunlight were breaking through the heavy roll of cloud to the east—the happy breadwinner home from work. It occurred to Andy that real breadwinners probably came home feeling just as sick, tired, and lousy as he did.

Few breadwinners were greeted at the door by anyone like Bleusette, however. She had come out onto the front gallery of the house and stood waiting for him. She was barefoot but wearing a very pretty and low-cut flower-print dress—clothes for the restaurant. Indeed, clothes appropriate enough for one of his Auntie Claire's afternoon garden parties. Even when she'd been in the life, Bleusette had habitually dressed like someone off to the Junior League.

Her day was now underway, too. She had what looked to be

her morning glass of Pernod in one hand, a card or envelope in the other.

Andy turned off the car's shuddering engine, then walked hesitantly up to the gallery. Bleusette was studying him with much suspicion.

"You got a postcard," she said, thrusting it forth.

The picture side showed a small wooden building set among tropical trees. The reverse bore the heavily inked circular postmark: "Hell, Cayman Islands, British West Indies." He glanced quickly at the message and the name of the sender.

"This just came?" he said.

"Yesterday. You got home so late I forgot to tell you."

He slipped it into a pocket of his shorts. The message was simple: "Here for fashion shoot. Miss you. Poor bears. Love you madly, Princess Astrid."

Bleusette leaned back against a pillar, folding her tanned arms. "This Astrid, is she one of those women you knew in New York?"

"New York, other places. Haven't talked to her in a long time. Not since I came back to New Orleans."

"Is she from here? Astrid is a French name, yes?"

Bleusette's world had two parts. There was New Orleans, and there was the rest of it.

"No. In her case, it's Icelandic. She's from North Dakota. Grew up there, anyway. She was an actress and a dancer and a model. Very big time for a while. Now she's a fashion designer."

"What is this 'princess' shit?"

"She was married for a while to a guy who claimed he was a prince. Mr. Montebello, a fellow she made the mistake of meeting in Cannes. She didn't like him very much, and I don't think he actually was a prince. They're divorced now. I helped her with that."

"How you do that, Andy?"

"I took some compromising pictures of the prince with another woman. He fooled around a lot."

"To show to a judge?"

"To show the other woman's husband. He was very rich—and in the arms business. A man with a bad temper."

"So she's single now, this 'princess'? Available for an unmarried *gentilhomme comme tu?*"

"Far as I know."

"Real good looking?"

"Yes. *Très belle.* Just like you. Only she has blond hair and blue eyes. And she's six foot two inches tall."

"*Mon Dieu.*"

"You should see her in heels."

"I don't want to. I know the Caymans. Beaucoup banks, rich tourists, scuba divers. What kind of fashion shoot they have way down there?"

Andy shrugged. "Probably bathing suits. Resort wear."

Bleusette gave him a quick and not at all friendly smile.

"At the end she say, 'poor bears.' What the fuck does that mean?"

He was tiring of this interrogation. He knew beautiful women all over the world from his fashion photographer days, as she'd long been aware. When he was living in the Quarter, he'd taken a lot of pictures of nudes, and many of the women had come to his studio to pose. Bleusette never said a thing about it, about any of them. Now this.

"Just an eccentricity. It's the last line in a play by John Osborne called *Look Back in Anger.* I took her to see a revival of it once and the line stuck in her mind. She uses it sometimes."

"Meaning what?"

"Nothing, really. Mostly when she's unhappy."

Bleusette's dark eyes looked like they were about to burst into flame.

"You haven't talked to this goddamn giant princess in, what, two years and now you get this? 'Miss you'? 'Love you madly'? 'Poor fucking bears'?"

"It's just a postcard, Bleusette."

"Don't call her."

"How can I do that? She didn't even put on a return address."

"I don't want you go down there, Andy. I know what this woman was to you."

"It was a long time ago. And it never went anywhere."

"You go down there and I will follow you with the biggest goddamn gun I can find and blow both your brains out. *Bien sûr.*"

"Look. I'm not taking any more fashion jobs, okay? She hasn't asked me to. It's just a postcard. For all I know, she's back in New York now."

"That's not what I see in your eyes. You got that look again."

"You don't know me as well as you think."

"Fuck I don't."

Andy sighed and put his arm around her. "Put on your shoes, *petite chatte*. Let me get a cup of coffee, and then I'll drive you to work."

She hesitated, then made a face and started with him back up the stairs. "Philippe Coquin, he dead for real?"

"Really for real. So is a woman who was with him."

"Working girl?"

He shrugged. "Something of the sort, I guess."

"I am sorry for her, whoever she was, but she should have known better. When I was in the life, I would stay a million fucking miles from Philippe Coquin."

Bleusette's restaurant was near Bourbon Street and its tourist crush, which was good for business but didn't endear the place to Andy. All the parking places along the block were taken, so he stopped the old Cadillac behind an idling, double-parked delivery truck, keeping his engine going.

A few cooks and busboys were loitering at the restaurant's door, smoking as they waited for Bleusette to open up. She let no one in the place unless she was on the premises, and she invariably stayed until everyone was gone. The restaurant had become profitable almost immediately after she'd opened it, but she was convinced it stayed that way only because she was always there to keep the waiters and waitresses from stealing and the cooks from drinking. To a degree this was true, but Bleusette was far too obsessive about it. What she meant by asking Andy to help out in the place was to have him spell her in watching over the staff. Andy didn't like being anybody's boss.

"You want to come in?" she said. "Nice, fresh beignets for breakfast—*tout de suite*."

"No thanks."

"Here I finally get the place of my fucking dreams and you don't step inside it but twice in three months, Andy."

"Every time this comes up I keep saying the same thing, Bleusette. Hire a manager. You can afford one."

"Who am I going to trust with that? Managers are biggest

goddamn thieves of all. I need you, Andy. Don't have to be all day. A little time in the morning, a little in the afternoon, a little in the evening. You hang out in bars. It's the same thing."

Andy stared at his dashboard, without speaking. There was a crack in the dusty plastic, over the defunct clock.

She threw up her hands. "Okay. Kiss me goodbye."

He did so. Her eyes stayed fixed hard on his as he pulled back.

"All these fucking women, Andy. You still get letters from that old girlfriend of yours in Texas, that rich model—what's her name, Candy?"

"I don't answer them."

"You keep getting phone calls from that movie star, Paris Moran. Now this goddamn postcard from this . . . this Astrid. When I move in with you, this is not what I had in mind."

"I understand, but it's nothing to worry about."

Bleusette studied him—too seriously.

"I don't have no heart of gold, Andy."

"Okay, okay."

"I gotta go to work now. I will talk to you later. We gotta talk, Andy."

He chided himself for thinking of Astrid while Bleusette was speaking.

"Okay, darlin'. *Bien sûr.*"

Instead of home, Andy went to where he always went when he wasn't sure of where to go: Long Tom Calhoun's Razzy Dazzy Café on Dauphine Street, up on the Rampart Street side of the Quarter. It took its name from what Al Rose and other reputable local historians had identified as New Orleans' first actual jazz band, a ragtag group of barefoot, turn-of-the-century street urchins with homemade instruments who were known to the sporting houses they serenaded as Emile "Stalebread" Lacoume's Razzy Dazzy Spasm Band. Long Tom kept a framed old photograph of the ragged ensemble on the wall behind the bar, enjoying the irony of the fact that every kid in the Razzy Dazzy Spasm Band had been white.

Long Tom was black—very light skinned and probably more white than black in heritage—but in every Southern sense of the matter, a colored man. A former state lawmaker who had been a friend and ally of Andy's late father when both were in the state legislature in Baton Rouge, Long Tom had been looking after Andy since he'd first started hanging out in the French Quarter as a teenager. Tom, who claimed ironic and illegitimate descent from the slaver statesman John C. Calhoun, no longer held public office but remained a figure of considerable political prominence and power, which he wielded now from his saloon's back room. Tom was a crook, of course, but a true and natural gentleman. Andy liked him enormously.

As to be expected that early in the day, Long Tom was not in evidence—neither out front nor in the back room. A drunk from the night before was sprawled snoring over a couple of chairs in a corner, and another lay asleep, stretched out on the pool table. The only conscious person in the place was the overnight bartender, Cue Ball Taylor, a bald colored man with a pigmentation affliction that had left his skin mottled but mostly albino white. Like Freddy Roybal, the day bartender, Cue Ball had done time— the larger part of it up at Louisiana's fabled Angola prison farm— but for nothing more serious than robbery and manslaughter. A lot worse drank in the Razzy Dazzy, and worked for Long Tom Calhoun.

"Mornin', Andy," Cue Ball said, blinking against the daylight revealed by the open door as Derain came through it. "You just gettin' up or about to turn in?"

Andy sat down wearily on his usual stool, rubbing his unshaven chin with his hand.

"Hard to tell, Cubie."

Cue Ball had a penchant for stating the obvious.

"Long Tom ain't here," he said. "Just a couple of drunks."

"I may join 'em."

"How about a nice cup of coffee—with a little help in it?"

"Okay. Looks to be that kind of day."

"How come you out in the world this early?" Cue Ball said, adding a few glugs of Wild Turkey to some thick New Orleans coffee made all the stronger by having aged in the pot overnight.

"A job. Shot some pictures of a murder over on Tchoupitoulas. Somebody killed Philippe Coquin."

"Crayfish Joe's boy?" The bartender shook his head in appreciation of the event, grinning broadly, if incompletely. Cubie had left some teeth up at Angola and various other unfriendly locales. "Always thought that was sure as shit gonna happen some day. Who done him?"

"He didn't say." Andy sipped, then glanced at the back bar tape machine, which was silent. "How come the quiet, Cubie?"

"Well, it ain't in honor of Philippe Coquin. I just turned it off 'cause weren't no one around to hear it." He picked up a tape cassette. "Here's somethin'. You want to listen to it?"

Andy nodded, not caring what it was, then sipped some more and reread his postcard, slowly. What he hadn't told Bleusette was that Astrid used "poor bears" as a sort of code. It meant she was very unhappy—or in trouble.

The tape was a Django Reinhardt jazz guitar piece from the 1940s. Andy listened to it idly a moment, then took out his wallet and set it open on the bar, turning to the small museum of plastic encased snapshots he carried in it. Most of the pictures were of women. Two were of Bleusette. One in the nude.

At the very back was his photo of Astrid Montebello.

Taken on the occasion of her first fashion show as a fledgling New York designer, it showed the two of them at a congratulatory party thrown afterwards by two of Astrid's legion of rich, chic, mostly European friends. Andy looked rather rich himself in the picture, wearing what he called his Eurotrash suit—a black pinstripe of Italian design—and a bright red tie. It amazed him now that he'd ever liked such clothes.

Astrid wore a long black gown of her own creation—an elegant confection of satin sheath with diaphanous sleeves and top. Her long golden hair, which she wore loose and down to her waist, was the color of dazzling winter sunlight. Her eyes were a bright robin's-egg blue, and her skin was incredibly fair. In all, a woman to make one believe in the goddesses of Norse mythology. She and he were holding hands in the picture.

There'd been a huge full moon that night, hovering just above the rooftops that looked down upon her Greenwich Village street when he'd taken her home, reminding him of the mordantly passionate song in Brecht's *Threepenny Opera:* "Moon Over Dock Street." At her door, he'd kissed her softly on the lips, held her close, then stepped back, his hands falling to hers as he looked into her eyes. They'd stood there like that for the longest time, but there'd been nothing more. There had never been anything more with Astrid. She was, after all, his own personal goddess, the only woman he had put on a pedestal who had stayed there.

Poor bears. What was her trouble?

He got up from his stool.

"I need to use the back-room phone for a long-distance call," he said. "Tell Long Tom to put the charges on my tab."

C h a p t e r
•4•

The House of Astrid, as the princess styled her fashion design es- tablishment, was a much talked about but still rather fledgling enterprise, run with a small and overworked staff. The phone rang seven times before someone finally answered his call. At least it was a living, breathing person. Andy had developed a nearly violent hatred of answering machines.

The young woman on the other end remembered Andy and readily gave him the number of the borrowed condominium on Grand Cayman Island where Astrid supposedly could be reached, but she quickly added that she herself had been unable to contact Astrid for nearly two days and was getting "like, maybe a little worried."

"Like, how little?"

"I don't know if they've been out somewhere on the shoot or what, but she just doesn't answer," the woman said. "I've tried, like, a couple dozen times, including twice this morning."

"Maybe you should be a lot worried." He should have said *we*.

"I don't know. She does this sometimes. What's worrying me is her new investor. He's real uptight about something and like, really, really wants to talk to her. If you get through to her, tell her to call the office. It's important."

Andy promised and, like, thanked her, then quickly hung up and dialed the Grand Cayman number. The connection was made surprisingly fast, but, as he feared, there was no answer for him, either, though he idiotically let the phone ring perhaps twenty times. He tried again, to make sure he had dialed the number correctly, but got the same result.

Shaking his head, he went back to the bar for another coffee-with-help. He had to serve himself, because Cue Ball was busy cleaning up for the day bartender, an effort that included dragging the drunk from the pool table outside onto the sidewalk. The other sot had recovered enough to stagger out the door on his own.

"You make your call?" Cue Ball asked, returning to the bar.

"No answer."

"It important?"

"Maybe. Probably."

"Then keep on trying. Long Tom won't mind."

The postmark on her card actually had been "Hell." Where in hell was Hell? Where in Hell was Astrid? If she had left Grand Cayman, surely she would have told the assistant in New York. Or would she have? For all her Nordic coolness, Astrid was highly impulsive—home in New York one day, then, almost on a whim, in Paris or Milan the next. She'd once called up at the last minute to break a lunch date they'd had at Le Cirque, explaining she was in Vancouver. Something to do with Japanese buyers.

But Astrid could also be infuriatingly indecisive. He recalled her taking nearly half an hour to decide what earrings to wear, while dressing for a dinner party she was attending with him one evening. When she'd finally hit upon a pair she'd liked, she'd almost immediately decided she needed a different dress to go with them and kept him waiting further while she changed. For all he knew, she'd been sitting there just now, staring at the phone, trying to decide whether to answer it.

For a long while, he sat contemplating the bar top, doubtless looking a little like one of the fellows Cue Ball had just removed from the premises. The bartender had put some Leon Redbone on the tape machine and was chatting with a couple of newly arrived morning customers. Redbone was singing a song about South Carolina.

The last time Astrid had used the code "poor bears" as a plea for help had been as part of a frantic, late-night message left on the answering machine Andy had of necessity used when he was still living in New York. Some Lower Manhattan club scene macho man who'd been hitting on her without success had crossed the line from unrequited infatuation to obsession, and turned stalker, threatening her with acts both vile and violent. Despite the haut monde life she'd led, Astrid was one of the most innocent and vulnerable people Andy knew. She tended to attract a really rum lot of men, swaggering predatory types who liked to feed their egos with amorous conquest.

Astrid was a hot prize for conquistadors. She had been the leading runway model in Milan for four seasons. Andy had photographed her for the covers of several New York fashion magazines, and other photographers had similarly enshrined her remarkable face and form. Her title of princess—however vague the claim—had its allure. And, if she was not an actual virgin, Andy knew of no man who could honestly claim to have taken her to bed, including the bounder who for so brief a time had been her husband.

It was not that she was frigid. Astrid was very affectionate, almost Southern, or at least French, in the reflexive way she was always touching and hugging. But, somehow, things never got beyond that—certainly not with him.

The macho stalker had been resolute—even to the point of climbing the fire escape outside Astrid's Greenwich Village apartment building and calling to her through the window. It was when he'd started that frightening stuff that she'd left her phone message. Andy had been able to get some quick action out of a friend on the NYPD, a detective who checked the records and found that the would-be swain was on probation from a date-rape charge that had been plea bargained down to something less onerous. The detective had the man returned to the slammer with great dispatch. Could that swinezoid be free again—and down in the Caymans? Had Astrid's "princely" ex-husband turned up, maybe looking for money? Was it some pirate, beach bum, druggie, or whatever kind of criminal they had down there? Or was she simply off in the boonies or on the beach, shooting pictures and refusing to let telephone calls intrude upon or distract from her creative moment?

The card had been postmarked three days before. Andy could not recall working very many fashion shoots that took much longer than that—unless there were unexpected problems.

Andy knew nothing about the Cayman Islands except that they were a British colony, south of Cuba, and expensive. A few of the Upper East Side swells he had known in New York had condos there.

Now the tape machine was playing Cajun—Austin Pitre's "Two Step à Tante Adele." Andy sat sipping and listening to it appreciatively, but kept going back to try Astrid again. After the third time, he decided he needed official help. An operator connected him with the headquarters of the Royal Cayman Islands Police. The English-accented Inspector Whittles who fielded his inquiry said he knew of no trouble involving a fashion designer or, for that matter, any visiting American.

"It's all very peaceful here, sir," he said. "Quite normal. Everything all tickety-boo. How long did you say this woman has been missing?"

"I'm not really sure. A day or two maybe."

"Hmmm."

Consulting the previous night's incident report, the inspector noted arrests of two ganja weed smugglers, the theft of an engine block from a garage storage room, and a domestic quarrel between the wife and the girlfriend of a local dock worker, in which the girlfriend had barely survived a deep cut to her throat.

"That's the lot," he said. "Nothing out of the ordinary, really, and nothing at all to do with Americans."

"Tickety-boo."

The inspector's affability diminished. "What is her address on Grand Cayman?"

"I don't know. One of the condominiums."

"We have quite a number of condominiums on Grand Cayman. If you don't know where she's supposed to be, sir, then how do you know she isn't there?"

"I told you. She doesn't answer her phone."

There was a pause. "This is an unusual occurrence?"

"I think so."

"Hmmm. If you could provide us with an address here, sir,

we might be able to make inquiries. But in the present circumstance, I might suggest that you simply continue telephoning the lady. We've a quite agreeable climate here, don't you know. Many of our visitors actually spend their mornings at the beach. I rather suspect your Miss Montebello is doing just that."

"Maybe, but—"

"Cheery-bye."

Andy didn't say Cheery-bye back. The woman in New York had said that Astrid had left no address, just a phone number. There was nothing more he could do, except to keep calling—or bother the inspector again awhile later.

When he returned to the barroom this time, feeling irked with all things British, he discovered that Cue Ball had gone home and been replaced by Freddy Roybal, the day bartender. Freddy made a substantial side income selling tourists lewd but exquisitely rendered ball-point-pen drawings on handkerchiefs. It was an art form he had picked up and mastered in a state prison in Texas, one that was enjoying a sudden vogue among gallery owners in the South and West.

The tape machine was now playing the Louisiana Aces' "Valse de Jolly Rogers."

"Mornin', Andy," said Roybal, glancing at Derain's empty cup. "You want some more breakfast?"

The Razzy Dazzy was beginning to fill up with morning drinkers, including a man and woman in T-shirts and shorts whom Andy took for tourists. Both their shirts had the word "Jazz" printed on the back.

"No thanks, Freddy. I'm going to stop by the paper to see if they're using some pictures of mine."

"Hear you and Paul Maljeux were out on a bad one, that's what they say. Philippe Coquin. That's a big-time whack."

"And a girlfriend, as yet unidentified."

"That ain't so, Andy. Her name was Felicie Balbo. That's what they say."

"Felicie Balbo? I never heard of her."

"Hell, you livin' in the Garden District now. Don't suppose you hear much of anything over there. This Felicie a real good-lookin' puss. Philippe brought her here from Miami a couple weeks ago."

"The city could have showed her better hospitality. I never

saw anyone shot up that bad. Bugs Moran's gang didn't get shot up like that in the St. Valentine's Day Massacre."

"New Orleans is a crazy town, sure enough, Andy, but there ain't nobody here so far outa their motherfuckin' minds they gonna clock the number one son of ol' Crayfish Joe. It had to be out-of-town talent. That's what they say."

"Do they say who the talent might have been?"

"Nobody know that. If they do, they don't wanta be saying."

The back bar music machine mysteriously switched to Nat King Cole's "I Love You for Sentimental Reasons."

"Got to go," Andy said.

"Have another drink for as long as this song."

Andy hesitated, then eased back on the stool. "Okay."

Freddy poured him a two-song drink, but Andy managed to get it down in the time of one.

The man on the newspaper's photo desk was profuse in his apologies. They weren't going to use Andy's pictures, fantastic examples of photojournalism that they were.

"Both the city editor and the photo editor think they're just too gruesome for a family newspaper," he said. "They're great shots, Andy. You're the best I ever saw. But you'd have trouble getting these into the *Police Gazette*. We're gonna use our guys' stuff instead. Got a good one showing the bodies being wheeled away."

"All your homicide stories have pictures of the bodies being wheeled away. I don't know why you don't just run the same one over and over."

"This shot's a little different," the photo man said, sliding an eight-by-ten glossy over for Andy's inspection. "See, they didn't zip up the body bag right and the woman's leg is hanging out a little, the shoe dangling off the foot. Kinda arty, don't you think?"

"Masterpiece. Weegee couldn't have done better."

"Who?"

"Never mind."

The man handed him a manilla envelope. "Here's your stuff. Negatives and prints, processed free of charge. Maybe you can use them in your book. You're still doing that picture book, right?

New Orleans street life and all that? Or was it nudes? You kinda got both here."

"It was both—a book on street life, and a book of nudes. But I lost all my pictures in that fire."

"So? Take some more. You got these."

"Not these."

"Andy. This town is full of pictures."

"Some day. Not today."

Eventually, Andy did sell his murder pictures—not to tourists, not to the Associated Press, which also found them in bad taste, or to the respectable photo agency that had bought his freelance stuff in the past. He took them to his market of last resort, the thoroughly unrespectable one-man outfit run by Bartholomew "Greasy" Griswold, located on the top floor of a sad little building off Canal Street. Greasy pounced on Andy's pictures with great glee, as though they were something to eat.

Greasy was as voracious an eater as Crayfish Joe Coquin but lacked the mob boss's gourmand taste. He was almost always to be found munching on something, usually fried, and fast-food wrappers accumulated on his desk and on the floor around his chair like droppings on the bottom of a birdcage. Andy had long wondered how Greasy was able to sell any pictures at all what with the thumbprints he continually left on them, but the man's clients were always happy to have what he offered. Perhaps they thought the thumbprints would reproduce as UFOs.

"Fucking terrific," Greasy said, holding up one of Andy's gorier shots to the light. "Wasn't sure what the hell you had the way you described this stuff over the phone, but shit, these are the real Toledo. In fact, I think I got a buyer already lined up."

"I don't suppose it's *Smithsonian* magazine."

Griswold gave him a quick dark look with his squinchy eyes, then shoved the uneaten half of a doughnut into his mouth.

"You know who it is," he said, during chews.

"*Crime Scene?*"

Greasy swallowed. "*Crime Scene.*"

Crime Scene was a lurid weekly tabloid that was to violent crime stories what New York's *Screw* magazine was to sleazy sex, though there was sometimes that in *Crime Scene* as well.

"They'll pay two hundred a picture, like always."

"Minus your fifteen percent."

"I can get you a hell of a lot more, Andy. You know that. Anytime. All you have to do is let them . . ."

"Use my real name."

"*Crime Scene* would kill to let the world know they got the famous André Derain shootin' for 'em."

"I'll never do that."

"So you keep saying. Two bills a pix it is. Done deal."

Andy wasn't going to shake hands.

"How many do you think they'll use?"

"This one of the broad for sure. Too bad they don't do color. And probably this one of Coquin. I don't know about more. If Philippe was a big-time New York or Chicago hood, instead of a local boy, they might do a big double-truck spread."

"How soon can I get paid?"

"On publication, like always."

"You wouldn't want to advance me . . ."

"Sorry, Andy. That ain't how I do business. Nothing personal. Anyway, what's the rush? I hear you and Bleusette are rollin' in dough."

"She is. I'm not."

Andy left Greasy's feeling as crummy as if he'd spent a night with a junkie hooker with dirty feet. His car was parked over on Camp Street, but in the mucky heat, it refused to start. Leaving his expired press card on top of the dashboard in hopes of warding off a parking ticket, he started walking up Canal. He hadn't yet made up his mind about going to Grand Cayman. He had no reason to offer that Bleusette—or any rational person—would accept. All he had was the compulsion to be there.

What he needed first was sleep. His brain was working about as well as his car. For all he knew, this notion of running off to the Caribbean on the strength of an ambiguous postcard from a woman he hadn't talked to in nearly two years was a really dumb idea.

He took the St. Charles streetcar home. Once there, he tried Astrid's number on Grand Cayman one last time from the phone in his kitchen. He let it ring so long that Zinnia, standing at the sink, began staring at him as though he was in need of urgent psychiatric help.

"You callin' somebody who can't hear, sugar?" she asked.

"No, Zinnie. Just got a little lost in my thoughts." He hung up.

His Auntie Claire was puttering about her rose bushes in the rear garden. He let her be and went upstairs, flopping on his big double bed. He actually managed to fall asleep, though fitfully, and for no more than an hour. Finally, he sat up. What was sleep when a friend like Astrid was in trouble? Either he was going or he wasn't. If he could scare up the money, he'd go. Absolutely, as soon as possible.

He showered, shaved carefully, splashed on some California, an inexpensive cologne he liked, and, though sticking with his boating moccasins and no socks, set about dressing more respectably, choosing a rumpled pair of white ducks, a striped button-down shirt, and his old navy blue tropical-weight blazer.

Looking presentable would help with his Cousin Vincent, a quite successful art gallery owner who fancied himself a traditional Southern gentleman—at least as Tennessee Williams conceived of Southern gentlemen—and held that a man should never appear in public without his jacket. Andy would oblige his sensibilities.

He found Vincent between customers, napping at his desk in the rear of his Royal Street gallery. He was indeed impressed to see Andy looking so natty but, uncharacteristically, was in no way inclined to be generous.

"I do sympathize with you in your difficulty, André," he said, his soft, slightly effeminate, upriver-accented voice full of amiable concern. "But I fear you've reached a point where my encouraging your further indebtedness is going to cause you far more harm than good."

"Vincent, just look at it as an advance on some picture sales."

"But I haven't sold any of your photographs. Not in weeks."

"I'm talking about pictures I've already sold—today—to a magazine. Four hundred dollars. Payable on publication, which should be in a few weeks."

"Which magazine?"

"Never mind."

"It doesn't matter. I simply can't do it." Vincent glanced down at Andy's camera bag, which he carried with him wherever he went. "Why don't you bring me some more nudes? We seem to have luck with those."

"The last nude I took was of Bleusette, and I'm not having much luck with her at all today."

Vincent only smiled.

It was like that all over town. Even old friends he'd grubstaked in his flush days turned him down flat. By midafternoon, he was down to just one possibility—Long Tom Calhoun.

This was a dim possibility. Andy's tab at the Razzy Dazzy was approaching serious money.

Long Tom was now on the premises, working on a glass of whiskey and a cigarette while he went over his accounts at the round table in a rear corner that he used as a desk. The stereo was playing a tape dubbing of what Andy recognized as one of Jelly Roll Morton's recordings from his Chicago days—"Fishtail Blues." Tom looked to have recently arisen and was dressed for evening—pearl gray suit, matching tie, charcoal shirt, and shiny black alligator shoes. He wore a big diamond ring, a gold wristwatch, and had a purple flower in his lapel. On the table was a wide-brimmed, old fashioned Panama hat.

He smiled and motioned Andy to join him.

"Thought you'd be in earlier than this," he said.

"I've been out trying to raise some money."

"So I hear. Lookin' to start a business? Thought you and Bleusette already got one."

The smile returned as a wry, broad grin. Tom had teeth as magnificent as Cue Ball's were decrepit.

Andy sat down. "I need to take a trip. A friend of mine's in trouble."

"A friend—or a lady friend?"

"She's a lady, and she's a friend. An old friend."

"What kinda trouble she in?"

"I'm not sure."

"But you want to go find out?"

"Yes."

"And where you have to go to do that?"

"The Cayman Islands."

Long Tom took note of this with a long, low whistle, then leaned back in his chair, eyeing Andy as he might a freshly dealt hand of cards.

"And you'd like to borrow the price of a ticket from your soft-touch old pal here, former State Senator Thomas C. Calhoun?"

"I'll get it back to you in a few weeks, maybe sooner. Greasy Griswold took a couple of pictures of mine. He figures they'll bring at least four hundred dollars."

Calhoun pulled a ledger from the papers before him and flipped through the pages till he found the desired entry.

"Says here you owe me in excess of nine hundred and fifty dollars, not counting today's refreshment."

"I guess I've let that get out of hand. I'm sorry. Haven't had a lot of work lately."

Tom turned to look back toward the bar. "Freddy, bring Mr. Derain a nice frosty cold gin and tonic on the house."

"Sure thing, Tom."

"Thanks," said Andy.

"Tell me more about this lady friend. She a looker? Model or something."

"Used to be. Now she's a fashion designer."

"Has she graced your sheets? And have you the expectation she might do so again."

"It's not like that at all. She's just in trouble."

"And she sent you this alarming news on a postcard?"

Andy stared hard at the man. "How do you know about the postcard?"

"You might as well know the truth. Bleusette's been callin' all over the Quarter telling people not to give you any money. She thinks you're going out of your fuckin' mind—or at the least, that you're going to skip town and throw her over for some high-class bimbo you knew in New York."

"One, that isn't what I told her. And, two, that isn't the way it is. And, three, this woman is no bimbo."

Roybal brought Andy his drink. It was gin and tonic as a martini was gin and vermouth.

"That Bleusette can tell what's on people's minds as good as any old conjur woman," Tom said, taking a delicate sip of his whiskey after Freddy had departed. "Now, you two supposed to get married soon, ain't that right?"

"I'm still willing. She's the one who's getting cold feet."

"Do you think running off to the Cayman Islands after this here princess is gonna warm 'em up any?"

"The lady's a friend. I've always stuck by my friends. Just like you."

"Too many of your friends're women, Andy. Like I always been tellin' you—even back when you were a young kid sportin' around the Quarter and it was expected of you—you just plain got too damn many women in your life. You got a way with 'em, sure enough. They fall for you real easy. And that's a fine thing for a man. But it don't mean you got to love 'em all back. Ain't time in this life for that. Most of them only going to get you into trouble. Sometimes real bad trouble. Like we've seen around here not all that long ago."

The woman who had burned Andy out of his place in the French Quarter was one he had picked up in the Razzy Dazzy.

Andy took a big gulp of his drink and pushed back his chair.

"Well, thanks anyway, Tom."

The older man laid a hand on Andy's arm, the flashy diamond in his ring causing a glitter that danced before Andy's eyes.

"Just a minute now," Tom said. "I want to ask you something. How much were you making when you were doing all that fashion and high-society shit up in New York?"

Andy knew the figure well. It had often haunted him when he'd found himself with nothing but a can of ravioli to eat.

"My best year I made three hundred and eighty-nine thousand dollars. But it all got spent."

"You had yourself a real good piece of the good life back then, sure enough, but when that long, tall Texas model girlfriend you had all those years up there—what was her name? Candy? When that evil-assed Candy of yours run off with that rich guy from Houston and left you with your back against the bottom of a ditch, you decided you were all through with that rich shit up there, right? So you come back home, deciding you were gonna be like that Ernest Bellocq who took all the pictures of the chippies in Storyville long time ago. You were gonna take pictures of working girls and street folk and musicians and all and put 'em into books. Be a real artiste. Bleusette set you up with that nice deal of a studio behind her house, and life was gonna be sweet."

"That was the idea."

"Only that all gone to shit, too. How much money you made this year?"

"I don't know. A few thousand."

"Lot of folks say you ain't made enough to pay for your drinks—not that it bothers me all that much. What riles me, Andy, is that the last few weeks you just been lyin' around drinkin' or dreamin' your way through your days. You ain't lifted a finger to help Bleusette with that fine new restaurant of hers. You hardly ever go out on a picture job anymore and you ain't worked up spit tryin' to get those books you were gonna do put together again. Seems to me you're beginnin' to find life down here the same piss bucket it was up North. So I wonder, and Bleusette wonders, and we all wonder if maybe you're fixin' to deal yourself out and move on, leavin' us stiffed like that long, tall evil-assed Candy stiffed you."

"That's not it, Tom. It's not."

"That Bleusette, she's a real fine woman, Andy—best I know in New Orleans. It bother you—deep down—that she was a whore?"

"Come on, Tom. I've known Bleusette nearly all my grown days."

"She's the best you ever ever gonna find, Andy. She ain't just the most beautiful thing walkin' around down here. She's damn smart, and she'll see you through the worst shit come your way."

"I know that. I just wish she'd see me though this."

They sat without speaking a moment. The bar was filling with regulars and a few more tourists coming in out of the heat. The back-bar tape machine was playing Louis Armstrong's "Mahogany Hall Stomp."

"If you go down to the Caymans," Tom said, "you swear you'll come back as soon as you fix up what's wrong? You won't run off with that 'princess'?"

"I'll swear it on a case of your best whiskey. Anyway, she lives in New York, and I'm not ever going back there."

Long Tom reclined in his chair again, tilting it back slightly, his eyes searching Andy's.

"Your daddy was the best white man friend I ever had," he said. "Hadn't been for him, I would have been just another up-pity nigger in Baton Rouge, the way times was then. When your daddy passed, it was a sorrow for me."

Andy vividly recalled the funeral. Thanks to Long Tom—and Andy's father's civil rights reputation—the street bands from seemingly half the black social and walking clubs in New Orleans took part in the procession, much to the consternation of the De-rain family friends in the Garden District.

"I promised him I'd look out for you, and I done that," Tom said. "I'll keep on doin' that. I don't care how big a tab you run up."

"Four hundred bucks, Tom. Make it three. I'll get it back to you as soon as I'm paid . . ."

Calhoun shook his head. "I can't give you a cent. Not for this. I promised Bleusette, and I ain't never gonna go back on my word to her. But maybe there's another way. Lotta traffic between here and the Caribbean. Some slow, some fast. Some legal, some maybe not so legal." He finished his drink. "I'll ask around. Pass the word about someone needin' a ride in a bad way. Get a lot of people wantin' to leave New Orleans in a hurry sometimes."

"I appreciate it. I really do. But wouldn't it be simpler just to loan me the money? Call Greasy Griswold. Really, I'm good for it."

"You get Bleusette to tell me it's okay, and I'll do it. Other-wise, you just come 'round here later on tonight. Maybe some-thin' will turn up. If it does, you make damn sure Bleusette don't find out I had anything to do with it. *Compris?*"

"*Entendu.*" Andy shook Tom's hand. "Thanks."

"And you make real damn sure you get your ass back to New Orleans, if it has to be on a goddamn conch boat."

"I'll swim if I have to."

"Let's hope you don't. With some of these people, that's al-ways a possibility."

Chapter
·5·

Back at his house again, Andy decided against packing a whole suit-case. There was something symbolic in that—much like going home to mother—and it might spook his Auntie Claire and Zinnia. If they told Bleusette he looked to be going traveling, she could be hot after him before he had a chance to get out of town—if there really was a chance of that. Long Tom certainly hadn't guaranteed anything.

His camera bag would do. He removed his big Nikon and most of the other equipment from it, leaving only his old Minolta and a spare long lens, an exposure meter, and a few rolls of film. Then he threw in a couple of fresh shirts, a pair of khaki shorts, and a toothbrush and razor. He seldom bothered with socks and underwear in the heat of New Orleans; there'd be no need of them whatsoever in the Caribbean.

He thought for the briefest moment of taking along his father's old .32 pistol, but decided to leave it in its drawer. As he'd had occasion to learn since coming back to New Orleans, guns invited trouble. Whatever Astrid's was, she didn't need more. The customs officials on Grand Cayman probably wouldn't appreciate the old automatic much, either.

Going into the kitchen, he took a bowl of gumbo from a fresh pot Zinnia had working on the stove, washing it down with a glass of iced tea. Refilling the glass, he went onto the back veranda and just sat a while, listening to the bugs buzz and bat against the screen and watching the lowering sun change the shadows on the lawn.

He wondered what his father might advise him to do, if he were alive and sitting there in one of the wicker chairs, wearing one of his white suits and sipping from his usual glass of Coca-Cola and Wild Turkey.

"Life's a real short time, boy. If you've got a serious yen to be with that gal down there, find a way to do it. New Orleans'll still be here when you get back. Nothin' you have here goin' anywhere else."

Andy's mother never walked out on his daddy. She was always there when he came home, sometimes at four or five in the morning, never complaining. She had pretty much everything she wanted: marriage to him and this house in the Garden District. His daddy's amorous adventures weren't important. She'd been the one who'd gotten the ring.

What did Bleusette want?

"You all right there, Andy?"

He turned to see Zinnia standing in the doorway behind him.

"Fine, Zinnie. Fine."

"You been workin' or drinkin' today?"

"A little of both."

Zinnia shook her head, in weary habit. "I see you been at my gumbo. Ain't anywhere near suppertime yet."

"I've got to go out tonight."

"Mizz Bleusette know that?"

"I'll leave her a note."

"There's some gentlemen here to see you."

She'd taken her time getting around to that.

"The only gentlemen I know in New Orleans are Cousin Vincent and Tom Calhoun."

"It ain't them, that for sure. Fact, they don't look like the kind of folks you'd want to have in the house."

"Where are they?"

"In the house. In the parlor."

· · ·

Zinnie's assessment proved correct. The two men were reasonably well dressed for New Orleans—one wore a double-knit brown suit and polo shirt, the other a tropical print shirt with palm trees on it, half unbuttoned, and white jeans—but they had the mean faces of the bad kind of street people Andy used to give wide berth to in New York. There wasn't a single good intention even hinted at in their expressions.

"You Derain the photographer?" said the one in the suit.

Both had scruffy chin beards, and the palm-tree-shirt guy wore several earrings. The two were surprisingly small for what Andy presumed to be their profession. Doubtless, equippage to even the balance was hidden on their persons. Andy had another urge concerning his father's .32.

"I am, but I'm closed," Andy said. "Photographs by appointment only."

"The photographs we want you already took," said the one in the suit. The other fellow's job, apparently, was not to talk.

Andy glanced through the window. A yellow stretch Mercedes was parked in the driveway, occupying most of its length.

Oh joy.

"Which would those be?"

"The ones you took this morning, down by the park. We'd like to buy them."

Andy looked again at the stretch. Was Crayfish Joe in the back? Did it matter?

"Uh, those aren't for sale."

"You're not shittin' me, are you? You ain't sold them yet? Thought that's what you did for a living."

Andy realized he was going to have to come up with nothing but right answers for the rest of this conversation. The right answer to this question was obvious.

"I haven't sold them. I was told they weren't publishable."

"That's good to hear, Derain. Very good to hear. Shows some respect. Now you just go get 'em for us. Like in about the next sixty seconds. All the prints. All the negatives."

He could try to stiff them, which might well lead to unpleasantness, which was the very last thing he wanted to occur in the house that was home to Bleusette, Auntie Claire, and Zinnie.

"I'll get them."

For a moment, he was afraid they would accompany him

down to his darkroom, but they remained in the parlor, as patient as real gentlemen.

Andy took the stairs two at a time, flung open the door to his darkroom and went to his lab table, where he had left the envelope the newspaper picture editor had given him. It contained the negatives and prints from the morning's roll, minus the prints he had turned over to Greasy Griswold. Andy was now even more pleased *Crime Scene* wouldn't be using his name.

He snatched up the envelope, then halted. There were more negatives than prints inside. They would wonder where the missing prints were. Quickly, he dumped out the contents, found the right strip of negatives, located the rest of the prints that went with them, and shoved them all into one of his wedding folders. The remaining prints and negatives went back into the envelope, and Andy went bounding back up the stairs, arriving breathless.

"Here they are. Sorry I took so long. Forgot where I put them."

The suit gave him a doubtful look, then shook the negatives and prints out into his hand, screwing up his face in disgust as though he had never seen the like of such things before. Sliding the photos back inside, he started toward the door. Andy felt relieved, then suddenly he didn't.

"Come outside," said the man. "Someone wants to talk to you."

Now Andy really wanted to be in the Cayman Islands. He had wanted to come home to New Orleans, he had told himself, to get away from the superficiality of New York, to get back to real life. This was a little more real than he had in mind.

They accompanied him out the door and down to the Mercedes stretch. In a moment, he was in the backseat, next to the immensity of Crayfish Joe Coquin. The mobster was munching something out of a white cardboard carton—from the sound of it, something fried. If they were crayfish, Andy didn't want to look.

This was one time Andy hoped Mrs. Boulanger next door would be watching. He wondered where Coquin was going to take him, hoping it wouldn't be anywhere near the river.

Coquin looked up at the suit, who had gotten behind the wheel. "You get 'em?"

"Yes, Mr. Coquin. Negatives and prints." He held up the envelope.

Coquin turned toward Andy, much as he might toward something he was about to eat.

"Why you take such pictures of my son?"

"I'm sorry. I didn't realize who it was." Andy was getting into some major falsehood here, but that was just the kind the situation required. "All I knew was that there was a murder."

"You didn't fucking try to sell them?"

"I talked about it with a guy at the newspaper, but we decided against it. Question of taste."

"*C'est vrai?* Taste?"

"Yes."

Coquin looked away, out the window, sadly. The suit leaned across the seat, breathing aromatic remembrances of his lunch into Andy's face.

"What did the cops tell you about the murder? They ain't told Mr. Coquin shit."

"Nothing, really. They didn't know much."

The face came closer and the aroma grew stronger. "You sure about that?"

"Hardly anything at all, except . . ."

"Except what?"

"They think the killers were after the girl, not, uh, your son, Mr. Coquin. They think she might have been two-timing someone. They also think Phil—er, your son, may have fired a shot or two at his assailants and hit one."

Andy didn't feel he was breaking any confidence. If he had been a reporter, he probably would have put that bit of information into the newspaper, though without attribution.

"That true?"

"The police think so."

"That all you know?" said Coquin, digging out what remained at the bottom of the carton with his fingers.

"Yes, sir."

"You got cop friends, right? Like Lieutenant Maljeux?"

"Yes, sir."

Coquin set the carton down carefully on the floor, on the plush rug, then burped. He reached for a glass of wine from an inset holder and sipped, decorously, smacking his lips.

Then he turned and leaned close to Andy. He smelled even more than the suit—rather like Bleusette's restaurant kitchen just before cleanup time.

"I want to know everything they know," he said. "Anything they tell you, I want to know. Anything, everything. *Compris?*"

"*Bien entendu*," Andy said, hoping their mutual French ancestry might count for something.

"Anything."

"Yes, sir. Uh, how will I let you know?"

"Your friend Bleusette Lescaut; she'll know how. You find out something, you tell her."

"I, uh, really don't see the need to get her mixed up in this. She's kinda busy and . . ."

"*N'inquiet, monsieur. Bleusette, elle est relation. Compris? Nous avons les mêmes cousins—au Bayou Vielle Père.*"

Andy had been out to the bayous with Bleusette to be with her kinfolk dozens of times, but he'd never explored her family tree. Crayfish Joe? One of her clan?

"I really don't . . ."

"She is family, Monsieur Derain. You marry her, you family, too. So don't worry, okay? Unless, well . . . *n'inquiet*. But you hear something from Maljeux or any them other cops, you make sure I know *tout de suite. Compris? Ça va?*"

Andy envisioned a wedding ceremony—*le tout ensemble* in St. Louis Cathedral, Long Tom, Paul Maljeux, his Cousin Vincent, Auntie Claire, and Zinnia on the groom's side of the aisle; and on the bride's, Crayfish Joe and all the boys.

"*Ça va.*"

"Go." Coquin wanted to get back to his mourning—or something of the sort. Andy got out, walking quickly to the house without looking back. He heard the limousine start up. By the time he reached his door, the stretch was racing away down the street.

In the kitchen, he poured himself a big slug of Bleusette's Pernod. Zinnia came in as he was lifting it to his mouth. It didn't mix well with the gumbo.

"You okay, Andy?"

"Much better than I thought I was going to be."

"Those boys didn't look like no magazine salesmen."

Andy set down his glass, deciding against another belt.

"Don't worry about them. Just some nice Cajun folk asking after Bleusette. Zinnie, I've got to go out of town, to help a friend. I'll be back—soon as I can."

Andy went to the counter and took a piece of notepaper from a pad by the telephone. He wasn't sure what to say.

"*Ma chère Bleusette,*" he wrote. "*Je t'aime comme toujours. Je retournerai bientôt.*"

"I like that girl, Andy," said Zinnie. "Didn't at first, but do now. Hope you be treatin' her right."

"Everything's fine, Zinnie."

"I sure hope so, but I sure don't know so."

"What do you mean?"

"She was sayin' the other day that maybe it ain't such a good idea, her gettin' married to you."

Chapter
·6·

The Razzy Dazzy was crowded by the time Andy returned, and his usual stool was taken by a short, fat woman wearing a too-tight halter top and jeans that made her flesh bulge out in an extraordinary number of wrong places. Moving on to an empty place at the far end of the bar, he ordered a Southern Comfort—a drink he hated. Not knowing how long he'd have to wait for whatever it was Long Tom might arrange, he wanted to have something in front of him that he'd be sure to sip slowly. Keep his head clear.

Southern Comfort didn't go well with the gumbo, either.

Tom wasn't around, but, to Andy's surprise, Paul Maljeux came strolling out of the men's room, looking police-manual perfect in a crisp uniform.

The conversation around Andy hushed as the lieutenant drew near.

"Still on duty?" Andy asked.

Maljeux yawned. "It's been a long one. You find an opportunity to restore yourself from this morning's labors?"

"Found the opportunity, not the restoration. Any developments?"

Both Cue Ball and Freddy Roybal were working behind the

bar. It was Freddy who brought down Maljeux's beer and uniform cap from where he'd been sitting. Maljeux waited for Roybal to go away again before he continued.

"Developments," he said. "Well now, the most encouraging thing is that Crayfish Joe Coquin hasn't killed anyone yet, though he and his boys have sure been tearin' up the town lookin' for someone to be unkind to. We got the bodies off to the morgue before Joe turned up, but only just. When he saw the way that sports car of Philippe's was shot up, I was afraid he might open fire on us, just for spite."

"Is he lookin' for anyone in particular?"

"Probably looking for a lot of people in particular. I don't know why, but he had quite a fondness for that boy."

Andy took another sip. "Paul, he came looking for me. Worse, he found me."

"Crayfish Joe?" Andy didn't like the glint of fear that came into Maljeux's eyes.

"Yes sir. Showed up at the house with two of his aides de camp. They unburdened me of my crime-scene pictures from this morning and suggested strongly that I had erred in taking them. They also suggested strongly that I tell them everything I learned about the shooting from you guys."

"*C'est vrai?* So what'd you tell them?"

"Everything I knew, of course. Namely what you said about it being a Frankie and Johnny and that Philippe might have gotten off a pop or two with his personal weapon."

"That last part's actual fact. We took blood samples off the pavement. The lab says there's three different blood types. I'd say Philippe scored himself a definite hit before expiring. Someone out there's probably bleeding pretty bad; may even turn up at a hospital, if not a funeral parlor. And there were definitely two perps. The brass we picked up checks out to two different firearms, not including the late Philippe's." Maljeux took a big swallow of beer, looked at his watch, and then daintily wiped his lips with a neatly folded handkerchief.

"Was the girl's name Felicie Balbo?" Andy asked.

The question startled Maljeux. "Where'd you hear that?"

"Idle conversation."

"That was her name, all right. We traced her to Miami, but the cops there have no sheet on her. Someone said she may be out of

Jamaica originally, though she looked to be a white woman. Only one who knew her well here was Philippe. You tell that to Crayfish Joe?"

"No. As a matter of fact, her name had slipped my mind. If it hadn't, I would have told him quicker than you can say Felicie Balbo."

"Well, I'll tell you what, Andy boy. I'm not going make you privy to any more about this."

"A little knowledge is a dangerous thing."

"Maybe you ought to stay clear of Crayfish Joe."

"Not about to argue with you. He said he was kin of Bleusette—that they had the same cousins or something out in the bayous. Can that be true?"

"Course it can. Hell, Andy, I got relations down in Thibodaux who are kin to Bleusette's people down in Houma."

"So you're related to Crayfish Joe, too."

"Let's not go that far."

Maljeux finished the rest of his beer in a big swallow, then set down the glass. He glanced at the big, long-barreled .357 Magnum revolver in his belt holster, running his fingers over the polished wooden grip.

"Guess I won't be pausing at Loomis's tonight. Not any night, till things calm down a little. Woman trouble like this, worst kind there is. Remember Troy, burned down and all? That was woman trouble just like this. Good luck to you, Andy."

"*De la bonne chance pour vous aussi, mon ami.*"

Maljeux grinned, though most of his face stayed serious. "Night then."

The conversation at the bar resumed full force when he had gone through the door.

"You want another Southern Comfort?" said Freddy, nodding at Andy's now empty glass.

"No, I sure as hell don't, but I'll take one. Did Tom say when he was coming back?"

"No sir. You waitin' for him?"

"Waiting for something."

"Well, I don't know you want to pass the time with too much more of this here sticky goo," Roybal said, refilling Andy's double shot glass.

"It grows on you."

"I knew a woman when I was livin' in California used to drink this stuff with Coca-Cola. Morning, noon, and night."

"What happened to her?"

"She moved to Oregon."

"Thanks for sharing that with me, Freddy."

Roybal leaned on the bar a moment, staring at Andy's face. His own, with all of its scars and leathery folds and creases, was a map of hard times and sin.

"You're lookin' real tired lately, you know?" the bartender said.

"I can't possibly look as tired as I feel."

"Still can't sleep?"

"Good guess."

"More of them nightmares about that woman who burned you out?"

"Those finally went away. Sometimes I wish they'd come back. Give me something to do at night instead of just lying there."

A customer was hollering for a drink. Freddy ignored him.

"What you need, Andy, is to get back to your work."

"What do you mean? I worked today. Shot those crime-scene pictures."

"I mean real work. Shit, anybody can point a camera at some stiff. I'm talkin' about that real fine stuff you done, like that picture you took in here of that saxophone player Bleusette used to go with."

"The one who drank himself to death in three days?"

"Yeah. The way you got all that in the look in his eyes, that was fucking profound, I mean, like, really fine shit."

"That was one of the pictures that got burned up."

"There's lots more saxophone players around, Andy. Lots more women don't mind showin' themselves naked. But you don't shoot nothin'. It's like you turned yourself off. Like you're drained dry inside—soul all gone, know what I mean? I hate to say it, Andy, but you're beginnin' to look like that saxophone player of Bleusette's."

"I'm not going to drink myself to death in three days—not with Southern Comfort, anyway."

"You gotta get back to work, Andy. It'll heal you."

Roybal reached into his pocket and took out a carefully folded handkerchief, opening it and laying it flat on the bar. On it was a ballpoint drawing of a seated naked woman with an entwining rose rising from between her thighs. The draftsmanship was so exact, it could have been a sketch by Egon Schiele, except that long-dead Austrian artist's nudes had been far more wanton and embittered. Freddy's ladies were more softly sensual, and they had a mysticism about them, as was true of so much Mexican art—even that learned in jails.

"That's brilliant, Freddy," Andy said.

"Did it today, on my afternoon break. Your Cousin Vincent says to keep 'em coming, so he'll get this in the morning. And Andy, I'm going to sleep real good tonight."

"How come you're still on duty?"

"Long Tom asked me to stick around awhile, just to make sure you get off all right."

"Off all right? How? With who?"

"He didn't say. Wasn't sure."

"So I just wait."

"There's worse places. We got lots of Southern Comfort."

The second drink didn't endear itself to Andy any better than the first. After a sip, he glanced along the row of stools, taking stock of the prospects for travel.

They looked decidedly dim. Most of those present were regulars, bound for no place more distant than the next bar or the police drunk tank. The rest appeared to be tourists, a few perhaps too wholesome and innocent to be so far from the riverfront hotels and so close to Rampart Street. At least, no one in the place looked to be in any way associated with Crayfish Joe Coquin.

Bleusette. He'd been fighting off thoughts of her all day, but now they came and ganged up on him. He didn't want to marry her. That fact stared him in the face. Married life, especially with each other, would drive them both bananas in a week. Yet he couldn't accept the idea of their not being together, of his coming downstairs in the morning and not finding Bleusette naked at the kitchen table, reading the *Times-Picayune* while she sipped her breakfast Pernod.

He sat through two B. B. King recordings, a Billy Lee Riley number from the fifties, Leon Redbone, and some raspy early rockster he'd never heard before.

"Who the hell's that, Freddy?"

Roybal checked the handwritten label on the tape cassette, then reported back.

"Big Boy Crudup," he said.

"Who the hell is that?"

"Memphis guy. Pre-Elvis."

"You still play jazz in this joint?"

Roybal looked back down the bar. "Not tonight."

"Wonderful."

He glumly returned to his Southern Comfort. When that was gone, he decided a switch to something else was in order. In honor of his father, and of his actually having thought about the man early that evening, he shouted down to Freddy to make him a Coca-Cola and Wild Turkey. Amazingly, he was getting a little sleepy. Maybe the caffeine in the soft drink would give him a jolt.

Roybal had been down at the other end of the bar; he lingered there a moment after acknowledging Andy's request, then quickly went about fulfilling it.

"You'll like this one, Andy," he said, setting down the glass. "Ain't gonna cost you nothin'."

"You mean Long Tom's extending my tab."

"Ain't goin' on your tab. It's on that lady down there."

Andy raised himself slightly on his bar stool, glimpsing only sun-bleached hair and a bit of tan face at the place where Freddy had been standing.

"Who?"

"Take a table, Andy. I'll send her over. I think she's what you've been waiting for."

The woman left the bar and came walking toward him nonchalantly, as if she'd known him all her life. She was very close to pretty, in an outdoorsy way, with a considerable tan, gray or light blue eyes, and short, tousled hair that would have been a light brown if it hadn't spent so much time in the sun. Taller than most— Andy guessed about five foot ten—she was slender but big boned and moved with the ease of someone who regularly played sports. She wore khaki pants, loafers, a pale blue man's button-down shirt with the sleeves rolled up to the elbow, and carried a lightweight beige windbreaker slung over her shoulder. In her other hand was her drink, which she set down on the table gently. It was as dark as his but contained no ice.

"Thanks for the refreshment," he said, as she seated herself.

"You're quite welcome." She rubbed her neck a moment, then folded her hands in front of her as she studied him. The eyes were definitely gray, and the look was unnervingly searching and thorough.

"Are you drinking Coke and Wild Turkey, too?" he asked.

"Just Coke. I'm flying tonight."

Her words were a bit chilly, almost reproachful.

"I'm Andy Derain," he said, extending his hand.

She shook it, firmly but briefly, her eyes still on his. "I know. I'm Glory."

"Glory?"

"As in Gloria. I don't particularly care for Gloria."

Her voice suited her—soft and a little husky, even sexy. But the accent was a surprise. He'd expected Midwestern, maybe even Western. She didn't look like a Southern woman. But what came out was almost British, the kind of British-rooted accent one might hear in South Africa or some other place where the British sun never used to set.

Like the Caribbean. The Caymans were a British colony.

"You're going to Grand Cayman?" he said.

She smiled, after a fashion, and sipped her Coca-Cola. "Your lucky night."

"You're a friend of Long Tom's, then."

"Mr. Calhoun? Not quite. We have mutual friends. They tell me you and he go way back and he trusts you. That true?"

"Yes."

She glanced down at his camera bag. "You don't have a firearm in there, do you?"

"No. Just a camera."

"Camera? I thought . . ."

"I'm a professional photographer. My camera and I are inseparable."

She sighed. "Bloody nuisance. Keep it out of sight, will you? Have you a passport?"

"Yes." She was making him feel like a small boy going off to summer camp.

She glanced around the barroom, her eyes lingering on the pool players for a moment, then returning to his. She wore very little makeup. Her eyes were large and quite beautiful. She didn't need any makeup.

"You're going to have to earn your passage, Mr. Derain," she said, leaning closer. "You're going to be my cargo kicker."

"What does that entail?"

"You off-load cargo. While we're airborne. You don't actually have to use your foot. Use whatever you bloody well like. It's the 'when' that counts. Just take care not to off-load yourself simultaneously. It's not a lot of work, but it has to be done well and fast and exactly when I say to."

He decided not to ask what the cargo was. "I'll manage."

"My regular man took ill of a sudden. I've had a hard time finding a suitable replacement. I'm rather behind schedule." She pronounced the first syllable of the word with a soft British *shh*.

"This is a scheduled flight?"

Like Queen Victoria, she was not amused.

"I'll be perfectly honest, Mr. Derain," she said. "You don't really strike me as a suitable replacement. Truth to tell, I don't quite understand how it is that Calhoun's friends suggested you. But I've not much bloody choice, have I? I can't wait any longer. You'll have to do."

"Thank you."

"Something I really must know, however. Why do you want to go to the Caymans?"

"See a friend. And I wouldn't mind getting out of New Orleans for a while."

"Spot of trouble?"

"Yes."

"Serious trouble?"

He recalled the smell of Crayfish Joe's breath. "Well, yes."

"Trouble involving the police?"

"After a fashion."

"Now you're beginning to sound a bit more suitable. Come along. Finish your drink. I'm tired of being on the ground."

Chapter

·7·

It was a quick cab ride up the freeway to New Orleans' Lake Front Airport. Rather too quick, as this mysterious English-sounding Glory might say. Andy wished now that he'd at least said good-bye to Bleusette. He didn't think she was really going to understand this. All he could do was promise himself that he'd call her when he reached Grand Cayman.

At the little terminal building, Glory stopped at the general aviation desk to fill out an aircraft declaration and some other papers and pay her ramp fees, then took him in tow and walked quickly out onto the field. They passed along a row of parked aircraft until she came to a long-nosed plane with a horizontal stabilizer at the top of the tail and funny-looking flanges sticking up from the end of the wings. It had an odd two-tone paint job—a dark marine blue on top and a pale sort of blue on the bottom—and was as big as any corporate aircraft Andy had seen or flown in. Something about it was disturbing, though.

"There's only one engine," he said.

"It works."

"We're going to cross the Caribbean with only one engine?"

She leaned back against the fuselage, folding her arms.

"This is a Pilatus," she said. "Swiss made, damn reliable. The engine's a Pratt and Whitney PT6A that has never failed me. It'll do two hundred seventy knots and has a range of eighteen hundred nautical miles. The aircraft's pressurized, has cabin oxygen, and will carry an entire ton of cargo. Best of all, you can land it in a bloody sandbox. I think you'll find that quite a bit more useful than dragging an extra engine around."

Why would he find it useful to land in a sandbox? "Sorry. I didn't mean to insult your engine."

"Make yourself comfortable up in the right front seat," she said, as she unlocked the cabin door and dropped a small set of steps. "I've got to do my walkaround."

He wasn't sure if this was British slang or pilot's jargon but did as bidden. Taking the copilot's seat, he watched out the window as she moved about the aircraft, stopping here and there to poke and prod, checking a cowling, running her hand over the leading edge of a wing, peering at a small tube that jutted forward from the side of the nose. She disappeared toward the rear of the plane, taking several more minutes to complete her ritual. Finally, she came aboard, pulled the door shut, and locked it behind her.

"I presume you can read," she said, sliding into the pilot's seat and handing him a clipboard, "unlike some of the assistants I've had on these runs."

"What's this?" he asked.

"Preflight checklist. Just start reading aloud from the top. When I sign off on each item, move on to the next."

He began the litany. Partway down the list, she gave him a sharp look.

"You skipped over carburetor heat," she said.

"Sorry."

"Say it aloud."

" 'Carburetor heat, on,' " he read.

She reached to the instrument panel and flicked a switch.

"Carburetor heat on," she replied.

"You don't need a regular copilot?" he asked, when they were done.

"Used to have one—briefly. They got pretty scarce. My employer prefers I make do with cargo kickers now. Usually, he supplies 'em."

"There's a big turnover with them?"

" 'Fraid so, love. Lucky for you tonight."

The engine grumbled, wheezed, whined, and then exploded into life. The aircraft trembled as, holding the brakes, she ran the engine up to full power, then eased the throttle back slowly. She reached for her seat belt.

"Strap yourself in and put on that headset," she said, sliding her own over her head. "Otherwise we can't talk."

Andy complied. Her voice came into his ears as though from another dimension, but intimately.

"Your microphone button's over by the side of the control wheel," she said. "Push it down when you want to talk, but for God's sake let it up again when you're through. And don't break in when you hear me talking to someone else over the radio. Now I'm going to check in with the tower. Keep quiet until we're airborne and out of the New Orleans TCA."

He pushed down the mike button. "What's a TCA?"

"I said keep quiet!"

Chagrined, he shrank back into his seat, watching and listening as she called the tower for takeoff clearance. Getting an immediate response, she shoved the throttle forward and taxied to the end of the runway. The lines of yellow lights converged in the murky distance. To either side of them and dead ahead were the night-shrouded waters of Lake Pontchartrain.

She ran the engine up to full again, then released the brakes. There was a steady, increasing thrum of tires on pavement, and a sudden silence as they became airborne.

"Tallyho," Glory said.

"That was fast."

"I told you. Marvelous aircraft."

She raised the landing gear and cleaned up the wings, then threw the rapidly climbing aircraft into a short, tight turn to the left. After straightening, they continued to ascend smoothly and passed through a thin veil of patchy cloud that did little to obscure the lights of the city below once they were above it. In a few hours, he'd be on the beach of a Caribbean isle—with Princess Astrid Montebello.

If he could find her.

"TCA," Glory said, her husky, honey-crisp British-colonial voice crackling into his ears, "means traffic control area. They're all over the place in this country. Bloody nuisance."

"Are we going to Grand Cayman nonstop?"

She looked over at him. He was becoming fond of her waspy little smile, but her eyes were full of amused scorn.

"I never said this was a direct flight. I filed a flight plan for Key West. It's four hundred eighty miles south from there to Owen Roberts."

"Where's Owen Roberts?"

"It's the airport on Grand Cayman."

"How long will it take to get to Key West?"

"A while. I have a stop or two en route."

He settled back further in his seat, supposing the "stop or two" would be to pick up the mysterious cargo. She hadn't explained why it required "kicking" once they got to their destination, which he assumed was an airport like any other. She'd reveal that in due time, he gathered. Feeling a little drowsy, he started to let his eyes close once more, but all at once they shot open again.

He remembered to push down the mike button. "Excuse me," he said. "Didn't you say those stops were 'en route' to Key West?"

"Right."

"But your compass heading shows 230 degrees. That's almost due west."

"A minor digression. We're going to drop by a little field I know south of Lafayette."

"But don't the air controllers care if you veer from your flight plan?"

"Usually they do. They follow your transponder number on their radar screens and like you to call in any changes in course and altitude."

"What do you do about that?"

She reached to the instrument panel and clicked another switch. "I turn off the transponder, and I stay off the radio. They'll assume I'm right on course. Now give your curiosity a rest for a bit, would you?"

But he couldn't. "Are we going to pick up the cargo at Lafayette?"

"Certainly not. We're going to pick up a couple of passengers."

"What passengers? You didn't say anything about passengers."

"Look, André . . ."

"Andy. I don't particularly care for André."

"Andy, then. I'm happy to help repay whatever favor it is my friends owe your Mr. Calhoun—and I gather it's considerable. You seem an agreeable enough fellow and I'm happy enough to have you aboard—especially when I think of the miscreants I've had along on these trips before. But I'd appreciate it very much if we didn't have all this chatter. This isn't a commercial airliner, is it? If you want to get to the Caymans, just accept what comes along and be quiet about it. All right? Make bloody do."

The first leg of the flight was extremely brief. What Andy assumed to be the lights of Lafayette appeared off in the haze to the north, then vanished as Glory banked the plane steeply and began a sudden plunge into a vast darkness below.

"There's an airfield down there?" he asked, forgetting her admonition to be quiet.

She hit him sharply in the arm. Realizing he had failed to release the mike button, he hastily did so.

"Yes, there's an airfield. Dead ahead. Now don't distract me."

The artificial horizon returned to level. Glory throttled back the engine and partially extended the flaps. In a moment, he heard the landing gear come down. But all he could see forward through the windshield was the black of night, broken only by a few pinpoints of light strung out in a line across the horizon.

She turned on the Pilatus's landing lights, which picked up the tops of trees below and dead ahead.

"Glory . . ."

"Do shut up."

The distant chain of lights on the horizon grew and spread until he recognized them as streetlamps. They flashed beneath. The rooftop of a house came next, then darkness again. The plane settled lower, and out the side window he saw grass rushing by. There was a bounce and then another and then they were rolling along rough ground at a mere sixty miles an hour. He had no idea what lay ahead of them. Glory apparently did. She was hitting the brakes hard. Changing the pitch of the propellor to something more wind resistant, she waited until the ground speed had lessened a bit more, then pulled back on the yoke, creating drag with the elevators.

Finally, they slowed enough to suit her. She kicked right rudder, spinning the plane around to the right, and headed obliquely toward the side of the field. Andy caught the outlines of a long, low shed with a galvanized roof and, next to it, the headlights of a car.

When they had stopped, Glory killed the engine, waiting for the propellor to cease its whining spin. Unfastening her safety belt, she slid out of her seat but paused to lean over him. He took off his headset.

"I want you to sit here and not say a word," she said. "You don't want to know these chaps, and I don't want them to know you."

"Whatever you say."

Glory went to the rear and opened the door, letting in a moist rush of heat and a cacophonous chorus of Louisiana night insects. Keeping his head down, he watched her run to the driver's side of the car. The headlights went out. It was a new car, and quite big. Andy guessed it was a Cadillac.

Far sooner than Andy expected, Glory came trotting right back again—alone.

"I'm sorry," she said, poking her head in the door. "I'm afraid I'm going to need your help. We have a sick man here. He has to be carried."

"There's no one else?"

"Just give me a hand. I told you you'd have to earn your passage."

There were two men in the car, one sitting behind the wheel smoking a cigarette and the other sprawled in the backseat, gazing upward. Andy gave the first one a quick, careful glance, noting someone fairly young, darkly handsome, flamboyantly well dressed, and in a bad mood. The fellow snarled something at Glory in a language Andy did not understand.

She opened the car's rear door. The other man's eyes were wide and staring and slightly crossed. His breathing was heavy and labored, making a dreadful rasping and sucking sound, and his shirtfront was covered with blood.

"Sick, you said," said Andy.

"Definitely not well. Come on. We have to get him in the plane."

The man behind the wheel got out and stood impatiently to the side, lighting another cigarette.

"Can't he help?" Andy asked.

"Just shut up and lift," said Glory.

They pulled the injured man out of the car, but he proved a little too heavy for the two of them to carry more than a few staggering yards—at least without a stretcher. The other man showed no interest whatsoever in assisting them.

"We'll have to drag him," Glory said. "I don't think he'll notice."

Each taking a foot, they pulled the man across the grass to the aircraft without much additional difficulty, but getting him up and through the door was a struggle.

"Just leave him in the back," said Glory. "He'll be more comfortable there."

"Shouldn't we get him to a doctor?"

"Right. First one we see. Get back in your seat."

She didn't join him but lingered by the door. He peered out the side window, searching for the man with the cigarette, but he seemed to have vanished. A moment later, the fellow abruptly reappeared, running toward the airplane with two small suitcases in his hands. Just as he reached the aircraft, there was a loud thump and a huge, incandescent ball of roiling orange flame where the car had been. It mushroomed into the night sky, spewing sparks and oily, coiling smoke, illuminating the small field.

When the man was aboard, Glory closed the door and hurried forward.

"He just blew up his car," Andy said.

"He was probably tired of it. Now buckle up and keep quiet."

She restarted the engine, and bumped the airplane with some haste back to the end of the runway by the streetlights. The burning automobile provided all the visibility they needed. On the whole, Andy could have done without it. He could see the trees at the other end of the field quite clearly. They were much too near.

"Can we make it?" Andy asked.

"Done it before. Piece of cake."

All but standing on the brakes, she revved up the engine until it was screaming and the prop seemed ready to spin off into the night sky. Then she let go, and the aircraft jolted forward, rolling and bumping and squeaking. Glory lifted it off the ground early, raising the landing gear the instant the wheels were clear of the grass. There was a moment of sickening terror as the plane sank a little, but Glory kept it whizzing along regardless, somehow keeping airborne, aiming dead for the trees. Slowly, foot by foot, they began to climb. As they cleared the trees, by no more than a yard or two, it seemed to Andy he could reach out and snatch a handful of leaves.

Another steep turn. Through a break in the thin clouds, Andy saw a star and waved at it, as though it had something to do with what appeared to be their miraculous luck. When Glory leveled off once more, the compass showed 185 degrees. They were heading south. Key West was not south.

"Glory, I think you need a new compass."

"The compass is fine."

"And you're happy with what it's indicating?"

"Everything's on schedule."

"Glory, no offense, but I have this funny notion that you may be a criminal."

Her look this time was very dark indeed. As there was nothing else to do, he sat perfectly still, staring forward, wondering why he wasn't more scared. In a few minutes, to his amazement, he found himself falling asleep.

He was awakened by a bump against his shoulder. Their well-dressed passenger was standing between the pilot's and copilot's seats, talking volubly to Glory in the same foreign language he had used before. It wasn't French or Spanish, which Andy understood a little of, though the man appeared decidedly Latin.

Whatever he was saying, Glory agreed with it. He took a step back, pausing to look at Andy as he might at a rat in his bed, then returned to his seat.

"Anything wrong?" Andy asked.

"Got another spot of work for you," she replied, easing back the throttle. "That other chap died."

"What work does that involve?"

"You can see to his earthly remains, or as our other traveling companion put it, without much lost to translation, you can 'get rid of the fucking stiff.' Open the cabin door and send the poor devil to his reward, which in his case is probably justly deserved."

"Kick him out like cargo?"

"Right."

"Where are we?"

She glanced at the instrument panel. "About a hundred and twenty statute miles south by southwest of New Orleans."

"Over the Gulf of Mexico."

"Quite. Separated from it by a mere sixty-five hundred feet. I'm going to go into a shallow turn to the right. That'll let gravity give you a hand. Just drag the fellow up to the door, open it up, and give him a shove."

"I haven't done this before."

"I know. I'd hoped we could get a little practice in before you had to do it for real, but it can't be helped, can it? Just make sure you look like you know what you're doing."

"The other guy still won't help?"

"It's not in his job description, I'm afraid. Keep out of his way."

"Shouldn't we say something—over the body?"

"You mean something religious?"

"Well, for starters, what was his name?"

"Don't know, rightly. All I ever heard him called was 'Looseballs.' Had absolutely no interest in finding out why."

"Did you know him?"

"Not well. He was the cargo kicker you're replacing tonight. On this trip he had some other business in New Orleans that did not go well."

Andy froze.

"Come on, Mr. Derain, get a move on."

Warily, he made his way back to the body and got behind it, bending to study the face a moment. The man was as dead as anyone he had ever seen. With a grimace, Andy reached under the arms and pulled. The man's shirt was still sodden with sweat and blood, and Andy slipped, landing on his rear with a thud. Getting back to a crouching position, he this time took the man by the wrists and yanked, and the body slid toward him.

Glory was watching him over her shoulder and put the plane

into a slight bank the moment he got the dead man to the door. It opened easily enough, just like those in commercial jetliners. The problem would be getting it closed again.

The sudden change in air pressure made him queasy. Clutching the back of one of the seats, he leaned out the doorway a little, catching a lot of whipping wind in the face but seeing nothing below that signified water—or much of anything. The black holes of space couldn't be any inkier than this.

There was no way to get the dead man through the door but to straddle him, lift, and shove. It took several tries. On one, Andy slipped again and almost went out all by himself, an irony the late cargo kicker might have appreciated—not to mention the regulars at the bar in the Razzy Dazzy.

Finally, once he had the man balanced upright on his knees in the doorway, lifeless head lolling onto the bloody chest, Andy completed the task with a quick shove. One of the fellow's shoes came off in the process. Andy quickly tossed it out after him, trying to recall what it was they said on navy ships when they had burials at sea. He couldn't quite, settling for: "We commit thee, Looseballs, to the waters. God have mercy."

Closing the door was every bit the struggle he had feared, but he somehow managed. The other man remained in his seat, sipping from a flask and leafing through the pictures of a men's magazine. Andy hurried by him without saying a word.

"Funeral's over," he said to Glory, once he had his headset back on.

"Go back to sleep now. I'll wake you when I want you."

"That sounds almost romantic."

"Well, it bloody well isn't intended as such."

As it turned out, Andy awakened all by himself. The pitch of the pro-pellor and speed of the engine had dramatically changed. There was a full moon high in the sky and, off to the right, he could see a glimmering sea and a dark, curving shoreline. Just beyond were mountains. Directly ahead of the aircraft were two clusters of lights. They were far from Louisiana.

"Where are we?" he said, after stretching.

"Mexico. That first bit of light there is Ciudad Madero. That lot just beyond is Tampico."

Andy looked again at the mountainous terrain along the coast.

"There's a good airport there, right?" he asked.

"Yes. Lovely airport. But we're not going there. We're going on a bit to the south."

"And what's that airport like?"

"It's not an airport at all. It's a road."

"Glory . . ."

"Just tighten your seat belt. And don't distract me."

The welcoming party on the ground had provided Glory with the best possible landing aids available. They amounted to exactly two vehicles—one parked at one end of a long straight stretch of road, the other, facing the first, down at the first curve. Both had their headlights on, helping Glory to make at least a good guess as to where the landing surface was. If she set down too late, her rollout would take her right into the second vehicle. If she tried to pull up to avoid it, she'd likely pile into the hillside just beyond, where the road curved. Andy vowed to do nothing whatsoever to bother her, wondering if he ought to hold his breath.

She lowered the gear, pulled full flaps, and reduced throttle to the tiniest fraction above stall speed. Then she crossed the controls and put the Pilatus into a sideslip. The aircraft began dropping rapidly. Andy closed his eyes. Seemingly a second later, the tires hit black asphalt with a screeching thud and bounce. He opened his eyes in time to see the plane waver to a stop some fifty feet from the headlights of a waiting vehicle.

It was a small truck, not a car.

"Don't move from this seat, and don't say a word," Glory said.

She removed her headset and stood up, just as her surviving passenger came up, threw one arm around her, pulled her to him tightly, and gave her a rather ardent kiss, which she accepted politely if rather limply, keeping her own arms behind her.

Andy stared, which proved a breach of etiquette. The man finally relented in his kiss, said something apparently affectionate to Glory in his strange tongue, then noticed Andy's upturned face.

"Who are you?" he said, in English, his eyes widening.

"I'm just the cargo kicker," said Andy.

"Nobody tell you not to fucking stare at people, you fuck, you piece of shit?"

"Sorry," said Andy, turning away.

He did so too late. The man whacked him on the side of the head so hard his neck made a slight cracking noise.

Glory stepped between them, speaking to the man rapidly in the strange language, edging him away. Whatever she had to say, it seemed to mollify him. A moment later, he was out of the plane.

"You all right, love?" Glory asked. She was touching the back of his neck gently, but not gently enough. It hurt, with a stinging pain.

Andy slowly straightened his head. "Not sure."

She moved her hand to his shoulder. "Won't be long. They'll be putting our cargo aboard now. You won't need to do a thing until later."

With great difficulty, he turned to watch. It didn't take long. The cargo amounted to a couple dozen plastic bags, each about two feet long. He heard Glory shout farewell, this time speaking Spanish, and close the door. She returned to her seat, carrying a large bottle of tequila.

"Isn't that sweet?" she said. "A little bon voyage gift."

"Can we go now?" Andy asked.

"In a minute. Don't worry, that chap who hit you won't be back. He wants to be far away from here, believe me."

"What language were you talking to him in?"

"Portuguese."

"But this is Mexico."

"Yes? So? You hear a lot of different languages in the export-import trade."

"You speak Portuguese well?"

"Not really. Just enough to hold my job."

"What's in those bags?"

She ignored this. "No more questions." She handed him the bottle. "Your head must hurt. Have some of this."

He took a large, heartening swallow, then sank back. "I want to be in the Cayman Islands."

"Oh you do, do you? Well, you can't want that any more than I do."

"The Caymans are due east of us, right?"

"Southeast. A couple hundred miles past Yucatán."

"Then it won't be too much longer."

Without replying, she started the engine and got the Pilatus turned around on the highway, taxiing back toward the head-lights waiting at the other end, so she could take off into the wind.

"Don't worry," she said, when they were again facing in the right direction. "That truck will be moving out of the way. Give us a little more clearance."

"That hill won't."

"Small hill."

Andy managed to get down two more healthy swigs before they were miraculously airborne again. When they had leveled off and were heading back out to sea, he peered at the instrument panel.

The compass was pointing north.

Chapter

·8·

If Andy had learned anything from all his years as a photographer it was how to read faces, yet he had no clear idea what this woman Glory was, aside from being an extraordinarily gifted and probably half mad aviator. She didn't strike him as that much of a criminal. There wasn't the malice, contempt, callousness, cruelty, and underlying paranoia he had seen twisted into the faces of the assorted bad guys he'd encountered in the company of Paul Maljeux and his law-enforcement colleagues. But she certainly got along well with them and hadn't been terribly upset by the bother of having to toss corpses with bullet holes in them out of her airplane. Long Tom owed him one hell of an explanation.

Once again, he was able to sleep. He was getting more slumber on this crazed, thrill-a-minute flight to nowhere than he had in weeks in his own comfy bed.

When he awoke, not knowing whether minutes or hours had elapsed, it was to the sound of a woman singing sweetly in his ear.

The music was coming through his headset. It was an old song, a sad and lonely yet lovely ballad, done in the clear, pure style of the 1940s—almost a torch song, though a little too ethereal for that. He listened as the woman returned to the refrain: "Be Still My Haunted Heart"—it had to be the title as well. Where had such a song come from? How had it found its way into his earphones?

He rubbed his eyes, then squinted at the instrument panel, discovering nothing that could be the source of the music. There was one oddity. Taped next to one of the dials was a cut-out photograph or print of turn-of-the-century artist Abbott Thayer's famous painting of his daughter as an angel, with huge wings and a beatific look in the innocent young girl's eyes and face. Andy had always liked the picture. He was about to ask Glory about it but was amazed to find her fast asleep herself. He assumed the aircraft was on automatic pilot. He hoped so.

The Pilatus continued thrumming contentedly on through the night, without falter or hesitation. Glory's head was tilted back against the seat, her face turned up, as beatific as Thayer's angel daughter. Her eyes were closed as though in reverie, her long hands folded decorously in her lap. The pale red glow from the instruments gave her skin a rosy aura. But for her casual flying clothes and headset, she might have been a painting by Jean-Antoine Watteau. Andy also recalled a magnificent pencil sketch he had once seen of Amelia Earhart, looking much like this, only with her eyes wide open.

He was struck by an impulse that hadn't visited him for months. Here, if he could manage it, was a marvelous photograph. The light was terrible, of course. He'd have to widen the lens aperture to its limit and hold it open for what amounted to a time exposure. It would be damned difficult, but the picture, if it came out, would be worth it. Saint Glory, in her heaven. She looked a little too sensual for the part, perhaps, but that didn't conflict with his idea of paradise.

Quietly, Andy edged out of his seat and went back to his camera bag for the Minolta. After checking the film load and changing to a fifty-millimeter lens, he returned to the copilot's chair and knelt sideways on it, careful not to nudge the control wheel. Glory stirred a moment, lifting her shoulders slightly, then relaxed, her lips forming a tiny smile.

Andy took a deep breath, wedging himself as tightly against the seat as possible, then pushed down on the shutter release, holding it for a full three seconds. The next shot, a little closer, was for what he judged to be two seconds. Making a slight adjustment, he reduced the time to about a second for the third picture. It was educated guesswork, but one of these exposures might be close to what he was after.

Relaxing finally, he stood, still unsure if he'd gotten any kind of decent image. The camera had a built-in strobe. He wanted the picture as he hadn't wanted one in a very long time. He'd try again with the strobe. Insurance.

The sudden flash awakened her instantly. She sat up blinking, as he quickly lowered his camera. She noticed it anyway. Furious, she tore off her headset.

"What the bloody hell are you doing?"

She wasn't merely irritated. She looked ready to toss him out after Looseballs. He'd have liked a shot of her like that as well, but he wanted to keep his camera in one piece.

"Sorry," he said, grasping for a useful falsehood. "I was testing my strobe. I was going to take your picture. You looked so beautiful. You still do."

She wasn't mollified by the flattery.

"Put that goddamn thing away and keep it away! If Fabio had known you had that aboard he would have killed you right then and there."

"Fabio?"

"Our passenger—the live one!"

Andy hurried to put the camera back. Glory was still a little livid when he returned to his seat.

"Just who in hell are you?" she asked.

Before answering, he buckled himself in and put on his earphones, compelling her to do the same.

"May I ask a question first?" Andy said. "Are we on autopilot?"

"You are a cretin. Of course we're on automatic pilot! How do you think I manage these long hauls all alone?"

"What happens if something goes wrong?"

"I wake up, as I've just now done. Just like Charles Lindbergh did when he fell asleep crossing the Atlantic. Now tell me who you are. What's going on here?"

"I'm André Derain. I was sort of famous once, as a fashion photographer. Celebrities, too. The rich and famous and all that. You know, magazine spreads."

"Well, terribly sorry to tell you this, but I never heard your name before tonight."

"Doesn't bother me. I didn't much enjoy being famous, or the people whose pictures I had to take to stay famous."

"But you are wanted by the police?"

"No. Sorry."

"What then? Why did you have to get out of New Orleans in such a hurry?"

"I've had a little trouble with a gangster—a New Orleans mob boss named Joe Coquin. You heard of him? A decidedly large man."

"Yes."

"More famous than me, I guess. Anyway, his son was murdered in New Orleans last night, along with a girlfriend. Joe thinks I know something about it that the cops aren't telling him. A friend of mine is a cop. He tipped me to the story so I could get on the scene early and shoot some freelance news pictures. Joe Coquin thinks the cops fill me in on everything."

"And do they?"

"Not at all. The only thing I learned of any consequence was the name of the girlfriend, and that was on my own—from a bartender. I'm pretty sure old man Coquin knew all about her anyway."

"What was it?"

"The girl's name? Felicie Balbo."

"From Florida?"

"That's what I was told. Miami. Did you know her or something?"

She was frowning and staring hard straight ahead into the night.

"I heard of her." She pushed a button on the underside of the instrument panel, the background music disappeared from the earphones, and a tape cassette shot out into her hand. Dropping it into a small plastic bin next to her seat, she fetched out another and put it in the slot. "Why do you want to go to the Cayman Islands? If all you wanted was to get out of New Orleans, there are a lot of easier places to go to."

"I have a friend staying on Grand Cayman, and I think she's in trouble. It isn't so much that I wanted to get out of New Orleans in a hurry. I want to get to Grand Cayman as soon as I can."

"It's very hard to get in trouble in the Caymans. They're about the most peaceful islands in the Caribbean."

"She's disappeared."

"That's even harder to do there. Grand Cayman's barely twenty miles long, and the population of all three islands is only about twenty-seven thousand. Stay there long enough and you get to meet everybody. Who is this person?"

"Astrid Montebello—the fashion designer."

"The *famous* fashion designer, no doubt. Sorry. Never heard of her, either. Don't move much in your pommy circles."

Her airborne stereo system was now playing a strange, raunchy, thumping sort of barroom music, almost Brechtian in its antic depravity. A male singer came on whom Andy recognized— Tom Waits, his voice sounding like he'd been drinking a mixture of whiskey, frogs, and gravel.

"I liked your forties music," Andy said.

"So did I, but now I'm in a mood for this. It's the sound track from *Night on Earth.* You remember the film? It had to do with taxicabs, working the night shift, all over the planet."

"A blind girl in Paris. A drunk in Helsinki."

"That's the one."

"Why do you play it up here? It makes me think of every dead-end saloon I ever got drunk in."

"It's perfect, don't you think? *Night on Earth?* I fly all night. I look down on Earth. The music reminds me of what's down there and how far away I am from it."

Andy studied her face again. With longer hair, a little less weight, and some education in the art of cosmetics, Glory could have done very well as a fashion model. He wondered at her age, guessing a year or two one side or the other of thirty. Her blouse was partially unbuttoned, revealing a curve of breast. It appeared to be as tanned as the rest of her. He wondered where she sunbathed on Grand Cayman.

"Why are you flying this plane?" he asked.

"What?"

"You're a very good pilot. You deserve a better job."

"What do you know about my job?"

"Well, the hours are lousy. You seem to have to put your life on the line every landing and takeoff. You carry cargo that looks suspiciously like something that could land you a long stay in do-

right city. And your passengers run to very well dressed repre-
sentatives of the scum of the earth."

"Not counting nosy riffraff like you."

"That too."

She flicked off a switch on the control column, releasing it
from the automatic pilot, and took the wheel lightly in her hands,
sitting more erect in her seat.

"I was going to be an airline captain, actually."

"Probably found it too dull."

"Nothing about flying is dull. Not for me. I wanted that job
for the longest time. I was six when I took my first airplane ride. I
started lessons when I was eleven and soloed—quite illegally,
mind—when I was fourteen. My mother insisted I go to college,
and I did for a year, but it wasn't a go. I dropped out and enrolled
in a commercial flight school in Florida. Worked as a flight in-
structor for a couple of years, then got a job flying checks."

"Checks?"

"Right. Canceled checks. Bloody bales of them. From city to
city, bank to bank, almost always at night. It's a great way to build
up hours. When I had enough, I went around to the airlines. One
of them was very anxious to get some women into its cockpits. I
flew copilot in props for their feeder line for a while, then got pro-
moted to second officer on a jetliner. Then the damn recession hit,
and it was last hired, first fired. Hell, they were laying off captains
with fifteen years. I took the first flying job I could get."

"Flying dope."

She shut her eyes, gripping the wheel tightly, but when she finally spoke, she was surprisingly calm. "I'm just the bus driver
here, all right? I've never looked into any of those bags. For all I
know, they're filled with marshmallows. I've never asked Fabio
or any of his associates what they do for a living. I fly for a corporation—a legal, American-registered company. I go where they
tell me, whether I'm carrying plastic bags or briefcases or party
girls in miniskirts."

"Or stiffs."

"That's a rare occurrence. I've really no idea what misadventure befell Mr. Looseballs."

"You were giving it some very serious thought though,
right?—along the lines of maybe he was involved in the shooting

of Philippe Coquin and his girl back in New Orleans? The police think Philippe got off a couple of shots before leaving this life. Mr. Looseballs stepped in the way of something."

"I know nothing about it, and if you're smart, you won't either."

"You scare me."

"Good."

"I mean, you make me afraid for you. I've only known you a few hours, but I really wouldn't like it if something were to happen to you. I wish you didn't have this job."

"I take care of myself."

"Lot of death associated with drugs, up and down the line."

She changed the subject. "Are you married?"

"Not really."

"What does that mean?"

"Cohabitation without the blessings of church or civil authorities. Shocking what goes on in New Orleans these days."

Glory looked to be thinking hard again.

"Are you married?" he asked.

"No. Was once."

"I don't even know your last name."

"Let's leave it that way."

"You sound English, but you're not."

"That describes me perfectly. Look. I'm going to be a bit busy now. We're coming onto a storm front up ahead, and I'm going to try to vector us around some thunder cells without help from the air controllers. Do me a large favor and go back to sleep. If it'll be any help, have some more tequila."

He obliged her by taking a pleasant swallow. It made him feel warm.

"When do I do my cargo kicking?"

"Soon enough."

But first the storm, which made an absurdity out of any thought of sleep. There was calm, then suddenly, a tremendous thrashing and bucking of the airplane. The windshield was nearly opaque with a sheet of thudding rain. Lightning was flashing all around them, illuminating towering clouds that enclosed them like the walls of some celestial canyon. Andy glanced somewhat fearfully at the instrument panel. The turn-and-bank indicator was swinging wildly back and forth like an amusement-park ride.

Glory looked very grim and serious now, but perfectly in control. Why would an airline let someone like this go?

"Is this vectoring?" he asked, as his seat seemed to drop from beneath him. It slammed back against his bottom almost instantly.

"Couldn't go around this one," she said. "I need the fuel to get where we're going. Damn it, tighten your seat belt!"

He did as instructed. Something like hail, sounding very much like tommy-gun bullets, rattled against the fuselage.

"Hang on," Glory said, as though talking to herself.

Andy's elbow banged painfully against the edge of the armrest. Absent her voice, the headset was noisy with static. Lightning exploded directly in front of them, and the aircraft veered sharply to the right. According to the artificial horizon, they were flying sideways. A moment later, he felt himself being pulled violently upward, the seat-belt buckle cutting into his belly. The instruments' message now was that they were upside down. He closed his eyes.

He didn't open them again until the hellish bouncing and jarring had ceased. There was nothing but darkness outside the window, and the lightning now seemed to be behind them.

Glory took her right hand off the control wheel and stretched her arm, flexing the muscles of her fingers. Then she did the same thing with her left.

"God almighty," she said. "We dropped four thousand feet in that one."

"How many feet does that leave?"

"Enough."

There was cloud about, but also large clear patches in the sky. The static had disappeared from his earphones. Andy was startled by the sound of a man's voice in his ear, saying with great casualness, "Delta (garble), cleared to twenty-seven."

"Where are we?" Andy asked.

"Approaching the Louisiana coast. The voice you heard was a New Orleans air controller."

He was angry. "You mean we're back where we started from?"

"We'll pass near. Don't worry. In a little while we'll be dropping our cargo; then we'll get on to Key West. Everything will be
all tickety-boo."

Andy tried to remember where he'd heard that phrase before.

"You didn't tell me about any of this."

"You signed on no questions asked," she said. "When we get
a little more clear of this weather, I'm going to drop down to a
thousand feet. Then I'll be wanting you to get by the door."

In a few minutes, some twinkling lights appeared low in the
distance. Glory throttled back to lose altitude, turning slightly to
the right, then steadied their course. To the east, there was a faint
glow of pale light showing above the clouds. To the west, the
twinkling lights now seemed to be receding.

"You're turning away from the coast?"

"I'm going exactly where I'm supposed to go. We just passed
over the mouth of the Mississippi River. Ahead is a chain of barrier reef islands—the Delta-Breton National Wildlife Refuge. The
northernmost island is where we make our drop. There should be
a boat waiting. Maybe two."

"You don't want to land?"

"No. I'll bring it down low and circle. When I give you the
signal, you drop the bags out the way you did Mr. Looseballs,
only a little more efficiently, please. The bags are reinforced. They
won't break."

"Pity."

"Then we'll be out of here, and you can forget all about
this."

He used the altimeter to judge their nearness to their goal.
When it read a thousand feet, he got out of his seat and headed to
the rear. The door opened to a gush of warm, moist air and the
smell of the sea. Below, he could see small lines of surf washing
against a narrow stretch of beach.

The beach vanished. Ocean intervened, then gave way to another point of land. The aircraft seemed to be sinking lower.

Suddenly, the engine surged and the plane began to climb. He
looked toward Glory. She was motioning at him frantically to
come. Leaving the door open, he did.

"We can't make the drop!" she shouted, her headset off.

"Why not?"

She extended her arm, but he couldn't make out what she was pointing to.

"Civil Air Patrol," she said. "They do surveillance flights for the Drug Enforcement Administration."

"How can you tell that's who it is?"

"By the way he's flying. I've seen that fellow before. Usually, he's gone home by now. Shit!"

"What do we do?"

"We get the hell out of here. There's an alternate drop site. Petit Bois Island. It's off the Mississippi coast, a bit south of Pascagoula." She looked back and off to the left. "But first I've got to lose that chap."

She banked the plane, and Andy almost fell into his seat. Righting himself, he buckled his safety belt.

"Shouldn't the door be closed?"

"Don't worry about it."

She said "Shit" twice more, explaining finally that the Civil Air Patrol aircraft had turned in pursuit.

"I don't know what he's got, but I'm afraid it's got some speed to it. And he's probably calling in help. Goddamn it. Why is he doing this?"

"Trying to stop the illegal flow of Mexican marshmallows?"

"You're so fucking hilarious." She leaned forward, squinting. "I think we're going to be all right."

"How's that?"

She pointed ahead and to the right, where he could vaguely see a lighter band of murk. "Fog bank."

"That's good?"

"Delightful, just so we don't have to fly too low to stay in it."

She went down to where the altimeter showed something between a hundred feet and death. He thought of closing his eyes once again, but in a moment it didn't matter. The windshield filled with an impenetrable dark gray.

"If we don't hit some goddamn tanker, we'll be just fine," she said.

"If this is fine, I'd like better than fine."

"Do shut up, love." She turned on the carburetor heat and lowered flaps a few degrees. Both actions caused their speed to drop dramatically.

"I'll do half an hour of this," she said. "That ought to get rid of him."

"Not to speak of us."

She hit him in the arm.

It was easily the longest half hour of Andy's life, surpassing even the time he had spent on a foot patrol with the British army in Belfast during a magazine photo shoot on Northern Ireland.

Glory pulled back on the wheel, and they broke free of the murk and swept up into the pink-orange glow of the rising sun. She had said she thought they might come out near the island. It, or one just like it, was directly ahead. They nipped over its shoreline just above some high trees.

"I'm going to try to circle over the beach on the east end," she said. "Get back there and throw out the bags as quickly as you can."

He looked out the window. "It's not a very wide beach. The stuff could end up in the trees—or the water."

"Too bloody bad. I just want to get rid of it. Now get back there!"

Andy watched the last of the bags tumble down from the door and into the eddy of a receding wave. Most of them, unfortunately, had landed in the sand. It occurred to him that, for the first time in his life—not counting a few traffic and drinking-hour violations—he had knowingly committed a crime.

Unless the bags really were filled with marshmallows.

Chapter

·9·

Low on fuel, they continued on across what remained of the gulf waters to the coast, putting down finally in the now bright morning light at what Glory called an unattended FOB—a small grass field between a swamp and farmland, with one hangar, a couple of sheds, and a gas pump.

The pump was locked.

"Goddamn it!" she said. "He's supposed to keep it open for me."

"Who?"

She ignored him and went back into the airplane, returning with a pair of bolt cutters.

"Here," she said. "You males have all the upper-body strength. Cut it free."

"And commit yet another crime?"

"We're in Alabama. Do you want to stay in Alabama?"

It took some effort, but, after three tries, the lock snapped. After he stepped back, Glory pulled it off the pump. The hose did not reach the wing fuel ports, but she went around the corner of one of the sheds and returned with two gasoline cans, setting them beside the pump.

"You fill 'em; I'll pour 'em," she said. "Be as quick as you can. It's not to our advantage to hang about here."

"This is a very impressive high-budget operation your corporation has."

She ignored him, clambering up on the wing.

By the time they were done, the morning air was beginning to fill with heat. Glory returned the refueling cans, pulled a fat roll of currency from her pocket, and stuck a hundred-dollar bill into a loose strip of metal on the gas pump. In a nearby field, they could hear a tractor start up.

"Key West," she said. "Let's hop it."

This part of the flight was uneventful—and very beautiful, the climbing sun glittering on the water like diamond dust, its rays shining through gauzy layers of cumulus cloud that the front they'd passed through had left behind as gifts.

Glory turned on the transponder. "We're official again. I'd better check in with the controller."

"Aren't they going to wonder where you've been?"

"If they ask, I'll say I had a mechanical delay. But they almost never do."

"You lead a charmed life."

"Don't say that." Her look was dark.

Glory had the briefest and most desultory of radio conversations with a bored male voice. The man seemed to recognize her and raised no question about her sudden appearance in his traffic flow.

"Thirty minutes," she said to Andy. "Maybe less."

"Then what?"

"We clean up a little, refuel, and then on to Owen Roberts. I telexed for a Cuba overflight permit when I was in New Orleans."

"We're going to fly over Cuba?"

"They let pretty much everyone do it except the military. All very routine. Otherwise, it's quite a long way round if you're going to Grand Cayman."

"Couldn't be any longer round than it's been tonight."

She slid another tape cassette into the tape deck and leaned back. As with her earlier selections, the music this time was entirely unexpected. Carl Orff's *Carmina Burana,* a choral hymn to angry gods, one of whom was called "Fortuna, Imperatrix Mundi"—which Andy had always translated as "Lady Luck, Goddess of the World."

They listened awhile—he curiously, she thoughtfully. The dark blue shadow of a cloud moved across the turquoise blue below, looking like a slowly moving island.

"I like this."

She made no reply. Andy watched out the window, observing a freighter steaming slowly south, creating an amazingly wide and long wake. Ahead, he could see the thin line of the distant coast—a row of cumulus clouds arrayed as though in parade formation above it, their tops a brilliant white in the sun.

He looked back at Glory. She was gently rubbing at her eye. He thought for a moment it was from lack of sleep, then noticed the tiny trickle of a tear on her cheek.

Andy shut up for the rest of the flight.

The Key West airport had only one runway, extending from northeast to southwest. Descending rapidly, Glory flew a pattern that took them past the field, skirting an area just to the north, where several hot-air balloons were rising over the water, then turned sharply right onto her base leg. With one more right turn, she was lined up with the runway. Squinting ahead, she abruptly dropped the gear, pulled on full flaps, throttled back to a very marginal landing speed, and then threw the airplane into a sideslip far more dramatic than the one she'd used landing in Mexico. They began dropping like the heavy object they were.

"What's wrong?"

"Got to get down fast," she said, gesturing forward with a nod of her head. "Damn birds. The cheeky little bastards will kill me yet."

Andy looked ahead to see a curving sweep of small white creatures rising from a marsh and turning across the runway about halfway down its length. Glory straightened the aircraft at the last second, hitting the pavement right on the numbers. They whizzed along the strip, passing just beneath the tail end of the seabirds' formation.

"John James Audubon used to shoot the things, you know,"

she said. "They're beautiful but so very stupid. I wouldn't mind them so much if they'd follow flight rules."

She parked the plane near a low building bearing a sign that said ISLAND CITY FLYING. Just down from it was a larger structure.

"That's the main terminal and U.S. Customs," she said. "We won't worry about them. We're a domestic flight, right?"

Then she did something he truly wished she hadn't. Reaching under her seat, she pulled forth a small automatic pistol and stuck it in her belt, at her back beneath her light jacket.

"Where are we going that you might need that?"

"Just to get some breakfast."

There was a rental car waiting for them—an innocuous white Ford Taurus. Glory drove the short distance to the main part of town cautiously, proceeding very slowly down Duval Street because of the pedestrian traffic.

There were a number of tourists, looking a little bored and hot, and a few young men walking in pairs, but most of the people out at that hour were elderly. Then Andy saw a tall blond woman with a little girl at her side and another in a stroller.

"Is that Kelly McGillis?" he said.

"My favorite actress," said Glory. "She has a rather nice restaurant down here. Stocks some of the world's great beers. Too bad we don't have time to stop. Not much time at all, really."

Instead they went to a grungy-looking joint near the waterfront, taking a table in the back, away from the window.

"I'm having a bowl of conch chowder, some Key lime pie, and coffee. It's all I'd recommend eating here. Everything else they cook in gallons of grease."

He nodded. After they'd given their orders to a tired-looking black woman, Glory pushed back her chair and picked up the gym bag she had brought with her from the plane.

"I'm going to wash up a little and brush my teeth," she said. "If you want to do the same, this is your best chance."

The men's room looked like a bacterial breeding farm, but Andy made do, standing fastidiously at the stained, multicolored sink and managing to wash his face, upper body and even feet. He brushed his teeth without benefit of the rusty-looking water, but completed a decent shave with it. An old man who looked like he hadn't had a decent shave in weeks shuffled in while Andy was finishing up and went to the urinal without greeting or comment, doing most of his business on the floor. Andy left speedily, hoping the man was not the chef.

Glory was already back at the table, looking much refreshed but very serious as she attended to her meal. She'd changed into shorts. As he set down his camera bag, Andy noticed that a large black vinyl briefcase had joined them, resting near her feet.

His spoon had soap stains on it, but Andy judged that an encouraging sign of an attempt at hygiene and set to the chowder, which wasn't bad. He nodded down toward the briefcase.

"Have you been in the luggage store?"

"Just eat," she said.

"I thought these deals were all done out of the back of stretch limos in warehouse parking lots. Not flying all over the Gulf of Mexico and making rendezvous in greasy spoons."

"You've been watching too many reruns of *Miami Vice*."

"How much money is in there?"

She glowered. "I haven't the faintest idea. It's locked. A man in a bank has the key. I'm just the driver, remember? This is freight."

"What bank?"

"Eat."

He finished his chowder and wolfed down the Key lime pie, which really was fresh and good. The coffee was at room temperature, which was to say, still quite hot.

"All right then," she said, putting down a fifty-dollar bill. "Let's go."

A hundred here. A fifty there. Glory was a very generous tipper.

She seemed in a very great hurry now, but instead of returning to the airport, drove east out of town, following a narrow road past a beach parking lot and then to the end of a clump of scrubby trees. Leaving the engine running, she turned to face him.

"Very well, Mr. Derain. This is where you get off."

He was stunned.

"That wasn't the deal. I need to get to Grand Cayman."

"Not with me." She pulled out her roll of bills again, and counted off ten hundreds. Hesitating, she then added ten more. Folding them, she thrust them into his shirt pocket.

"That's the going rate," she said. "Plus a bonus—for being a good sport. And, I trust, keeping your mouth shut. You've got to do that. Not a word to anyone. Just disappear."

"I guess I'm not making myself clearly understood. I'll be happy to keep my mouth shut, but I went through all this crap so I could get to Grand Cayman."

"You can't go with me. Sorry. My apologies to Mr. Calhoun."

"Look—"

"Goddamn it! Fabio told me to kill you!" She pulled her little automatic out from her belt, not aiming it at him but holding it pointed near enough to his general direction. He felt ill. Buckets of acid seemed to be gushing into his stomach. Otherwise, he felt perfectly numb.

"Have you done that? Killed people?"

"What matters is that Fabio thinks I have—and expects me to, if told to do so. Don't you understand? He's a very bad man."

"Really."

"It's not bloody amusing! Do you want to die?"

"What have I done to him? All I did was watch him try to give you a hickey."

"He didn't like you. He tends to view the general run of humanity as just so many cockroaches anyway. Listen to me, Andy. I don't want you to go down to the Caymans. It's not a good time to be there. Take your money and get on back to New Orleans and forget you ever took this trip. Please."

"Joe Coquin's back there."

"He's Santa Claus compared to Fabio and his friends. Now go. Please."

"My friend Astrid . . ."

Now she pointed the gun with great exactitude. He opened the car door a few inches.

"Just one thing."

"What?!!" She was exasperated. She glanced back out the rear window.

"A kiss."

She shook her head. "God almighty."

"You gave one to that scumbag. How about one for the forces for good?"

"You're utterly mad."

But her expression had gentled. He leaned toward her, reaching to touch her cheek with his hand as their lips met. The kiss was very brief but soft and gentle—and, he thought, quite friendly. He wondered why she did it, feeling quite heady. If only he didn't also feel the metal sharpness of the gun barrel against his ribs.

She pulled back brusquely. "All right. Out. Run down the beach a ways and wait till I'm gone. Go. Goodbye."

Andy swung the door open wide, but lingered. "I don't even know your last name."

"Out!"

Camera bag in hand, he began trotting over the sand toward the water. On impulse, he glanced back. She was leaning out of the car, her arm extended. The gun was still in her hand.

There was one shot. It missed him by a good twenty feet, but he began running all the faster.

Chapter

·10·

By the time Andy returned, somewhat warily, to the Key West airport, Glory's two-tone Pilatus was gone. Presumably she was en route to the Caymans, though, for all he knew, she was on her way back to New Orleans—or maybe to Bolivia, or to Easter Island. He was relieved to be free of her and the rather constant excitements of her life but, at the same time, wistful and sad. When she wasn't shooting at him or making him toss corpses out of airplanes, there was quite a lot that was appealing about this very singular woman.

She had come into his life with a whoosh, and now she was gone as swiftly. He was curious to know her secrets—some of them anyway. He wanted to learn the reason for that tear. He was pleased with himself for having taken her picture but unsure of how successful he had been at getting a true portrait. Behind Amelia Earhart's brave angel face, he'd been told, was a very mercenary woman.

He did very briefly consider taking Glory's advice to hotfoot it home but without much anguish decided against it. Whatever anger he'd stirred up in Bleusette by making this trip wasn't going to be much lessened by an early return, and he certainly wasn't going to take a walk on Astrid before finding out the nature of her trouble. He was a law-abiding U.S. citizen—at least he was when he wasn't in Glory's company. He had every right to go visiting the Caymans if he chose. And anyway, they'd left the fearsome, foppish Fabio back in the wilds of Mexico, and only hours before. The swine was probably amusing himself with a bedful of Tampico hookers.

Without too long a wait, Andy caught an afternoon feeder-line flight to Miami. During the short layover there, he tried Astrid's number on Grand Cayman again, more from habit than justifiable hope, charging the call to his New Orleans phone. To his astonishment, he got a busy signal. Excited, he tried a couple times more, with the same frustrating yet encouraging result. He had a quick drink at a bar just down the concourse, then hurried back and made one last call.

Joy. It rang. But it kept ringing. And ringing. He let it ring a dozen times. His happiness vanished as quickly as Glory had. Astrid might not have been there at all. The busy signal could merely have meant that all the phone circuits down there had been taken up for a while.

There was no way of knowing—except to be there.

His flight was the last into Owen Roberts that evening, arriving shortly after sunset. When he handed his passport to the Caymans customs inspector, he was surprised to note it was going to expire in three weeks.

"You didn't put down a departure date on your immigration card," the customs man said.

"Sorry." Andy quickly scribbled in a date a week hence, just on a guess.

"This says you're a commercial photographer. I'm afraid you can't be employed here without obtaining a work permit."

"Understood. I'm on a busman's holiday."

"A what?"

"I'm going to take pictures for my own pleasure. Palm trees. Bathing beauties. Tropical fish."

There was a card on the counter listing prohibited items, including "dangerous drugs and hallucinogens, firearms, mechanical spear guns, Hawaiian slings, or pile spears." It occurred to

Andy that Glory's plane might have been carrying all of those things.

"This is all your luggage, sir?"

"Yes. I'm going to buy some clothes here."

The inspector eyed him curiously but not with any great suspicion.

"I'm not carrying any pile spears," Andy said.

The man shook his head, then stamped Andy's passport and slid it back to him. "Enjoy your stay, sir."

Owen Roberts' various facilities occupied several buildings connected by walkways. The money exchange was up one flight in the building containing the restaurant. He converted five hundred American into Cayman Islands dollars, somewhat dismayed to find the exchange rate provided him with only four hundred in local money, though it was very pretty currency.

Putting it in his wallet, he left the exchange and was about to leave the building when he felt a hand slip into his. For the briefest instant, he thought it might by Glory's, but it quickly occurred to him this would be unlike her. She'd doubtless greet him with a punch in the arm.

He knew damn well who it was. The woman was gifted with a special sense about people moving around her. He remembered once passing behind her backstage at a fashion show and then again at some party. Each time she had reached out without turning her head and taken his hand as surely as if she had been staring at it—drawing him near, pulling his arm around her waist. She did it now. He felt a little light-headedness—the giddiness of relief—and joy.

Their hug was very close. Her perfume seemed to penetrate to his brain, intoxicating him. It was a scent of her own concoction, unmistakably her.

"Princess, Princess."

"Andy, Andy."

In the worst of his fears, he'd imagined Astrid tied to some heavy weight a hundred feet under the Caribbean. Here she was coming out of a restaurant.

He stepped back. It was as though not a minute had elapsed since he had last looked into her eyes from this distance, outside her Greenwich Village apartment building that long ago moonlit night—the same large arctic blue eyes, the same long, lustrous

Nordic blond hair. She was wearing a low-cut, floor-length dress, as she had been then, as she almost always did, morning or night. This one, though, had a floral print; the other had been as dark as her hair was light.

"How in hell did you know I was coming?" he asked.

"I didn't. This is serendipity. I was having coffee, and I looked up, and there you were. Voilà. Magic. My heart was beaming wishes that you'd turn up. You must have caught one."

She looked perfect, everything in place, nothing to indicate fear or anxiety. It hadn't exactly been a pleasure cruise getting here, and Bleusette was going to provide him with a one-woman demonstration of the guns of Balaclava when he got back to New Orleans. He needed a better reason to be here than heartbeams.

"All I got from you was a postcard. From some place called Hell. Why didn't you call?"

Astrid sighed, glanced down, then looked up again. She was wearing high-heeled sandals and stood measurably taller than he.

"I didn't really want to bother you with my troubles—at first. I wasn't sure how serious they were or what was really happening. Sometimes things just go wrong, especially on location shoots."

"You wrote, 'Poor bears.' "

"I was feeling 'Poor bears.' I still am, worse."

"I've been trying to reach you on the phone for two days. Your office in New York has been trying, too."

"I know. I didn't mean to worry them. I just didn't want to take any calls. That's part of my troubles, too. Someone keeps calling me I don't want to speak to."

"Who?"

She gave him a weak, sad little smile. "Harvey Fitch."

The long and short of Harvey Fitch was simple. In the way of "long" were the several office towers, hotels, and residential high-rises he owned in Manhattan and other expensive places. The "short" was Harvey himself. He was more diminutive even than Henry Kravis and Laurence Tisch, New York moguls with far more stature and money, though Harvey was working hard to catch up with them. His bottom line was a hard guess. Everyone assumed he was carrying enormous debt and that his liabilities probably exceeded his assets. But he always seemed to be buying something new, and always something big.

Andy considered the notion of Astrid and Harvey together, coming up with the image of Henri Toulouse-Lautrec and one of his willowly demoiselles from the Moulin Rouge. Each of Fitch's three wives had been taller than he—and, successively, taller than each other. It had been a joke on the Upper East Side that the more money Harvey made, the more woman he could afford. Astrid was of greater height than any of them. Was Harvey thinking of moving up again?

"Why is that creep phoning you?"

"You remember when I told you my fashion business might take off if I could get a big investor? Well, it took off, and he's the big investor. He owns so much stock in my company I should probably be calling him boss. And now I think he wants to marry me."

"Marry you? He's already married."

Ramona Fitch was just the wife the man deserved. When Andy was still living in New York, she had been the most flamboyant, outrageous, notorious trophy wife to be found on the Upper East Side—an imperious, designer-draped Park Avenue Catherine the Great, with movie-star legs and body and a glamour-puss face attended to by plastic surgeons kept on retainer. It had taken Ramona four upwardly mobile marriages to get to the level where she could get her hooks into Harvey. Andy couldn't imagine her withdrawing said hooks very compliantly. Andy had shot her portrait once and come quickly to dislike her intensely. He would have despised her even more had he not come to the conclusion she might well be insane. Ramona had odd little idiosyncrasies, such as her fondness for the color gold.

Practically everything she owned—excepting Harvey—was gold: clothes, jewelry, the decor of her apartment. Even the pricey Impressionist paintings on her walls had gold as the dominant color in them. Andy knew of a nice if eccentric woman in Dallas who had a penchant like that for the color yellow, but that was Texas.

"I think she may be here—on Grand Cayman," Astrid said.

"Ramona Fitch?"

"Yes. And I think she may be part of my troubles, too."

Astrid gave a nervous little laugh. It was what she did when she didn't like what she was feeling. Andy decided she might be pretty scared after all.

They were still holding hands.

"Would you like a drink?" he asked.

"I thought you'd given that up."

Whenever had he said that? "Not today. It's been a thirsty day."

"All right. But not here. It's too bright and noisy. And public. There's a restaurant Chef Tell owns on the island, not far from here. It's very beautiful. Right on the sea. And quiet."

"Sounds perfect."

"Nothing's perfect anymore, Andy."

Without relinquishing his hand, she led him out the door.

She had a white Jeep Wrangler in the parking lot, emblazoned with the rental car company's name and logo on the rear. The steering wheel was positioned in the American manner, but driving in the Caymans was on the left-hand side. She managed this without difficulty, slipping into the stream of traffic heading along the airport road into town.

"Shouldn't you call New York? Your office must be really nervous about you."

"I will, but not tonight. Anyway, they'll just tell me that Harvey Fitch has been calling. And I already know that."

The landing lights of an airplane were boring in from the west. Andy watched its approach, deciding as it whizzed over some nearby rooftops that it was much too big to be Glory's.

"Why were you at the airport?" he asked. "Were you planning to leave?"

"I don't know what I'm planning," she said, expertly shifting gears. In Europe, in her star-modeling days, Astrid had driven a Maserati. In New York, she had an old heap of a Honda. She drove all her cars the same, very fast and very well. She roared through an intersection just as its traffic light changed to red.

"I went to the airport," she continued, "because now my models are missing."

She told her story carefully, pausing from time to time to get her facts exactly right. With a photographer and three New York models in train, she had flown down six days before to shoot pictures for her spring catalogue and some resort-wear ads she was going to take out the next buying season in *W* magazine and *Women's Wear Daily.*

Things had gone wrong from the start—at first, mostly small things. While they were at dinner the first night, someone had broken into the three adjoining condominiums she had taken for the week and stolen some of the camera equipment. Then some young rowdies having an all-day beach party had ruined their first day's shoot. And when they moved to the other end of Grand Cayman's Seven Mile Beach, she thought she saw someone following them. Then, for a day and a half, it had rained.

"Sounds like a typical Caribbean vacation," Andy said.

"That's not supposed to happen here. These are the best islands in the Caribbean."

The following day, the photographer threatened to quit, saying he thought the shoot had become jinxed.

"Anyone I know?" he asked.

"Yes. Ernst Konig. Very expensive guy, but I wanted the best—anyway, the best since you dropped out of the business. This resort collection is very important to me. It's the first time I've gotten some nibbles from the big chain department stores. There've been hints I might get some big orders. Up till now, I've only sold to boutiques. There's so much competition. I'm up against top people like Anna Sui and Maria Snyder."

Konig was a very good photographer—probably better than Andy at pure fashion. But he was an irascible, temperamental man, with a considerable drinking problem. And he liked to fool around with the models.

"What happened to your models?"

"Same thing that happened to Ernst Konig, I guess. Whatever that was."

Astrid gave him a long, hard look, as though trying to make him understand the whole thing by concentrating hard and beaming it all to him.

"You'd better explain, Princess," he said, relieved when she turned back to the road.

"Last night, we were all getting on each other's nerves, and Harvey kept calling, and I was becoming more than a little nervous about Ramona being here, and, well, I just couldn't take it anymore. I moved out of the condo for the night and checked into a hotel. The Hyatt. Very nice. I felt safe."

"I'm sure. What about the others?"

"Harvey was bothering me, not them. And they certainly have nothing to worry about from Ramona. It's me she's upset about. Honest, Andy, I thought they'd be fine. I just had to get away. Get a decent night's sleep."

"Okay. Then what happened?"

"This morning I went back to the condos and they were gone. All of them. Ernst and the three girls. *Disparu.* And they left their luggage behind."

"Maybe they were just out looking for you."

"If they were, no one's seen them, and they never came back."

"Perhaps they got fed up with everything and went back to New York."

"I thought about that, but I told you, they left their luggage. Everything. And the girls wouldn't have walked out on the money. I'm paying top New York dollar."

"You tried the airlines?"

"Yes. That's why I was at the airport. I also went to the police. I didn't report them missing or anything. I didn't want some wild story to get into the *Women's Wear Daily* gossip column. I'm trying to get Seventh Avenue to take me seriously, Andy. I can't afford anything like that. But I did ask if they'd gotten into trouble or had an accident or something. The police hadn't a single report of anything like that. Actually, they weren't very helpful."

"I know. I called them myself—when I couldn't get you on the phone."

She took his hand. "That really was sweet of you, Andy."

"I talked to an Inspector Whittles."

"I know. He told me. He was very nice, but he didn't think anything was wrong. He said that you'd been worried about me being gone but then I'd turned up, so maybe the same thing would happen with Ernst and my girls, that maybe they'd moved to a hotel. As though we flighty New York fashion people were just amusing ourselves playing hide-and-seek. Practically no crime in the Caymans, don't you know. Nothing untoward could possibly have happened. I'm scared, Andy. Poor bears, poor bears, poor bears."

"Did he say 'Tickety-boo'?"

"What?"

"Inspector Whittles, did he say everything was all tickety-boo?"

"Yes. I think he did."

"Maybe he's right. Who are your girls?"

"The best. Annie Albrecht, Vilma, and Beth Hampshire."

"Beth Hampshire."

Andy had worked with all three, including the outrageously buxom Vilma, who had no last name. But he had once dated Hampshire—very seriously. A very long-legged girl with soft, sensitive eyes and long chestnut hair, she'd be over thirty now. He gathered she was still in pretty good shape if she was doing bathing-suit shoots.

Astrid reached and patted his knee. "You two were an item once, right?"

"Long time ago."

"Well, now you may have a reunion—I hope."

Chef Tell's restaurant was called the Grand Old House, and it was—a sprawling structure built on coral rocks overlooking the sea. They took a table out in back on the wide veranda. The water was very calm, and there was moonlight coming through the shifting clouds. Very romantic. Too romantic.

"I forgot," he said, after they'd ordered their drinks. "There's a call I have to make. I should have done it at the airport."

Bleusette was not at home. Zinnia was.

"She's lookin' for you, all right, Andy," Zinnie said. "But I don't think you want to be found too soon. She goin' kind at a boil as concern you."

"Well, tell her I made it to the Caymans, and I'm all right."

"I think she be a lot happier to hear you got yourself chomped on by a shark."

"Tell her I found my friend, and after I take care of a few problems, I'll be heading back home."

"Take your time, boy."

"Anyone else looking for me?"

"Those gentlemens who come callin' on you was back again."

"They do anything?"

"One of 'em kicked over a pot of begonias on the front gallery when I told 'em you'd gone off on a trip."

"Gangsters are hell on flowers."

"Lieutenant Maljeux come by lookin' for you, too."

"Gotta go, Zinnie."

"You sure you all right?"

"Yes. Everything's all tickety-boo."

There was a pause. "I do believe you lost your mind, boy."

Astrid was at the railing, drink in hand, looking out at the inky sea. Andy picked up his whiskey and water from the table and joined her.

He stood close, studying her face, feeling its magic. Actresses—at least good ones, like his friend Paris Moran—had ever-changing faces, expressions coming and going like wavelets of water in a flowing stream. Models tended to hold their expression, making a fascinating surprise of any change in it.

Astrid's expression was somber and wistful, all Nordic perfection. Even in the dim light, her lustrous blond hair shone. Ramona Fitch spent a fortune on hairdressers to keep her hair matching the golden hue with which she was so obsessed, but compared to Astrid's, it looked cheap and brazen.

"Are you married now, Andy?"

Her voice was as cool and Nordic as her beauty. Andy moved even closer, till their arms touched. He'd forgotten how overpoweringly magnetic this woman was. No wonder Harvey kept calling.

"Married? Me?"

"You."

Women were always asking him that, but the question coming from her was surprising. He shook his head.

"I would have told you—invited you to the wedding."

She kept her eyes on the dark horizon. "I'm amazed you're not. You always had so many girlfriends. That Texas model—Candy Longstreet. Weren't you pretty stuck on her?"

"She married somebody else. A rich guy in Houston named Browley."

"Was that hard for you?"

"For a while."

"Is she happy?"

"I'll say. He got killed this year."

Instead of amused, she looked a little sad.

"I want to walk on the beach," she said.

He looked down the shore.

"Not here," she said. "This is all sharp coral. We'll go back to those condos. They're right on Seven Mile Beach."

"You won't be frightened there?"

"No. You're with me now. I'm feeling better about everything."

The way there took them through George Town, the principal munici-pality on the island. There were a number of shops and stores, but mostly it seemed to be a place of banks. Nothing was open for business. It was quite late.

The tourist spots along Seven Mile Beach were looking lively, though—a glut of bright lights and signs on both sides of West Bay Road, with lots of married and college-age couples ambling along the roadside.

"The postmark on your card said 'Hell,' " he said. "Just where is that?"

"Not far from my place, up at the north end. It's a little place on a hill near the Turtle Farm. It's named Hell because of the weird coral rock formations there. They look like an illustration from Dante's *Inferno*. But it's nice. A lot of the natives live there. I was going to say black people, but there isn't really black and white here. Just a lot of people of all different colors. I like it that way. Color doesn't really seem to matter. This is a really lovely place."

She pulled into the parking lot of the condominium complex at some speed but thereafter proceeded slowly, looking about at the bushes and other cars cautiously before turning off the Jeep's engine.

"You stay here tonight. There's plenty of room, isn't there?"

"Unless they're back."

She checked the two adjoining apartments first, shaking her head sadly when she found them both still empty. Her own was on two levels—two big bedrooms above and a living and dining area and a kitchen beneath. The living room opened onto a wide patio that led directly to the beach. Pushing back the sliding door, she stood gazing out a long moment.

"Do you want to change clothes?" he asked.

"No. I'm fine."

She slipped off her sandals, and he removed his shoes. The sand was cool and silky. A number of boats were anchored in the water beyond, their riding lights twinkling happily. The clouds had moved off, and the moonlight was now very bright.

"It's nice up at this end of the beach," she said. "Not so many people. There are no hotels from here on till you get to Hell."

She took his hand and they went to the water's edge, then turned north, strolling along as shallow shrugs of sea dabbled over their bare feet.

"Are you sure Ramona Fitch is here?" he asked.

"Harvey told me he has a house on the island. It's up on the north side, at some place called Rum Point. I saw her car parked at Freeport Plaza. That's a little shopping center in George Town. One of the boutiques there carries some of my clothes. I think Harvey had something to do with that. He owns a lot of things on the island."

"But how could it be her car? She couldn't very well drive here."

"It was a gold Jaguar. She keeps the same model gold Jaguar at all their houses—the same color as her hair. Brassy gold."

"Maybe some servant's just using it," he said.

"I don't know. I suppose you could be right. Seeing it there made me feel creepy, though. I've never given her any reason to worry about me, but I'm afraid Harvey has. It was his idea for me to come down here for the shoot instead of doing it in Florida. He owns the condos we're in. I'm not paying any rent."

"And you say he's been calling?"

"Yes. Persistently."

"How can you tell it's him if you don't answer the phone?"

"Because I took the first five calls. First he wanted to know if I was settled in all right. Then he wanted to know how the shoot was going. Then he called to tell me how much he missed me. After that he called to apologize for all the other calls. The last one was to tell me that he loved me. That's when I stopped answering the phone. I disconnected all the extensions except the one in the kitchen. It's bolted onto the wall. I was going to leave it off the hook, but I didn't want to do that in case Ernst Konig called me."

"Just a thought, Astrid, but if you weren't answering the phone anyway, what difference would that make?"

She gave a nervous little laugh. Astrid had a very high IQ, but sometimes her brain operated on very different frequencies.

"You're right, Andy. I told you I've not been thinking straight."

They walked on. The shore ahead curved to the left, ending at a point in the far distance where there were many lights, and what looked to be a hill.

"Harvey thinks Ramona is out in California," she said. "I don't know. Maybe I should have told him about what's been going on. Maybe he could do something about it. He likes to think of himself as the most powerful man in the world."

"Maybe it wasn't so wise to get mixed up with him."

"I had nothing to do with it! He just pushed himself on me, the way he does with everybody. It all started last year. He saw me at some party at the Plaza and was at my elbow all evening. Then there was a dinner at Tiffany's, and he had the seating re-arranged so I'd be next to him. We talked a little about my com-pany, and the next I knew—the very next day—he made a stock offer that was unbelievable."

"You could have said no."

"Andy, it was the break I'd been waiting for! God, I was about to go under. This is a hard, nasty business. I'd no idea, back when I was a mere brainless model."

"How much did he invest?"

"Nearly two million. It put us on the map."

Harvey wasn't buying into her designer firm. He was buying her. And now he was probably looking for his first dividend.

"I know what you're thinking," she said.

"Princess, I would never think that," Andy said. "Not with you and Harvey Fitch."

"I gave him a couple of kisses on the cheek is all, the way everyone does in our business. That's absolutely all. And always in public places with people around. I've never gone out with him, though he keeps asking me to. A couple of business lunches maybe. I went to dinner with him once, but I brought another man along. Bobby Mellon."

Bobby was a fashion-show music coordinator, a genius at his trade, and as gay as a vanilla daiquiri.

"That made Harvey really angry," she said, "but didn't stop him. He never gives up. Lord, the gifts. He even bought me a BMW—'company car,' he said. Sent the keys and title and everything over. I've never gone to the dealer to pick it up."

"How can you be sure he wants to marry you?" Mistresses were still in some vogue on Park Avenue, though the trophy-wife syndrome was rapidly supplanting the need for them.

"Because he asked me—the very first night we met. I thought he was joking. Now I don't."

"And Ramona knows about all this?"

"I'm pretty sure. She has people working for her. Strange people. One of them turned up at my studio once, spying on everything. Ramona's gone into the fashion design business, you know."

"Ramona? She has the worst taste in New York. All her dresses would be gold lamé."

"Doesn't matter. She looks upon having her own salon as another de rigueur Upper East Side status symbol. Carolyne Roehm had her husband—he was Henry Kravis—set her up as a designer. Georgette Mosbacher had that cosmetics company. Ramona just wants to be one of the girls—and have people like Ivana Trump and Dominick Dunne come to her fashion shows."

"They'd be the ghastliest carnivals in town. The fashion writers would cream her."

"You know better than that. She'd invite a few of the big ones to one of her dinner parties or out to her place in the Hamptons, and they'd be eating out of her hand. She's been after Harvey to do this for a long time. He kept saying no, but after he bought into my company, she really lit into him. You know, 'If you can do it for her, you can do it for me.' "

She leaned against him, her silky, straw-colored hair blowing across his face, along with the scent of her fantastic perfume.

"In the morning," he said, "I'll go to the police again."

"Okay."

"And everyone will live happily ever after."

"I don't even want to think about it anymore."

He kissed her cheek. "Then don't."

She sighed and looked out over the water. "I want to go swimming."

Her condominium was far back down the beach.

"I don't have a suit," he said.

"We'll go skinny dipping, like we did that time on the Riviera."

She stepped to the side, unzipped the back of her dress, then let it fall to the sand. She'd been wearing nothing underneath.

This could signify nothing. Andy had been in hundreds of fashion-show changing rooms in his career, going about his business in the midst of models wearing only underwear or nothing at all. He'd been with Astrid like that a couple of times.

But this was not a fashion show.

That time on the Riviera had been his first real opportunity to get somewhere serious with Astrid—to make something a little more glorious of their relationship than an occasionally flirtatious friendship. But she had just been married to the spurious prince then, and Andy was involved with Candy, and the idea seemed kind of sleazy.

Now there was Bleusette—but was there? Whatever happened here on the Caymans, Bleusette would likely treat him as though he'd been playing Errol Flynn to a yachtful of romping nymphets. She might not even be there when he got back. It was not a great stretch to imagine her this very moment moving back into the French Quarter—maybe taking up with another of her saxophone players.

There was this marvelous moonlight, this deserted beach, these warm Caribbean waters. Life, the man had said, was nasty, brutish, and short. Tonight he could do a little something about the nasty, brutish part.

He told himself he wasn't being self-indulgent. What was about to happen could answer a compelling question. If he felt guilty afterwards, then perhaps he should marry Bleusette after all. If not, then indeed there should be no marriage.

Zinnie said Bleusette was having doubts. Anyway, the man hadn't been born who could walk away from a naked Astrid.

He'd always wondered what it would be like to make love to

a goddess. Astrid even bore the name of a Norse god, Thor. She'd
been christened Astrid Thorsdottir.

Leaving his clothes next to hers, he went running quickly into
the sea after her.

They went out to where they could barely stand and floated
and paddled about a little. Then his hand touched her arm and
she reached and grasped his shoulder and they came together. He
pulled her back a bit to where they had real footing, then held her
close and hard, kissing her wantonly and repeatedly. What nature
intended to happen in these circumstances happened, and very
quickly.

At the first touch against her belly, however, she stiffened and
then pushed herself back.

"No, Andy."

"No?"

Her head went back and she looked up at the moon, closed
her eyes, then opened them again.

"Not tonight."

"Astrid, this is a wonderful night."

"No it isn't, Andy. Not for me, and it shouldn't be for you."
Her eyes now sought his, conveying the indulgent reproach she
reserved for times when he'd done something silly.

"You belong to someone else."

"Astrid. I truly am not married."

"I know that, but you still belong to someone else. I can tell. I
could tell the minute I met you at the airport. I can always tell."

She was crazy. Bleusette hadn't been on his mind at all.

Following Astrid back up to the beach, he caught himself forgiving
every swine and lothario who'd gone nuts trying to get his hands
on her. King Tantalus with his ever-unreachable grapes could not
have been more frustrated. He felt like Sisyphus, watching the
rock tumble down the mountain again.

They dressed without speaking and remained silent all the
way back to the condominium.

"I'm sorry," she said, once they were inside. She turned on a
light, then came up and kissed him, sweetly. Afterwards, she held
him—gently but affectionately. "You're very, very dear to me. You
know that."

"Right."

She stepped away. "We both need some sleep. Tomorrow, we'll put everything right."

"Sure."

She was the fairy-tale princess again, vulnerable, in need of a shining knight.

"You can take the back bedroom."

"Will you be all right?"

"I think so. Sure. You're here." Tiny, tiny smile.

"Lock your door."

"Good night, Andy."

He went to the back bedroom meekly, switching on the lamp and then sitting on the bed, feeling a little dazed. He listened to Astrid swishing down the carpeted hall, then her door closed, tight.

He could still smell her perfume. Or someone's.

Chapter

·11·

Andy awakened in the morning naked but alone, lying in warm sunlight on a silken sheet. He stayed there a long luxurious while, utterly still, listening to the breeze rustle palm trees outside the
window and thinking of Astrid as he had dreamed of her during
the night.

The truth was inescapable. He was back in his old, fashionable, self-indulgent and supposedly glamorous life. He had been
from the moment Astrid had slipped her hand into his at the airport. Worse, he was enjoying it.

He sat up, swung his legs over the edge of the bed, and
looked around the room. He'd not noticed the night before, but
there were women's things scattered here and there around it.
He'd been sleeping in one of the models' beds—probably Beth
Hampshire's. Of the three, she had been the most friendly with
Astrid, and it was logical that they might share the same digs.

There was a handbag on the dresser—a very smart, stylish,
and expensive creation that Andy guessed might have come from
Prada or Fendi. He went to it and snapped it open. Lipstick,
makeup, money, wallet. New York driver's license: Elizabeth R.
Hampshire. She was a knockout even in that Polaroid ID photo.

A museum brochure was in the bag, too, from the Metropolitan—a just-opened exhibition of nineteenth-century American watercolors. Beth was mad for art. She had been taking art history courses toward a master's degree and planned to retire from modeling to become a curator—a job paying one-tenth what she made as a big-league model.

He hadn't thought Beth was serious about this at first, but he had since heard that she'd been taking long breaks between modeling assignments to work without pay as a docent at the Smithsonian's National Museum of American Art, in Washington, where she had grown up. It kept her near some of the paintings she loved—American Impressionists, mostly, especially Childe Hassam, and the later realists of the Ashcan school.

Andy had dated her only a few times, back during the dark interlude when he'd had his first falling out with Candy. Following their reconciliation, he'd tried to keep at least a friendship going with Beth, but she'd never gone out with him again, not even to museums. A very smart girl in all respects. She wasn't one for trivial relationships, or for anything trivial.

A memory found him—Beth in a light summer dress, walking with him by the garden fence of the Frick museum in New York after a morning rain. She'd been reciting some lines from a poem by Edna St. Vincent Millay. He recalled wishing at the time that Candice Longstreet would never come back. But she had.

Now, oddly, here he was with Beth again.

Except she was gone. Disappeared. He'd been worried so about Astrid, safe in the next bedroom. What about Beth? What about them all?

Annie Albrecht was not so smart as Beth. He recalled her as a stunning, slender woman who looked as aristocratic as a duchess, but who chewed gum, did drugs, and was by now probably working on her fifth or sixth rock-star boyfriend.

The voluptuous Vilma was a creature from another planet. Andy wasn't sure she could read the labels of face-cream jars. Yet on a fashion runway, all these "girls"—Astrid, too—were quite the same: dazzling celestial beings deigning to walk among the mere mortals of the earth.

Andy tried to make himself believe, as Astrid had tried, that the three women were off somewhere with Ernst Konig, who was that odd sort: a man who got more cheerful, charming, and generally agreeable the drunker he became. Annie and Vilma might be up for a frolic with Konig, but Andy knew such cavorting would not be at all like Beth.

And Beth wouldn't have left her handbag behind. She was a very careful person.

He sighed. He'd been feeling almost euphoric.

Before anything else, he'd decided, he ought to attend to his appearance. He'd gone to bed looking at least like a close relative of the late Mr. Looseballs and couldn't have improved much during the night. After a quick hot shower in the bathroom's enormous tub, he brushed his teeth, shaved, and carefully combed his hair. Peering into the mirror now, he found the bleary vagabond gone and a reasonably kempt gent in his place. With more of a tan, he might look a little like one of his own celebrity portraits, might resemble more the man he'd been when Astrid had known him in New York.

"Gent." That had been Beth's word for him.

He opened his camera bag, pulled on a clean white shirt, his khaki shorts, and his boating moccasins, pausing to splash on some expensive men's cologne he found among a vast assortment of bottles on the bathroom shelf, enjoying the idea of indulging himself with something paid for by Mr. Fitch.

For all the years he'd known Astrid, Andy had scant knowledge of her morning habits, but he did recall that she liked to begin her days with music to help set her mood—much, he supposed, like Glory in her airplane.

Andy stepped into the hall. The condominium was utterly silent. Astrid's bedroom door was open. Knocking on it politely, and getting no reply, he peered inside.

Empty. Bed unmade. No sounds coming from the bathroom. He thought she might be down in the kitchen, but that was deserted also—lights off, clean and neat, demonstrably unused. The living room's sliding door to the patio was open. It was a glorious, sunny day. There was reason to hope she'd simply gone for a walk on the beach.

Andy went out onto the patio and then down to the water's edge, looking up and down the shore. There were people walking and lying about, but none were tall and blond.

He made breakfast. Mr. Fitch kept the food shelves well

stocked, and Andy quickly found the wherewithal for a New Orleans–style omelet and a pick-me-up Bloody Mary, both of which
he heavily flavored with fiery Tabasco. His mind was very clear
now, but fretful. By the time he had washed up the dishes, Astrid
still hadn't returned.

Trudging down to the shore again, Andy looked about, then
sat down on one of the several deck chairs set out on the sand.
There were a wide variety of boats moving about on the water—
scuba-diving boats heading out to what he assumed was the reef,
small Sunfish sailboats, annoying Jetskis, and an odd, gray war-
like craft, with the word *Parasailing* painted large on its side.

The parasailing rig prompted thoughts of Glory. He looked
off to the western horizon. Mexico was over that way. Yucatán.
She could be there. More likely, she was aloft, somewhere high in
the sky. That's where she belonged. It was her visits to the earth
that seemed temporary.

Too many women in his life, Long Tom had said. Not to
worry. They all seemed to be vanishing.

After a few more minutes in the increasing heat, he returned
to the condominium and searched through it very thoroughly,
even looking behind the water heater in the laundry room just off
the kitchen. The purse Astrid had had with her the night before
was on her bedroom dresser, the keys to both the condo and the
Jeep still inside, along with a lot of cash. Looking out the window,
he saw that the vehicle was where she had left it in the parking
lot.

He checked the two adjoining apartments used by Konig and
Annie and Vilma. Nothing. In the one with two double beds, lots
of women's things—and two full handbags.

It was nearly noon. He could now allow himself some really
serious worry. Returning to Astrid's kitchen, he called her office
in New York.

"It's Andy Derain again," he said to the female assistant who
answered. "I'm in the Caymans."

"You are? Did you find Astrid?"

"Yes. Last night."

"Put her on."

"Uh, she's not here. I was wondering if she might have called
you this morning."

"No, she didn't. Where is she?"

"I'm not sure. Went out someplace without telling me. I'm in her condominium."

"Do you know when she's coming back?"

"She didn't say."

"This is getting, like, kinda weird, right? You found her, but now she's gone again?"

"I'm sure she'll turn up."

"Hey, the minute she does, have her call us, okay? And have her call Mr. Fitch. She'll know what it's about. He really, really wants to talk to her."

He certainly did. Almost instantly after Andy hung up, the phone rang. Andy stared at it stupidly for a moment, as though it were something that might explode. Then he picked up the receiver.

He remembered the man's voice from dozens of New York black-tie parties—gruff, amazingly deep for such a little fellow, and commanding, but in a forced, contrived way, as though the effect were entirely pose—and maybe the result of speech lessons.

"Astrid's not here,"Andy said.

"Who's this?"

"This is her, uh, photographer."

"That you, Konig? This is Harvey Fitch. Where the hell's Miss Montebello? I've been trying to reach her for goddamn days."

"It's Princess Montebello. The 'Miss' goes with Thorsdottir. Her maiden name."

"She's not married, is she?"

"No."

"But she goes by Montebello."

"Yes."

"So she's Miss Montebello."

"No. She was Mrs. Montebello, but she prefers 'Princess.' "

"Goddamn it, where is she?"

Andy stood there.

"Mr. Fitch?"

"Yes?"

"Why don't you leave Mrs. Montebello alone?"

"Listen you Kraut sonofabitch. Don't you realize who you're talking to?"

Being Konig for the moment had its advantages.

"Let me put it this way, then," Andy said. "Why don't you go fuck yourself?"

He hung up. The phone immediately began ringing again. Andy ignored it. If something untoward had happened to Astrid—and to Konig and the girls—it was at least obvious that Fitch had nothing to do with it.

Little was going to be accomplished hanging around the apartment. Andy went back to the beach, which was extremely hot now, and looked forlornly up and down the shore again. He started walking, a mile or two in one direction, then even farther in the other. He brought along his camera this time. The long lens he had with him was an eighty-to-two-hundred-millimeter slide zoom, which served as an excellent telescope. He found himself examining a lot of tanned, exposed flesh with it, but none belonging to anyone he knew. None that looked a goddess.

He was sweating heavily when he returned to the apartment. Someone was singing in the kitchen, but his joy evaporated when it proved to be the maid. She hadn't seen Astrid since the previous morning.

Andy went to Astrid's purse and got the keys to the Jeep. Glory had said Grand Cayman was small. He'd find out what that meant.

His first stop was the small village called Hell, at the end of Seven Mile Beach. Though he had some difficulty with the left-hand driving, he found the tiny post office there with ease. It was a one-story wooden building in the Caribbean style, complete with porch. Next door was a souvenir shop with a large cutout devil at the entrance beside which tourists could pose for photographs. Andy looked into both places, where both the postal clerk and the sales clerk remembered Astrid well, but not from any visit that morning.

Behind the post office, a wooden walkway led to the black coral formations that gave Hell its name. They were indeed Dantean—macabre and grotesque in every detail—but in miniature, the twisting gorges and hellish canyons no more than four or five feet deep.

They matched his mood. He drove on to his next destination, the airport, feeling glum—glummer still when ticket agents and baggage handlers alike gave him the same response: They recalled Astrid vividly from the night before and earlier visits but had not seen her that day.

Next was the police station, located just up from the George Town harbor on the same road as the building housing the governor's office.

From their telephone conversation, Andy had expected Inspector Whittles to be rather like one of those tweedy police detectives one saw all the time on public television's British imports—and so he proved to be, right down to his Oxonian air, briar pipe, and morning tea. The only difference was that he was black, his complexion at the far end of the Cayman color spectrum.

"Montebello," he said. "Astrid. Princess. Yes, she was here yesterday, wasn't she?"

"You don't remember?"

"Yes, I do. Of course. A quite attractive woman. Quite. You're the gentleman who phoned, to report her missing. But as I say, she was here yesterday."

"Well, now she's missing again."

"How long has she been missing this time, Mr., er, Derain?"

"I don't know. A few hours. Maybe more. She wasn't there when I awoke. Her purse was there, most of her clothes as far as I can tell. Her car keys and rental Jeep, too. That's what I came here in. But no Astrid."

"You explored the possibility she might be on the beach?"

"I explored it a good two miles in both directions."

"Shopping?"

Andy shrugged. "I've been up and down the beach road. This is really quite serious, Inspector. Last night she told me her photographer and her three models were missing, too."

"Yes. That's why she came by here—to ask about them. Have they returned?"

"No. And they left all their things behind as well. As everybody keeps saying, it isn't that big an island."

"Hmmmm. Are you acquainted with the particulars of these persons? Names, ages, descriptions, and all that?"

"More or less. I'm a photographer myself. I've worked with all of them."

The inspector rose from his desk. "Then I'd like you to fill out some missing-persons complaint forms, if you please, sir, and we shall launch a general inquiry."

"Inspector," Andy said, "do you know a Ramona Fitch?"

"Fitch?"

"Wife of Harvey Fitch."

"Oh yes! The financier. They have a house up at Rum Point. Rather quiet people, as I recall, although Mrs. Fitch has a most flamboyant car."

"Astrid thought Ramona Fitch might want to do her harm."

"And why is that?"

"Because Mr. Fitch is a business partner of Astrid's and has, well, amorous inclinations toward her."

"Old story, what?"

"Yes, but I wonder if you might want to go talk to Mrs. Fitch about this."

"I shouldn't think so, Mr. Derain. Quite respectable people. Own considerable property on the island. And they've dined with the governor, I do believe. You just fill out those forms, and we shall proceed with this inquiry step by step."

Whittles provided Andy with directions to the Fitch house, though with the admonition that he ought not make a nuisance of himself, and that he certainly shouldn't accuse Mrs. Fitch of anything untoward until such time as the official inquiry produced information indicating that was warranted, which the inspector doubted would ever be the case, thank you very much.

Right. The route there was simple enough. The western half of Grand Cayman had a large bite taken out of it in the form of a large body of water called North Sound. Rum Point was on the north coast, just at the eastern edge of North Sound and five miles across its mouth from the knob of land on which Hell was situated.

Andy drove east out of George Town, following the shore road through a village called Bodden Town and, not long after, finding the A4, the cross-island highway, just where Whittles said it would be. He turned left, reached the north coast at a town called Old Man Bay, and headed west toward Rum Point. He encountered a number of large, expensive houses and ultimately came to the end of the road at a Hemingwayesque open-air bar called the Rum Point Club. A waitress directed him back down the highway to what proved to be the largest of the houses he had earlier passed by, set back off the road behind a yellow stucco wall with large steel gates at both ends of the driveway.

Parking on the shoulder, Andy walked through the one open gate and resolutely up the drive, reminding himself that, if Ramona was up to mischief in this, he might soon be in the same difficult circumstance as Astrid, whatever that was. At least he'd then know what it was.

The door was answered by a very large, muscular, and light-skinned black man, who politely but firmly told Andy that Mrs. Fitch was not at home. Just that moment, both heard through some open door at the back of the house a loud splash and a woman's laughter, which Andy recognized all too well.

"I believe you're mistaken," Andy said. "I think if you'll go to wherever that swimming pool is, you'll find Mrs. Fitch. Tell her André Derain is here to see her—the photographer who took her portrait in New York. Tell her I'm looking for Astrid Montebello."

The man pondered this briefly, then told Andy to wait and closed the door.

When it reopened, Ramona was there, wearing a gold terry-cloth robe and gold sandals and dripping slightly.

"Andy, darling! I didn't know you were on the island. How nice of you to drop by. Please come in."

The gracious spider, all hospitality. He followed her down a wide, parquet-floored hall and into a bright Florida room that was filled with lacquered wicker furniture, mostly gold, and looked out over a flower-filled garden, with a glimpse of sea beyond the shrubbery. She moved so quickly he had no opportunity to speak until she stopped and turned to face him, but even then she didn't give him a chance.

"I've only a minute," she said. "I was doing my laps. Girl's got to keep her figure."

She let her robe fall open a little, showing off her enormous and much adjusted breasts, which seemed as tanned as Glory's. Plastic surgeons can do nothing about hands, of course, and Ramona's looked as bony and veined as one would expect of a woman her age, whatever it was, but their condition was disguised by a very deep coat of tan, which may well have been augmented by a tube or bottle. Noticing the direction of Andy's gaze, she stuck her hands in the pockets of her robe.

"You said you were looking for someone?"

"Yes. A friend of mine. Astrid Montebello. Princess Astrid Montebello." He emphasized the title, rubbing it in a bit that Ramona had none, much as she yearned for one.

"I'm afraid I don't know her."

"Yes you do. She's a fashion designer. Used to be a model. And an actress. She's in business with your husband. I gather he's her principal backer."

Ramona shrank back a little, leaning against a wicker chair. Her toenails were golden. They looked like something from a model airplane kit.

"Harvey owns simply scads of companies. Can't really keep track of them. I'm sure he has no personal dealings with this woman. A dressmaker, you say? A seamstress?"

Ramona, Andy knew very well, had originally been a truck-stop waitress in Wilkes-Barre, Pennsylvania. He wondered if her hair had been golden back then.

"Ramona. You know damn well who Astrid is. She's been in *Vanity Fair, Vogue, Town & Country.* I know you read *Town & Country.*"

"Perhaps I do know her. Very abnormal looking girl. Eight feet tall or something? Should have been a volleyball player. If Harvey was talking to her, it may well have been to hire her for *my* company. I'm going into the fashion business myself, Andy, in a very big way. Couture. Accessories. Perfume. I'm going to make Carolyne Roehm and Georgette Mosbacher look like pikers, not to speak of Ivana Trump. Harvey's been talking to people on QVC for me. It's the coming thing."

"That's all wonderful, Ramona, but—"

"And I'll certainly have need for a photographer, Andy. I'll keep you in mind. I'm very generous when it comes to help, as you know. I hear you could use some generosity these days."

Something was terribly wrong here, something preying on his senses, but Andy couldn't quite decide what it was.

"Gee, thanks, Ramona. Now look. Astrid's a very active partner of your husband's. I was just now talking to him on the phone. He knows she's on the island and he really wants to get ahold of her. He seemed quite upset that she's disappeared and I gather would be extremely unhappy if anything happened to her. Are you going to help me out or not?"

Ramona stared at him. Her latest face-lift was very recent, and the skin was stretched so tautly over her cheeks it resembled plastic wrap pulled over a bowl of leftover macaroni and cheese. There was no way of telling from her frozen expression what she might be thinking, though her eyes were no longer at all friendly.

"I really don't know what you're talking about, and I do not like at all the way you're badgering me. I want to go back to my swim now, so, instead of helping you out, I'm going to have Christophe show you out. Christophe!" The light-skinned black man appeared at once. "Mr. Derain is leaving, now!"

"I want Astrid, Ramona." Christophe had taken Andy by the arm with a grip like an automobile clamp.

"I do believe you've gone absolutely bonkers, Andy. They were saying in Mortimer's more than a year ago that you'd cracked up."

She disappeared somewhere behind him. Christophe steered him on to the front door and then gave him a little shove out of it. Andy tottered down the steps, not regaining his balance fully until he was in the driveway.

Hurrying out the gate, he wondered if he had jumped to a wrong conclusion—indeed, if maybe he truly was losing his mind. But as he climbed back into the Jeep, he realized what it was he had sensed in the house. The aroma had been faint but definitely detectable, and quite unmistakable. There was nothing in the world like Astrid's home-brew perfume.

A cosmetics executive had once told him that the scent of even the very best perfumes lasted no longer than six hours.

Andy started the Jeep's engine.

Chapter
·12·

Andy rumbled off down the highway, wondering what to do. If he returned to George Town to fetch Inspector Whittles, he'd give Ramona an awful lot of time to do something with or to Astrid, assuming the princess was still there. And Whittles might not want to be fetched, especially if all Andy could offer as evidence was something he thought he'd smelled. The olfactory was not the most reliable of senses. Police tended to give it credence only if one were a dog.

Before he did anything else, he had to determine exactly where Astrid was—at the least, whether she was or was not in Ramona's house.

The trees were thick on both sides of the road, but those on the left abruptly gave way to a wide expanse of sand extending down to the shore, which was surprisingly near, spray kicking up from the coral rock. Andy slowed, then braked sharply. The wide sandy area was littered with huge stone rectangular boxes, some with flowers on them. It was a Caymanian cemetery.

He glanced back down the road. A white car was approaching rapidly. Andy tensed, cursing himself for not getting out of the Rum Point area at maximum possible speed. It occurred to him too late that he probably ought to leap out and hide behind a tomb.

The white car—an Infiniti—sped by, the man and woman in the front seat arguing about something and paying him no mind. Andy returned his attention to the cemetery, taking note of a narrow lane of crushed shells that led around behind the burial vaults to the sea. He ground the Jeep into gear and bumped it down the lane to the cemetery's far side, pulling it to a stop in back of one of the flower-bedecked stone boxes and dropping to the ground beside it.

A black car went by now, a Mercedes with two serious-looking dark-skinned fellows sitting hunched forward in front. More employees of Ramona's?

They didn't notice him. If they had indeed come from the Fitch house, that would mean two less there to observe his approach if he returned, which he just then decided to do—this time on foot, along the shore. Pulling his Minolta out of his bag, he slung it around his neck. He'd try to look like a tourist and not alarm those in the other houses he had to go by.

He stopped three times, pretending to take pictures of seagulls. Finally rounding an outward curve of shoreline, he saw the gold-trimmed roof of the Fitch house just above a line of palm trees.

There was a side wall running between the house and its nearer neighbor but stopping just short of what Andy assumed to be the high-tide line, leaving the rear of the place open to the sea. If one were going to pay big money to have a house on the water—and this one looked like it cost at least a couple of million—one would want the investment to include a decent view. This was a spectacular one.

Moving to the wall, he scrunched down behind it and waited quietly for a moment. No one was visible up or down the shore.

There were two boats standing off the reef at some distance— one quite large, almost a ship; the other offering a much more slender silhouette—but he didn't think he could be seen from them.

He lifted his head above the wall. Immediately in front of him and extending down the shore were some clumps of tropical foliage with a path winding back through them from the water's edge. Just beyond this shrubbery was a wide lawn of what looked to be Bermuda grass. The sprawling terrace of the house lay beyond that, dominated by a long swimming pool. Two figures, very close together, lay at one end.

Still crouching, Andy slipped around the end of the wall into the tropical shrubs, moving through them as stealthily as possible until he had a good view of the terrace. The two figures, a man and a woman, appeared to be alone—and not at all dressed. He lifted his camera to his eye, sliding the long lens out to its full two hundred millimeters. The figures leapt magically into very near focus.

They were reclining, if that was the proper term for it, on a large, thick gold plastic mat. Ramona, minus her robe, was kneeling over a man, her rump pressed down against his face. Just in front of her, another part of the man's anatomy, of remarkable size, gave ample evidence of his excitement.

Andy scanned the rear of the house but perceived no face or movement at any of the many windows. The two by the pool were being accorded the fullest privacy.

They needed it. Andy refocused on them, holding them in his sight as clearly as in a movie close-up. A XXX-rated movie. Leaving her rear planted on the happy fellow's mouth, Ramona lowered her own head to his forward extension—not all that far to go, really—and proceeded to bob up and down with great enthusiasm, her golden hair flopping about like a cheerleader's pompom. Whoever this gentleman was, she was working very hard to please him. Maybe she'd found some improved marriage prospect after all—someone wealthier even than Harvey. Ramona was not a person to waste sex on mere pleasure.

Since returning to New Orleans, Andy had declined several generous offers to employ his photographic talents assisting divorce lawyers and private investigators in the acquisition of steamy evidence, figuring that such labor was much closer to rock bottom than he really wanted to go—and dangerous besides. But he did have film in his camera now, and there was always the chance these action shots of Ramona could prove useful. Certainly Harvey would find them interesting.

Andy shot off a few quick frames, pausing to make sure the sound of the camera motor didn't spook the lovebirds. It didn't seem to. They were much too preoccupied. Ramona's head ceased its bobbing and lifted. She looked back at her companion and then slid forward, lifting her haunches and then easing them back down again. She gave a little wiggle, then recommenced the lifting and lowering with increasing frequency, her eyes closed now, her big breasts bouncing so wildly they looked as though they might tear loose from their surgical moorings, her taut face expressing more zeal than ecstasy. Andy kept shooting.

Suddenly, at the high point of a bounce, she stopped, her head jerking back, her mouth in a clenched grin. Andy snapped this magnificent moment, too. It was a picture he'd love to put on one of the rest-room doors of the Upper East Side's ultrachic Mortimer's—probably the men's-room door, which the last he'd looked had been decorated with paintings of designer Bill Blass's lapdogs.

He was almost out of film. He waited for more action. He wanted to see who the man was.

Slowly, her strained expression returning to normal, Ramona pulled herself free from her sexual connection and came forward. Click, whirr. She shook her hair out, took a deep breath, then lifted herself over the man's body and stood up. Click, whirr. The man, smiling wickedly, rose on his elbows. Click, whirr. Andy recognized him at once. Scared now, he fired off the rest of his roll—five or six shots—then dropped to his knees and crawled backwards through the shrubs as fast as he could. Reaching the wall, he crept around to the other side of it, then got to his feet and began running back toward the cemetery. He ran faster than he thought possible.

The man whose picture he had just taken was Fabio.

Chapter

·13·

Strolling in and out of the Razzy Dazzy Café twice or three times a day
was not an exercise program designed to put one in the most terrific shape. Gripping the camera tightly to keep it from banging
against his ribs, Andy pounded along the hard, sharp coral, his
breath coming with increasing difficulty, his speed decreasing the
farther he went. As the shoreline began to curve, he took a quick
glance back.

As he feared, someone was behind him, far back but gaining
on him—a man wearing sunglasses and a tan suit. Andy kicked
back into high gear, swinging closer to the trees to his right, his
chest sounding like a malfunctioning steam engine. As the shoreline straightened again, he could see the cemetery and Astrid's
Jeep just ahead.

Another look back. The man was still behind him and had
greatly shortened the distance. He didn't seem to have a weapon
in his hand. More curiously, he kept looking over his own shoulder. Perhaps he was expecting reinforcements.

He had very short hair and very little on top.

In high school, Andy had run track and been famous for his
stretch run in the mile. He summoned it up now, only to discover

that, at age thirty-seven, it was no longer there. In fact, as he came nearer the Jeep, his steps began to falter. He slowed to a clumsy, panting trot.

His pursuer was now just behind him. In another ten yards, he pulled even. Andy waited for, what?—a punch, a gunshot, a knife? The man appeared to be maybe thirty and in very good condition. He made no threatening move at all. He just kept thumping along, as though they were out jogging together.

Confused, Andy lumbered on, all but staggering when he reached the Jeep. He leaned against it, indulging himself with a few deep breaths, then turned to look back down the shore. There was no one coming, but the balding man was clambering into the passenger side of the Jeep.

"Come on!" he said. "Get going!"

Andy didn't have breath enough for questions. He heaved himself up into the driver's seat, found the right key, and jammed it into the ignition. A moment later, the engine roaring, he ground the vehicle at high speed up the narrow track, slipping and sliding, bits of crushed shell flying into the air behind him.

"We had a good head start on 'em," said his uninvited passenger. "But they'll be switching to wheels real fast."

Skidding the Jeep up onto the pavement, Andy jammed the accelerator to the floor, then, frightened by his sudden speed, eased it back a little.

"Don't you work for Ramona?" Andy asked.

The man took off his sunglasses, revealing the kind of pleasant, innocent face mothers like to see on their daughters' first dates. He wore a white shirt and black tie with his tan suit, along with desert boots. He loosened the tie, then put back the sunglasses. What was he doing in a suit? The only others Andy had seen wearing jackets on the island were Inspector Whittles and a ticket agent at the air-conditioned airport.

"I don't work for Ramona Fitch," the man said. He looked at Andy. "Who are you?"

"My name's André Derain."

"What were you doing with that camera?"

"Taking pictures?"

Andy swerved, taking a sudden curve too fast. The left-hand tires dug into the shoulder, kicking up sand.

"Who for?"

"For myself. I'm a professional photographer."

The man studied him. "You're not law enforcement?"

"No."

"A PI? Working a divorce case?"

"No. I'm a photographer."

"Just out here doing nature studies, right? Mating rituals."

If he meant it as a joke, he wasn't laughing.

"Did they see me?"

"Heard you first, I think. Sure fucked things up."

"'Things'?"

The man said nothing.

"And just who are you?" Andy asked.

"Never mind. Up ahead on the left is a resort. Cayman Kai. Pull into the parking lot. And be quick about it."

"I don't want to stop. You said they'd be coming after us in cars."

"I want you to drop me off there. You'll see a little nondescript green Nissan. Only take a second."

"You sure you don't work for Ramona Fitch?"

"I wouldn't be this friendly. Or in this big a hurry to get the hell away from there."

"How about a guy named Fabio? He work for Ramona?"

The man gave Andy a peculiar look. "You know Fabio?"

The details of his flight with Glory from New Orleans were not something Andy wanted to share with strangers who went around beach resorts in suits.

"I know who he is, that's all. That was him with Ramona."

"You think so?"

"Yes. I got pictures of him."

The resort appeared just ahead. Andy waited until they were almost at the entrance, then slammed on the brakes and whipped into the drive.

"I'd like to talk to you more about this," said the man, when they'd stopped. "No time now."

He hopped out.

"Just keep going the way you came," he said. "Fast as you can. No sightseeing."

He started walking toward his car, fast.

The road before Andy ran straight and level, and he pushed his speed up to what he thought was a tolerable limit for Jeeps, not knowing exactly what that was. They were the opposite of sports cars—great for bumbling about in low gear over rough terrain but dangerously unstable as racing machines.

No vehicle of any kind appeared in his rearview mirror.

By the time he'd reached what passed for the suburbs of George Town, a few enterprising notions had occurred to him. Turning onto Crewe Road, he headed for the airport, dumping the Jeep in the parking lot and hurrying quickly to the terminal complex and the upstairs currency exchange, where he converted a full thousand of the money Glory had given him into Cayman Islands dollars. He guessed he might be staying here quite a little while.

The second-floor deck had a view of the long single runway and the ramp area. On impulse, he went to the railing. There were two jetliners, both American, and a long row of business and private aircraft. None was blue. Maybe Glory really had gone to Yucatán.

He had money enough for his own wheels. There were several car-rental offices. He picked a different agency than the one that owned the Jeep, acquiring his own nondescript Nissan, this one colored gray.

Driving out the Seven Mile Beach road, he thought it wise to avoid Astrid's condo for the moment. The first thing he had to do was take care of his interesting snapshots. He remembered seeing a one-hour photo shop in one of the little roadside shopping centers. He drove to it sedately, like any other tourist.

As he set his film roll onto the counter, it occurred to him this might not be so easy. In the United States, the film labs had long before come to accept the sexual revolution as concerned intimate snapshots but had generally adopted what Kodak among others called a "no insertion" rule. Ramona and Fabio had been indulging in every form of insertion imaginable.

Here in the very British Caymans they might be even more skittish about such matters. But there were always ways to encourage tolerance.

"I'd like two sets of prints," Andy said to the friendly, coffee-colored man behind the counter. He wouldn't mind having three, but that would really look funny.

"Very good, sir." He had an accent much like Glory's.

"Uh, these are, er, honeymoon pictures."

The man stood there smiling, saying nothing.

"They're, uh, rather personal, requiring special handling, if you know what I mean." Andy set a very pretty Cayman Islands hundred-dollar bill on the counter.

It disappeared. "Very good, sir. No problem. Very happy to oblige."

He was promised the prints within the hour. The lab had a steady trade with cruise-ship passengers whose visits on the island lasted less than a day and who needed their scuba- and snorkel-diving snapshots printed up in a hurry.

After that, Andy stopped at the Hyatt Regency gift shop to buy some sunglasses of his own, then drove quickly back to George Town.

If Inspector Whittles thought Andy completely daft, he did not allow his expression to show it. He listened calmly and courteously, as though Andy had dropped by to ask for advice on lodgings, pausing from time to time to jot down notations on his pad.

"I telephoned your Lieutenant Maljeux," he said, when Andy had finished his tale. "He certainly does vouch for you, but he seemed quite curious as to how you came to be here in the Caymans."

"Yes, well, spur of the moment."

Whittles cleared his throat and looked down at his notepad.

"To return to the matter at hand, Mr. Derain, you are accusing Mrs. Ramona Fitch of holding Miss Astrid Montebello and possibly four other persons described earlier against their will at Mrs. Fitch's residence on Rum Point Drive. You state that you believe Mrs. Fitch to be in the company of a drug smuggler named Fabio, family name unknown, and that he may pose a threat to the safety of Miss Montebello and, possibly, four other persons."

"That's about it. Actually, Montebello's her married name, though she's divorced."

"Is it her legal name?"

"Yes. Far as I know."

The inspector cleared his throat and continued. "You say you observed Mrs. Fitch, er, entertaining this alleged drug smuggler through your camera lens while they were on the rear terrace of her residence on Rum Point Drive."

"Right."

"That is, mind, a violation of Crown law—observing people in a clandestine manner, trespassing, and such."

"My apologies to Her Majesty, but, as I've tried to make you understand, I'm really, really worried about Miss, er, Mrs. . . . Princess Montebello. I didn't come all the way down here from New Orleans just to go trespassing."

"But you offer no evidence of Miss Montebello's presence at the Fitch residence, other than to say you recognized the unique aroma of her own perfume."

"Inspector, she's a fashion designer who mixes her own perfume especially for herself. It's quite distinctive, unmistakable. I'm sorry to be imposing upon your valuable time, but when you throw in Miss Montebello's disappearance, and the four other persons earlier described, and the presence of this Fabio guy, who I think may have murdered some people back in the United States and who knows how many other countries . . ."

The inspector eyed him very directly now, tapping on his desktop with his pen. "How are you familiar with this Fabio?"

Andy hesitated. "A friend of mine in the export-import business told me about him."

"Hmmmm." The inspector stood up and went over to a file cabinet. A moment later, he returned with a Spanish-language picture magazine and laid it open on the desktop, pointing with his pen to a photograph of Fabio and a dour-looking older man. Fabio had his arm around the other's shoulders and was smiling, broadly. The other man, who had the same dark complexion and general countenance as Fabio, was not.

"Is this the Fabio you observed at Mrs. Fitch's residence?"

"Yes. Sure is. Who's the other guy?"

Whittles closed the magazine and returned it to the file, then stood there, gazing back at Andy as he thought upon something.

"There isn't the time, and I haven't quite the inclination to bother a magistrate just now about a warrant, which at all events we might not obtain until tomorrow. But this does pique my curiosity, and I do think it would be worthwhile to call upon Mrs. Fitch this afternoon."

Call upon her? By appointment? With flowers or something?
"Tickety-boo," muttered Andy.

As much as he was now impatient to get back to Ramona's, Andy felt
some apprehension and perhaps even futility driving back to the
place from which he'd been trying so desperately to escape just a
short time before. But this time, at least, he was sitting beside
Whittles in the backseat of an official police sedan, with a plainclothes sergeant driving and a burly uniformed officer up front.
The sergeant was white and the uniformed man a dark-skinned
black, but as Astrid had observed, that didn't seem to matter. It
was something of a surprise to find the kind of tolerance exempli-
fied by the French Quarter here in the last remnants of the British
Empire.

Andy didn't say much during the trip, which was made at an
irritatingly sedate speed. Whittles handily deflected his further
inquiries about Fabio and blithely carried on like a chamber of
commerce representative trying to impress a tourist agent or real
estate developer.

"We have a genuine pirate cave here in Bodden Town," he
said, as they rolled through the village that he said had once been
the island's capital. "All the great pirates of the Caribbean used
the Caymans as a base at one time or another—Blackbeard, Captain Henry Morgan, the whole bloody lot. It was the trade winds,
don't you know. As you may have noticed, they're from the
southeast in this part of the Caribbean. To sail back to England
from Jamaica, ships had to course west past here and go around
Cuba, passing through the Florida Straits to get back to the Atlantic. Easy marks they were, for the pirates here."

This led to a discourse upon the natural lack of surf-tossed
seaweed along Seven Mile Beach on the leeward west end of the
island, and then to detailed remarks about the sea-turtle population, and then to a complaint about United States environmental
laws forbidding the importation of turtle meat. Whittles was prat-
tling on about the island's principal golf course when they finally
pulled up at Ramona's gate.

To Andy's surprise, it was open. There was no Mercedes of
any kind parked within, only Ramona's gold Jaguar.

She answered the door herself—dressed in a chaste silk

blouse, Bermuda shorts, and expensive sandals, everything in gold. Whatever else she'd been doing in Andy's absence, she'd found time to wash and dry her golden hair, which was now so fluffy it resembled meringue.

If superficially cordial, her demeanor was otherwise extremely haughty. She gave Andy only a sidewise glance, such as one might briefly accord a filthy and diseased street person one had to walk near, devoting her attention mostly to Whittles.

"Inspector Whittles, how nice," she said. "We met at a party at the governor's last spring. Darling man, your governor. Such a good, good friend of my husband's."

Those last words were uttered in the manner of bursts from a machine gun, though they seemed to have no more effect on the inspector than the breeze.

"We are looking for a Miss or Mrs. Astrid Montebello, Mrs. Fitch. She has been reported missing. We have been given reason to believe she may be here."

"That's ridiculous. Nobody's here. Nobody's been here. I'm on a holiday. All by myself. I don't even know the woman, except that she does business with my husband. This idiot here came around a while ago with some crazy story about her, but it's all nonsense. I'm here alone. You ought to know that Mr. Derain here has had treatment for mental problems."

At the suggestion of friends, during his deep despond after Candy had finally ditched him for good for her Texan, Andy had gone once to a therapist. The woman had listened to his troubles less attentively than most bartenders, and that first visit had been his last. How Ramona had found out about it, he could not say. As Astrid had noted, she had strange people working for her.

"This is an official inquiry, Mrs. Fitch," said Whittles. "We'd like to ascertain if Miss Montebello is on the premises."

She gave Andy another quick, dark look, but then smiled at the inspector—as much as her petrified cheeks would permit.

"See for yourself," she said, gesturing toward the interior of the place with sudden equanimity. "I love to show off this house. I've heard *Architectural Digest* is interested in it. They did a spread on our place in the Hamptons."

In the manner of a tour guide or museum docent, she led them on, room by room, saying nothing when the two policemen with Whittles began opening closets and peering into alcoves. She said not a word about their lack of a warrant.

There was no basement. There was a cabana and changing room by the pool, which the sergeant dutifully poked into also. They looked into the big, three-car garage. Nothing. No sign of Astrid, Fabio, or anyone. There wasn't even a servant in the house.

Whittles thanked her politely. Much as she could, Ramona grinned wickedly in farewell.

"Sorry," said Andy, as they got back into the car.

"I detected no scent of perfume of any kind," said Whittles.

Andy pondered this. "She had all the windows open. She had a sea breeze blowing through the place."

Whittles smiled. "Our inquiry is not concluded, Mr. Derain."

The driver started the engine. As they drove by the cemetery where he'd parked the Jeep earlier, Andy glanced out to sea. The two boats he'd seen out there were gone.

Chapter

·14·

His pictures were ready when promised. Turning away from the other customers at the counter, Andy opened the package and quickly looked through the prints. He was surprised and delighted to see that, though two of his shots of the sleeping Glory had come out overexposed, the third was fine and the fourth truly magnificent. As for the telephoto snaps of Ramona and friend in various gymnastic forms of insertion, they were sharply in focus and probably of better quality than were sold in porn shops. Greasy Griswold would love them, but Andy had decided on a much better customer.

It was a short run up to the post office in Hell. He used the back of a money-order form for stationery on which to jot his friendly little note—citing the place and time the photos were taken—and slipped a half dozen of the shots of Ramona and Fabio with it into an Express-Mail envelope. He couldn't recall the street number of Harvey Fitch's Park Avenue penthouse so he sent them to his office, hoping "The Fitch Building, Third Avenue, New York, New York" would suffice. The friendly postal clerk promised delivery the next day.

The remaining pictures of Ramona at play and the four of

Glory he stuck in the pocket of his shorts. The envelope with the other complete set of prints and the negatives he slipped under his car seat.

There was a fancy Holiday Inn down the road back toward George Town. He found a pay phone just off the lobby and charged another call to his long-in-arrears AT&T account. He was put on hold and then transferred upward through several levels of flunkies. But, invoking Astrid's name throughout the process, he finally got Harvey Fitch on the line.

"Who is this?" Fitch said. "What do you know about Astrid Montebello?"

"I'm André Derain, the photographer. I took your wife's picture once."

"You what?"

"I shot her portrait. Four years ago. In your apartment."

"Oh, yeah. What do you want? I paid that bill. It was outrageous, and the pictures were lousy. You made her look like a two-dollar whore dressed up like a queen."

He had indeed paid the bill. It was one time Andy'd let his integrity get the better of him, though, as it turned out, Ramona had loved every shot.

"I've just taken some new pictures of her, Mr. Fitch, and sent them on to you. Should get there tomorrow or the next day. I think you'll want to see them. She's entertaining a gentleman friend in them. And she's not dressed up in anything."

"What do you mean?"

"I mean naked."

"Ramona?"

"And the gentleman."

"What are you, some kind of blackmailer?"

"No, I told you, I'm Andy Derain."

"Wait a minute. I know your voice. I talked to you this morning—when I called Astrid's. You're not Derain; you're Ernst Konig. What has this got to do with Astrid?"

"Sorry. I was just pretending to be Konig this morning, since you were being so uncivil. Look, Mr. Fitch. Astrid's missing. I've been looking for her all day. Your wife is down here, and I think she may have had something to do with this. I took some pictures of her—with a long lens—on your terrace, with a guy named Fabio. Topless and bottomless. Both of them."

"Fabio? The guy on the covers of all those romance novels?"

"Not that Fabio. This one's a handsome devil, all right, but more along the lines of what Marlon Brando would call 'a scum-sucking pig.' He's a drug smuggler and a murderer."

"Drug smuggler? Murderer? What the hell are you talking about? You're on Grand Cayman? And Ramona's down there with a guy named Fabio? She's supposed to be in California!"

"She's here. With Fabio. Fucking."

Was this guy completely dense, or just stupefied in amazement? Maybe he'd been drinking.

"Where's Astrid?"

"Mr. Fitch, Astrid's missing. Ernst Konig and the three models Astrid hired are missing. Your wife's down here with this very nasty guy, who I think killed somebody in New Orleans. It doesn't add up to anything good."

A pause, then, "What do you want?"

"I want you to do something about this. Get ahold of your wife and put a stop to whatever she's trying to pull. I'm a very good friend of Astrid's, and I'm getting mighty goddamn worried about her. If you want a little leverage with your wife, you can tell her about the pictures."

There was only silence on the other end.

"Mr. Fitch, this call is costing me a lot of money."

That was a real compelling argument to use on Harvey, who could probably afford to buy AT&T, if he hadn't already.

"Don't go anywhere."

"You want me to camp out here by this pay phone?"

"Go to the condo. Where you were when I called this morning. Have you gone to the police?"

"Yes."

"Shit."

" 'Shit'? Mr. Fitch, I think Astrid's been kidnapped!"

"Goddamn bitch."

Andy wasn't sure which woman Fitch had in mind, so he refrained from comment.

"Mr. Fitch?"

"Go to the condo. I'll take care of everything."

"What are you going to do?"

"I'm going to call my lawyer. I'll be talking to you." He hung up.

·   ·   ·

The condo could wait. Andy was a little nervous about going back there anyway. Instead he stopped in the hotel's bar. Feeling perverse, he ordered a Coca-Cola and Southern Comfort. The bartender, used to weird tourist drinks, set one up for him as casually as if he'd ordered a beer.

The room was quite full of tourists, listening with varying degrees of attention to a white reggae singer who called himself "the Barefoot Man." He wasn't bad, but he wasn't quite the genuine article, either. Andy wondered if he'd worked his way to the Caymans on cruise ships.

As sad and depressed now as he was frustrated, Andy sat staring into his drink, resting his elbows on the highly polished bar. He felt guilty. He'd been right there in the condo. He shouldn't have allowed Astrid to be snatched while he slumbered away. Of course, if she'd let him spend the night in bed with her, this might not have happened.

Or they both might now be wherever she was.

Which could also be where Beth was.

He drank.

Someone took the stool next to his. Andy didn't pay much attention, but, lifting his glass again, he noticed a tan suitcoat sleeve. He shifted his eyes to take in his uninvited companion, then turned them back to his drink.

"Before we go any further," Andy said, "I think it's about time we introduced ourselves."

"Name's Jim," said the man, removing his sunglasses and smoothing down the few hairs on the top of his head. "Jim Kelleher. I'd like to see those pictures."

"What pictures?"

"The copies you kept of the ones you just mailed off from that post office in Hell. The pictures you took of Ramona Fitch. You say you're not a PI, but I think you are—or at least that you're working for one. You took those divorce court specials of Mrs. Fitch fucking her brains out, had them developed, and then shipped them off to parties unknown. That's what PIs do."

"I'm not in that racket."

"What, you're down here on vacation?"

"Something like that. What racket are you in?"

"Law enforcement. That's all you need to know."

"You've been following me. Why?"

The bartender came over. Andy's uninvited companion ordered a beer, waiting until it was poured and served before resuming the conversation.

"I was just keeping an eye out," said Kelleher. "What were you doing with the local police? I didn't expect that. That's not what PIs do."

"A friend of mine is missing. Inspector Whittles is trying to help me find her. Why do you want to see my pictures?"

"They're material to an ongoing investigation."

Andy studied the man's face. He made a guess.

"You with the DEA?"

"No."

"CIA?"

Kelleher gave him a weird look. "Hell, no."

"Okay, badge me."

"What?"

"I read that line somewhere. As in, show me your badge. Then maybe I'll show you the pictures."

"Nobody talks like that. 'Badge me.' Jeez." Kelleher took out a leather case and briefly held it open. The ID photo was too terrible to be anything other than authentic government issue.

"FBI," said Andy. "I thought you fellows didn't have jurisdiction outside the United States."

"We have a small international presence, and we liaison with other agencies with big ones."

"Like the DEA?"

"Sometimes."

"Why were you at the Fitches' house?"

"Ongoing investigation. You're asking too many questions. Come on. Let me see those pictures."

"In a second. How long were you hanging around there behind the Fitch house?"

"Couple of hours—till you came along and spooked them. Why?"

"You didn't see a tall woman with long blond hair—maybe in a real long dress?"

"Not from where I was on the beach. Blond?"

"Very. And she's six foot two."

"I'd have noticed. I didn't."

"If I show you the pictures, will you help me find my friend? Her name's Astrid Montebello. She's a fashion designer. She's in a partnership of sorts with Harvey Fitch, and I don't think Mrs. Fitch likes the idea."

Kelleher frowned. "I'll do what I can. But, like I said, I don't have any official jurisdiction here."

"Except for ongoing investigations."

Kelleher cleared his throat impatiently.

"Promise you'll help me," said Andy.

Kelleher finished his beer. "Okay, okay."

Andy couldn't manage the rest of his drink. "They're in the car."

They sat in the parking lot as Kelleher went through the prints one by one. The agent held his door open slightly to keep the overhead light on. Darkness was falling fast.

He licked his lips as he stared at one, which showed Ramona looking down smugly at her extremely happy outdoor companion.

"That's him all right," said Kelleher. "Fabio Machado."

"You know him?"

"Never met him, but I know all about him. He's half of the Brazilian Brothers."

"Tag-team wrestlers?"

"Nothing so nice. Andao and Fabio Machado. Last couple of years, they've taken over most of the drug business in the Caribbean. Guys are worth billions, probably, if you could lay hands on their assets. Andao's the older and smarter one. Fabio's the younger and crazier one. When he isn't fucking he's killing somebody. Always leaving bodies around behind him, the way gorillas leave fruit peelings. You took your life in your hands getting this close to him."

"I think my friend Astrid was in that house."

"Then let's hope she's not Fabio's type, though it sounds like she is."

Kelleher continued on through the remaining prints, then suddenly froze. He was looking at one of Andy's pictures of Glory. "Who's this?"

"Just a woman I met on the way down here."

"Where'd you take her picture?"

"Florida." It was close enough. "I came down here from Key West."

"You met her in Florida?"

Kelleher was asking too many questions about Glory. "Yeah," said Andy, lying. "Airport bar or something."

Kelleher turned the picture sideways, then back straight again. "What's she sitting in?"

"An airplane seat."

"She's asleep."

"You never sleep in airplane seats?"

"What's her name?"

This was something he didn't want Special Agent James Kelleher to know. Glory had been pretty decent; she'd given him two thousand dollars and missed when she shot at him.

"Daisy."

"Daisy?"

"Daisy Buchanan," Andy said, seizing upon the name of the heroine of *The Great Gatsby*, one of his favorite books.

"Daisy Buchanan. She has nothing to do with these other pictures you took of Mrs. Fitch and Fabio?"

"No."

Kelleher slipped the photos back in their envelope.

"These others are very interesting. They place one of the biggest drug guys in the hemisphere right here on Grand Cayman—island of banks. By the way, the focus is great. You're a pretty good photographer."

"Thanks."

Kelleher swung the car door open wide. "Well, good night then. I'll catch up with you later."

"What about my friend Miss Montebello?"

The man got out and shut the door, then leaned down to the window. "I'll keep an eye out."

He still had the photo envelope in his hands.

"Wait! My pictures!"

Kelleher started walking away.

"Hey!"

Andy opened his own door, but by the time he got out from behind the wheel, Kelleher was running—heading for the hotel entrance. Andy started after him but never caught up. He wandered around the lobby for a few feckless minutes, then went back outside.

The parking lot was full of little Nissan Sunnys, but there was no sign of Kelleher. Andy got back into his own rental car, hit the dashboard hard with the side of his fist, then sadly turned on the engine.

He drove up and down the Seven Mile Beach road a couple of times, to absolutely no point. It was fully night now. He could either go back to the George Town police station and have another friendly chat about the scenic sights of Grand Cayman with Inspector Whittles, or he could hit the nearest bar and get drunk, or he could return to the condo. The last choice seemed the best. Fitch had told him to wait there, and there was still a chance, however slim, that Astrid might turn up—or one of her models might. He was as worried about Beth Hampshire and her friends as he was about Astrid.

The parking area in front of the condo entrance was empty. No one seemed to be skulking in the bushes.

Andy listened at the apartment door a moment, then turned the key.

A lamp was on in the living room. Andy was sure there'd been no lights on when he left.

He wished now that he had brought his father's old automatic. Or had thought to borrow a gun from Glory.

Quietly—or so he thought—he crept up the carpeted stairs. The door of the bedroom used by Astrid was closed. He'd left it open.

He turned the knob and slowly pushed. "Astrid?"

There was enough light from the stairway for him to see the woman on the bed. She turned over, her gray eyes blinking.

"Where the hell have you been?" she said.

Chapter
·15·

Glory sat up, turned on the light, and rubbed her eyes. "God, I'd kill for another hour's sleep."

He took her word on that. Prominent on the night table was a pistol that most definitely hadn't been there before. It wasn't the pretty little purse gun she'd had in Florida but looked to be one of the big Glock 10-millimeter automatics some of the New Orleans police were now carrying. Elephant-stoppers.

"I'm glad you weren't using that thing when you shot at me in Key West."

She yawned, politely covering her mouth. "You needn't worry about that. I was just going through the motions."

"Just what is a nice girl like you doing with a howitzer like that?"

"Please, Andy. I'm utterly exhausted."

He shifted his eyes to a sight more pleasing. Glory was wearing only blouse and panties.

"Yes," she said. "It's true. I'm a woman. Now if you don't mind, old sport . . ."

"How did you know I was here?" he asked, not moving.

"This is where Astrid Montebello's staying, isn't it? I presumed you'd be where she was."

"And just how did you know she was staying here?"

"I know bloody everybody on Grand Cayman—including real estate agents."

She swung her legs over the side of the bed. They were long and muscular, very trim. And perfectly tanned.

"She's gone."

"So I noticed. I had to pick the lock."

"No. I mean she's disappeared. And I think your friend Fabio's had a hand in it."

"Fabio? What are you talking about? He couldn't know your friend. I don't think he's ever been to a New York charity ball."

"I think he knows her now. He certainly knows Ramona Fitch."

"The real estate mogul's wife?"

"Yes. I thought you were completely unaware of the rich and famous."

"I'm aware of the Fitches. They have a big house on the island."

"At Rum Point, which is where I just this afternoon observed Ramona and Fabio engaging in fellowship on her terrace. They engaged in fellowship from one end of Ramona to the other end of Fabio. I'd call it a quite intimate acquaintance."

Glory stared at him the way Zinnie often did, only a little more dangerously. "Fabio said he'd be coming this way. Which is why I strongly suggested to you back in Florida that you not make the trip."

"Glory, Astrid's been kidnapped. She was at the Fitch house. I could smell her perfume. And your Fabio—"

"Look, I'm not at all sure what you're talking about," she said, heading toward the bathroom, "but I can't deal with it in my present state of mind. I need a hot shower, and I desperately need some coffee. Would you be a nice man and go make some? Take the pistol with you—just in case. I'm afraid Fabio and I are no longer friends, and this is a small island."

The door shut behind her.

When she emerged from her shower and general freshening up a few minutes later, he was still in the room, sitting on a corner of the bed. She had obviously expected him to be downstairs, as she was wearing nothing but a towel over her shoulders. If surprised, she did nothing to cover herself. In fact, she walked nonchalantly past him to the dresser mirror, standing in front of it while she began combing out her damp hair. His eyes wandered. Here was another picture he'd like to take, but there were far more important things to deal with first.

"That doesn't look at all like a coffeepot in your hand," she said, glancing at him via the mirror.

"It's not. It's your gun."

"Yes. I rather recognized it, though this is the first time I've ever seen it aimed at my very own backside."

"Awfully sorry, as you would say," he said, moving the barrel slightly to the side.

"I accept your apology. Now if you'd please go downstairs and attend to that coffee, I'd—"

He hadn't realized how angry he'd become until he found himself throwing the pistol at the wall beside her in a sudden, mad, explosive motion. Then he jumped to his feet, grabbed her by the shoulders, and flung her onto the bed. Stunned, she lay there, staring at him wildly, like a woman who thought she was about to be ravished.

Andy's mind was as far from ravishment as could be, oddly enough. He simply stood over her, breathing like a fire engine. The automatic had bounced all the way across the room. He was amazed it hadn't discharged.

"Just listen to me," he said, calming himself. "Astrid Montebello is one of my oldest and dearest friends. Her fashion design business is being bankrolled by Harvey Fitch, who even owns this condominium we're in."

"I know that. You're in love with her, aren't you? And Fitch has made you insanely jealous."

"Shut up. Please. Mr. Fitch has the hots for Astrid, and I think wants to marry her. His current wife, Ramona, who is one of the rottenest swinolas ever to haunt the slow-food joints of New York's Upper East Side, doesn't like the idea. She turns up here on Grand Cayman, where Astrid is trying to do a fashion shoot. Astrid's three models and her photographer disappear, snatched by persons unknown who I think were after Astrid. Then, this morning, Astrid disappears. Persons unknown finally succeed. I went to the Fitch house, and though there was no Astrid, I could smell the scent of her perfume. She'd been there, I swear it."

Glory's face was a complete blank.

"Now maybe, with a little help from the local police, I might be able to handle this," he continued. "But not with Fabio Machado and his merry men hanging around as rotten Ramona's houseguests. And believe me, they looked like they were very welcome there."

"How do you know his last name is Machado? I never told you that."

"Be quiet. I saw what happened to Fabio's ex-girlfriend Felicie in New Orleans. So I'm really, really scared about Astrid, okay?"

He was shouting, also trembling. He sat down on the end of the bed. Glory sat up beside him, pulling her towel over her lap and folding her arms in front of her bare breasts.

"I'm sorry," she said, with what sounded like geniune sadness. "You must truly be in love with her."

"What would Ramona be doing with a weasel like Fabio? Her goal in life is to become Queen of the Upper East Side—at the least, a lifetime guarantee of the best table at Le Cirque. Those snoots wouldn't hire Fabio as a busboy."

"I've absolutely no idea. The relationship completely mystifies me."

"You work for those bastards!"

"No, I don't. Not anymore."

"What? You're flying their plane."

"I told you, Fabio and I are no longer chummy. I appear to have been fired. You recall the island where we had to drop our cargo? It was the wrong bloody one. I misplaced the right one in that damned fog bank. We dropped those bags where my erstwhile employers couldn't find them but the Drug Enforcement Administration could."

"Pity."

"I heard about it from Fabio in highly colorful Portuguese over my aircraft radio. He had a welcoming committee waiting for me at the terminal at Owen Roberts. Happily, I noticed them before they noticed that I'd noticed them. I took my Pilatus back down to the other end of the runway and left it there. Then I hopped it over the fence into my briar patch."

"Briar patch?"

"You know, as in Br'er Rabbit and his briar patch? The Uncle Remus tales? Mine's Grand Cayman."

"You could have taken off in your plane again."

"I was quite a bit low on fuel, actually. And I've some unfinished business here. That's why I came looking for you. I could use your help."

"There were two boats."

"Boats?"

Glory had very pretty feet.

"Lying offshore near Ramona's house when I first went there. One was a great big tub, the kind you see tied up in Monaco all the time. There was a smaller one with it—a kind of giant-sized speedboat. They were there when I first went to the house but were gone when I came back. It didn't occur to me at the time, but I wonder now if Astrid might have been on one of those boats."

Glory leaned forward, resting her elbows on her knees.

"I'm worried," he said. "If she was on one of those boats, I fear she's not anymore."

"The big one, was it rather modern looking? Very sleek lines? Flying bridge?"

"Something like that."

"The smaller one would be one of their cigarette boats. They've got a bloody fleet of them working the Caribbean."

"Who does?"

"Fabio and Andao Machado. The big tub's Andao's yacht. They're brothers."

"I know," Andy said.

"How do you know?"

"I made the acquaintance of a federal agent. He gave me a fill on the Machados."

"A U.S. agent? Here?"

"Yes. FBI. His name's Kelleher."

"And what did you tell him?"

"Not much. I'm afraid I showed him your picture, though."

"What picture?"

He pulled one of the prints from his pocket and handed it to her. "I didn't mean to."

"I don't have fluffy gold hair."

"Sorry. That's Mrs. Fitch and Fabio." He gave Glory one of the pictures of herself sleeping in her pilot seat. "It was one of these. I took it on the airplane. I had two sets of prints made of everything, and this fellow Kelleher snatched one of the sets, including some shots of you. He seemed interested in you."

She sighed. "God, Andy. Why couldn't your Mr. Calhoun have just supplied me with another Looseballs? Why do I end up with a camera bug?"

"The pictures may help. I sent some of the hard-core shots to Harvey Fitch. He was quite disturbed just hearing about them. He may even come down here."

"So this peaceful little island is going to have among its guests the Machado brothers, Mr. and Mrs. Fitch, and a federal agent."

"And my friend Astrid Montebello. I hope. And the others. I knew those three models. One of them I liked a lot."

She bit down on her lip briefly. "We'll have to help each other."

He pondered that. The only other person on the island he could turn to was Inspector Whittles—the tour guide.

"Which means we'll have to trust each other," she said.

"Why?"

"Andy, if I was the kind of person you're perhaps thinking I am, you'd be dead now—just part of the beach detritus on Key West. I told you, I got mixed up with these people just to keep flying. All I've done for them is fly airplanes and deliver packages. It's the truth."

"All right. But if we're going to be so trusting of one another, you might at least let me know your last name."

She stared at him warily a moment, then relaxed. "It's Newlands. Very old Cayman Islands name. There aren't so many of us as Boddens and Edens, but the name dates back to pirate days."

"You're Cayman?"

"The term is Caymanian. The answer's yes. My father's ancestors were English. He ran a dive shop here, until he ran off with one of his wealthier, prettier scuba customers. My mother's American. She has an art gallery in George Town. I was hoping to see her this trip, but she's gone off to Florida, so I'm rather on my own. I'll tell you how much I trust you, Andy. I trust you enough to tell you I'm scared stiff."

"Oh."

"I'm in way over my head."

"Well, me too, I guess."

She pulled the top of the towel up to cover her breasts. "I'd like to get dressed now. Wait for me downstairs. If you need to throw anything in that camera bag of yours, do so. I want to get out of here."

He stood up. "You still want that coffee?"

"No. Pour us a couple of stiff drinks. Or better, just grab a bottle for the road."

Andy started for the door, then stopped. On the carpet next to the dresser was the briefcase she'd acquired in Key West.

"Isn't that . . .?"

"Yes. Contents undelivered. Another reason the Machados are more than a little peeved with me."

Glory came downstairs dressed in a fresh blouse and shorts. Her feet were in a pair of Sperry Topsiders much like his own boating shoes. She had her canvas bag over her shoulder and was carrying the briefcase. With a quick move, she turned off the living-room lights.

"We can be seen from the parking lot."

"Sorry."

They went out the patio door and down to the beach, joining the flow of couples and groups walking in both directions along the warm, slapping surf. Glory chose to head north, toward Hell.

"Where are we going?" he asked.

"I borrowed a car. I left it in the parking lot up at the public beach."

"Then where?"

"For a boat ride, I hope."

"Do you have a boat?"

"No, but I have friends who do."

Glory's borrowed car was a battered old Chevrolet as aged and disrep- utable as Andy's Cadillac. She kept the headlights on only for the five or so minutes they were in the traffic of West Bay Road, then killed them the instant she turned into the long drive of a big yacht club, relying on the moonlight to reach a distant jetty on the south side of the harbor. There was a flat-roofed houseboat tied up at the end. Its lights were on, and there was reggae music playing.

"We're in luck," she said. "That's the boat."

"And your friends?"

"Sounds like they're aboard. During the day, they take tourists out to the reef on North Sound to snorkel and play with the stingrays," Glory said. "At night, they charter for parties. If they haven't any customers, they party themselves. That seems to be the case tonight."

"Who's 'they'?"

"Toby and Joey. They used to be commercial fishermen, but Joey got a bit banged up and Toby decided to retire. He owns the boat and Joey's his mate. They live on it." She glanced at her watch and sighed. "By now, I'm afraid they may be a bit into their partying, but don't let that rattle you. They know the waters here better than the fish. I've known them both since I was a little girl."

Toby and Joey looked a little like pirates, but friendly ones. Both had beards. Joey's arms and legs had the look of knotted ropes wound around metal rods and were covered with more old scars than Andy had ever seen gathered together on human skin.

"Sorry to disturb your pleasant evening, Toby," Glory said, "but I need to charter you, and right this very minute."

"Sure, my darling Glory, you want to go for a little party time?"

"Something like that."

"Where you want to go, Glory?"

She puzzled a moment, then looked to Andy. "Out to Rum Point?"

Andy nodded.

"Rum Point, then," Glory continued. "Out past the reef."

"I think maybe tide is rather low, darling Glory," said Toby, moving toward the helm. "Bit of a scrape getting through the reef at Rum Point Channel."

"We'll take the cut through Main Channel and go around."

Toby grinned, then turned up the volume on his tape deck. "Party time!"

It was a good half-hour chug out to where Glory wanted to go. As soon as they were beyond the yacht harbor and into North Sound, she went out on the forward deck, leaning against the rail in the moonlight. Andy poured some of the Tortuga rum he had brought into a couple of plastic cups and then joined her.

"The stiff drink you asked for."

"Thank you very much." She knocked back about half of it, then took a deep breath. "Yes, just the ticket."

"Moonlight cruise."

"Lovely bit of water. That point just off to port there is Head of Barkers. There's a nice bar near there at Morgan's Harbour. Across the sound to starboard, that's all marsh and mangrove swamp. Quite wild and altogether deserted. Those lights off the bow a little to starboard are Cayman Kai, with Rum Point just the other side of it. Where we're going, straight ahead, is Main Channel, the principal cut through the reef."

"What do we do when we get to Rum Point?"

"I haven't the foggiest. Thought I'd leave that up to you, Andy—depending on your Astrid's situation. But if Andao Machado is back there again with that great bloody tub of his, we might be able to get close enough to see if your friend's aboard. How attractive is she?"

"Extremely. She has men all over the world panting after her."

"That'll help with Fabio. He'll want to keep her around awhile. Believe it or not, taking a woman by force offends his machismo. If for some reason they don't throw themselves at his feet, he talks them into it. He has great technique at seduction, or so I'm told."

"Astrid's a hard seduce."

"Good. That'll buy her time."

"Are you?"

"What are you talking about?"

"You kissed Fabio on the plane."

"He kissed me, rather. You did, too."

"I mean . . ."

"My love life is truly none of your bloody business, Mr. Derain, but I'm not so dense as to allow myself to get involved with Fabio. It's taken some artful dodging, but I've stayed out of his bed. He's not one for long romances. The chase is the thing."

"Felicie Balbo . . ."

"Let's not talk about it anymore."

She gulped down the rest of her rum.

• • •

Glory helped Toby navigate the houseboat through the cut, then returned to the forward deck with Toby's binoculars, turning them to the east as Toby steered right onto a course paralleling the reef. The sea was moderate, but there were big swells and a bit of a roll, bumping their bodies together.

"There's a big bloody silhouette about a hundred yards off Rum Point," she said. "I'd say a bit to the northeast of it."

"The Fitches' house is a mile or so down the road from Rum Point," Andy said.

"Well, that could put it directly opposite. It's showing lights, too. Not many, but I daresay there're a few people aboard." She lowered the binoculars.

"What're we going to do, just putt-putt right up to it with all this reggae music blasting away?"

"That's the essential idea. Not quite right up to it, but near enough. Can you swim?"

"We're going to swim up to that yacht?"

"No, but the outboard skiff Toby and Joey have on this boat is quite small, and you never know. Accidents do happen."

Chapter

·16·

They continued on east toward the yacht, deciding to keep up the act of a party boat out for a night's cruise along the reef, while passing as close to the big boat as possible. The full moon was still rising in the northeast. It would brighten the yacht's port side, but the side of Toby's and Joey's craft that faced the yacht would be in shadow.

"Come outside," said Andy. "We'll stand at the starboard rail and whoop it up a little. Add to the verisimilitude."

"That's not very smart, is it?" said Glory. "They'll recognize us."

"No they won't. If we stand in front of the windows and all the cabin lights, we'll be in silhouette. They'll have no idea who we are."

"Unless they turn a searchlight on us."

"Why would they do that?"

"Why do you think?"

"Let's risk it."

"I'm bringing a gun."

If the yacht was in fact Andao Machado's, it would have weaponry aboard of far more consequence than anything at

Glory's disposal, but Andy indulged her. Toby turned up the volume of his tape deck to teenage decibel levels, while Joey, bottle in hand, commenced cavorting in the main cabin, whirling about like some crazed sword dancer. It was very effective.

Standing at the starboard rail with Glory, and invoking again the need for "verisimilitude," Andy slipped his arm around her, wishing this embrace did not include the big Glock automatic she had stuck in the waistband of her shorts at the back. The huge yacht began to increase in size as they drew nearer, its superstructure ascending fully four decks above the waterline. From their perspective, it looked almost a cruise ship, but it had a draft accommodating enough to be anchored in fairly shallow water just to the ocean side of the reef, the bow pointing east into the prevailing trade wind.

The sounds of the breeze and the sea breaking against the reef were lost in the blast of recorded music, which had shifted into the fast rattles and bangs of a steel-drum ensemble, the beat having a very encouraging effect on Andy's adrenaline flow.

As they came within a hundred yards of the Machados' yacht, the music was joined by what sounded much like a dozen or so Indianapolis 500 racing cars warming up. Suddenly the cigarette boat, engines throbbing and burbling, came around the big yacht's bow and headed toward them.

"Just like a navy destroyer on convoy duty," said Andy, raising his voice and leaning close to Glory to be heard.

"They'll have a searchlight or two aboard that thing as well," she said.

"I have an idea."

"Go back inside?"

"No. Something better."

Indeed, it was a marvelous idea, inspired in part by their little sit together in the condo's bedroom. As the cigarette boat rumbled up to them, cutting between them and the big yacht, Andy turned Glory around, yanked her blouse up and over her pistol, and then pulled her close with both arms, kissing her with great vigor and ardor.

She was muttering something angrily. He was holding her too tightly. The heavy pistol was digging into her spine.

He relaxed his hold on her just as her fears proved true. A dazzlingly bright light came on forward of the cigarette boat's helm and swiveled to catch them in its incandescent glare, treating them like performers in a Times Square sex show. Burying his face in Glory's hair, Andy pretended to be oblivious to it.

Then another marvelous idea occurred to him. Sinking to his knees, he pulled her down with him.

"Andy!"

"Verisimilitude, verisimilitude!"

Still holding her, he lay down on his back, pulling her on top of him. With the searchlight bathing them in its hellish brilliance, he put his hand to the back of her shorts. It would look more realistic if he slipped his hand inside them, but that might reveal her automatic, among other things. Thus far, no one seemed to have recognized them. It would be hard to in their present embrace.

There was laughter from the other craft, and then the light went out. The cigarette boat proceeded on past. Andy looked back to see it beginning a slow circling turn behind them.

Glory was catching her breath.

"I think they're going to follow us awhile," he said. "Just stay here. I'll be back in a second."

Remaining on his hands and knees, he scurried into the main cabin, snatched Toby's binoculars down from the control console, and crab-walked his way back to Glory again.

They were drawing near the wide stern of the yacht. It had a built-in swimming platform at the waterline, just below the aft deck, with a descending ladder dipping into the sea and an ascending one leading to the main deck. A hanging lifeboat kept the platform in shadow. Farther along the hull, there were intermittent patches of warm, yellow glow from the cabin and stateroom windows.

"Get back on top of me," he said, lying down and turning his head sideways toward the water as he brought the binoculars to bear.

She did so, resting her weight on her elbows. "I've never felt so ridiculous and so terrified at the same time."

"Then you've never been to Mardi Gras."

The rising and falling swells and roll of the sea made it difficult to keep the binoculars trained on the yacht's windows as they slowly chugged by it, and those above the main deck he couldn't see into at all. But he saw enough.

In the aftmost cabin below the main deck, the ubiquitous

Fabio was once again shed of his flashy garments and having his way with a woman—this time standing. Andy couldn't see enough of the lady to recognize her, except to note her hair was red—not the metallic gold of Ramona's, nor the Nordic blond of Astrid's, nor Beth Hampshire's deep chestnut, but a flaming auburn. Vilma had been a two-tone streaked blonde last time Andy had seen her, but she changed her color, sometimes weekly, and she was as good a guess as any. Certainly she was Fabio's type.

The next two staterooms were brightly illuminated but apparently empty. The one after that was dark, but the lighted window that came next provided a gladdening sight. The sea's movement allowed him only a quick glimpse, but it was a marvelous one, of floral print dress, bare arm, and flow of long blond hair. Guest of Ramona and the Machados as she might be, Astrid was alive.

No Beth, or Annie or Konig, but they had to be aboard, too.

Andy lowered the binoculars to see where the window was situated in relation to the rest of the yacht, then quickly turned his head away and pulled Glory down close upon him again. There were three people standing at the rail up on the yacht's sundeck, just behind the bridge. One of them was Ramona, as unmistakable as a channel marker. With her were two men, both shorter than she, one a darkish fellow Andy did not recognize and the other the extremely diminutive Harvey Fitch, who had lost no time jetting down from New York after Andy's call.

"It's the Fitches," he said, into Glory's ear. "And some guy I don't know."

"Andao Machado."

"Do you think they're looking at us?"

"She was, but not anymore. They're talking about something. Arguing."

"Do you see anyone else?"

"Quite. Couple of men on the bridge. Another at the bow. Two standing at the stern by the aft ladder. And those chaps are definitely looking at us."

"They won't see much, but let's not take any chances."

Andy pulled her head back down. For the heck of it, since her mouth was so convenient, he kissed her again. This time, she relaxed a little, and after a moment, responded more than a little.

Then he felt a hand on his shoulder. It was Toby.

"Hey, hey," he said. "We are past the yacht now. What you want me to do, darling Glory?"

She got to her knees and looked back over her shoulder at the larger craft, now beginning to recede behind them. The cigarette boat was idling beside it.

"Just go on down the coast a bit," she said, "like this is all we had in mind."

"Party, party."

"Party, party," she repeated, then turned to Andy, her eyes rather serious. "After a while, we'll turn around and make another pass by them. Do you want to try to get aboard?"

"With all those thugs there? And Fabio?"

"It's up to you. We'll have surprise on our side. They won't be expecting this."

Glory's suggestion affirmed that she was every bit as crazy as he had supposed, watching her land her plane on a dark, coastal highway in Mexico. They could both be shot into étouffée the instant they set foot on that yacht. Or worse, banged around a bit for sport by Fabio and his friends, after which would come the sharks' turn.

But there was Astrid, as big as six-foot-two life, and he could think of no other way to get her off that floating palace than in person. His friendly acquaintance with Inspector Whittles might at least deter Ramona from rashness, and, for all he knew, he might even have Harvey Fitch on his side.

Certainly the yacht was big enough to get lost in for a brief while, and the better part of the Machados' Cult of Thugee maritime detachment seemed to be stationed abovedecks. If things went too terribly wrong, Toby and Joey had a radio aboard their houseboat. There were other pleasure craft back along the reef by North Sound.

All this was rationalization. What impelled him mostly was that Glory was willing to do this.

Toby stowed their two bags and the briefcase in a locker belowdecks, with instructions to bring them to Glory's mother's art gallery in George Town if Glory and Andy did not make it back to the yacht harbor in the skiff by morning.

They'd been twenty minutes on their course down the coast. Glory had Toby come about for the return trip past the yacht. At

Andy's ardent request, the volume of the tape deck had been turned down temporarily.

"What are these Machado guys doing on this nice respectable island here anyway?" he asked.

"Goodly sums pass through its nice respectable banks, many of them the Machados'. They like to keep an eye on their money, especially Andao. He runs the business end of things. Fabio handles the rough stuff."

"But why would Ramona get mixed up with them?"

"That's probably what husband Harvey came down in such a hurry to find out."

"No. He came after Astrid."

Glory looked at him. "Rather like you."

"Why are you doing this? You don't even know Astrid."

"I don't like the Machados, I'm curious about the Fitches, and I'd like to know exactly how much trouble I'm in. Also, I suppose, in a very small and trivial way, I'm coming to like you."

She bestowed upon him the sweet smile of a high schooler giving her date a boutonniere to wear to the prom, then handed him her pretty little purse gun.

"I don't like these things."

"It'll grow on you."

He stuck it in a pocket of his shorts. "What we really ought to do is bring in the police."

"If you haven't kept track of the various laws I've broken in recent days, they're not exactly misdemeanors. You've broken a few yourself."

"Not intentionally."

"Right. Tell that to your friend Agent Kelleher. No, I'd rather not do any jail time just yet, thank you very much. Let's just see how much of this we can handle ourselves."

Toby and Joey managed to get the skiff into the water and Glory and Andy aboard it without the little thing capsizing. Keeping it on tow, Joey payed out its bowline until it was bobbing along a hundred feet or so behind the houseboat, shifting from side to side in the bigger craft's wake. Andy, crouching forward in the bow, had to hold tightly to the gunwales to keep from falling over. Glory sat hunched in the stern by the skiff's outboard motor. She'd started it but kept it idling in neutral.

The plan was for Joey to let slip the line just as the houseboat drew within hailing distance of the yacht. He and Toby would pass on as merrily as before, music at full volume, making for the cut in the reef they had come through before on the way out of North Sound. Fireworks were popular on Grand Cayman, and the houseboat had some bottle rockets aboard, not to speak of an ample supply of empty bottles. Once past the yacht, Joey would set a few off to add to the distraction.

If any of the Machados' crew happened to notice that Glory and Andy were no longer on deck, the surmise as to the lovebirds' whereabouts wouldn't stretch their imaginations much.

Or so it was to be hoped. Glory was looking scared again, but no less resolute. Andy was feeling numb, rather like he had on that job in Northern Ireland years before. He was going to make it or he wasn't, he told himself—as he had at his Belfast moment of truth. In the meantime, he'd try to keep his fear generator shut off.

They saw Joey at the stern of the houseboat. The knot he'd tied came loose in an instant, and the skiff drifted free, slowing. As Andy pulled in the line, Glory engaged the little outboard and turned the skiff toward the now hulking form of the yacht. The music from the departing houseboat was still so loud Andy could barely hear the outboard's putt-putt.

Glory was as good with small boats as she was with aircraft. When she had the bow of the yacht dead ahead, she cut the engine and let the skiff drift along with the breeze and swells. In a moment, they'd come up against the big boat's anchor chain.

Crawling up beside him, she snatched a length or two of their bowline and tied it fast to the chain, then looked up. The yacht's bow was almost directly above them.

"Can you climb this?" she whispered.

"Think so." He lied.

"Take off your shoes."

He obeyed.

"You remember which cabin she's in?"

Andy thought upon it. Second back from the bow. "Yes."

"Okay. Wait."

The cigarette boat, on station to seaward of the big yacht, once again went prowling after the houseboat, but with less curiosity this time.

There was a reddish flare of light, above and aft of the yacht. Joey had shot off one of the bottle rockets, aiming it seaward to draw the eyes of the Machados' crew away from Glory and Andy's location.

Glory patted Andy's bottom. "Now."

He remembered the rope climbs he had done in high school gym. Given his height and slender build, they'd been whizzes, but this was not. The anchor chain links were big enough to provide excellent handholds, but the heavy metal hurt his knees and ankles.

Glory clambered along impatiently behind him. Despite her comment about male upper body strength at that airfield in Alabama, she had a considerable amount of the female variety. She'd said her father had run a diving equipment shop. There was no need to wonder how she'd spent her free time when she wasn't flying.

The opening in the hull through which the anchor chain ran wasn't quite big enough for a human being to crawl through, but it gave Andy, who'd made most of the climb hanging upside down, a place to perch his feet as he reached upward and grasped the wooden top of the rail. With both hands upon it, he slowly lifted his head above the edge.

The sharp forward curve of the hull had masked them from two men leaning against the rail a short way distant down the deck. Both were staring intently at Joey's fireworks show. Andy felt a sharp pain in his right buttock, where Glory jabbed him— presumably with the Glock. Taking a deep breath, he pulled himself over the railing, dangled a bare foot down to the wooden deck, then eased himself into the shadows behind the anchor capstan.

Glory got aboard with far more ease, but did not join him. Holding the Glock by the barrel, she slipped like a rat along the rail, stood up, swung back, and then sunk the gun butt into the nearest man's skull, the dull thwack audible despite Toby's recorded reggae concert.

As that unfortunate fellow began to crumple, she swung again, this time sideways, hitting the other man in the mouth. Instead of crumpling, he only staggered. A second whack took care of that. He collapsed onto his mate. But then he commenced a wheezing, moaning, groan. There was a third *thwack!*

Andy saw Glory shift the gun to her left hand and shake the right one vigorously, as though it were stinging. She looked back to him and gestured vigorously with her head. He was supposed to be leading.

His photographic work for fashionable magazines had taken him aboard a number of yachts, including the late tycoon Robert Maxwell's, a high-decked tub as fat as its owner had been and one that much resembled the Machados'. He had a fair idea of the way around one.

There were doorways on this deck to either side of the super-structure. With Glory anxiously following, he went to the one just below the bridge, on the shadowy side of the yacht, peering cautiously inside the well-lighted companionway. One set of stairs led down to the staterooms; another went up to the sundeck where they'd seen the Fitches and Andao.

The numbness had not yet abandoned him. He could think in the vacuum it provided. Prudence urged reconnaissance. Pausing to listen a moment, he put foot to the upward leading stairs and raised himself just high enough to look out onto the sundeck.

Ramona was there, drinking and pacing back and forth like a zoo animal. The man Glory had said was Andao was seated on a high canvas deck chair, also drinking—and smoking a long cigar. He looked rather like Fabio, only there was a lot more to him.

Andy could hear snatches of Ramona's side of the conversation, which was neither casual nor happy and definitely not Upper East Side: "Fucking bastard . . . got to kill them, Andao . . . you gotta . . . him and his goddamn lawyers and . . . " No one else was with them.

Machado's contribution to the discourse seemed to consist mostly of patient and indulgent repetitions of Ramona's name. Then he became less patient and stood up—his white loafers thumping to the deck. He grabbed Ramona by the shoulders and leaned into her face, fuming cigar inches from her much-surgically-adjusted nose. It sufficed to quiet her instantly.

"We let him be for now, okay?" Machado said, removing the cigar. "Let him have his fuck! He can do nothing to us . . . nothing he can do. He don't dare do nothing."

"Not to you!" said Ramona. "What about me?"

"What about you, Ramona? I get tired . . ."

What in hell were they talking about? Kill who? Which fuck-ing bastard? Ramona knew so many.

There was a bar on the sundeck. Puffing his cigar furiously, Andao retreated to it and reached for a bottle.

Andy felt another sharp jab, this time in his left buttock. He looked in its direction to see Glory grimace at him and start down the stairs to the deck below, her bare feet moving soundlessly. She was holding her pistol right way around now, and quite expertly.

He quickly followed, catching up with her as she reached the doorway that led to the yacht's main interior corridor. There were doorways all along it.

"Which?" she said, inches from his ear.

"Follow me." What brave sounding words.

He counted three doors where he expected only two. The first door was narrower than the others, however. Andy went to it and turned the knob. It was a closet.

He moved quickly two doors down. The knob refused to turn. It was locked. Of course. It would be.

Andy stood there, puzzling at it, till Glory shoved him gently but decisively aside. Moving her automatic to her left hand, she produced a penknife from her pocket, pulling forth from its small cache of blades a long, awllike jimmy. In a moment, she swung the door open.

He leaped passed her, wanting to get to Astrid first so she'd not cry out. It was a large stateroom, tastelessly furnished.

Astrid wasn't in it. No one was. He and Glory sought each other's eyes, his astonished, hers questioning. There was a door at one end of the room that Andy correctly assumed led to a bath-room. It too was empty.

"Shit," Glory said. "We haven't much time."

"Try another cabin."

They crept back into the corridor, then went to the stateroom just forward. It was unlocked, brightly lit, and perfectly empty. They hurried down to the door just aft of the cabin he'd thought was Astrid's.

Locked. When opened, dark. With light turned on, it too proved empty.

"Triple shit."

"The next one."

It was not locked, nor was it empty. The insatiable Fabio, still bereft of garment, was reclining spread-eagled in a lounge chair, while a naked red-haired woman knelt before him with her mouth around his member, perhaps attempting to revive it. Whatever Fabio's mood, it quickly changed.

It changed yet again as Glory stepped forward, thrusting the Glock at Fabio's handsome, furious, yet bewildered face.

"Is this your Astrid?" Glory asked, a little frantically.

Vilma looked up, emptying her mouth, scarcely comprehending. "Andy Derain?"

"No," said Andy.

"Where is she?" Glory snarled at Fabio. "Astrid. Where?"

"Gone. Fuck you."

The Glock moved closer. "Where, dammit?"

"Gone. Fuck you, you fucking cunt!" Fabio continued his obscene commentary in Portuguese.

"Shall I hit him?" Andy asked, remembering Felicie Balbo.

"No time. Have to go."

"Astrid. Beth Hampshire . . ." He looked to Vilma. "Where . . . ?"

"Now, Andy! Now!"

Vilma, still confused, was on her feet. Andy snatched her hand and yanked her with him out the doorway. Glory, backing up behind them, kept the Glock aimed at Fabio's head.

"You take one step out of this cabin and I'll blow your bloody head off!" she said, then pulled the door shut.

"The other girls," Andy said. "We have to look for them."

"Not this visit, love. We've got seconds at most."

Fabio hadn't believed her. They were pounding down the corridor almost to the stairway when Andy heard the door to Fabio's cabin slam open. A second or two later, there was the explosive crack of a gunshot. Andy heard a sound as much bleat as groan and felt wetness against his bare arm as Vilma's hand slipped from his grasp. She fell, rolling into a heap against the mahogany paneling.

Glory whirled about, raising the automatic in both hands as she pressed herself against the opposite wall. The shot she got off missed Fabio but drove him back yelping into his cabin.

There was a rapid thumping on the stairs above them. Glory turned quickly again and fired, her bullet hitting a huge, dark-skinned man in the belly. He shrieked, clutched his horrible wound, and tumbled headfirst past them.

"Move!" said Glory.

They reached the landing by the open door leading to the main deck just as the raging form of Ramona came tearing down at them from the steps above. Andy shoved her against the bulkhead, but she came leaping back at him in banshee fashion almost at once. Glory swung back, then drove her pistol barrel-first hard into Ramona's liposuctioned belly.

She could have used more padding. Ramona gasped, fighting to refill her lungs with air, then threw up, coughing desperately.

The brief fracas delayed them much too long. Suddenly, Fabio was mounting the stairs behind them, gun in hand, but in too great a hurry to stop and aim a shot.

It was time for Andy, as Glory would say, to do his bit. There was a fire extinguisher in a bracket on the bulkhead. Andy grabbed it up and, like a batter hitting a bunt, shoved it hard into Fabio's face. He heard the crack of breaking teeth and felt the squish of tissue.

Glory was already out on deck. Andy pulled the pistol she'd given him from his pocket and lunged along after her, reaching the bow area just in time to see her leap over the port railing. There was a loud crack, and a bullet fired from somewhere above whizzed near his head en route to somewhere else. He hurdled the rail like a track star.

It seemed to take forever to hit the water.

Chapter
·17·

By the time Andy reached the skiff, Glory had the line free and the
outboard running. She slammed it into gear with Andy still half
hanging over the side, reaching to grab him by the belt and haul
him in. Somehow, he still had the little pistol in his hand.

"Hang on!" she said.

He'd thought she'd head directly away from the yacht, but
she was too clever for that. Not wanting to give their angry ene-
mies a clear shot, she roared along the side of the hull toward the
stern, sheltered somewhat by its curve and catching the crew by
surprise. They heard shouting and running but no more gunshots, at least not until they had careened past the stern and were
weaving in zigs and zags over the open water.

The way Glory was soaring and slamming the little boat over
and into the swells, their feet were already aslosh in seawater. A
hole in the bottom would take them down fast. Nothing came
near them.

Andy looked behind them. The cigarette boat had been summoned into action but had headed for the yacht's bow. Informed
of the skiff's westward course by those on the yacht, the cigarette's helmsman came about with a great swoosh of wake but

had to complete a wide arc because of his craft's great length. Once the boat was pointed directly toward them, the helmsman dug the stern into the water and made up his lost time fast.

Glory heeled them over nearly on their side as she turned their bow toward the coast.

"I'm heading for the reef!" she said.

"I see that! We could smash up there!"

"Right! Tide's still low! But I don't want to go near Toby and Joey!"

Andy looked west again. The houseboat was still brightly visible, if no longer audible, but far enough away to seem uninvolved in the action. The riding lights of other boats, probably fishing craft, dotted the dark waters just beyond. In a few minutes, Toby and Joey would be well among them.

"Is there a break in the reef here?" Andy asked.

"Only at Rum Point."

She was steering directly for the reef—at top speed.

"Glory!!!"

"Do shut up!"

The cigarette boat was bearing down on them, whomping and planing and throwing up spray in spewing cataracts. It was bouncing too much to afford anyone aboard a clear shot at them, but apparently its crew had something just as lethal planned: They were going to run them down.

Glory was apparently aware of that. It suddenly dawned on Andy what she had in mind. She was going to lead the cigarette onto the reef at full tilt, hoping to dart the more nimble skiff away at the last second.

It almost worked, but the cigarette's skipper was smart enough to see it. With deep water to spare, he stood his sleek craft on its tail, spinning it off to port. Glory had flipped the skiff around to starboard, but they got caught in the bigger boat's rooster tail of seawater.

"What now?" he shouted, wiping off his face with his arm.

She, too, was drenched. Her hair was a mop. "I'll keep as close to the reef as I can! Hang on!"

The numbness had gone. His fear was almost chewable. He had to do more than sit there. Cupping his hands, he began bailing out the skiff, bracing himself against the forward seat with his knee.

The work kept him from looking at the reef, but as she turned them back toward it, the sound of the breaking waves grew louder. When he finally did look up, it was to see a swell roll up into a huge mound and then explode over the coral with flying spray.

Glory yanked on the outboard's steering arm. Like a skier on a slalom course, she began her run along the reef, swinging the skiff up and over and around the swells, heaving off to windward just as they appeared about to break. It was guesswork by inches, made on a tiny platform bouncing about the water like a bucking bull.

They took water with every broach, but Andy was making progress. Pausing briefly, he looked back over his shoulder for the cigarette boat.

It was coming up fast—not toward them, but on a parallel course back off in smoother water that kept it away from the reef.

But still within gunshot range.

The first two bullets came from pistols or rifles, buzzing overhead like speedy insects. Then they brought in an automatic weapon. With the distance between them and their constantly changing movements, accurate fire would be nearly impossible, but there was always the chance of what Glory would call misadventure.

As she made one quick turn, a burst of gunfire made six or seven sploshes in the water where the stern had been. A swell lifted them then and heaved them sideways, back toward the reef, the outboard's propellor spinning in air for a moment.

"It's no use!" she shouted. "I've got to go across!"

"The reef?"

"Yes! You ever do any white-water rafting?"

Not a lot of rapids around Louisiana.

He shook his head. "Only brown water!"

"Okay! Get your legs under that seat—and hang on!"

She headed back out toward the sea for a few seconds—in part, he guessed, to throw off the cigarette-boat bastards, but also to give herself a chance to choose her spot for crossing.

Whipping the skiff around again, she set it rushing toward a breaking swell at an oblique angle. The wave blew itself apart on the coral just ahead of them, exposing the hard black rock like a row of bad teeth. Holding them steady, Glory throttled back, and a moment later they were lifted by a following swell. Just as its leading bulge began to froth into spray, she straightened the skiff and gunned the motor, shooting them forward into the air. They hit the eddying flatness ahead with a smack, and banged against some unseen bit of rock that skewed them slightly sideways, but the great rush of water from the broken swell lifted them again and shoved them on. A few seconds later, they were in clear water. And not sinking.

Glory wasted no time, turning the throttle up full and speeding away on a diagonal course that kept her moving west but away from the reef and the cigarette boat. They wouldn't dare try shooting now. Ahead, quite near, were the lights of the outdoor bar at Rum Point. There were small boats along the beach and several larger pleasure craft anchored just inside the reef. Toby and Joey had turned their houseboat through Rum Point Channel and were heading into North Sound.

The cigarette boat's engines rumbled and roared angrily. It veered away from the reef and began accelerating, making course for the same channel taken by the houseboat.

"They're coming in here after us," Glory said.

"We can make it to shore before they get to us."

"Not by much. They'd only hunt us down. Or they might go after Toby and Joey. I've got a better idea."

It didn't seem like a better idea at all. She was steering away from the land and for the channel, as though trying to get to it in time to greet the cigarette.

"Where are you going?" he asked.

"Watch!"

It was a hot night, but he was shivering. So was she. But she grinned.

She zipped them along the landward side of the reef just at the edge of breakers. The cigarette boat was a spectacular sight as it raced opposite them toward the channel, planing and throwing up a big bow wave. Andy couldn't tell if its crew could still see them, but they were hell-bent on finding them regardless.

Glory's course was straight. The bigger craft had to make a wide circle to make the turn through the channel at that speed, giving Glory the time she needed. The cigarette finally straightened, then came charging through the cut. Just as it did, Glory skidded the skiff around the last nub of reef rock and sped past the cigarette in the opposite direction, making for open water.

"Did they see us?" Andy asked.

"Don't know, but I'm not going to wait to find out."

She steered westward again, heading across the mouth of North Sound on the ocean side of the main stretch of reef. The cigarette boat, hesitant, fell to idling. The searchlight came on and began glancing over the water in a frantic series of arcs. All at once it swiveled aft, toward the ocean, then shifted from side to side, seeking them.

"Can they see us?"

"You keep asking that. I don't know, but I think they've figured it out." She paused and grinned, patting his arm. "This is good."

"It is?"

"It is if there's as much gas in this thing as I hope there is. It's not a bad little skiff, but I wish we had a Boston whaler. Then we'd lose 'em for sure."

He didn't pretend to understand but accepted it all with awe and amazement. Nothing seemed real anymore. Despite all that had happened, he found himself beginning to feel giddy. He watched the cigarette boat rev up again and begin another circle to get back out through Rum Point Channel. Andy felt as removed from the scene as though he were looking at it on film.

They didn't speak. There was nothing to do but skim along and keep on course and wait, hoping that all of Glory's calculations, whatever their intended result, were correct.

As Andy expected, the cigarette boat, quite a bit behind them now, returned to the ocean side of the coral barrier and, with searchlight aimed forward, came growling toward them. He was heartened when he saw the beam shift left and right a couple of times, signifying uncertainty.

"We've about a mile to go!" said Glory.

Andy eased back onto the middle seat and turned to face her so she wouldn't have to shout so. Water was sloshing about their ankles, but no more was coming in.

"A mile to what?"

"To the Main Channel. Andao doesn't hang about here much,

and I'm going to bet his people aren't real familiar with Cayman waters."

"What difference does that make? They're closing the distance. Pretty fast, too."

"That's all right. I want them to spot us. I want them to follow us through the channel. I'm going to go straight through at full bore—right at Fisherman's Rock."

"'Rock'?"

Another grin, but showing strain. "Don't worry. It's an underwater shoal—a long one—just beyond the channel. I'm guessing the tide's in enough to give us a couple feet of clearance. At the least, one foot. I'll pull the motor up a bit, and we should make it easily."

"And?"

"If they're hot behind us and don't know the shoal's there, they won't make it quite so easily."

They stared at each other, letting each see the other's weariness and fear and hope. On an odd impulse, he took her free hand and held it. She squeezed his, then pulled hers away, turning to look back at their pursuers.

"Well, here they come!"

Once the searchlight rediscovered them, the distance between the two craft began to diminish inexorably. By the time Glory turned them into the channel, bullets began spattering in the water around them with great fury.

Andy ducked down. Glory had done the same. There was another zing and crack and a sudden stinging in the back of his right hand. One of the shots had hit the metal rim of the gunwale near the bow, sending a splinter of something into his skin.

He pressed himself against the bottom of the skiff, the side of his face going into the salty water. The searchlight illuminated everything around him. He could see bits of things floating before his eyes.

"We're coming up on it!" Glory shouted. "Hold on!"

He heard the outboard grumble as she tilted it partly out of the water. It seemed to him the skiff was slowing. But it kept on over the shoal. Much sooner than Andy expected, Glory jammed the propellor back down again. He heard a couple of scrapes against underwater sand, but they skipped free and were quickly up to full speed once more.

Andy started to lift his head.

"Stay down!"

The cigarette boat struck the shoal with such force it sent a great wave washing forward. The sound of the crash was unlike anything Andy had ever heard before, a gathering *moooosh* followed by a sharp and rattling crackle. Bits of wood and metal sang through the air and fell splashing near and far.

Now Andy looked back. In the movies, there'd doubtless be a huge fireball and explosion. Here, nothing like that happened. The big boat had been transformed into a monumental wreck. It had been planing when it hit the shoal, and the impact had broken its keel, shoving the bow section up into the air and twisting the rest of it over on its side. The engines had stopped, but the electric was still functioning. The searchlight pointed skyward like an advertisement for a Hollywood premiere.

Glory slowed the skiff, steering a bit to port to better view the carnage.

"Are you all right?" he asked.

"Darling Andy," she said. "I'm quite ecstatic."

If true, that wasn't all she was. She took a deep breath, then leaned over the side and began throwing up.

Chapter
·18·

Andy waited for her to finish, saying nothing. Finally, she washed off her face and resumed her place by the motor, opening up the throttle again to put the wreck far behind them.

"What about survivors?" he asked.

"If there are any. It's shallow there. They won't drown unless they lie down."

"Right."

"I don't care if they do lie down. I don't care if there are any survivors. They're all sons of bitches. Not at all worth the vomit."

"I guess not."

"Your friend Vilma wasn't a survivor, was she?"

"No, she sure wasn't."

"Did you know her well?"

"Not really." A memory came to him of Vilma staggering out of some downtown New York all-night club, stoned to the moon. He'd thought then she might not end well, but this?

"I'm worried about Astrid. And the others."

"I don't think their status has been changed any."

"I want to know if they're still on that yacht."

"For the moment, Andy, use your wants on us."

Obliquely, they were moving closer now to the eastern edge of the sound, cruising in quite gentle water. He could see the lights of George Town far off to the west, many compass points off their present course.

"In case you're wondering," Glory said, "I'm not going back to the yacht harbor. Not just now."

She was steering toward a long, low, dark silhouette of land lying just ahead across the moonlit waters.

"Okay. How come?"

"All that great bloody smash-up accomplished was to buy us a little time, and much less than you'd think. That yacht of Andao's has two outboard inflatables on it, plus a twenty-one-foot runabout with an engine probably ten times as powerful as ours. They'll be all over this sound in a few minutes. If we had pitch darkness, it might be all right. But in this damnable moonlight, we'd be spotted quick out in open water. Got to get under some cover."

"But won't the police be coming? Or the Coast Guard or something?"

"All the RCIP has is this one patrol boat. It's rather fast, but if it's coming from George Town it'll take a while. And anyway, we don't want to get mixed up with the police, do we? Especially now."

"So where are we going?"

"Booby Cay."

"'Booby'?"

"Booby. It's that low-lying island just ahead. All marsh and mangrove swamp. Completely uninhabited. Lots of cover. Good place to hide."

"For how long?"

"The Machados are going to be very displeased with us—especially Fabio, and especially with you. You've grievously offended his machismo. That fire extinguisher bit will keep him away from mirrors for a very long time. So they'll come looking for us in very serious fashion—checking out every foot of shoreline. But I doubt very much they'll hang about all night. They've got dead bodies aboard that yacht, and the police will get here eventually. I'm sure the Machados will be well clear of the area by daybreak. We can try for the yacht harbor then. Or George Town."

"Then what?"

"I don't know. Depends."

"And in the meantime?"

"Into the mangroves. As far in as we can get. It won't be terribly pleasant, but with all this moonlight, I can't think of anyplace else to go."

She took them down the side of the swampy cay, into water as shallow as that at Fisherman's Rock but considerably muckier. When Andy went over the side to help her push the skiff into the mangrove thickets, his feet sank into ooze that came up over his ankles.

A small boat, following the curves of the shoreline, was approaching them from the direction of the reef—carrying a light that was moving about busily.

"That's got to be them," she said. "Come on, shove!"

It was hard and painful work. The mangrove branches clawed at them as though angry at the intrusion. Andy was reminded of Humphrey Bogart hauling his boat through the marsh in *The African Queen,* only it seemed to him that Bogie had it easier.

Once they managed somehow to get the boat and themselves fully within the mangroves, they crawled into the skiff, rolling over and lying side by side on their backs. If there was a less comfortable position, it had to be strapped into one of the interrogation devices of the Spanish Inquisition. Their heads were against the hard edge of the boat's rear seat and their backs and buttocks lay in water. The canopy of mangrove branches and leaves pressed down almost to their faces. In a moment, he began to detect an added nicety: Creatures tiny as well as amazingly large began crawling about his face, neck, and arms, and then into his clothing. He thought of Humphrey Bogart again, wondering if there were leeches here, too.

"Son of a bitch," he said, "I've got little visitors."

"Me too. Mangroves are full of life. They support an extraordinary number of insects—also snakes."

"Oh, goody."

"Shhhh. I think it's them."

"The snakes?"

"Quiet!"

The approaching motorboat, of course, could be merely some late-night fishermen, looking for a favorite spot. There was an equal chance it could be the Easter Bunny. The engine noise was slightly muffled, suggesting it might be an inboard, which suggested it was the twenty-one-foot runabout Glory had mentioned, which meant it might have three or four thugs aboard—four pairs of searching eyes.

The boat's spotlight was nothing so powerful as the cigarette boat's, but its beam was able to penetrate the outer mangrove branches, outlining Glory's face with a hazy glow. He took her hand. She pulled him close to her side and held tight.

But nothing happened. The light moved on, and so did the motor sounds, diminishing gradually, sounding more muffled and distant as the boat rounded a curve of shoreline just to the south of them.

Something very nasty bit Andy's waist beneath his cloth belt. He hit at it with the heel of his free hand, but it only moved lower, and then into his crotch.

"Keep still," Glory whispered.

"Trying. Damn beastie."

"Shhhh."

Ten or fifteen minutes passed. It might just as easily have been two hours. They'd been left in darkness again, and there was no way of seeing his watch. He wasn't even sure it still worked. He concentrated on the touch and feel of Glory's hand. Whether he lived just a few more minutes or another fifty years, he doubted he'd ever forget this particular tropical interlude.

Another ten years went by. The creepies and crawlies were now everywhere on his body, each and every one of them moving. His bottom, still lying in the soaking salt water, itched terribly. What he wanted to do more than anything was give out a piercing primal scream. Instead, he gripped Glory's hand all the more tightly, so much that it hurt. She was doing the same—the equivalent of biting the bullet.

The speedboat returned, passing by a bit faster and a little farther out, the searchlight this time not penetrating so deeply.

There was a frightening moment of hesitation, the boat's motor abruptly idling.

"God," said Glory.

She pulled her hand away. Andy wondered if she was reaching for the automatic. All it would be good for in their situation was committing suicide.

"I love you, Gloria Newlands," he said. He chose them as last words.

She muttered a few syllables in response. He couldn't understand them, but it didn't matter. She was cut off by a marvelous sound—the runabout's inboard going full blast and away from them. A wild and joyous feeling surged through him, increasing in reverse proportion to the dwindling engine noise. The only disturbing element now was the realization that the speedboat was moving off to the southwest, not north toward the reef and the open sea and the yacht, where Andy desperately wished it to be.

At length there was silence, which was to say, a madness of insect and wildlife noises. He hadn't paid much attention to it, but now it grated on his nerves. The itching was overwhelming him. He'd pulled the metal splinter from his hand, but the wound was hurting. It needed a thorough washing.

"Glory, I can't take any more of this."

"Soldiers in Viet Nam did."

"I was never in Viet Nam."

"My uncle was. My American one, my mum's brother. He was killed there."

"I'm sorry."

She sighed, a long, sad sound. "I never killed anyone before tonight."

"It's okay."

"They're dead, those men. The one I shot—I'm sure he's dead. The ones I hit on the head . . ."

"They had it coming, just like you said. Don't worry about it."

"Did you ever kill anyone?"

"No, but I tried to once."

"I think I have that man's blood on me."

"Come on, Glory, we're getting out of here."

He rolled out of the boat, carefully, easing himself into the soupy mush. Obediently, she did the same on the other side.

Somehow it was much easier pulling the skiff out of the mangroves than it had been pushing it in.

They went straight out to where the water was waist deep, towing the skiff along with them. Except for a few twinkling lights far in the distance to the north, and a red one to the south, the sound was empty wherever they looked, darkening a little as gauzy clouds passed over the face of the moon.

"I'm sorry," he said. "I've got to get this insect zoo off me."

He pulled off his ruined shirt and soggy shorts and tossed them in the boat. Then, naked, he plunged underwater, furiously running his hands over his skin and scalp. When he came up for air, he saw that Glory was emulating him.

"All right," she said, when she was done. "What do you want to do?"

How nice. Now things were up to him.

"I want to go to a clean, dry beach and curl up and go to sleep."

"There's nothing but swamp between here and Cayman Kai. There is a nice beach up there, but it's not far from Rum Point and the Fitches' place. A bit south of here, though, where you see that red light, that's Head Sound Barcadere. There's a resort development with some hard ground along the shore."

"Not too hard, I hope."

"I shouldn't think. And at one end I remember it being rather secluded."

"Oh, goody. This time I mean it."

It was only a mile and a half, but it took awhile. Glory held the outboard nearly at idle to keep down the noise and conserve fuel. Their gliding passage was so gentle Andy began to doze. Wakefulness returned just as the bow slid through some reeds and plumped up onto a bank of soft grass.

"We're here," she announced softly.

Off to their left, there was a road running out to the shore from the development, extending into the water on a tiny peninsula apparently used as a boat-launching ramp. Ahead of them in the darkness were the distant shapes of houses, a few with lights faintly showing.

"Up on that hill is a little village called Newlands," she said.

"Your ancestral home?"

"Couple of centuries ago, perhaps. Apart from my mother, I have no close relatives on the island now. I'm the last of my line. Help me pull the boat up. The tide's coming in."

When they had the skiff fully out of the water, they just stood a moment, looking at each other.

"I don't feel like getting dressed," he said.

"I don't suppose it matters much now, does it?"

"It's warm here on dry land, almost hot."

She took a slight step forward. "I'm still a little chilly."

He reached and pulled her to him, putting his arms gently around her. "I'll warm you."

"What I said about your not being suitable," she said, "that was wrong. You're quite suitable."

"Thank you." He kissed her forehead.

She leaned her head back to look into his eyes. "Do you know what I'm thinking?"

"I'm thinking the same thing."

"I can tell."

He had feared he'd be too exhausted. "Sorry."

"Don't say sorry." Her lips came up against his, softly at first, then with more ardor. Now he felt very warm indeed.

"My mind's been full of so many fears and horrors," she said. "I want to wipe it all away."

"Me too."

"I don't want to think about anything for a while."

"No thoughts."

He kissed her once more. They settled to their knees and kissed again. His head was beginning to spin a little. He brought her down to the grass, still in his arms, her breasts tight against his chest. Everything was suddenly, extraordinarily, bewilderingly beautiful, the world all around them sharply clear in its perfection and nocturnal grandeur. He was amazed at his happiness. He hadn't been this happy in years. A matter of minutes before, he'd been miserable.

He didn't hear the word "love," but she kept calling his name. He murmured hers. It sounded good in murmurs.

Then he was on top of her. Her strong, trim legs enfolded him.

Her face pressed hotly close to his, and everything around them vanished from his mind.

It wasn't until much later, as he was lying wakeful with the sleeping Glory's head on his shoulder, that the fears and horrors returned, along with thoughts of Astrid. And Beth.

And of Bleusette.

Chapter
·19·

They were awakened at first light by a few drops of rain, which were quickly followed by many millions of them. Andy lifted his head to see a squall line descending upon them in an almost solid curtain of murk and drenching downpour, accompanied by whipping, whirling winds. The nearby palms were thrashing about like torture victims.

"Good bloody morning," Glory said.

"A bit British out," he said, patting her wet bottom.

She didn't laugh. Brushing away his hand, she stood up and went groping for her clothes.

They shook out whatever insects still remained in their wretched garments, then quickly pulled them on. The skiff was rapidly filling with rainwater. Andy started to lift it up on its side to empty it, but she shook her head.

"I don't want to go out in this bad a blow," she said. Bending over the outboard motor, she opened the lid to the gas tank, wiping the rain from her eyes. "No bloody petrol to speak of anyway."

"So what do we do?"

"We walk. There's no real bus service here."

"Walk to where?"

"To George Town. If we're lucky, someone may give us a ride."

She'd lost one of her boating shoes in the previous night's adventures.
Andy offered her one of his, but she preferred to limp along half
barefoot. They trudged up the road past the houses, moving on
over a low hill. As they were passing a school, a small truck carrying two Jetskis under a tarpaulin came up behind them, slowed,
then halted.

The rain had abated somewhat. Instead of a million drops a
minute, the rate had decreased to perhaps half a million.

A smiling black face leaned out the window. "Would you be
needing transport this morning?" His accent was the marvelous
musical British English of the islands. Andy hoped the man's
cheerfulness would be contagious. Glory's mood looked very
dark indeed. As he thought upon it, his own wasn't so joyful, either. If they were in New Orleans, he'd be taking her for a happy
breakfast at Brennan's. A lot of joy to be had in a serving of Bananas Foster.

The truck driver actually was going to George Town. Of
course, there weren't many other places to go on the island. He
looked something of a Rastafarian, and the truck radio was playing music to match—with much static.

The little truck had a manual transmission and seating only
for two, so Glory rode on Andy's lap, bending over somewhat for
headroom. He hoped she wasn't uncomfortable; he didn't mind
at all. The downpour had provided them something of a vigorous
shower bath. They both smelled very damp, but clean.

Glory told the driver their boat had sprung a leak in the storm
and they'd been compelled to put into shore. He accepted this.

"Quite a bad bit of weather this morning," he said. "They say
on the radio it's a low pressure trough over from Jamaica. A wa-
terspout was seen off Jackson Point. Have you ever seen a water-
spout?"

Glory stared straight ahead, saying nothing.

"Yes," said Andy. A memory had come to him: He and his father in a small day sailer in the Gulf of Mexico off Grand Isle; a
black sky to the east, an eerie white and blue-gray funnel rising

like a rope trick to the angriest of the towering clouds. His father enjoying himself immensely, sipping from a flask and raising it in a toast to the heavens.

"A wonder to see," said the driver.

"Yes."

"Something most peculiar," the driver continued. "There was a very big wreck last night—by the reef on North Sound. Did you see it—when you were out in your boat?"

"No." Glory's voice was very flat.

"Great big speedboat yacht, it was. Broke into two pieces. But it happened in clear weather! Full moon! They must be very great fools, these speedboat people. More money than brains, eh mon?"

"Too goddamn much money," said Glory.

The truck driver was going up toward Seven Mile Beach a ways but dropped Andy and Glory on George Town's main street by the harbor, whose formal name was Hog Sty Bay. It was a small facility, a deep but narrow inlet with concrete quays on each side, capable of accommodating nothing larger than the boats and barges that brought the cargo containers in from the freighters and the tenders that ferried passengers to and from the cruise ships. There were two cruise liners present that morning, lying perhaps half a mile offshore. They'd be gone presently, doubtless quickly replaced by others.

The storm was moving out to sea now, to the west, the dark sky accompanying it a macabre greenish color. Elsewhere, especially behind them, the sun was breaking through. The wet pavement and rooftops sparkled with its light.

"Maybe it's a good omen," Andy said.

"Fat bloody chance."

Tired of limping, Glory took off her remaining shoe and led him barefoot up a side street to a pale green stucco one-story building with freshly painted dark green trim and a sign that said THE NEWLANDS GALLERY, and below that, ISLAND ART. Glory looked carefully up and down the street, then hopped to the top step and quickly unlocked the door, pulling him in behind her. She relocked the door, checking to see that the hanging CLOSED sign was still facing outward.

"My mum's in Florida for the month," she said, leaning back

against a display case containing highly polished dark coral jewelry. "There's a woman who takes care of the gallery for her, but she won't be here to open up until ten."

"So what do we do?"

"Just relax a moment. Dry off. Catch our breath. Clean up. We must look beastly. You certainly do."

"Not you. Is there a shower?"

"No." Her eyes looked for something in his, something, perhaps, she was hoping not to find. "I've become fond of you, Mr. Derain, but that has nothing to do with what happened last night. Understood?"

"You're sure?"

"Have you ever been married?"

"Engaged a few times."

"Doesn't count. I was married for three years. To an airline captain. He was a walking stereotype. Girl in every airport. Drove me altogether mad. I like you, Andy, but you strike me as a chap with at least two women in every port. I just can't handle that sort of thing."

"Oh."

"I don't believe you can handle it, either."

"Glory . . ."

"So let's just chalk it up to a highly emotional evening, not to be repeated anytime soon, all right? And we'll get on with this."

"*Bien entendu.*"

"I'm going to check in back."

Andy glanced about at the gallery's wares. The coral jewelry was lovely, some pieces quite exquisite. But most of the pictures, prints, and odd pieces of sculpture and painted china would have been considered fairly crass junk on the Upper East Side of New York. The proprietress even had T-shirts for sale.

The closest thing to really fine art in the shop was a group of half a dozen watercolors hanging on the wall near the door. They were island scenes, mostly, but done with a deft and telling touch and imbued with a very haunting, lonely quality. Not junk at all. He peered at the oddly scrawled signature.

"Your mother do these watercolors?" he asked.

"No," she said. "I did. I paint a bit when I've the time. Haven't done any for months."

She was rummaging around in the back room. He heard a closing drawer and the clink of keys.

"They're magnificent."

"Codswallop. Just some trite sunsets for the tourists."

Now he heard a door open, squeaking on its hinges, and then a screen door open and slam. "Bloody marvelous!" she said, from some distance.

Marvelous? He went through the back room, which apparently was used as much for storage as for bookkeeping and paperwork, and stood at the doorway. Glory was in a small, flower-filled and now sunny backyard bordered on one side by a high wooden fence. At her feet were their two bags and the briefcase.

"Toby and Joey have been here already, bless them," she said. "Which means they're likely all right—probably en route to Stingray City with a boatload of snorkelers this very minute." She slung Andy's camera bag over one shoulder and picked up the other two pieces. "Lovely place to leave them, isn't it?—right where any layabout could amble by and make off with them. Your expensive camera, my dirty undies, and a briefcase full of money. Andao would truly love that."

Andy opened the door for her. She set the bags inside, then stepped back out into the little yard.

"I'm going to nip down the lane back there and see where my mum left her car," she said. "Be right back."

When she returned, very quickly, it was with a sort of plan, the first part of which appealed to him greatly. After taking turns using the gallery's small bathroom to complete their *toilette*, they'd go up the street for some coffee and breakfast, then down the street to buy some clean clothes.

"I really do think the Machados are well clear of the Caymans," she said. "At least Grand Cayman. Otherwise, I wouldn't have had us strolling about the way we have."

"How can you be so sure they've left us?"

"They had their shot at us and they missed. All they ended up with was a bloody bunch of corpses, and none of them us. Now they've got to lick their wounds and think of what to do next.

And they have to be damned careful after this. There's rather a good governor here. He's the one who got the police force that patrol boat, and he's shut down a couple of banks for dealing in drug money. I doubt he has any idea he has such big sharks swimming in his waters, and Andao won't want him to find out. The Machados can't afford to fuck up again."

"I want to find Astrid and the girls."

She looked at him and said very bluntly, "I know that. You've made me anxious about them myself. I'm particularly interested to meet this Astrid. It's my guess she was gone from that yacht by the time you and I got back to it. I think she may well have gone off somewhere with Mr. Fitch. From what you said, he wouldn't leave that tub without her."

"He came down here to get her away from Ramona."

"So there you are. The alternative's unthinkable."

He stared at the floor. "The alternative may be what happened to the others."

"Maybe not."

Andy sighed. "I'm running a little low on hope. A lot of real bullets whizzing around last night."

"Come on," she said. "Once we get freshened up and refueled, we'll take my mum's car and check out the airport. See who's on the tarmac and who isn't."

"How will you know if Fitch's plane is there?"

"Aren't too many Learjets painted gold with a big fucking black *F* on the side."

"And if it's not there?"

"Then, love, take heart. That could very well mean he's already flown back to New York with your Astrid. And maybe her friends. They might be dancing the light fantastic or whatever at the Stork Club."

"The Stork Club closed decades ago."

"Ah well, at the Peppermint Lounge, then."

Their meal was at a very utilitarian establishment that served a "full English fry-up"—British breakfast—complete to kippers and bangers. Glory ate even more heartily than he, as greedily as one of the waifs in Oliver Twist's orphanage. He wondered when she'd last eaten and how she'd kept going so indefatigably without.

The slacks and blazer he'd left wadded in his camera bag were not very wearable, so their shopping stop included for him the acquisition of a pair of white polyester trousers and a white polo shirt with a Caymans sea turtle emblazoned on the front. The outfit was a bit touristy, but when the thick, heavy, menacing sunglasses Glory picked out for him were added, he gained something of the aspect of a tackily dressed hired killer.

"Perfect," she said, proceeding to buy fresh shorts and blouse for herself, along with a new pair of aviator sunglasses. And a pair of canvas deck shoes. A thin, light-blue boating jacket covered up the Glock at her back nicely.

The airport was barely stirring at this early hour. Leaving her mother's bright red Sterling fastback in the lot, they made their way along the chain-link fence to where they had a good view of the terminal apron. The Pilatus had been moved from where Glory had abandoned it at the end of the runway back to an aircraft parking area on the ramp near the commercial jetliner gates. Not far distant was Harvey Fitch's business jet—as ridiculously painted as she'd said. A couple of men whom Andy took to be crew or security were loitering next to it. Nothing about them suggested any urgency or unusual concern. Harvey might know nothing at all about the previous night's carnage. Harvey—and Astrid.

"I still have the keys to the Pilatus," she said. "They can't have changed the lock. A hop over this fence and I could be in the left seat and the hell out of here before the tower knew what was happening. I just wish I knew how much fuel's in the tanks. I don't know if they topped them off or not."

"I should think you'd want to wait until dark."

"Quite. But who knows what might happen in the meantime? The Machados might send someone after it. I'm surprised they haven't already. I'm going to have be out of here rather soon, Andy. A bit of unfinished business, and then I'm gone."

"Fitch's jet is here. Astrid's probably still here."

"I'll wager he took her to his condo or checked into a hotel. They wouldn't be at that house with Ramona."

"But Astrid can't stand Harvey."

"She has no idea where you are. She has to turn to someone."

"I'm not leaving without her."

She grumbled, gazing at the airplanes opposite rather like a lioness contemplating a herd of fresh meat. "You do what you have to. But right now, I really, truly need your help. And may I remind you that you had quite a lot of mine last night."

"What is it you want from me?"

"I want to deliver this briefcase to the bank—just as I was supposed to yesterday, as I normally do."

"That's crazy."

"I'm only twenty-four hours overdue. That's happened before. It's the last thing Andao would expect. I'm hoping it might mollify him a little. Don't you think? Putting this highly prized possession of his precisely where it's supposed to be, as though last night never happened?"

"There's still the misdelivered 'marshmallows.' "

"A lesser crime."

"What bank?"

"It's quite near."

"Why do you need me?"

"There's a protocol. I'm always accompanied by one of the Machados' men. Whoever's assigned to it meets me at the airport and drives me to the bank. He comes with me into the vault—to keep an eye on things. The bank expects this. The man changes sometimes. This time it's going to be you. If you'll do it."

"Just hand over the briefcase? That's all?"

"It takes a while. The bank chap has to go through the contents and sign some papers. But then we'll be free to go."

"I'm supposed to be one of the Machados' goons?"

"All you have to do is keep your mouth shut and look mean as possible behind your sunglasses. Do you still have the small pistol?"

" 'Fraid so."

"Stick it somewhere he'll notice it. Add to the verisimilitude, right?"

"Then what?"

"We get the hell out."

"With Astrid. And the others."

"Whatever's possible." She spoke with no enthusiasm.

The bank was up the next side street and one of several in its block. It was air-conditioned, but badly. The interior was only a little less

warm and damp than the out-of-doors. There were two customers in the establishment, a tourist exchanging currency with
one teller, a local Caymanian, apparently making a deposit,
standing by another. A third teller was drowsily toying with a
computer keyboard.

The only bank officer present—a neat black man wearing a tie
and short-sleeved shirt—sat at a desk to the side, going over a
computer printout with a ballpoint pen. Glory went up to him
and stood at the edge of the desk.

"Good morning," she said, quietly.

He looked up, brows rising in both curiosity and frown.

"You're very late," he said. "An entire day."

"Terribly sorry, but it absolutely couldn't be helped. Ran into
some dreadful weather. Had to divert. Other problems. At all
events, here I am. Let's get on with it."

The man rose but then stood there, staring at Andy.

"What's wrong?"

"I don't know this man."

"I don't either. They sent him to the airport to meet me. A lot
of turnover lately."

Andy started to smile but then remembered how mean he
was supposed to look. He scowled.

"Very well," said the man in the shirt and tie.

He led them to the counter, pausing until one of the tellers buzzed open the lock of the little gate. The door to the
vault was open, though the steel gate beyond had to be unlocked.
They followed him through it into the vault's outer room.
Standing by a bare metal table and the only chair, Andy began to
sweat.

The bank officer shut the gate, then crossed to a larger steel
door in the rear of the room and began working the combination.
Glory set the briefcase on the table.

"I'll be with you in a moment," the black man said, swinging
open the steel door and stepping into the chamber it protected.
He returned with a large metal box, setting it gently next to the
briefcase. He unlocked both, then seated himself.

The briefcase contained just what Andy had expected it
would: neatly packed stacks of U.S. currency, each bound with a
paper band. They were hundred- and thousand-dollar denomina-
tions, and there were a very great many stacks. The fact that Andy

had assumed this was what the briefcase contained didn't make it any less fantastic to see.

To Andy's surprise and dismay, the bank officer began counting the money, efficiently but laboriously, stack by stack, using his thumb in practiced manner to separate each bill. When satisfied, he'd set each stack in a row on the table, then take out another. Andy wiped his forehead with his palm. It did no good. The sweat kept coming.

It took a very long time for the briefcase to empty. When he was done, the man at last opened the metal box, lifting out a sheaf of folders and selecting one. From it he extracted an ordinary, old-fashioned ledger and began making a complicated entry. No computers to access, trace, or jigger with in this part of the operation.

They were almost through. Andy began thinking of how soon he might be seeing Astrid. The bank officer paused to look up at Glory, who'd been staring at him intently. She smiled, perhaps too warmly.

The man hesitated, then returned to his work, a bit more briskly now. Finally, he took what looked to be a receipt book from the box and removed two of its sheets, filling them both out in precisely the same way. When done, he turned to hand Glory her copy, but she was standing beside him, the big Glock aimed at his head.

"What are you doing?" he asked.

Glory reached over him and lifted up one of the folders, spilling its contents on the table. "Keep your voice down."

"Those are bank papers," he said, angry now, but also scared, and sweating as much as Andy was.

"And interesting reading they are," she said, picking up one of the documents. She sensed the fellow moving and turned to shove the pistol up to about an inch from his right eye. "I'm taking them."

"That's robbery! You'll go to jail."

"You're going to call the RCIP? I don't think so. They'd find all this quite fascinating reading as well." She looked quickly over her shoulder at Andy. "Put it all in the briefcase."

He did as bidden, glancing at the top sheet. Whatever information the documents contained, it was obvious it would require an accountant to comprehend it.

"All of it," Glory said. "Everything in the folders. The ledger, too."

"You can't do this," the bank officer said. "You know what will happen."

"But I am doing it. Don't be a bother now, all right? This is the last time I'm going to call on you. Don't make it the last time anyone does."

"I can't close the briefcase," Andy said.

"Sit on it! I want all those papers."

Andy gave her an unhappy look but managed to carry out her orders.

She turned to the black man. "Now, sir. You stand up—slowly, if you please, and go into that other room, the one you got this box from."

"Don't put me in there."

"Shut up." She nodded to Andy. "Try the gate there, just to see if it opens. There's a switch by the wall."

He went to it and pressed. There was a muffled click, and the gate eased toward them slightly. "It opens."

"Just hold it there, so we don't get locked in." The bank officer had risen but hadn't budged further. She put the Glock up against his temple and used it to move him along. "All right. Into the back. Be nice about this, love. I'm getting tired of killing people."

"Your colleagues will be very angry with you, miss. You are quite right that we won't be meeting again."

He was moving, though, not quite as fast as she wished. Once inside the inner vault chamber, he had to jump to avoid her hurried closing of the heavy steel door.

She took a deep breath, slipped the Glock under her jacket, then grabbed up the briefcase. "Put the money into one of those folders. What won't go in, put in your shirt and pockets."

"We're going to steal the money?"

"I don't want them to have it. They have enough money."

"But this is bank robbery." He was working feverishly. The folders were expandable. It looked as though he could get most of the cash into one of them.

"We're the depositors, aren't we? We've just changed our minds about making the deposit. Now hurry up."

He crammed the folder full, then pulled its elastic band

around it, careful not to stretch the band beyond the breaking point.

"There are five stacks left," he said.

"In your pockets. Come on. I don't want to leave anything for them."

Andy tried, but his pants pockets bulged like Harpo Marx's. Shaking her head, she relieved him of some of his burden, sticking them in her own jacket pockets.

"All right, laddie, let's go. We're going to stroll out of here as calmly as we came in."

"Won't they miss him?"

"We'll find out presently. Come on."

The customers were gone, but the three tellers had been joined by another bank employee—a white man in shirt and tie, with a bad haircut. Andy could feel all their eyes on him and Glory all the way across the room.

Just as Glory put her hand to the front door, it clicked shut. Andy wondered what was happening, but Glory knew at once.

She had the big pistol out again, aimed directly at the white man's chest.

"Open it or you'll be as dead as the chap in there!"

He stared, thinking.

"Now!"

The man's hand moved, very carefully. Andy heard the click again.

Glory was out the door in an instant. As Andy followed, an alarm began to ring.

"Run!" she cried.

Chapter
·20·

The gun in Glory's hand startled some of the pedestrians as they hurried by, but she managed to get it back under her jacket by the time they rounded the next corner. They pounded along for another block and then across a vacant lot and into a winding sort of alley, brushing against large bushes that crowded in from the side. There was an opening in the shrubbery. Glory darted through it, leading Andy along a grassy path even narrower than the alley.

"You planned that bank thing," he said, between breaths. "From the beginning."

"No. Thought about it. Didn't make up my mind till this morning."

"You could have told me!"

He was running just behind her, appreciating this view of her despite their dicey circumstance.

"No. Couldn't. Wouldn't have worked."

"What're those papers in the briefcase?"

"Records. Stuff Andao and Fabio need."

"Stuff they don't want us to have."

"Right."

"So now they'll really want to kill us."

"Told you. Don't think they're on the island."

He looked back, relieved to find no pursuers yet in view. They were moving across another street now, then up the opposite sidewalk. At the corner, Glory swerved right once more, trotting down a slight hill past a house set close to the road. Reaching the hedge that bordered it on the other side, she turned again. Andy realized her circuitous route had taken them around to the lane in back of her mother's gallery.

"Shit!" she cried, her feet sliding as she stopped.

The Sterling was there, just where she'd put it upon returning from the reconnaissance of the airport, but someone had parked a big Land Rover up flush behind it and another thoughtless motorist had jammed a Nissan just as close in front. Unless they waited, there was no way to get the Sterling out except by rolling it over.

She looked at the rental license plate of the Nissan. "Bloody fucking tourists!" Her fist came down hard against the car's front fender, then she banged it with the briefcase.

"Shall we go back into your mother's gallery?" he asked.

"No." Pulling car keys from her pocket, she opened the Sterling's trunk and tossed in the briefcase and folder, slammed it closed, and then paused to look up and down the lane.

"Don't want to be anywhere near here for a while," she said. "Come on!"

"Where?" he said, catching up to her.

"We'll head down to Church Street and the harbor. Maybe there's a cab."

"To where?"

"I don't know. Maybe to Hell."

There was a taxi, but it had tourists in it. Glory stood in front of it, glaring at the driver. For a moment, Andy thought she might pull out her automatic again and highjack the damned thing. But she finally stepped aside and the cab drove off.

"We have to get off the street," he said.

"I know." She looked quickly around the street and harbor. There was a seagoing barge, laden with oil drums, moored on the far side of the inlet. Tied up at the nearer quay was what looked like a large excursion boat. A sign at the side said *atlantis.*

"Come on," she said.

"Where?"

"Underwater. The deep."

"You want to jump in the water?"

"Just follow me."

She led him toward a large one-story building just above the boat landing. It bore a much bigger sign with the same name on it: *Atlantis.* Through a set of glass double doors, Andy could see a crowd of people. The place resembled a small passenger terminal.

"The *Atlantis* is a submarine," Glory said. "A real one, but for tourists. Takes them down a hundred feet and out to the reef, which is quite a bit under the surface at this end of the island."

"I don't see any submarine."

"They keep it offshore, down near the big oil storage tanks. That boat'll takes us out there."

He caught at her arm. "You want to take us on a tourist ride?"

She pulled him along. "Have to get scarce, Andy. Fast. I'm just worried they may be all booked."

And they were. The *Atlantis* was one of the most popular attractions on the island, and reservations had been made for every seat for the rest of the day. Glory stared at the young woman behind the ticket counter about as amiably as she had at the taxi driver.

"You're absolutely sure?"

"Yes, miss."

"No possibility of cancellations?"

"No cancellations. Everybody's here. Next dive cruise leaves in ten minutes. Sorry. Maybe tomorrow."

Tomorrow would be entirely too late. Through the glass doors, Andy saw the two men from the bank moving along the other side of the street. Neither of them seemed to have a specific idea as to where Andy and Glory were, but they were certainly getting warm.

"Glory," he said quietly, nudging her.

She turned in the direction to which he nodded. Her expression became grim.

"Thank you," she said to the ticket clerk, backing away and

then pulling Andy to the side, behind a large group of waiting passengers.

"I don't think they've seen us," Andy said.

"Not yet, but they will after this lot moves off—if we're still hanging about here."

She glanced over the group around them, as a cowboy might, looking to cut a heifer out of a herd, fixing finally on a young couple wearing shorts, T-shirts, and cheap sandals.

"They don't look like they have a lot of money, do they?" Glory said.

"I don't recall ever bumping into them at Le Cirque."

"Expensive place, Grand Cayman. People are always running through their money before they know it. Let's go talk to them."

She was a good actress. In a short time, she had the couple convinced she and Andy were man and wife on the last morning of their vacation—scheduled to leave for the States that afternoon but desperate to get in a ride on the *Atlantis* before they did so. Desperate enough to pay the couple two hundred dollars each for their tickets.

The woman appeared dubious, even a little apprehensive, but her male companion, a demonstrably overfed fellow, greedily overruled her. Four hundred dollars would not only buy the two a submarine trip the next day but a couple of magnificent dinners at Chef Tell's.

The man handed over his tickets, then took his still-uncertain lady by the hand and led her outside, perhaps heading for Chef Tell's that very minute.

The remaining tourists kept milling about, every so often exposing Andy and Glory to view from the street. Their pursuers were now working the near sidewalk.

At that moment, the submarine people announced it was time to depart, urging everyone out onto the dock. As the crowd began to move, Glory dashed to the souvenir counter. The stock included a number of *Atlantis* T-shirts and sweatshirts. She seized upon two of the latter and a couple of *Atlantis* baseball caps, dropping a hundred dollar bill and waving off the change.

Both sweatshirts were sized extra large. Andy's fit reasonably well but Glory's was ridiculous. With a baseball cap scrunched down over her tawny hair, she looked like one of the waifs of old-time silent comedies.

They were the last ones out the door. Waiting with the group on the quay to board the excursion boat, they didn't want to look back toward the town, but when at last aboard, Andy risked a quick glance.

Their pursuers were now getting extremely warm. They were coming down the steps to the quay.

One of the *Atlantis* crew, natty in nautical whites, began man-handling the gangplank off the boat while another freed the aft line from its mooring post. The two men from the bank were now running.

A good six feet separated the boat from the dock by the time the bank creeps got to the rail. The black man, his face still showing anger, appeared willing to leap the distance, but his colleague restrained him. Both then stood there, watching fixedly as the boat finished backing off the dock and, in forward speed, began moving out to the open water.

The white man grinned meanly, staring at Glory, making clear what sort of greeting would await them when they returned from their undersea journey. The trip took an hour or more—ample time for others to be added to the welcoming party.

The *Atlantis* carried forty-six passengers and a crew of three, including the pilot. Once the submarine had disgorged those from the dive just ended, and those people had transferred onto the excursion boat, Glory and Andy's bunch were allowed aboard, descending into the sub's passenger compartment through hatches both fore and aft. Glory hung back, maneuvering them to the end of the group using the forward entrance.

The seats inside the submarine ran back to back in two rows along the center, facing out toward big round portholes that lined each side of the hull. As Glory had calculated, she and Andy ended up at the very front, just behind the man at the controls and the mate who was their chief host and spielmeister for the voyage.

Glory appeared to know him, and they chatted briefly until the pilot got the submarine underway and the fellow had to start his running commentary. He did so in chipper, humorous fashion, putting the passengers at ease. Andy supposed some of them might not be so comfortable having a hundred feet of water over their heads.

Most of the tourists looked positively eager, however, and sat hunched forward to see as much as possible out the big viewports. Andy and Glory just sat, looking like a couple of weary commuters. An irony occurred to Andy. Aside from the crew, he and Glory were the only ones aboard without cameras in their hands. His was still in his bag, which he hoped was still in the trunk of Glory's mother's car with all their other interesting treasures.

The sub was now fully submerged and descending as it prowled forward. Andy leaned closer to his own porthole. The ocean floor in these relatively shallow waters was white and sandy, with only the occasional rock. A few fish swam by his window, most of them singly. He could see clearly enough, but the sunlight reached them filtered and hazy through the water, giving things seen at a distance a pale turquoise hue.

"We're going out to the reef near Jackson Point," Glory said, quietly. "It's a good hundred feet down, but there'll be enough light to see quite well."

"All I want to see is the bar at the Razzy Dazzy. If I get to, I'll drink Southern Comfort the rest of my days."

"Shhhhh!"

The woman next to Andy was trying to hear the crewman talk about barrel sponges. She was middle-aged, very large, and sweaty. The humidity in this underwater bubble was oppressive with all the clothes they were wearing. Andy took off the now useless sweatshirt Glory had given him. She removed her own but left the boating jacket on to cover her pistol.

They were already nearing the reef. Andy could see it on the ocean floor's horizon, rising like one of the jagged ridges of the Dakotas' Black Hills.

"On the other side of the reef is the Cayman Wall," said Glory.

"Anything like the one in China?"

"It's an underwater cliff, you cretin. It slopes gently at first, then plunges some twelve hundred feet. They don't have a submersible around here that can reach the bottom. I think their best one only goes to eight hundred or a thousand."

"Shhhhhhh!!!!"

The sweaty woman nudged Andy with her elbow. They were quite close to the reef now, and the crewman was talking about a large creature out there he called the jewfish. People were pressing their faces flush against the double glass. Andy stayed where he was and saw a sudden dark blur sweep by his window.

"That's only for starters," Glory continued. "A bit beyond the Cayman Wall is the Cayman Trench. It's twenty-five thousand feet down—as far down almost as Mount Everest is up. You remember the film *The Abyss?* That's it. They shot that movie here."

"Must be black as night at the bottom."

"Blacker. Good place for a grave. No one would ever bother it—for the rest of time."

The crewman on the public address system began encouraging the passengers to call out their sightings. One excitedly proclaimed an octopus. Someone else followed with a sea fan. Another, a little girl, saw a couple of starfish. Although the underwater colors were far more beautiful, the reef reminded Andy a little of the hills near Los Angeles—the barrel and bottle sponges looking like some of the houses at Malibu. He was surprised there weren't more sea creatures along here.

So was the crewman. He said the pilot was going to try farther up the reef.

Glory was staring down at her hands, looking sad. He put his arm around her, feeling her muscles stiffen but then relax. She let herself come against him, resting her head against his. He felt like saying, "Poor bears."

Inadvertently, he did.

"What?" she said.

"Nothing. Thinking out loud."

"Bears." She laughed, but sadly.

The submarine skipper wasn't happy with the pickings in the new location. His mate announced they were going over to the other side of the reef, calling it a special treat, as they'd get a look at the Cayman Wall.

"There's a sort of saddle they go through," Glory said, "like a mountain pass."

The sub made a sharp, clanking turn, then halted, as its whirring engine went into reverse. The pilot shifted into forward again, and they proceeded through the cut in the reef. Before turning again, the pilot moved the sub out into the deeper water beyond to gain more clearance. Slipping his arm from Glory's shoulders, Andy leaned forward to peer down through the porthole. The Cayman Wall dropped so steeply he had the feeling he was atop some mountain, that if they dropped something off the submarine it would fall forever.

The slope from the top of the reef down to the edge of the cliff was gentle, however. Scuba divers could walk along the ledge it provided, like hikers following the rim of the Grand Canyon.

Andy sat back. Glory did not resume leaning against him, so he took her hand.

"We'll be heading back soon," she said.

"Don't worry. We'll think of something."

"I am thinking of something. I'm thinking we may not get out of this."

"I have every confidence in you."

"It's bloody misplaced."

The crewman holding the public-address system microphone was facing forward now, looking over the pilot's shoulder and out the round front window. "Looks like we have some divers over there on the ledge," he said.

Everyone on their side of the sub had their faces up against the portholes.

"That's funny," said the crewman.

The pilot was steering obliquely toward the reef, coming ever nearer the ledge. The red digital depth indicator sign was showing 100 FEET.

"Oh my God," said the crewman, "they're not wearing any oxygen tanks!"

Now Andy moved close to the porthole, still holding Glory's hand. There was room for both of them at the glass, but she hung back.

The first of the figures came into view. Glory's hand suddenly tightened on his.

It was the man she had shot, his clothing rippling in the water, his feet bound and roped to a concrete block, his arms floating free but angled down. His head was canted forward. Little fish were nibbling at his face.

The big woman next to Andy screamed. So did others. Most

just stared in rapt, horrified silence. The crewman also was too stunned to speak.

The submarine moved on to the next body, similarly bound and weighted. Andy recognized it as Ernst Konig's. He was being nibbled at also. Bones were showing through the flesh of his face.

Next came Vilma, still naked, long hair flowing, head tilted back as though she was looking up at the surface. Then, quite close to her, was Annie Albrecht, wearing a bikini bathing suit, looking ethereally beautiful, except that her mouth was open, and some small sea creature was emerging from it.

The last was Beth Hampshire, her naked form suspended at the very edge of the ledge. One leg had come loose from her bonds, and she seemed almost in a ballet stance. Her hair streamed sideways, much in the manner of a sculpture of the drowned Ophelia from *Hamlet* Andy had once seen in a New York museum. Her head was tilted sideways, toward them. She seemed to be looking at the submarine, looking at him, her eyes wide, staring.

And unforgiving.

Chapter
·21·

"Yes. That's Elizabeth Hampshire."

Andy was kneeling beside her body, which had been laid out on the quay with the others the divers had brought up and was partially covered with a blanket. He paused to wipe his eyes with the back of his hand.

In the sea, Beth had seemed somehow alive, as though her spirit had lingered and was inhabiting some part of her, if only her eyes. Here on the concrete dock, laid out like a fisherman's catch, she was completely dead, her skin the bloodless color of the drowned Caucasian. Her eyes were still beautiful, still jewellike, but they no longer saw him.

You meet a woman. It takes. You never know how it will play out—in the case of Beth, not for very long at all. But Andy wouldn't for the saddest or angriest moment have figured his last time with her would be anything like this.

Inspector Whittles cleared his throat.

"Yes," said Andy again, rising. "That's her."

"You knew her well, I gather."

"Yes, but it was a long time ago."

One of the many policemen on the scene moved to cover Beth's face. Hers was the first body in the row they'd laid out. Whittles, putting his hand to Andy's arm, moved him on to the next.

The police had brought the blankets. Andy supposed that a department dealing with such a low murder rate didn't stock many body bags.

"And this is . . .?"

"Anne Albrecht."

"You're certain?"

"Yes. God, yes." They moved.

"And this is Vilma—last name unknown?"

"Yes." On to the next.

"Ernst Konig?"

Konig had died very unhappily. "Yes."

"And this man?"

"Haven't the faintest idea."

"None? He's in no way connected with the other people?"

"Not that I know of—unless you want to pursue the possibility that he might have been in the employ of Ramona Fitch or her pals the Machado brothers. I believe I may have mentioned to you my incredibly strong fucking belief that she's up to her last face-lift in this bloody mess."

"There's nothing here to suggest the possibility that this man was employed by Mrs. Fitch, other than your strong, er, belief. And I've received strict instructions that we are not to bother Mrs. Fitch again without first obtaining a search warrant. You certainly haven't provided me with new grounds for that, have you? Now, would you have any idea as to the next of kin of any of these unfortunate people?"

"Sorry, I don't really. Astrid might have something about them. Or her office in New York would. Miss Hampshire's from some town in Northern Virginia, the Washington suburbs. I can't remember which."

"We in the Caymans have never experienced a crime of this magnitude," Whittles said. "It hearkens back to pirate days."

Andy feared he was about to launch into a travelogue spiel about the island's buccaneer relics, but instead the inspector looked over the shrouded bodies one more time, then nodded to a sergeant, who with two other uniformed men began moving the remains to a waiting ambulance. They apparently were going to pack all the corpses into the one vehicle.

It seemed that every policeman on the island was down at the harbor. The submarine crew was standing uneasily but patiently by the entrance to their little building, along with the two divers who had so quickly retrieved the bodies. Most of the passengers had gone, after giving brief statements to the police. But a few lingered with the crowd of tourists and passersby that had gathered behind the police tape up by the street. Some of the gawkers were jumping up and down or standing on tiptoe to better see the bodies.

Andy needed to be someplace else—in a dark bar with a lot to drink. Some music playing. "Lush Life," maybe—one of Beth's favorites. Long Tom had a good half dozen different recordings of that song among the back-bar tapes at the Razzy Dazzy.

Glory had departed the instant she could get clear of the police, all but pretending not to know Andy, taking off without a word of farewell and leaving him to deal with the grisly business of the identifications by himself. Glory doubtless had her reasons, and she certainly had her own problems. She was responsible for one of the corpses, the unnamed thug she'd shot on the Machado yacht. Andy was feeling very much alone.

He could only hope the big congregation of cops had sent the men from the bank scurrying into hiding. Another, unhappier guess was that those creeps were tracking Glory—or possibly had even found her. He wished the Cayman cops would be a bit swifter with this. They had the slows worse than anyone in New Orleans.

"Whoever did this made rather a stupid mistake, don't you think?" said Whittles, who now was looking off toward the sea. "A few meters more and the bodies would have gone into very deep water indeed. We'd never have recovered them."

"I guess that's what they had in mind."

"Odd they were so careless."

"They were in a hurry," Andy contributed.

"There will be autopsies, of course, as soon as we locate a pathologist. Perhaps we shall know much more when the procedures are complete. But already I find all this quite curious."

Andy moved away a few steps, glancing toward the street. He wished he knew where Glory had gone.

"Do you know what I find most curious?" Whittles asked.

He reminded Andy of Paul Maljeux. "I'm not a detective, Inspector."

"The causes of death, Mr. Derain. Such a wide variety of fatal circumstances. This one man, the chap you can't identify. He has a gunshot wound—entry through the lower abdomen, exit through the middle of the back. He appears to have been shot from below. And the woman you call Vilma? She was shot twice in the back with a much smaller caliber weapon. And she was completely naked. This man Konig, found dressed, dead of knife wounds in the back, chest, and throat. Miss Albrecht and Miss Hampshire, from all appearances, were simply drowned. The others, clearly, were dead when they went into the water. But these two women, I think they were thrown in alive. Miss Albrecht in a bathing suit; Miss Hampshire nude. Why?"

Andy felt very ill. He clung to a single, perhaps callous thought and spoke it again, now aloud. "Astrid wasn't with them."

"Unfortunately, Mr. Derain, we can't be sure of that. The victims were dropped into the sea in something of a line, one after the other as the boat or vessel carrying them crossed beyond the reef. The last one, Miss . . ."

"Hampshire."

"Yes. Her body was recovered from the very edge of the underwater precipice. The possibility exists that one or more bodies were dropped after that and went down to unrecoverable depths as intended."

"Thanks for sharing that with me, Inspector."

"There was another odd occurrence last night. A large high-speed motor yacht, what is called a cigarette boat, piled up on a shoal at the outer edge of North Sound. Terrible smash. The boat was broken in two, but we found no one. No survivors, no injured, no dead. In point of fact, the boat was stripped of its possessions by the time our patrol craft got to it. I don't suppose you know anything about that?"

"No."

"There were witnesses of a sort," Whittles said. "Some people aboard a charter boat anchored at some distance down the reef. They said a big yacht came to the rescue of the wrecked boat but sailed off not long after."

Andy shrugged.

"Did you know the cement blocks they used to weight the bodies were stolen from the waterfront last night?" Whittles said. "From a storage yard just up from the customs house. A man saw them do it—saw them put the blocks in an inflatable boat and take them out to sea. We thought the fellow a bit daft, and he was quite drunk. Now it all makes sense."

"I'm not giving up on Miss Montebello, Inspector."

"We haven't closed our inquiry. Not at all." Whittles paused. "Where were you last night, Mr. Derain?"

"Here on Grand Cayman."

A brief wisp of a smile. "This is intended as amusing?"

Andy now wanted desperately to get away from there. "I was at Miss Montebello's condominium for a while. Then I drove around looking for her. I ended up on some beach. I spent the night on the beach. I was awakened this morning by that big storm."

Whittles was studying Andy's eyes. "Are you acquainted with Miss Gloria Newlands?"

"Why do you ask?"

"She was aboard the submarine. When she left here she acted as though you were complete strangers, but several of the *Atlantis* passengers told my men you came aboard as a couple and were behaving oddly. Also romantically."

"I recently made her acquaintance. She was showing me the sights."

"Including this tourist ride, when you've supposedly been searching desperately for Miss Montebello?"

"Let's just say we were taking a break."

"Do you know where Miss Newlands was last night?"

"With me."

"On the beach."

"Yes."

"The entire night."

"Yes."

The uniformed men had lifted all the bodies into the ambulance and were shutting the doors.

"Miss Newlands is related to one of the oldest families in the islands, Mr. Derain. I myself have cousins who are Newlands—descended from one of the African lines. Miss Newlands' father was something of a rogue, perhaps, but her mother is quite popular. Very charming. Lovely lady. Quite respectable."

"Right. Sorry I haven't had a chance to meet her."

"Gloria, however, is not held in such high esteem. She was rather wild and reckless as a girl—kept with bad companions. Always in trouble. I fear she has worse ones now."

"Spent too much time in America, right?"

"She hasn't matured much at all, really. Still disrespectful of authority. Still breaks the rules. I've an official complaint at the office lodged against her by the airport manager. She left her employer's aircraft parked in an unauthorized place—where it might have interfered with or endangered other aircraft. Very irresponsible of her, but typical. She's supposed to appear at a magistrate's hearing next week. If she fails to do so, we'll be required to take her into custody."

The ambulance had driven off.

"I think I'll be wandering on now, Inspector."

"If you please, Mr. Derain, I'd like you go to the police station now and make out a statement—a full, comprehensive statement. Absolutely everything you know about this."

"I gave you a statement when I filled out the missing person report."

"Now that we've found the missing persons—and found them deceased—I should like one much more thorough."

"Let's get it over with."

"I've a bit to do here still," Whittles said. "I need to talk to the *Atlantis* people additionally, and I think the governor may be coming along. I'll have one of my men take you up."

"I know where it is. I can go myself. It's what, two blocks?"

"Just up Shedden Road there, and then right on Elgin Avenue."

Andy stuck his hands in his pockets and started to walk away.

"Mr. Derain."

Andy stopped, turning. "Yes?"

"Do go there directly, please. No digressions. If we should have to go looking for you, as I fear we must now do for Miss Newlands, I will be most unhappy. Her Majesty's Government views this affair with the utmost seriousness."

"Right." He took another step.

"Mr. Derain . . ."

"What?!!"

"Something you might want to know about Miss Newlands. I told you we were proceeding with our inquiry. The corporation Miss Newlands flies for? We've discovered it's owned by Mr. Harvey Fitch."

Andy headed up the street, moving quickly and glancing warily about for the disagreeable bankers. He wanted his camera bag. Glory and that red Sterling would doubtless be long gone—along with his Minolta. He loved that heavy old camera dearly. He'd been through a couple of wars with it.

This adventure was turning into something of a war. He'd already taken pictures of it—those fascinating action shots of Ramona and Fabio. He still had them, jammed into his pocket with his wallet. Pulling them out, he discovered that a few of the prints had become hopelessly stuck together, but the others pulled apart easily, the images still largely clear and unmuddied, though the edges were a little marred. As he walked, he looked at all of them again, including those of Glory, then returned them carefully to his pocket. The police station was almost in view.

They might keep him for hours, even days, behind bars if he didn't get rid of the pistol he still had in his pocket. He began looking for a place to ditch it.

He'd forgotten the Caymans' left-hand driving rule and was startled when an oncoming car screeched and skidded to a halt beside him.

It was red.

"Get in!" Glory said. "We're getting out of here."

Andy kept walking. "I'm going to the police station. You'd better not. They're looking for you. You're crazy to still be here."

She began backing up, matching his pace. "So are you. Get in. There's no time to waste."

He looked over his shoulder. Back down on the corner was a tall black man, watching them. The police station was just ahead. He stopped.

"Why did you leave me like that?"

"Because I didn't want any trouble with that inspector, and I still don't."

"I would have thought you'd have taken off in your flying machine by now."

"I've been waiting for you, you cretin! Now come on, please!"

He didn't really want to go to the police station. Not any police station, ever again. He got into the car. She was roaring off down the narrow street before he'd even closed the door.

"You really don't want to have anything more to do with those coppers," she said. "They're not a bad lot, really, but they can't help you out of this mess. And once they let you go, if they are so inclined, you'd be here on your bloody own. I can't wait any longer."

"I'll manage. I came here to help Astrid, and I'm not leaving until I find her."

"Oh, knock off the chivalry bullshit, all right? You can't do her any good now."

"I can try. I might still be able to do her more good than I did poor Beth."

Glory turned into a shopping-center parking lot, zooming diagonally across it. Reaching the road on the other side, she turned east, toward the airport.

"Look, love. There are three possibilities—and only three. One, she's on that yacht with Fabio and company somewhere out in the ocean, course unknown. Two, Harvey took her back to New York . . ."

"His plane was still at the airport. So much for 'two.' "

"All right, scratch two. Three is that she's still on the island—with Harvey, or with Fabio and Ramona, or with all three of them. If you go near them, they'll kill you. You won't have a chance. You've seen how serious they are about this. After what you did to his face, Fabio is going to be extremely brusque with you."

"You're going to the airport, aren't you?"

"Obviously."

"I want to get out. And I want my camera bag."

"Andy!"

"I helped you at the bank. I've helped you commit all kinds of crimes. Just let me out, please."

"Not here. You'll be a sitting duck."

"Then take me to the condominium."

"What?"

"To Fitch's condo, where Astrid was staying. Square one."

"Why?"

"I don't know where else to go."

"How about with me? Right now! Off this bloody island be-fore we end up scuba diving without a tank like your friends."

"I can't leave it like that, Glory. She asked for my help and in-stead I let all this happen to her."

"But you don't know what's happened to her!"

"Exactly."

"Andy! They could have my plane locked up in a hangar now for all I know."

"Why did you wait for me? You could have been long gone by now."

"I feel responsible for you. Like you and your Astrid."

"You don't have to. I got into this all on my own. Just let me out and you go off into the wild blue yonder. May you have happy landings the rest of your days."

"Let you off here?"

"Anywhere. I don't care."

"Triple bloody shit." She hit the brakes and gave the steering wheel a sharp turn to the right, throwing the car into a skid. Just as the Sterling's rear swung backwards into the opposite lane, she spun the wheel back again and hit the gas. The car straightened. They were heading back toward George Town—fast.

"Where are you going?"

"Down the road to Hell, as it were. I'm going to risk my neck and waste my precious time and take you to that goddamned condo. Then we're quits."

Glory bumped into the condominium parking lot and stopped just be-hind the Nissan Sunny he'd rented. She had the Sterling's trunk open and his bag out of it in a handful of seconds.

"That's it, then," she said, moving for the driver's seat.

He reached to touch her shoulder but she slipped by him.

"Glory, I . . ."

"Stuff it!" She rubbed at her eye, then turned the ignition key. "Get in there before someone sees you." With a squeal of radial, the Sterling was speeding out to West Bay Road again.

Andy looked up at the rows of balconies and apartment doors ahead of him, then slung his bag over his shoulder and started toward the steps.

It took him a while to find the key to Astrid's, what with having all that money and a pistol in the same pocket. When he finally had it in hand, he discovered it was unnecessary. The door had already been unlocked. He pushed it slowly open. A stiff breeze commenced blowing in his face. The sliding doors leading to the terrace were apparently open.

This sign of occupancy encouraged him. He stepped into the entrance hall and called out Astrid's name. He thought he heard a reply, then realized it was someone out on the beach.

He called out again. Nothing.

He turned in to the kitchen. No one there.

The phone was there, reminding him pointedly of a responsibility he had neglected again.

As usual, Zinnia answered on the New Orleans end. Bleusette avoided doing that whenever possible. Occasionally, she still got calls from old clients, and they made her furious. After all, she lived in the Garden District now.

Zinnia was happy to talk to anyone.

"Zinnie, it's me, Andy. Whatever you may be thinking, I'm okay. I'm alive."

"Well I figure you must be if you callin'. People say there a heap of ghosts in New Orleans, but I never hearda none of them ever use the telephone."

"Is Bleusette there?"

"No. She at her restaurant."

"There's been a lot of trouble down here."

"Well, there's been a mess of it up here, too, boy. Them gangster mens that came around looking for you the other day? They been comin' on back. One of them, that big fat one, he had a big shoutin' match with Miz Bleusette right here on the lawn. Terrible fuss, till she finally run him off. And that police lieutenant, Paul Maljeux? Ah remember him from when you two used to sneak out back here in the garden and smoke cigarettes and drink your daddy's whiskey when you was in high school. He come by, that Maljeux, and said to tell you that your friend Mr. Griswold—ah think he called him 'Greasy Griswold'—he say this man Griswold he got beat up real bad and put in the hospital by maybe the same gangster good-fer-nothin's that tangle with Miz Bleusette. Somethin' about pictures of a red Italian automobile?"

Andy swore, but to himself. "Is Bleusette all right?"

"Ah think so. She kept at 'em till they run off, even that big fat one, but they say they be back."

"Gosh."

"You say 'Gosh'?"

"The word I want to use is not one of which you approve."

"Somebody broke into your Cousin Vincent's art gallery, too. Messed around with some of your pictures there. He real upset, Vincent."

"I'll be back as soon as I can, Zinnie. Tell Bleusette."

"She says she got somethin' real important to tell you, Andy. Maybe she's fixin' to run you off like she did that fat gangster man."

"As soon as I can."

"Ol' New Orleans gettin' all stirred up like this, an' it still be halfway around the year till Mardi Gras."

"I'll call as soon as I know when I'm coming in."

"You take care now, Andy."

"Right. You too."

He stared at the kitchen wall, furious, and utterly frustrated. Somehow Crayfish Joe had found out about the sale to *Crime Scene*. Maybe he had connections in New York who could drop in and tear up that esteemed periodical's editorial offices.

There was nothing Andy could do for the moment. He had some more immediate concerns. Where was Astrid?

Moving on into the dining area, he saw in silhouette the figure of someone sitting in a chair in the living room, facing toward the open glass doors and the sea. If it was Astrid, she was deeply asleep. But the sitter seemed much too short to be her.

Unless she was slumped down.

Andy took a deep breath and started forward. At least he'd know her fate. There'd be an end to this.

But it wasn't Astrid. Andy stepped around to the front of the chair and looked into the dead, silent face of Harvey Fitch. There was an odd twist of a smile on his small lips, but his eyes showed astonishment—were frozen in the midst of surprise.

Fitch had three eyes, actually. There was a huge red one in his forehead, just to the right of center.

Who could have killed him? Wasn't he one of the bad guys? Or was he really a good guy, who'd made a uniquely bad marriage? Andy stood looking at him, stupidly, as though waiting for him to speak. But Harvey had nothing to say.

Andy was wasting time. Setting down his camera bag, he hurried for the stairs, bounding up them to Astrid's bedroom.

The doors to its balcony were open, too. The bed was made. A bathing suit and some of Astrid's clothes were on the floor, but her purse was gone. So was her small suitcase.

He flung open the bathroom door and clicked on the light. A tube of toothpaste and some expensive shampoo were by the basin, but otherwise the shelf had been swept clean. Astrid's bag of bathroom essentials was missing.

Back in the bedroom, he went to the closet. A long dress was hanging in it, but there had been a good half dozen or more in there.

She'd been in the apartment. Now she was gone. Those were facts. With less haste, Andy checked out the back bedroom that had been used by Beth Hampshire. Its bed was made, but otherwise it was just as he'd left it.

Sadly, he poked around a little in some of Beth's things, deciding finally to take her handbag with him, along with whatever small personal effects he could find. There weren't many.

Returning to the living room, he jammed Beth's belongings into his camera bag. The phone in the kitchen began to ring.

He decided to answer it. He'd learn a lot more from whoever was calling than he would from Harvey.

Indeed. He recognized the voice at once. How many times had he heard it blaring brassily across the tables at New York's snobby Mortimer's?

"This is Mrs. Fitch. I want to talk to my husband."

Her husband? Didn't she know he was very, very dead?

"Mr. Fitch is not available just now." Andy tried disguising his voice, aiming for an approximation of the island British of Glory and Whittles but making a mess of it.

"Who is this?" Ramona asked. "Are you with the police?"

Now why would she presume the presence of the police?

"No, ma'am. I'm not with the police. Do you need the police? I'll look up their number."

"Who is this?"

Andy let his speech fall back into his natural Garden District New Orleans. "Well, I can't very well be Ernst Konig, can I? You people sliced him up pretty good, Ramona. And then filled him up with water."

"Derain? Andy Derain? What the hell are you doing there?"

"I'm staying here, remember? Guest of the Princess Monte-bello, who's the guest of your husband. You haven't seen her by any chance, have you? Someone's broken in and taken her things. Maybe I should call the police."

"Where's my husband? Where's Harvey?"

He wondered if she could imagine him smiling. "He's in the living room, enjoying the view. Do you want to talk to him, Ra-mona?"

A pause. "Yes, please." Like she was talking to a waiter.

"Okay." He turned toward the dead Mr. Fitch. "Harvey, it's that gold-digging gold-haired bimbo wife of yours. I think she's through screwing Fabio for today and wants you to come home." He waited. "Sorry, Ramona. He doesn't want to talk to you. He just sits there. Won't say a word. "

Another pause. "What's going on there? I want my husband, damn it!"

"Let's knock off the crap, Ramona. I just walked in. Your hus-band's dead."

There was a sudden, startled gasp. She needed more practice at it.

"Dead? What are you talking about?"

"Harvey's dead, Ramona. As dead as my model friends were when they were pulled out of the ocean this morning. Harvey has a bullet in his brain. It's often fatal."

"He's dead? Really dead? Harvey?"

Was the surprise feigned? Andy could not recall a time when he'd been certain she was telling the truth, so there was no way to make a comparison.

"I said, knock off the crap," Andy said. "I don't know what occasioned this call, Ramona, except maybe you were hoping there would be police here by now. Smart move, asking for your husband, but I'm not the police."

"I loathe you, Andy Derain."

"Very posh word, 'loathe'—especially for Wilkes-Barre."

"All right, fuck you. How's that?"

"More in character."

"Why don't you ask your dear sweet Astrid what happened to Harvey? She spent the night with him."

"Last I saw her, she was with the whole bad bunch of you."

"That was you on the boat last night, wasn't it? You and that bitchy flygirl."

Andy said nothing.

"You did some very, very bad things, Andy Derain. You hurt someone. You hurt him in the worst way imaginable. That's going to cost you."

"It's already cost me. Did you know Beth Hampshire, Ramona? One of the nicest fashion models in New York. Friend of mine. I was just down at the dock, identifying her body. Seems to me I didn't hurt your pal Fabio anywhere near enough. Should have aimed lower, like between his legs, so I could have crushed his brains."

"You're a horrid man, you know?"

"'Horrid'? Jeez, Ramona. I'm overwhelmed by all this class. Let's get back to the 'fuck' and 'shit,' shall we? So I know it's you."

"All right. Fuck you, you shit."

"Now that you're in the proper mood, shall we get down to business? Your husband is dead. Thoroughly deceased. I don't think this really comes as a surprise to you, but there it is. Consequently, Astrid's no threat to you anymore. Harvey's no longer her swain. All that's finito, just like him, leaving you the grieving widow and the presumptive heir. You know the word 'heir'? As in 'inherit'?"

Only silence.

"So I want you to let her go."

"I don't know what you're talking about."

"Astrid Montebello. The Princess Montebello. The lady you kidnapped and were holding on that yacht with the others. Is Astrid alive, Ramona? Or did you drop her into the deep the way you did her photographer and those models?"

"This is outrageous. If you think I'm going to conduct a conversation like this over the telephone, you're nuts."

"Where would you like to conduct it?"

A long pause here. "Wait there, at the condominium. I want to talk to you. Are you sure the police aren't there?"

"I want to know if Astrid's alive, Ramona."

"Why shouldn't she be? She was a friend of Harvey's, wasn't she? I'm always nice to Harvey's friends."

"I want to hear from her."

"She's not here. I swear it."

"Where is she?"

"Why should I help you?"

He thought upon this. "I have pictures. Of you and Fabio. Divorce court masterpieces."

"Divorce court? Like you said, we're talking probate court now, right? And if you're talking about those pictures you Express Mailed to Harvey in New York, I know all about them. They're destroyed. Burned. I had it taken care of before he could even look at them. So you can forget that shit."

"That was one set. I had another made. Shot nearly a whole roll, Ramona. There's enough to share with several people."

"Like who?"

More thought, quickly. "A federal agent I know, for one. Maybe the editors of *Town & Country*, *Vanity Fair*, *W* magazine. Fabio isn't even as socially acceptable as Claus von Bülow, Ramona. He's a known drug scummie. You won't be able to get a table in Mortimer's men's room with him on your arm. You may think you can get away with killing all those people, lady, but as far as your social life is concerned, you're dead."

A long silence.

"Ramona?"

"Wait there."

"What?"

"Wait there. I'm going to try to help you. Just stay there and I'll call you right back."

"What are you thinking, Ramona? That I've been in the sun a long time? That I'm crazy enough to just sit here and wait for more fun with Fabio?"

"Trust me. You want Astrid. I don't want you to send those pictures. We'll try for a happy ending. Just wait."

Andy didn't believe her. He had never believed Ramona about anything. He had the most powerful urge to fling himself out of the condo like someone fleeing a time bomb in its last few seconds of predetonation. But miracles did happen. Maybe, just this once, Ramona was telling the truth.

He'd give himself just a minute or two to think about that—think hard. If she wasn't lying, it might be his only chance left.

"Okay, Ramona. If I don't hear from you or Astrid in five minutes, you can kiss Park Avenue goodbye."

She hung up.

Andy nervously poured himself a quick gin and rejoined Harvey by the open rear door. The view outside was total travel poster—nearly cloudless sky, turquoise waters, white sand, waving palm trees, people in bathing suits. The breeze was warm, lush. Perfect. A woman and a little girl were drying off from a swim not far distant.

Actually, there had been a time when Ramona had told him the truth. She'd once confessed to a friend of his that her father had been a mere mailman.

There was an odd, tiny sound slipping into his perception, something that reminded him of a movie—an English movie. Listening intently, he realized it was the alternating whoop of a British police siren, approaching at some speed. In New York, sirens had been a constant part of the background. This was the first time he'd heard one in the Caymans.

As he thought upon it, Ramona had lied about her old man as well. His friend had later learned that Ramona's father had worked in a mailroom, all right—as a trustee convict at Attica.

Listening to the siren grow louder, he glanced into Harvey's face, at the tycoon's silly, ironic, twist of a smile; the fixed, widened eyes; the garish, ghastly wound.

The siren was getting closer now, very close.

Harvey was trying to tell him something. He was telling Andy to get the hell out of there.

Andy grabbed up his camera bag, then froze. The phone was ringing.

He reached it on the third ring, calming himself before speaking.

"Yes?"

"Andy, this is Ramona. You can't speak to your Astrid now. She's not on the island. But I got a message from her, to let you know she's alive, all right?"

"What message?"

"'Poor bears.'"

Was it true? Had Astrid told her that? How could he know?

The siren had stopped. He heard car doors slamming outside.

"Gotta go, Ramona. Sorry."

He slammed down the phone. Outside the kitchen window, he saw an RCIP patrol car stopped beside his Nissan. Two uniformed men were crossing the lawn, heading toward the condominium. Here he was about to welcome them with a gun in his pocket and a dead millionaire in the parlor.

Hard to explain. As someone apparently intended. Who? Ramona?

He was going to be out that back door to the beach in about five seconds, but not without leaving behind something in the way of explanation—something to give Inspector Whittles a little push in the right investigatory direction.

Harvey was wearing an expensive blue blazer. Andy took out his remaining photos of Fabio and Ramona, selecting one that showed her in the act of fellatio but still revealed both their faces. He slipped it into the blazer's breast pocket.

Chapter
·22·

Holding tightly to the camera bag, he headed up the beach, the heat slowing him as much as the sand. He was almost to the end of the row of condominiums when Glory came running around the corner toward him, a steely, take-no-prisoners look on her face—until she saw him. She smiled, skittering to a halt. They almost collided.

"Harvey Fitch is dead," he said breathlessly, steadying himself with a hand on her shoulder.

"You're sure?"

"As you would say, Quite. I'm not the only one who knows. Someone called the police."

"I saw them pull in. That's why I came round this way—to warn you if I could. Let's go. We need to disappear fast."

She led him into some shrubbery. They plowed through it, then ducked under the long branches of a tall bush and emerged on Bermuda grass. In the parking area opposite was the old green Chevrolet she'd had the night before.

"I decided to ditch my mum's car," she said, hurrying him along. "Too obvious."

"Why did you come back for me?"

"Saw those constables coming along the road. Thought you might have a problem."

Glory reached the car first, flinging open her door. She had the engine started by the time Andy was in the passenger seat.

They drove toward Hell for a short distance, then pulled into a small supermarket parking lot and turned around. In a moment, they were in the left-hand lane heading toward George Town, this time proceeding circumspectly.

The police car was still in the condominium parking lot. Another, lights flashing, was speeding toward them.

"You ready for the airport now?" she asked.

"Yes. I need to get back to New Orleans. Some bad things are happening there."

"What about your precious Astrid?"

"Ramona called while I was in the condominium. She said Astrid is alive and somewhere off the island. Normally I wouldn't believe Ramona if she told me this was the planet Earth, but she repeated a phrase Astrid uses—something Ramona wouldn't know."

"Something from the Lord's Prayer, no doubt."

"Anyway, I believe her."

"Off the island it is, then. Let's just hope my Pilatus is still where I can get to it."

"You mean Harvey Fitch's Pilatus."

"How do you know that?"

"Inspector Whittles made what he called an inquiry. A complaint was filed against you by the airport manager about your bad parking habits."

"I imagine the complaints against me are rather a large stack just now."

Another police car flashed past. The black man in civilian clothes in the backseat was Whittles. If he noticed Glory and Andy in the old Chevy, there was no sign of it. The police car didn't slow.

"What did Ramona have to say about her husband's demise?" Glory asked.

"I think the best word to describe her is 'nonchalant.' "

·   ·   ·

The airport fence was more difficult to surmount than they'd antici-
pated, but they managed it with no more injury than a rather revealing rip in Glory's shorts and a tearing scrape across a couple
of Andy's ribs. Once on the other side, they simply walked on
steadily toward a hangar, veering toward the parked aircraft only
when they were sure no one was paying any attention to them. It
wasn't until they were at the rear door of the Pilatus that anyone
called out. Glory was in the pilot's seat and had the prop turning
over before some ramp rats started running toward them, and
prop wash was all they got for their trouble.

"No preflight, no checklist, no run-up, and about half a pint of
fucking gas," she said, moving out to the runway.

"What's that?" said Andy, clambering into the seat beside her.

She leaned forward to look past him out the right-hand window. "What fun. A jet on final." She swung the Pilatus onto the
runway anyway. "Hang on, we're going to set a new world
record for short takeoff."

Andy closed his eyes until he felt the wheels lift from the
ground and heard the thump and clank of the landing gear folding into the fuselage. Then he reopened them.

They were in a shallow climbing turn over North Sound. In a
moment, he saw the mangroves of Booby Cay beneath them. Suddenly, there was a thundering roar, almost directly overhead, and
a huge shadow flashing by.

"It's that jetliner, doing a go-around," Glory said. "We must
have spooked them."

"Another complaint against you."

"A great bloody big one." She grinned. She seemed as happy
as a little kid.

Andy was not. He knew they had to leave, but he felt helpless
in this thing—unable to do anything about Astrid, or about whatever was happening back home in New Orleans.

"Is there any of that tequila left?"

Glory groped through a storage bin next to her seat with her
left hand, finally producing the bottle. No one appeared to have
been nipping at it in their absence.

He took a very big drink, then mustered the courage to look at
the fuel gauge. The needle was resting just above the "E."

"We can't make New Orleans or even Key West on this," he
said.

"Right you are. We couldn't make bloody Cuba. We'll put in at Cayman Brac or Little Cayman. They have FOBs in both places."

"How far?"

"Ninety miles tops—if we make it."

Another big swig. Andy stared at the magazine print of Abbott Thayer's *Angel* that Glory had taped to the instrument panel, wondering if the daughter who had posed for it could possibly still be alive as an old woman. He preferred, he supposed, that she was up above them now, in all that blue, looking down upon them with that same beatific smile.

Chapter

·23·

He managed to stay awake and even sober all the way to Cayman Brac, his alert state encouraged by the fuel gauge needle, which was resting motionless at bottom by the time the island came into view. But the engine miraculously continued to churn along smoothly, so Glory elected to go another five miles to the smallest of the Caribbean trio, Little Cayman.

It was very little indeed, barely ten miles long, more sandbar than inhabited place.

"Only a couple dozen or so people live on it," Glory said. "One of them serves as customs agent. I don't think he'll bother us."

With the engine throttled back to near idle, Glory started the landing approach at a high altitude, keeping the nose down and the glide angle steep so she could maintain sufficient airspeed if the motor sucked dry.

The fuel held through the landing and most of their rollout. Then, as though protesting that it had put up with enough, the engine abruptly died. Glory kicked right rudder and steered the plane to a rough stop on the grass.

"Bit of a walk and some jerry-can lugging," she said. "I'll have you do that while I make a few telephone calls."

They were on the ground only about twenty minutes, but it was enough to dampen Glory's mood. She barely spoke to him until they were airborne again and had leveled out at ten thousand feet.

She clicked on her headset mike.

"I talked to Fabio."

"How did you manage that?"

"It required two other phone calls to his associates, and then he insisted on calling me at that pay phone number, so he knows where we are."

"Then let's go someplace else."

"We are. Don't you want to know about Astrid?"

"Of course I do. I'm just afraid of what you might have to tell me. Your eyes are full of bad news."

"Call it doubt. He says she's alive, that she's all right, that she's with him and his brother, wherever they are, which is on that yacht of theirs somewhere in the Caribbean or the Gulf of Mexico. He says he wants to trade."

"Astrid's life for that million dollars or whatever?"

"Andy, that million or whatever is pocket change to that lot. What they want is the bank papers we stuck in the briefcase."

"Those files we took?"

"Right. Hot stuff. The U.S. confiscation laws for drug traffickers are quite serious—and all inclusive. The *federales* can grab your every asset if they can prove smuggling or peddling or even possession. The Machados break every narcotics law on the books every day."

"But they're not U.S. citizens. All their assets are in other countries."

"No they're not. They're on Wall Street, Park Avenue, all over Manhattan. Also Los Angeles, Texas, and Miami. Plus, I think, a hotel in Hawaii."

"The Machados? On Wall Street?"

"Not them. Their silent partner. Really silent now. Harvey Fitch."

"Harvey may have been a swindler and a swine, but no one ever accused him of being into drugs—outside of a little recreational cocaine in the fabled Hamptons."

"What those bank records show, as well as I can reckon it, is that drug money has been his principal source of capital for years. The Machados haven't been letting the ungodly sums they take just sit there in that little Caymans bank, or any of their banks. It's a transfer point—one of several—from their accounts to Harvey's accounts. That's what these records show, what they prove. Fitch's assets are really the Machados' assets. They've been shoveling hundreds of millions into Harvey's real estate empire and all that. If the feds were to get hold of these records, it would all go down the drain, which is to say, into the U.S. Treasury."

"Are you a cop?"

She gave him a funny, exasperated sort of smile. "No, I'm not a cop."

"I mean a federal cop—some sort of agent, like that Kelleher I ran into."

"I am not a federal agent. I got into all this just the way I said I did. I needed a job as a pilot, and this is what I wound up with."

"All right, let's go back."

"Back?"

"For Astrid."

"Andy . . ."

"We'll give them back their goddamn briefcase and take her home."

"No, love, can't possibly."

"Why the hell not?"

She kept on flying, looking extremely troubled now.

"You're making me kind of unhappy here, Glory. What you might call mad. What is it you want, the money?"

She was fighting her own anger. It showed in the grip of her hands on the control wheel, a paleness where there should be deep tan.

"The reason I'm doubtful," she said, "what has me worried, is that I don't believe him. I daresay the man lies all the time, but there's a pattern to it. What I'd expect in this situation is a lot of threats—bloodcurdling stuff about chopping her into shark food, or decorating her feet with concrete blocks the way they did the others. Instead, he carried on about how well and happy she is, except he wouldn't let me talk to her."

"Do you think she's already dead? Whittles said there could

be more bodies down there, bodies that went all the way to the bottom of the Cayman Wall."

"I don't know. You said Ramona knew some secret phrase of hers."

"That doesn't mean Astrid's still okay. Let's go back and find out. Give him the briefcase and the money and see what happens."

"He means to kill you, Andy—much the same way I gather he did that girl in New Orleans. You deprived him of a couple of teeth. He liked his teeth."

Andy took another drink. "I didn't like his teeth. I should have shot the son of a bitch."

"That's something I don't think you have in you. Anyway, I tried to dampen his blood lust a little. I told him Astrid didn't matter that much to you. That he'd already murdered your girl-friend—that poor Beth Hampshire. Bit of truth in that, right?"

"Yes."

"Just how many girlfriends have you?"

"I'm not one of those guys, Glory. I'm not like Fabio."

"So, it's only Astrid then?"

"She's a friend—kind of special."

"Special. 'Goddess,' you told me?"

"Something like that."

"Astrid's no different from any of us, Andy. Her hair gets dirty and she has her time of the month. If you want to go through all this crap for her, do it because she's a decent human being in a lot of trouble she doesn't deserve, not because you think she's a goddess."

"Actually, you're something of a goddess yourself."

"You spread that compliment around a bit thinly, sir. Or should I say, thickly."

"I mean, like her." He tapped the picture of Abbott Thayer's *Angel.*

"How fucking sweet."

"What's wrong?"

"Our interlude in the mangroves wasn't trivial for me, Andy. Never is. That's what my ex-husband couldn't get through his thick airline captain's skull, poor devil. That's why I worked so hard to keep out of Fabio's bed. I thought you might have figured that out."

He took her hand, then kissed it. "Glory . . ."

"I'll see you through this, Mr. Derain. We'll get back to the States and see what we can arrange with Fabio. But after that, we're quits."

"Why does it have to be quits?"

"It just does, that's all. Do you want to go to New Orleans? That's where I'm heading."

"I have no interest whatsoever in any other place. How long will it take?"

"A few hours, depending on head winds."

"A few hours," he repeated. He put his head back, staring at the seemingly limitless blue ahead of them. "You can put it on autopilot and get some sleep."

"I don't want to sleep. Give me a drink, Andy."

Andy wished she'd opted for sleep but handed her the bottle nevertheless. "Aren't you breaking your rule?"

"With a vengeance."

"Why?"

"Because life is unfair." She drank, took a deep breath, daintily wiped her mouth, then drank again. Returning the bottle to him, she rummaged in her storage bin, found a tape cassette, and pushed it into her console player. Then she carefully set her speed and trim, and clicked on the autopilot switch.

"You don't want to sleep?"

"No."

The aircraft began to fill with music—a very twentieth-century classical piece, but still dated, a sadly sweet violin passage reminiscent of the 1920s.

"What's that music?" he asked.

"I don't know. Something by Ravel. Sonata or étude or something. I'd forgotten I had it." She was staring at him.

To his amazement, she then pushed herself out of the pilot's seat, backing into the aisle. He looked up into her eyes, and found tears.

"What is it?"

"Make love to me."

"Here. Up here? Now?"

She was unbuttoning her blouse. She seemed quite frantic. "Yes."

"The plane will be all right?"

She nodded. Her blouse came off. Then her shorts. She sat down in the aisle, then lay back.

"I don't understand."

"I've gone mad. I'm scared silly. I've had almost no sleep and I just had a drink. I don't know what's going to happen in New Orleans, or who will be waiting for us. What do you care why?"

He didn't. Managing somehow not to touch the control column, Andy extricated himself from his seat. His own clothes came off clumsily. Naked, he looked unhappily at the empty pilot's seat then back to the lovely, insane woman before him. He knelt over her.

"Glory . . ."

"All right, I love you. Very bad idea. Damn stupid of me." She reached for him, and the languorous music enveloped them both. He tried to tell her he loved her, but the words couldn't make it past the music.

Chapter

·24·

They'd reached New Orleans after midnight and now it was past noon.
There was jazz music coming through the curtained hotel room
window—a little mainstream and contemporary, David Sanborn
or Kenny G, but a lovely saxophone nonetheless, and it did very
nicely. Andy was home. Life was good again—or could be, once
matters were settled. Astrid and the Machados. Bleusette.

Glory.

He put his hand on the bare back of the sleeping woman next
to him. She gave a gentle murmur but did not stir. Glory had
fallen asleep so exhausted she'd hardly changed position during
the night. He pulled the sheet up over her shoulders, then slipped
out of bed. They'd taken one of the hotel's best suites; moving
quietly, he went into its sitting room.

There was still some tequila in the bottle they'd brought from
the plane. He poured himself a drink and took a sip, the warmth
spreading through him. Then he took another. It was a little late
for beignets and café au lait.

The day was warm, but the New Orleans summer heat had finally gone. The Caymans seemed a million miles away. The flight

had certainly seemed to take that long. Andy had somehow stayed awake, devoting his energies to keeping Glory in
that state. They hadn't spoken much—just played a lot of loud
music, Tom Waits grumbling through the night sky at high
decibel.

The saxophone jazz was coming through the sitting room's
windows as well. Andy sat down in a plush armchair by the
room's French doors and sipped again.

He'd decided what he was going to do—at least what he
wanted to do—but he had hours yet. If all went as he hoped, if
Astrid was indeed alive, if he and Glory could persuade Fabio
and Ramona to accept the arrangements, they'd make the exchange the next day—early in the morning, just at sunup—in
Jackson Square opposite St. Louis Cathedral.

Andy could see it happening. The scene was almost a photograph in his mind: he and Glory sitting by the wrought-iron fence
that bordered the square's central garden, the briefcase between
them; Astrid, surrounded by several murderous-looking men,
walking along the galleries of the shops on St. Peter Street—
everyone looking apprehensive. A great photograph—or, at least,
a decent movie scene.

The hotel he had taken them to in the middle of the night was
one of the most discreet in the French Quarter, and their suite was
in the hotel's even more discreet annex across the street from the
main building. The annex had been a private residence once,
a large house wrapped around a central court complete with
fountain, and the suite was on its ground floor, on the opposite
side of the court from the entrance gate that led to the street. The
French doors looked directly on the fountain. Andy opened one
of them.

He'd made a number of calls, but not to Bleusette yet. He
didn't want to do anything to complicate his plans for dealing
with Fabio and getting Astrid back, and Bleusette could complicate a walk across the street if she was of a mind to—as she well
might be, given his truancy.

Zinnie had said Bleusette had something important to tell
him. He certainly didn't want whatever that might be riding on
his mind while all this dicey stuff with Fabio went down.

"Went down." Did drug folk still talk that way? Had they

ever? Most of the druggies Andy had heretofore had contact with had been prostitutes and street people, and down here they spoke languages all their own.

The saxophone stopped. Nothing was making a sound outside but the burbling water.

Glory had stuffed all the money she had taken from the Machados' bank into her canvas gym bag, except for a few thousand set aside for expenses. It mattered not to Andy; he had no interest in the Machados' money.

The bank papers had been left undisturbed in the briefcase, which lay flat on the table next to him. A sense of evil, magical power emanated from it, as from a voodoo effigy. The contents could save a human life or destroy a huge financial empire—or, if one looked at it from the Machados' point of view, accomplish the reverse.

He found his khaki shorts and put them on, then set the small automatic pistol he still carried on the table next to the briefcase. He could hear an automobile moving along the street. When it was gone, there was only the fountain again.

Their two rooms looked more house than hotel. The once fine, flowery wallpaper was fading and stained in spots. The furniture was genuine, if slightly mismatched, antiques. The space was commodious, intended for more than travelers' rest. The framed prints on the walls were of decades-old French Quarter and Mississippi River scenes.

Andy had called the Razzy Dazzy as soon as they'd arrived. Long Tom was off with one of his ladies, but Cue Ball had found the saloonkeeper and passed on the word of Andy's return and need for help. Tom had called back within the hour, listened to what Andy had to say, and promised to help him without equivocation or qualification adding that he'd come by Andy's hotel hideaway by lunchtime. It was getting on to later than that, but his father's old friend had never failed him.

Andy finished his glass of tequila and, encouraged by it, took up his camera. Guessing at the exposure required for the shadowy available light, he began moving about the room, seeking and shooting pictures, looking for hints of the multitude of stories that must have unfolded in these chambers—some doubtless even stranger than his and Glory's.

Halfway into a roll, he found himself at the doorway to the bedroom. Leaning in, he saw a nice picture in the way the gauzy window light fell across the sheet upon her body. All he could see of Glory was the tousled hair of her head, a hand on the pillow, and a full length of tanned leg. He began shooting, moving closer with each frame. An irresistible impulse prompted him to try to gently pull the sheet away without awakening her, so that he might have for always a photograph of her nude, but just as he touched the cloth he heard a rapping at the suite's door.

Returning to the sitting room, he grabbed up the little pistol and went to answer the summons.

There was Long Tom Calhoun, dressed in a gray double-breasted suit, white shirt, purple tie, tan-and-white shoes, and a broad-brimmed light brown fedora. Happily, he'd brought with him a bottle of Wild Turkey and some Jax beer in a paper bag. Less happily, he'd also brought along Lieutenant Paul Maljeux.

Andy stuck the gun into his belt.

"If you're going to be packing a piece, Andy," Maljeux said, "you probably be wanting to wear a few more clothes. Kind of conspicuous there."

His policeman friend grinned and took a seat next to the table with the briefcase on it, while Calhoun poured whiskey into clean glasses. Maljeux shook his head at the offer, and instead reached for one of the bottles of Jax.

"How y'all are?" said Long Tom, after he had seated himself and sipped.

"Alive, and that's saying something. The Caymans must be a wonderful place to visit as an ordinary tourist, but nothing about my stay was ordinary."

"It's an amazement how a guy like you could end up taking on the Brazilian Brothers. That's big-time bad."

"It wasn't my idea," said Andy. "When it comes to brothers, I much prefer the Flying Karamazovs."

He went to the bedroom door and quietly shut it. Calhoun gave him a wink and then a shake of his head.

"I've got some official communications back in the office concerning you," said Maljeux. "There's a detective fellow in the

Caymans named Whittles. Says you're wanted for questioning in a multiple homicide and that he also has an arrest warrant on you."

"For homicide?" Hadn't the inspector found that photo of Ramona and Fabio?

"For unlawful departure and customs evasion. Also a warrant issued on a Miss Gloria Newlands." Maljeux's eyes went to the bedroom door. "Whereabouts unknown but last seen in your company. There's a stop-and-detain order out from the FBI in Miami. On both of you. You sure been busy, boy."

"What do you plan to do about those things?"

"I'm taking it real serious, Andy. I've put all that stuff in a case file I made up on you. It's in my active bin, and I'm gonna put a man on it first thing next week." Maljeux took a couple of glugs of Jax, then leaned forward. "What concerns me a lot more is this plan you're cooking up with Senator Calhoun here—for some kind of high-level swap with big-time drug smugglers right on our own historic and tourist-packed Jackson Square."

"No drugs involved. A briefcase full of business papers in exchange for one kidnapped young woman."

"The one you went down to the Caymans to help?"

"Yes, I didn't make out too well."

"So now you want to draw that whole troublesome crew up here to try again on your own home ground."

"Yes, I do."

"Well, I'm here to ask you not to do it."

"Can't not do it. Won't."

"Why not go off to some nice quiet place out in the bayous to take care of this?"

"Because some nice quiet place like that is where I'd get killed—and not just me. Here, this is public. They'll have to watch themselves. That's the idea."

"What did you say the body count was down there?" Calhoun asked.

"Six, including four people I knew from New York. One of them, she was a very close friend."

"And one of them that rich Harvey Fitch," Maljeux said. "That's what they want to question you about in the Caymans."

"It's already on the news," interjected Long Tom. "A lot bigger story than Philippe Coquin. The kind of mess to stay real far away from."

"That's what has me kinda hot and bothered, Andy," said Maljeux, who was now halfway through his beer. "I don't intend to share any of this with my colleagues, beyond dealing in some way with all that official paperwork. But I've got to think of the Quarter. *Le tout ensemble,* Andy. The common good. We take care of our own. I can't have gun-toting Caribbean druggies runnin' around 'mongst all the folks in shorts and T-shirts. Bad for business. And we might lose an innocent life or two along the way."

"I want to do it early—say around seven, when there won't be any people around. It'll be a quick, simple exchange, Paul. We'll see them coming from one end of the square, and they'll see us sitting at the other. As soon as Astrid is walking free and clear we'll get up and leave them the briefcase. Then everybody goes home."

"What's in that briefcase? Drug money? Evidence against them?"

"Nothing that should involve the New Orleans Police Department."

"All right," said Maljeux. "I'll throw in—but, mind, it's gonna be discreetly. Now, how long you figure it'll take those fiends to show up in our fair city once you get the word to them?"

"Six hours maybe, max. I consulted a, er, pilot friend. An expert on such matters."

"Just one more thing, Andy," said Maljeux. "This Fabio Machado fellow right now happens to be our *primo suspecto* in the demise of the late Philippe and one Miss Felicie Balbo. Are you expectin' me to just sit back and watch him walk in and out of here?"

"Yes. Until I get my friend Astrid well out of there. But I don't intend for that to take very long."

"Crayfish Joe Coquin ain't gonna just sit back and watch."

"He won't know about it unless you tell him, and you won't do that if you're worried about all those folks in shorts and T-shirts. Anyway, I don't think Fabio'll show up in person. He can't be that crazy."

There was another rapping at the door. Andy left his pistol in

his belt. Maljeux had his Magnum, and he was fairly certain Long
Tom had a gun, too.

It was Freddy Roybal, fresh from the Razzy Dazzy and carrying a picnic basket, which he set down on the table next to the
briefcase. Inside were some plastic plates and utensils and a couple of casserole pots, plus more Jax.

"Got here some shrimp Creole and Cajun chicken and
dumplings," Roybal said.

"I figured you'd be hungry after so many days away from
anything worthwhile the eating," said Calhoun.

There were six plastic plates. Maljeux took one and began
helping himself to some of the chicken and dumplings. Andy
hadn't eaten in twenty-four hours but couldn't find an appetite.
He sipped his whiskey. He'd finish that first.

To his surprise, the phone rang. It was Cue Ball, over at the
Razzy Dazzy, filling in for Roybal while the latter accomplished
his errand.

"Your Cousin Vincent called, Andy. Wanted to know if we'd
heard from you. Was wonderin' if you were all right. I told him
yes on both scores."

"Thanks. You didn't tell him where I was."

"Shit no."

"Please don't. Not anyone, Cue Ball. Okay?"

"I hear what you're sayin'."

As Andy hung up, he saw the bedroom door open, revealing
a glowering Glory standing there with the sheet wrapped around
her like a figure in a classical painting.

They all fell silent.

"Simply marvelous hideaway you've picked, Mr. Derain. 'No
one will ever find us,' I believe you said."

Long Tom stood up and bowed in courtly fashion. Maljeux set
down his plate to do the same.

"You, I'm guessin', are Gloria Newlands. I'm Tom Calhoun. I
believe we have some mutual acquaintances."

Glory nodded to him in recognition, then turned to look at
Maljeux, who was in a fresh, crisp uniform.

"Fear not, mademoiselle," he said. "I'm here as a friend. Not
officially."

"I'm Freddy," said Roybal, grinning in gap-toothed splendor.
"I'm an artist. Like Andy."

Again there was someone at the door. Maljeux, unsnapping the holster strap on his Magnum, went to it and slowly pulled it a few inches open.

An instant later he jumped back as the door swung wide, banging against the wall. Bleusette, wearing a black, low-cut dress and an apron, stood there a moment, glowering as darkly as a storm cloud rolling up from the gulf, then stepped inside.

C h a p t e r
·25·

Bleusette required only a few seconds to make her assessment of the
situation. Taking in the people present, their state of dress, the
luggage and dirty clothes, and the food and drink on the table in
a few sweeping, unhappy glances, she marched past Maljeux and
Andy right up to her presumed rival. Glory, though startled, did
not lose her composure. She looked down at the dark-haired
woman from her six-inch height advantage much like a weary
nanny confronted by an obstreperous child.

Bleusette stared back for a long defiant moment, then commenced to examine Glory as though she were an object for sale,
touching her hair, glancing over her breasts and body, pulling the
sheet aside slightly for a glimpse of her leg. Glory stood her
ground, not moving, not at all amused.

"So, you are the fucking Princess Astrid," Bleusette said, lifting her head again to challenge Glory's wide, impassive gray
eyes. "You don't look like no fashion model to me. You look like
you eat *très bon.* I cannot believe Andy goes all the way down
there to the goddamn Caribbean to bring back you. He scare us
all to fucking death for three days, risk his poor excuse for a life,
just for you? *Incroyable!*"

The men in the room looked at each other helplessly, as

though they were watching an accident about to happen and were powerless to do anything about it.

"Bleusette," Andy said quickly, stepping forward. "This isn't Astrid."

"What? *Je ne comprends pas ce que tu dis.*"

"She's not Astrid. The princess isn't in New Orleans. The bad guys still have her. We're trying to work out an exchange. That's why we're here."

Bleusette whirled around. "Who is this woman then?"

"I'm Gloria Newlands," Glory said, in a flat, clipped, crisp English tone. "I'm a friend." She pulled the sheet higher around her chest. "And you are . . .?"

"I are Bleusette Anne-Marie Genevieve Toulon Paquerette Lescaut. I am Andy's . . ."

"Glory's a pilot," Andy said quickly. "She flew me out of the Caymans."

"*C'est vrai?* You go down there for this Princess Astrid and cannot find her so you bring back another one instead?"

"This woman saved my life, Bleusette."

"So? You have saved my life. I save yours all the time. A lot of fucking work, trying to stay alive in New Orleans. Not been so easy, last few days." Bleusette peered past Glory at the rumpled bed. "And now I find you where? Shacked up just five blocks from my restaurant, with this pilot woman I never know anything about before."

She paused for breath. No one in the room was moving.

"I do not think you really want to marry me, Monsieur Derain. And I know *bien sûr* I do not want to marry you. That's all I have to say. *Au revoir. Je ne veux pas dire 'À bientôt.' *"

Bleusette went to the door leading to the courtyard, opening it wide, then hesitated, turning about, hands on hips. "And where is this poor Princess Astrid, Andy? Eh? You leave her down there? You forget all about her, too? *Merde!*"

She left the door to the suite open. It was the wrought iron gate she slammed. They probably heard it all the way across the Mississippi in Algiers.

Glory was more decorous. Returning with great dignity to the bedroom, she closed the door quietly but firmly.

"How in hell did Bleusette know I was here?" Andy asked his male guests.

"I guess she's got her spies at the Razzy Dazzy," said Long Tom, eyeing Freddy Roybal, who simply shrugged.

"That lady's got spies in every bar in New Orleans," said Maljeux. "She ought to be working for us."

Long Tom finished his whiskey and got wearily to his feet, reaching for his hat. He paused. "You goin' through with this thing tomorrow morning, or are you thinkin' now of maybe movin' on? Everyone in town seems to know you're back."

"Of course I want to go through with it."

"Okay," said Calhoun, still a little doubtfully. "Call me 'round midnight to let me know what's what. By then I'll be able to tell you what we've got workin' in the way of backup." Calhoun turned to Maljeux. "But that ain't goin' to include you, right, Paul?"

"I'll keep my boys out of it, but not too far out. And Andy, if these Machados don't show in, like, fifteen, twenty minutes of the appointed hour, that's gonna have to be the end of it. You just get out of there and let life get on like normal. We can't keep the French Quarter closed down just for you. *Le tout ensemble*, Andy. *Le tout ensemble*."

"Twenty minutes. Fine."

"You want someone around this place tonight?"

"That would be appreciated."

"Happy to oblige. Happy to oblige. And I'll instruct 'em not to hang around too close, so you won't be disturbed." He produced a grin, but it vanished. "I don't know your plans for afterward, but you might tell that nice lady in there that next week I really am going to have to put a man on your case. And that means carrying through on all that paperwork I got waiting—deportations, extraditions, arrest warrants, whatever. *Compris?* We are not just tour guides over there at the Vieux Carré station."

"*Entendu.*"

Maljeux shook Andy's hand before going out the door. So did the other two. It was as though they were paying their last respects.

Glory remained in the bedroom for a very long time. Andy then heard the shower running, also for a long time, but when she didn't emerge immediately after that, he finally set to eating, taking a second helping of chicken and dumplings. When she still didn't appear, he refilled his whiskey glass and sat down in the chair by the window, propping his feet up and gazing out at the fountain.

At last the bedroom door opened. Glory came near and put a hand on his bare shoulder. She hadn't yet put on any clothes.

"Those people all gone?"

"Yes. Some time ago."

"I've been making some phone calls. In a few minutes, I'm going to have Fabio on the line. What do I tell him?"

"Shouldn't I talk to him?"

"You'll only argue. He'll start screaming obscenities at you. Macho cockfight. Won't do."

"All right. Tell him this: We'll be in Jackson Square near St. Louis Cathedral at seven tomorrow morning. We'll have the briefcase. He's to bring Astrid and come down St. Peter Street. When he gets to the corner that opens onto the square, he's to stop and let Astrid keep on walking. When she's far enough away from them, we'll get up and leave the briefcase behind. Then both sides go their own way. We'll never bother him again, and he better never ever show his broken-toothed face in New Orleans again."

"I'll amend that last bit a little. Ramona Fitch is in on this thing, too, Andy. She's been acting as his go-between with me just now."

"I was kind of hoping Inspector Whittles would have her locked up or something by now."

"I'm afraid Whittles isn't much of a match for that woman. It would seem she's moved into full partnership with the Machados in poor dead Harvey's place."

"I don't know which to feel sorry for."

"Save that for our side."

She squeezed his shoulder, then her hand was gone. He turned to watch her go back in the room. A moment later, he heard her talking on the phone.

With the door open, Andy was able to follow most of the conversation. The long pauses and silences between Glory's sentences, representing Fabio's side of the exchange, unnerved him some, but he was pleased to find little worry or concern on her face when she finally hung up and rejoined him, standing by the table, her naked hip just inches away.

"Is this any good?" she said, lifting the cover of one of the casserole pots.

"*C'est le mieux, Mademoiselle. Mais ce n'est pas très chaud.*"

"If it's good, cold's aces with me." She put small portions of both dishes on a plate and then gracefully sat down, tucking her bare feet under the chair. "It's a go, Andy. Seven tomorrow morning. Jackson Square."

"Fabio didn't want any changes?"

"He tried to make some. I knew he would. Screw over our minds. In response, I just repeated everything you told me very quickly again and hung up. If he wants that briefcase, he'll be here. If he doesn't bring the lady, no briefcase. He understands."

"But do you think he'll do it?"

"I don't know, love. It's our last chance, isn't it? We'll just have to take it. Surely Ramona wants all this done with. And she can't like having that beautiful Astrid around."

"Can Fabio get here by tomorrow morning?"

"I daresay. He's in Houston."

"Houston?"

It seemed so frighteningly close. How did a homicidal creep like that just stroll back into the United States?

"Yes. And Ramona is definitely with him."

"And Astrid?"

"He said we'll see her right where you said. Seven tomorrow morning."

"You don't have to be there."

"Of course I do. I'm the one to deal with Fabio. At all events, you went into that Cayman bank with me. I'm returning the favor."

"I don't understand why you're so willing to give up the bank papers. You could accomplish a lot for yourself with those—trade them with the feds for a walk out of all this."

"If I did that . . . what if something happened to Astrid?"

He looked away.

"You'd hate me for that, Andy. Wouldn't do. Lot of bad things I'd endure before your hatred."

He pondered this, allowing Glory to consume her meal in silence. When she finished, she pushed away her plate. "I'll have a bit of that Wild Turkey now. Perhaps two bits."

He filled a glass halfway. "Not flying tonight, are we?"

"No, we're not, thank you very much."

"Will you be flying tomorrow?"

"What do you mean?"

"When it's all over."

"I shall want to be going as far away from here as I can bloody manage—as far away from Fabio as there is."

"What about us? 'Quits,' I believe you said."

She took his hand. "Here we are now, Andy. Let's not think about anything more."

"Okay."

"Tomorrow, you've got to deal with Astrid."

She leaned forward, elbow on the table, chin on hand, eyes heavy lidded as she watched the afternoon light dying in the courtyard.

"I want to take your picture," he said.

Her eyes moved, nothing else. "You're mad."

"Not mad. Just a photographer."

He got the camera out quickly. After changing lenses, he went to work, shooting from his chair, from his knees, standing by the window facing her, from a rear corner of the room with her seated body a silhouette against the window light, then back to the table for a close-up. She gave him a soft, dreamy smile. It was at that moment he realized he wanted to start work on his book again.

"I should like you now to tell me about that woman," Glory said. "The small, dark beautiful one, who looks like she's perhaps killed people."

"Bleusette."

"Bleusette. Yes. And all those other names." Glory leveled her eyes at him, her smile all gone.

"I've known her all my adult life. From when I first started hanging around in the French Quarter."

"Have you two been living together?"

"She's staying in my house. It's a great big place, over in the Garden District."

"Is she a prostitute?"

"Was."

"Andy, that girl was talking like someone breaking off an engagement."

"I suppose she was."

"And what does that mean?"

"She and I have been through a lot over the years. I owe her. A lot. You were wondering why I'd go through all this for Astrid. With Bleusette, it's like a hundred times that."

"Do anything for her."

"Right."

"Even marry her."

He'd shot his last frame. He hit the rewind motor button, then set down the camera.

"That was the idea, I guess."

"It's none of my business."

"Sure it is."

"You and women, Andy. Every time I turn around I discover another. I don't know how you can discuss marriage seriously with any of them."

"My problem is that I always seem to discuss it with the wrong ones."

She looked at him with vague, sad eyes. "I don't want to discuss anything just now. I'm going back to bed."

He reached for her.

"No," she said. "I just want to sleep."

Chapter

·26·

Glory slept, with Andy lying unhappily awake next to her, until well
after midnight. When she finally stirred, her mood was little improved. Grumpily untalkative, she went into the bathroom and
took another shower, then returned to the bedroom and announced she wanted to leave the hotel.

"I'm getting jumpy," she said. "I don't want to be in this place
anymore. I want to be where I can see around me."

"Like up in your airplane."

"No. We'll go through with this. I told you that."

They dressed, slung their bags over their shoulders, picked up
up the briefcase, then left, going out the French doors into the
courtyard and from there into the New Orleans night.

Mostly they walked after that, two solitary figures passing
along from one circle of streetlamp light to another, passing from
the Quarter across Esplanade and Elysian Fields into Faubourg
Marigny, strolling that neighborhood's quieter precincts for a
long while and then stopping for an after-hours drink with
Loomis Demarest at One-Legged Duffy's. After that, they wandered along the river, sat and talked, sat and said nothing, stood
at the embankment and watched the waters roll on to the sea
from which they had just come.

They went to all manner of places as familiar to Andy as his life, but whose memories now would never be the same. She finally let him kiss her again, on a wharf, just as the first light began to glow at the bottom of the muddy dark sky visible beneath the high span of the Mississippi River bridge. What they never brought up was that in a few hours—if they survived—she would be flying out of his life again. Given all the criminal charges against her, it would likely be for good.

But, if all went as planned, he'd have Astrid. As Katharine Hepburn liked to say in her inimitably snappy way, "Oh, goody."

Things had gotten all twisted around. There had been a time when Astrid Thorsdottir had been all he could conceivably desire. Now she was simply a life to be saved, a promise to be kept.

He'd do it—as he wished he could still do it in the maddening instance of one Elizabeth R. Hampshire.

As the lady said, woulda, coulda, shoulda.

Andy kicked a rock far out into the river. Glory didn't understand the anger behind the gesture.

"Come on, love," she said. "Let's get it done."

They arrived at Jackson Square at nearly half past six, selecting a spot along the square's central garden that faced St. Peter Street. They sat on the concrete ledge quite close together, the briefcase and two bags in front of them. Glory had her Glock automatic just under her jacket. Andy's smaller weapon was in his pocket. He looked forward to getting rid of it.

"I used to smoke," she said. "Quit four years ago. This is the first I've wanted a cigarette in a very long time. But I do, desperately. I'm mad for one."

He looked at his watch. Only four or five minutes had passed since they'd arrived. There were more people out and about the square than he had anticipated. Some of the shopkeepers opposite were cleaning off their sidewalks. An artist was setting up a folding chair and easel in a familiar spot down near Decatur Street and the river. Looking elsewhere, Andy could see some joggers, a dog walker, a half dozen derelicts, and an elderly tourist couple, the latter seeming to have no place to go but tottering around like happy children in toyland.

There was no one present who could possibly be in the employ of the Machados, Long Tom Calhoun, or the New Orleans Police Department—unless one or two of the derelicts were faking it.

"Do you want me to get you some?" he asked.

"What?"

"Cigarettes. There's a store around the corner."

"God no. Anyway, it's too close to seven. You stay here close to me."

Andy took her hand. He tried to think of Astrid, to remind himself of what he was doing here, but her image kept slipping away.

He stood up. His peripheral vision had caught movement. Turning, he saw two more joggers coming around the corner of the square, both young men, collegiate types in T-shirts.

"Do you know we've been together almost constantly for almost two days?" he said, seating himself again.

She said nothing.

"I feel a little like we're married."

"Don't." She stared down at the pavement.

He did the same, then looked again at his watch. Somehow, it had gotten to be five minutes of seven. Nervously, he put his hand to the gun in his pocket, though he knew very well it was still there, then pulled the briefcase in front of his legs.

How could Fabio be sure there was anything inside? Or that he and Glory hadn't made photocopies of everything? Andy knew the answer: Fabio had no choice. It was his only chance to get his all-important bank records back and he had to take it.

Suddenly Andy saw them, a tiny group coming down St. Peter Street—on the opposite side—a blond woman in a long floral print dress to the fore. Andy nudged Glory.

"I see them," she said.

There were three men with the blonde—all dark haired, one wearing a suit, the other two in trousers and short-sleeved shirts. Everyone in the group, including the woman, was wearing sunglasses.

"Push the briefcase out a little where they can see it better," Glory said.

Andy did so. The blond woman had a model's walk, but exaggerated, almost a prance. She was tall, but no more so than the men behind her. Fabio was relatively short. Andy began to feel unsure.

No, it had to be Astrid. Who else could it be?

"Fabio isn't with them," Glory said.

"How can you tell?"

"Nobody walks like Fabio walks."

"What does it mean—his not showing?"

"It means he's not stupid. This is your briar patch, not his."

The group stopped at the corner of St. Peter and Chartres streets, looking both ways like schoolchildren—only furtively, like schoolchildren looking for truant officers. Then, at the prodding of the man behind the blonde, the four moved on.

She held her head high. When Astrid was troubled, she always looked down. Her hair was much fuller than Andy remembered.

Reaching the other side of Chartres Street, the three men halted, moving apart a little, each of them turning toward Andy and Glory. The woman kept walking.

Andy heard someone running, off to his right—another jogger, moving with quick steps, coming nearer. Ignoring whoever it was, he kept his eyes on the approaching blonde. The hair looked like Astrid's—was exactly the same color—but there really was too much of it. Why didn't she look in his direction? What had they told her to do?

He could hear the jogger coming around the corner of the fence.

Andy looked at the blond woman's feet. The dress's long skirt dragged a little on the ground, but with each step her shoes protruded—gold shoes, with pointed toes.

Astrid wouldn't wear gold shoes unless paid to do so on a fashion runway—and she didn't do that anymore. Not in years. Nowadays, she always wore black shoes, or silver. Always.

"Glory, that's not her."

"You're sure?"

The jogger was coming very close.

"Andy, you're sure?"

Andy stood up. "Yes! That's not Astrid."

An instant later, the dark-haired form of the jogger swept into

Andy's field of vision. It was Bleusette, moving at a run. Without slowing, she snatched up the briefcase and hurried on, shouting over her shoulder to Andy: "Follow me! *Vite, vite!*"

Glory was on her feet. "What the bloody hell?"

"Come on, goddamn you!" Bleusette shouted, still running. "Joe Coquin is coming here! Hurry!"

The three men were now coming toward them from the street corner. The blond woman was glaring at them from the shop galleries opposite, her sunglasses off.

It was goddamn Ramona.

Andy and Glory grabbed their bags, slinging them over their shoulders on the fly. Ahead, Bleusette reached Decatur Street and turned left, swinging the briefcase behind her.

They followed her as fast as they could. They had little choice. Glory slipped a little rounding the corner, but Andy caught her arm and steadied her.

They were closing on Bleusette. Where were their own pursuers?

Andy had no idea where Bleusette could be headed. If she kept going down this open street, they'd lose this race to something, quite possibly a bullet. Then Andy saw his old white Cadillac, top down, parked at the curb just ahead.

They were going to die. The car would never start.

But there was oily smoke curling up from behind a rear tail fin. The thing was running. Through the dirty windshield, he saw a long-haired figure behind the wheel.

Bleusette had the curbside door open and the seat folded back by the time Andy and Glory thumped up to them. The long-haired figure in the driver's seat was a man. He turned and smiled.

"In back, quick!" Bleusette said. "I tell you, Joe Coquin is coming! *Vite!*"

They tumbled into the back. Bleusette jounced onto the front seat and yanked the big door closed just as the man behind the wheel pulled out into traffic, making a U-turn to the left with a wrenching shift of balance and a squeal of worn tires.

"This is my cousin Jean-Robert," said Bleusette, leaning over the front seat. "You remember him, Andy? From the party after Tante Juliette's funeral in Lafayette?"

The man glanced back and smiled again. Andy nodded to

him. Glory had her pistol out and was looking toward the square. Two of the men had come around the corner of the fence but had no weapons showing.

"What's all this about?" Andy said to Bleusette, with more anger in his voice than she'd probably ever heard from him before.

"I am saving your fucking life, that's what is happening!"

Jean-Robert had the Cadillac up to forty-five miles an hour, horrible noise and oily smoke billowing out behind them. People along the sidewalk turned to look.

"What made you think Joe Coquin was coming?" Andy shouted at Bleusette. "How would he know what was going on this morning?"

"Someone tell him."

"Who?"

"Me!"

Chapter

·27·

"I am sorry, Andy," Bleusette said, leaning closer to him over the back of the front seat. "Coquin is a fat, no-good gangster bastard, but he is kin and I cannot ignore him."

The wind from their speeding progress blew her dark hair about in all directions, the wildness fitting everybody's mood and making her look all the more bewitching.

"But you screwed everything up! Why did you do this?"

"That *cousin cochon* made me promise to tell him soon as I know something about what you are doing with that Fabio, who Joe says shot Felicie Balbo and his no-good son Philippe. How he knows what you do with these Fabios down there in the islands I don't know, but Crayfish Joe he is very, very mad. He come around the house, Andy. He threaten me. I throw him off the property, but he make me very scared, you know? So I help him."

"I shouldn't have left you on your own. I thought you'd be okay."

"I am okay. I told him like he asked. That's why I'm okay." She glanced to Glory, then back. "You left that Astrid back there at Jackson Square. *Pourquoi?*"

"That wasn't Astrid. Fabio was pulling a fast one. It was a woman named Ramona Fitch, wearing a wig. Very bad news."

"So this gonna go on, then?"

"I don't know."

"Maybe she's dead now, the real Astrid. I didn't mean for that to happen, Andy. I never want to get no one killed, except maybe these Fabios."

"She wasn't there, Bleusette. I don't know where Astrid is."

He could barely see Bleusette's eyes through the tangle of hair. He had no clear idea of her mood.

"If she is dead, then maybe Crayfish Joe whacks this Fabio and we can all go back to normal life, maybe."

"Fabio wasn't there, either. Those were was just some of his men."

"*Merde,*" said Bleusette, and she turned around to face forward in her seat.

Jean-Robert wheeled onto Elysian Fields at the intersection where the river bent east, following the broad avenue north toward Lake Pontchartrain. Andy for some blithe reason assumed they were going to the Lake Front Airport. Glory would be gone from him very soon now—in just a very few minutes. They'd drop her off, and it would just be him and Bleusette again, though everything seemed to have changed.

Jean-Robert suddenly spun the wheel once more, catching Andy by surprise. They were turning from Elysian Fields onto Interstate 610, the freeway that led west out of the city.

"Where are you going?" Andy said. "Her plane isn't at New Orleans International. It's at Lake Front Airport."

"We're not going to no airport," Bleusette said.

Glory touched his arm. "It's all right, Andy."

"No, you've got to get out of here. You helped me, just as you said you would. I had my chance. It didn't work. You should get the hell out now. I don't know what kind of trouble we left back there at Jackson Square or how quick it's going to come after us. But it will."

"What about Astrid?" Glory asked. "She has to be somewhere. 'Poor bears,' remember? I'm going to stick with you, all right? One more time. We'll give it one more bloody shot."

Bleusette muttered something Andy could not hear with all

the auto noise. He could see Lake Pontchartrain off to the right, a flat blue gray in the hazy morning light.

"Where are we going, Bleusette?"

"You know that shitty old place I inherit from my Uncle Hercule over down near Houma last year?"

Houma was a friendly bayou town some sixty miles southwest of New Orleans. It was popular with tourists looking for a quick taste of Cajun life—and cooking—and a glimpse or two of alligator, but her Uncle Hercule had been something of a crazy recluse and had lived way out in the marshes. There wasn't even much of a road to his place.

"I know it. I thought you sold it."

"Who would buy it? That is where we go. We hide out there for a while." She glanced at Glory. "Maybe you can work out another meet with these Fabios. This time with the help of Bleusette Lescaut and her many friends and family, so maybe it won't get fucked up."

They stopped at a country grocery a few miles the other side of Houma for Bleusette to notify her nearby relatives of her presence in the area and to buy the victual wherewithal for a stay in these parts, if necessary. Glory had enough money in her bag to buy the little town surrounding the store and a couple more just like it, but Bleusette insisted on paying for everything. She was an excellent cook. Andy had heard that Jean-Robert was even better.

After Bleusette was through making her several calls, Andy took the opportunity to call Maljeux from the outdoor pay phone on the store's front porch. The lieutenant had unhappy news, if not quite a catastrophe to relate. Ramona and her three companions had run into a carload of Crayfish Joe's street crew on Decatur as they were trying to leave the Quarter. There were some gunshots, and one of Fabio's men was wounded or killed. Though there'd been considerable panic around the waterfront, no civilian had been hit, but the entire matter was now top priority police business. Maljeux wanted Andy and all concerned to come in and make out statements. They might as well be back in the Caymans with Inspector Whittles.

"From what interesting place are you calling me, Andy boy?" Maljeux said.

"Never mind."

"Somewhere no more than a two-hour drive from New Orleans, I figure."

Andy hung up.

He called Long Tom as quickly as he could. The news from him was no better. Crayfish Joe's people were all over the Quarter and neighboring environs looking for Machado types, and nervous uniformed police were turning up everywhere, too. The local radio news had already linked the otherwise minor shootout with the Philippe Coquin murder and were making a major gang war out of it—and making *le tout* New Orleans jumpy, as well as fascinated. The mayor had even felt called upon to issue some fool statement urging calm.

And, no, Tom was not about to lend Andy some "friends" for any last stand in the bayous with South American druggies. He urged Andy to have Glory take him to some nice quiet place like the North Pole for a few months until matters quieted down, and to hide Bleusette somewhere with her numerous Cajun kin.

Andy thanked him. When the others came out of the store, he related the news to them.

"*C'est vrai, j'ai beaucoup de famille ici*—*beaucoup* cousins, and two half brothers and my Uncle Étienne," Bleusette said. "They will look out for us."

"My sister Claudine," Jean-Robert added, "she has a husband who weigh two hundred fifty pounds and has four shotguns."

"Everybody here have guns," said Bleusette. "But if Crayfish Joe show up, we don't want no trouble with him. That becomes *très sérieux*, you know? Family business. Go on forever."

"Andy," said Glory. "Let's take a little walk."

Bleusette watched carefully as they went around to the side of the grocery. At the edge of the parking area was a grassy path leading down to an eddy of the local bayou. The water was so dark and soupy and covered with green plant scum it seemed an extension of the mushy ground. The life teeming in it was so rich, a cup of it could get an entire plant and animal kingdom going on some other planet.

Andy had his camera. He saw a picture in the different shades of moss hanging from the trees near and distant—lush curtains of green falling to the chartreuse of the bayou. He focused on a black oak rising on higher ground at the end of a mossy corridor, then moved left slightly to improve the perspective and depth.

"Do you have to do that all the time?" Glory asked.

Click, whirr. "Yes. Went too long the last few months not doing it at all. Be happy for me."

"So your mind's back on your work?"

"My mind's on you. Stand on this board and let me shoot a few frames and then I'll put it away. *Ça va?*"

She shook her head, but indulged him reluctantly with a tiny smile, and, finally, compliance with his request. He had her look away, off toward toward the unseen end of the bayou.

"I think it's worth another try," she said. "Another exchange—out here. But if you don't get delivery of your princess this time . . . I'm sorry. I have to leave. And the briefcase will have to come with me, okay? I mean to sink them, Andy. Whatever it takes."

"I'm amazed and grateful you've stuck with me this far, Glory. Now please turn around and face toward the camera, but look off that way, toward the road. That's it. Head a little higher. Great." Click, whirr.

"I think maybe this time we can persuade Fabio himself to come. He should be more comfortable with things out here—no New Orleans gangsters. No police. I think there's a good chance of it. He'll have incentive. I'm sure he'd like to kill us both—in a personal way. Especially you."

"As long as he brings Astrid. I don't know how I could have mistaken Ramona for her."

"You were wishing it was her. Clouds your judgment, wishing things were so. But we'll have to convince him the area is full of armed Cajuns who won't let him get out alive if anything goes wrong."

"It'll be the truth. Alligators, too."

"He'll appreciate that touch. Can you provide me with some sensible directions to give him?"

"Bleusette can."

Andy came up to her, slinging his camera back over his shoulder.

"I'm through taking pictures."

"Let's go back, then."

"I want to kiss you."

"Be brisk about it. This isn't that hotel room. Your Bleusette is making me nervous."

They weren't brisk enough. As they started up the path, Andy saw Bleusette leaning against the wall of the grocery, her dark eyes like a wary animal's.

"I'll make the calls," Glory said.

Uncle Hercule's house sat half on stilts at the edge of a bayou. There were thick woods to either side—especially just across the water, but the ground immediately around the house was open and fairly firm. A wide wooden veranda ran along two sides and extended out over the water. A neglected skiff, nearly full of old rain yet somehow still afloat, was tied to it. On higher ground behind the house were a couple of sheds. The rusty ruin of a thirty- or forty-year-old pickup truck sat wheelless and windowless in the center of the wide, weedy yard. Uncle Hercule had seldom been troubled by visitors.

They'd brought plenty to eat, and Jean-Robert set busily to cooking up a late lunch of rice and boudin shortly after their arrival. There was no electricity, but the pump worked and the kitchen had a cast-iron stove with plenty of old chopped wood beside it. The living room and back bedrooms had a mouldering look and smell to them, doubtless from sizable leaks in the roof, but the wide deck over the water was bright and sunny, and they all sat out there.

Glory had gotten Fabio to agree to an eight o'clock meet, which would be just after sunset—providing them some darkness in which to retreat if necessary. Andy hadn't decided on the exact procedure of transfer, but there was time enough for that. They had all afternoon.

Jean-Robert brought the hot sausage out in its cast-iron frying pan, then went back for the rice and four plates, and returned once more for three bottles of Jax beer. Bleusette, who only drank Pernod or water, had brought some of the former.

"If we had some music," said Jean-Robert, "we could have us a *fais-dodo* today."

"A what?" asked Glory.

"A little party," said Andy. "Music and dancing."

"I am in no mood for no *fais-dodo*, Andy," said Bleusette.

"Next time, perhaps," Glory said.

"There gonna be a next time for you, mademoiselle?" said Bleusette.

If Bleusette was looking to begin a scrap, Glory wanted none of it. "No, probably not."

"I am very particular about with who I make *fais-dodo,* you know?"

"I'm sure you are."

They took a long time eating their meal, managing a fairly pleasant conversation afterwards, mostly thanks to Jean-Robert and his willingness to answer Glory's questions about Cajun life and the countryside around them. Then he and Andy pumped some more water and washed the dishes.

When they were done, it was agreed they'd all just laze around for a while until they'd decided on some sort of plan. Jean-Robert opened some more Jax. Bleusette sat on the edge of the deck, dangling bare feet in the warm water. Glory stretched out on her back. He imagined she wished she had no clothes on.

Jean-Robert sipped his beer, smoking a small cigar.

"You say they gonna be coming at sunset, Andy?" he asked.

"A little after. Eight o'clock."

"Maybe I go start gathering up the others now. We get ready."

"We have a couple hours or more."

"I want to make sure we have everybody rounded up. Plenty of guns."

"Not too many. We don't want them to see you."

"This is our country, you know? Nobody gonna see us."

"You be very careful, Jean-Robert," Bleusette said. "Like we talk about."

"*N'inquiet, chère cousine. Entendu.*"

He set off across the yard toward the road, on foot, leaving Andy's car behind. It was a good two miles to the last house they had passed, but as Andy recalled, that belonged to one of Bleusette's relatives as well.

Left alone, the three of them fell silent, and finally, the two women dozed off. Andy crossed over to where the skiff was tied up and pulled on the line, bringing it close.

"What you do, Andy?"

"I'm going to bail this out."

"*Tu es fou, bien sûr.*"

"It's something to do."

It was tiresome work, but it seemed to get his mind to functioning. He'd put the briefcase in the boat. Leave it out where Fabio could see it but not get at it—at least until Andy had hold of Astrid and was headed with Bleusette and Glory into the woods. If Fabio tried going after them, Bleusette's relatives could do their stuff. Quite frankly, Andy hoped that would be the case.

When he decided he was finished bailing, there was still an inch or so of water sloshing idly in the bottom, but nothing coming back in.

He sat in the boat and let the line pay back out till he was floating twenty feet or so out on the water. Glory turned her head, squinting against the lowering sun.

"What's the name of this bayou?" she asked.

"Bayou Terrebonne," Bleusette said.

"I'll remember this place," Glory said.

"You seem happy," said Andy.

"Considering everything, I am."

Considering everything, Andy was, too. He lay back in the skiff and made himself comfortable, gazing across the water into Glory's eyes for a time, until at last she closed them. He did the same. Hours to wait.

An odd, misplaced sound began to creep into Andy's hearing—a distant chattering, gradually increasing. He scanned the sky, but the tall trees on the other side of the yard limited his view.

"Helicopter," he said, sitting up.

Glory sat up, too. "What would a helicopter be doing out here?"

"Fish and Wildlife Service," said Bleusette, seemingly unconcerned. "They come out here all the time in helicopters, checking on the gators and snakes."

The noise suddenly stopped. Andy listened harder, but there was nothing more. He relaxed. Glory was still lying down, Bleusette still dabbling her feet.

Then Glory abruptly sat up again, giving no sign of what bothered her. A moment later, she got to her feet and went into the house.

"Glory?"

"Quiet!"

Bleusette turned her head, an apprehensive look on her face. Andy began pulling on the line to get back to the dock.

It broke, with a loud crack, sending him onto his back into the water in the boat's bottom.

The crack hadn't come from the old rope. It was a gunshot. The bullet struck the water with a splash just a few feet away.

Chapter
·28·

There was a second and much louder splash. Andy looked over the side of the boat and saw that Bleusette had dived from the deck and was swimming for the opposite shore.

Then came another gunshot. Andy heard the bullet's raspy singing in the air beside his head, saw it strike the surface scum a few feet shy of Bleusette. He couldn't tell which of them the shooter was aiming at. It didn't really matter. They were all at risk. He pulled the small pistol from his pocket and wildly fired two shots from it in the general direction of the attackers.

From inside the house, he heard a much greater, more percussive explosive crack, recognizing it as Glory's automatic. The sound was followed by that of someone crying out in pain. Then there was shouting.

Suddenly Glory appeared at the house's kitchen door, briefcase and her canvas bag in one hand, the Glock in the other. She fired again, at something behind her and bolted through the screen door with such violence it came off one of its hinges after banging back against the wall.

Her feet thumping hard on the old wood of the deck, she was across it in two seconds. The briefcase and bag came sailing through the air; the latter hit the boat bottom next to him but the hard briefcase landed on his stomach. He gasped, sitting up, just as Glory struck the water in a shallow dive, disappearing into the chartreuse murk. A man Andy vaguely recognized came running along the side of the house, carrying a large, squarish, odd-looking weapon in both hands. Andy raised his pitiful little pistol and fired. Some perverse inhibition kept him from aiming lethally. He tried for one of the man's legs, but the short-barreled gun was so inaccurate it almost didn't matter where he pointed it. Amazingly, he did hit the man—in the groin or lower belly. The fellow dropped his own weapon, doubling over and clutching himself and screaming before losing his balance and toppling into the bayou.

Glory's head whooshed up just beside the boat. "Get out of there!" she shouted.

Andy saw her point. Placing the small pistol on the forward seat, he rolled over the side into the wet.

The water tasted as mucky as it smelled and looked. He spat some out, wiped off his mouth, then propelled himself with a single swimming stroke up to the bow of the skiff.

Glory was already there, one hand on the prow, the other pawing into the muck. "Come on, pull!"

He grasped the bow just to the other side and began to swim. The outward curve of the boat shielded them somewhat from the shoreline by the house. All they could hear from that direction was one man swearing.

"I think that was the advance guard," Glory said, the words coming in bursts between strokes. "Small chopper. Maybe only two or three men. I think there's another one coming. Probably bigger."

Andy looked ahead. The bayou here was narrow. There wasn't that much water separating them from thick woods.

"I'm so goddamn stupid," Glory said. "Thought they'd come in cars. Never thought about helicopters."

Bleusette, moving ahead of them, was almost to the shore, her hair glossy and sleek. Glory's was sleek, too. She looked different, classically beautiful.

There was that chattering sound again, with an echoing resonance. The noise increased.

"Reinforcements!" Glory said.

Another stroke, another. He counted ten of them before looking up again. Bleusette was in waist-deep water, reaching up to pull herself into the thick greenery of the bank.

The echoing soon explained itself. There were two helicopters—one very large and the other small. The big one settled into the yard behind the house, barely missing the rusty old abandoned truck. The other kept coming, canted over a few degrees, then slowly floated outward over the water.

Whoever was aboard the aircraft seemed to be concerned with the man Andy had shot, who was still in the water. Then they took note of the skiff. The chopper lifted suddenly, tilting to the right, circling toward them with the passenger side down, the door open.

Andy and Glory had towed the skiff almost to the shore. They began swimming with all their might.

The pilot, seeing he could not complete his circle without brushing the trees, leveled and then reversed the turn, flying out over the bayou and then making another pass from the opposite direction.

Glory, watching the maneuver, stopped swimming, bringing herself close to the boat and reaching in for her weapon.

"Keep pulling!" she said. "If they get close enough, I think I can worry them a little."

Someone began firing from the house. Through the gunfire and helicopter noise, Andy heard Bleusette from somewhere in the woods, swearing in French.

A bullet from somewhere whacked through the side of the boat a foot or so back from the prow, the exit hole sending splinters into Andy's arm and hand. Another struck the boat bottom, making a duller thwoping sound. The helicopter was coming on fast, a man in a sports shirt, gray pants, and sunglasses crouching in the open doorway with a rifle. He leaned forward, firing and hitting the skiff's bottom again, but coming nowhere near Andy or Glory. The man sat back, holding the rifle loosely against his shoulder. The chopper slowed, hovering.

"He's waiting for us to try to make it out of the water," she said. "Then we'll get a couple of quick shots in the back."

Andy kept stroking. It had become much harder.

"The boat's sinking."

"Hang on," she said. "Maybe he'll get a little bit closer."

The chopper settled low and near enough for its rotor wash to begin spreading and stirring the water, some of it coming into Andy's mouth. He stopped watching what was going on and concentrated on moving the skiff.

The Glock barked twice. There was a metallic *prang!* and the helicopter began coughing. It rose for a moment like a rearing horse, then fell away onto its other side, dropping into the bayou with a tremendous splash and roar as the rotor blades ripped into the green muck.

"I broke something with one of those shots," Glory said. "A round from one of these will chew up a lot of engine parts."

The helicopter had gone down canted sideways but nose first. The water was too shallow for it to sink fully, and the tail was left sticking up into the air, with much of the cockpit section above the waterline as well. Only one man came out of it. He glanced once toward Andy and Glory, then began swimming furiously toward the house.

Andy stood up. The waters they had reached came only to his chest. He lugged the sinking skiff a few feet farther, then reached in and grabbed Glory's bag and the briefcase. She took the latter from him and began splashing on ahead. Andy followed, just as a bullet hit the water behind him. Another whistled through tree leaves above and a third whacked into the wood of a high branch.

Once on shore, he began running. The women were well ahead of him. When he caught up with them, the bayou behind him was hidden from view.

"Hercule had an old fishing shack other side of this high ground," Bleusette said. "It's on a creek that run into the bayou further down. I think I remember how to find it. These cocksuckers won't know."

"A fishing shack?"

"*Oui. Poissons.* I think it used to smell all the time like piss, but what the hell. Good hiding. Maybe."

"It's going to be dark in a little while," Glory said.

"*C'est bien,*" said Bleusette. "We won't see the snakes."

The wood of the shack was so old, unpainted, and rotten it almost seemed part of the undergrowth. There was one frameless window, facing the creek. The door next to it had fallen out onto the ground, extending into the swampy water like a ramp. Inside, it was murky and damp, and very small. An ancient water-rotted mattress lay in one corner. Andy thought of sitting on it but realized it would be full of every imaginable kind of crawling vermin.

Instead, he went to the rear wall, eyed the old wooden boards carefully, then, with a few quick, sharp kicks, knocked two of them out.

"What the fuck you doing, Andy?" said Bleusette, seating herself with extreme care by the doorway.

"I want to be able to see out both sides of this thing."

"Shit, in a little while, nobody see anything," Bleusette said. "Those sonsofbitches just gonna thrash around out there going nowhere. Then it get dark and they gonna be real sorry they come here."

In the gathering gloom, it was hard to see her face.

"They double-crossed us again," Andy said, forlornly. "I don't think they have Astrid."

Glory was near enough to him to touch his hand. "It's time you accepted the worst."

"Can't prove anything."

"Andy, if she's anywhere, it's probably in that water off Grand Cayman, where the others were."

"I don't want to think that."

"Look, you tried, all right? There's nothing more to be done."

"We'll see."

Andy stared out the open door. Some large night bird with wide white wings swooped low over the water, making a quick quiet splash as it gathered up its meal and began ascending again, large wings flapping.

"Don't worry, Andy," Bleusette said. "That Fabio prick is not going to get out of these bayous alive. I see to that, *bien sûr*."

"And how, pray, are you making sure of that?" Glory asked.

"Crayfish Joe Coquin and his boys on their way out here now," said Bleusette, "and this time they are going to fix that Fabio *longtemps*, like they suppose' to do this morning in the Quarter."

"You told Coquin we were coming here?" Andy asked.

"*Vraiment*. I call him from that grocery where we buy the boudin. He should be here *bientôt*."

"*Bientôt* may not be soon enough."

"That's your fault. You don't say fucking thing about these helicopters, that these Fabios gonna come *très vite comme des oiseaux.* Now it will be *plus difficile,* but, don't worry, Coquin will kill them real dead, *bien sûr.* I never know of this man being so mad before. It is like *dérangé*—his anger stuck in his mind. Won't go away until he take care of Fabio. Not good for a man to have so much *de la fureur.* It makes for indigestion. After this Crayfish Joe will be happy again. Everything will be as before."

"All tickety-boo," said Andy.

"I didn't expect the helicopters," Glory said. "Should have done, damn it. With all the money that swine has at his disposal I shouldn't be surprised if he'd rented an entire goddamn air force."

There was a mosquito whining near one of Andy's ears. He slapped at his cheek. The whining stopped. It was fully night. Completely dark. Except for the frog and insect noise, perfectly quiet.

"This isn't going to work, Bleusette," Andy said. "Fabio got here first. Crayfish Joe and his boys are going to walk into an ambush. They're the ones who are going to get whacked. And who cares if they are?"

"*Mais non.* Never happen. I have Jean-Robert waiting out by the highway to give Joe the warning. And I care if Joe get whacked. He is going to help me set up a new business. I am tired of that fucking restaurant. *Toujours travail. Rien de joie.*"

"What new business?"

"Never mind. We'll talk about it later."

"I thought he was threatening you." Andy said.

"That, too. They have big temperament, these Coquins. Anger for everybody."

Andy stood up. "Sorry. I'm not going to leave my fate in the hands of those goofballs. We're getting out of here."

"How? Where?"

"Does this creek lead back toward the house?" he asked Bleusette.

"*Oui,*" she said. "It wind some but it go back there. The road that goes from Hercule's house out to the highway? The creek comes up to it—just to the other side of the house."

Andy remembered that stretch—creek on one side, bayou on the other, the road little more than a causeway.

"How deep is it along the bank?"

"We gonna get wet, *très fort*."

The going was slow and laborious but steady, their feet making mushy sucking sounds when lifted, with gentle sloshes accompanying the forward swings of their legs. Andy stumbled once, going to his knees. Bleusette fell twice, each occurrence followed by long, obscene mutters in French. Occasionally, they heard splashes nearby but had no idea as to what kind of creature was causing the sound—not that they wanted to know.

They kept going. A vague dim glow began to illuminate the swampy landscape as the moon ascended through the hanging clouds. They could see each other's silhouettes now, and after a bit, the lightness of their clothes and skin.

At length, the trees to the left gave way to an open flatness. Andy could see a glint of water just beyond it. This had to be the road. They had gone around and past Hercule's house. If they kept going in this direction, they'd soon join Jean-Robert at the highway. They'd be safe.

Andy led them up onto the narrow roadway. Looking back toward the house, he could see a faint swath of light lying over the ground and a few pinpoints of brightness around it. He knelt, motioning the women to him.

"Bleusette," he said, whispering. "I want you to go back up to the highway and Jean-Robert. You go with her, Glory. Stay out of this."

"And just what are you going to do?" Glory said.

"I thought I'd go up close to the house and see what's what. See if they have might have Astrid after all. Maybe get back my car."

"Your car?"

"*Merde*," said Bleusette.

"I love that car. It's family. And my camera's in there. There are some shots on that roll I don't want to lose."

"You're crazy."

"They may all be off in the bush looking for us. It might be easy. Then we can get out of here fast. All the way home."

"If you go up there," Glory said, "I'm going with you."

"You're both fucking crazy," said Bleusette, too loudly.

"Shhhh."

His admonition came too late. Preoccupied with what he could see of Hercule's house, he failed to note the shadowy figures coming upon them from behind. By the time he heard their squishy footfalls, the intruders were on them, swiftly and expertly grabbing their arms and twisting them backwards, putting heavy hands on their mouths.

Their captors dragged them back along the road all the way to the other end of the causeway and a clump of moss-bedecked trees. There, looking unhappy from his exertions, was Crayfish Joe. It was not often one saw the man standing up.

The fat gangster addressed his remarks to Bleusette.

"What the fuck you doing, creeping around here?" he said. "This is not what we agree."

"Just trying to get out of your way, Joe. Get the hell out of here."

"That's them up there? Them Brazilian *cochons?*"

"*Oui*. My Uncle Hercule's house. *Celui-là*. They got helicopters. Came real early. *Quelle surprise*, eh?"

"How many are there, these Brazilian fucks?"

"Enough," said Glory. "They've got the jump on you. A lot of your people are going to get hurt if you go in there. Maybe us, too, and we haven't done anything to you."

Crayfish Joe nodded, not to Glory, but to one of his thugs, who stepped up to Andy and decked him with a carefully measured blow to the side of the head. Andy dropped to his knees.

He got up slowly, a ringing in his ear, wondering what came next.

"You shit bastard, you sell pictures of my poor dead Philippe to a fucking cheap tabloid, you prick. You saw what this Fabio do to him. You think I can forget this? Just go home and let that bastard *Portagee* live? *Je n'oublie rien*. I will kill him, right now."

"I have to pee," said Bleusette. She and Coquin exchanged a few sharp but not threatening words in French, then she went off into the shadows.

"I should kill you, too, Derain. *Peut-être*, I should break your hands so you think *très fort* next time you pick up a camera what you do with the pictures. *Compris?* But maybe I leave you alone if you now do something for me."

"What?"

"This briefcase you got is what Machado wants, yes?"

"Yes."

"What's in it, money?"

"No. Bank records. Evidence that could be used against them."

Coquin pondered this. "Okay. I want you to go down this road to that house and give the briefcase to this Fabio. Tell them you are coming with it so they don't shoot you before you get to them. He will want to look in it at once, yes? See what's inside? See what you have? So, while he do that, we move in. Bang, bang, bang. *Finis. Très bon.*"

"Not 'bon,' " said Glory. "They'll kill Andy before he ever gets close."

"You let that happen, Joe Coquin," said Bleusette, "and your name going to be shit in the Quarter—an *homme déshonoré.* Andy is the son of Doc Derain, who take care of *beaucoup* working girls. Andy is *bon vieux ami* of Long Tom Calhoun. My family, we will hate you very much *longtemps.*"

"I'll do it," Andy said.

"Don't be bloody stupid."

"If Astrid's there, maybe we can still work something out."

"No, Andy," Glory said.

"It's okay," said Coquin. "We'll be right behind you. *Beaucoup* guns."

As he neared the outer limit of the circle of light around Hercule's house, Andy did hear someone coming behind him, but it wasn't Coquin and his men.

Glory slipped her hand in his.

Andy halted. "Go back," he whispered, urgently.

"No. I can help."

"You're crazy."

"Fabio knows me. He used to like me. I can stall him. Please, I know what I'm doing. You do not."

They were making too much noise.

"All right. Into the valley of death."

"Would that we were six hundred."

· · ·

Their first greeting was a gunshot. It came from somewhere near the house, striking the mushy ground beside them with a splat that scattered watery mud against their legs. Andy could see lanterns and flashlights in the near distance. Most of them went out.

"Fabio!" shouted Glory. She began hurling forth a flurry of angry words in Portuguese.

A flurry of Portuguese came back. Glory responded. Then there was silence.

But no more shooting. Some of the lights came back on. Into their circle of illumination stepped Fabio. He motioned to Andy and Glory to come forward.

The closer he came to Fabio's face, the more Andy realized what gigantic trouble he was in. Fabio had ceased being a handsome man. There was a deep, scabby gash across his right cheek and a purplish abrasion spread across his brow. His nose was big and swollen and pulpy—an animal's snout. It would doubtless take an entire team of plastic surgeons to put Fabio into original form again.

Fabio might not want to kill Andy after all. He might just settle for having Andy pounded on and mashed up until he could play Quasimodo without stage makeup.

Andy glanced at Glory. If she had indeed managed to avoid becoming one of Fabio's conquests, she wouldn't be able to boast of that much longer. Then what?

All they had to count on was Crayfish Joe's bloody-mindedness. Still, that came in inexhaustible supplies.

"Give it to me. Now," said Fabio, quietly. He took a drag on his cigarette, then dropped it to the ground.

Andy handed him the briefcase. Fabio said something in Portuguese to Glory.

"He wants to know if you made any photocopies, took pictures of the stuff, anything like that."

Andy looked into Fabio's scabby, puffy face.

"Yes, I did," Andy said.

Fabio smiled gruesomely, then kicked Andy's shin.

"All right, all right," Andy said, wincing. "I didn't make any copies. There wasn't time."

For this he got a kick in the other shin, harder, and almost slumped to the ground. He hung on to Glory's shoulder.

"Where is my money?" Fabio said to Glory.

"I hid it. Back there. Up the road."

"Where?"

"Back there, on the other end of that little causeway, under some trees."

"You think I forget about a million fucking bucks you steal from me, you cunt?"

Without a second's hesitation, he stepped forward and swung the briefcase hard against Glory's pubic bone, then lifted his knee into her belly. Amazingly, she didn't cry out except to gasp and moan a little, but she crumpled. Andy caught her, pulling her to him, moving to shield her. He thought, very briefly, of snatching Glory's Glock out from under her jacket and emptying it into Fabio, but that would just get them both killed very swiftly, instantly.

He truly wanted to do it, though. As far as Fabio was concerned, Andy considered himself a certifiable homicidal maniac.

"You should have hit her in the face, Fabio," said a woman's voice, coming from behind them. "She's much too pretty."

The voice was highly recognizable. As Andy should have expected, it was Ramona. She came striding out of the shadows almost in parody of one of her New York charity ball grand entrances. Surprisingly, though her hair was still its usual flamboyant gold, she was dressed all in black—slacks, pullover, and what looked to be expensive black sneakers. Maybe she'd developed a Cat Woman complex, or thought this was Brazilian chic.

Ramona stopped in front of Fabio, her look full of adoration and admiration, doubtless well practiced.

"This is it?" she said, touching the briefcase. "You've got it?"

"They say so. Maybe they lie."

Ramona took the briefcase from Fabio and carried it to Andy's Cadillac, which was still sitting in the middle of the yard. She set it on the hood, showing no concern for any scratches she caused, the witch, and then snapped it open. One by one, she took out the papers, holding each up to the lantern light.

"You and Andao shouldn't have kept these in that bank, Fabio."

"Where else you keep fucking bank records?"

"They're atom bombs, Fabio. The U.S. government could

seize every one of Harvey's properties. Every brick and beam. Just using these papers. It's all in the drug laws."

"But they're your bricks now."

Ramona smiled, continuing her perusal of the papers. "As soon as we're through probate."

"Did you kill Harvey, Ramona?" Andy asked.

"Shut your mouth, Andy. You're not going to live very long here. Don't waste your time annoying me."

"Just tell me."

"Why?"

"So I know who didn't kill him."

Ramona turned, her eyes agleam. "What, afraid your precious Princess Astrid did it?"

He stared, waiting. Ramona was vastly enjoying the completeness of the power she now had over him. She reminded him of a wildlife film he had once seen—the glint in a lioness' eye as she put teeth and claws to the rear of a zebra.

"I'm not going to tell you," she said. "You know why?"

"Why?"

"Because I don't like you."

"How did you know about 'Poor bears'?"

"What?"

"'Poor bears.' You told us Astrid had passed on a message to me, 'Poor bears.' How did you know about 'Poor bears'?"

"She kept saying it, over and over, when we had her on the boat. I thought it was some code she had with Harvey, but he didn't know what it meant, either. I just took a chance it might mean something to you. Clever of me, wasn't it?"

"Where is she?"

"Astrid?" Ramona smiled. "Not going to tell you that, either."

"You've killed her, haven't you? Just like you killed Harvey."

Ramona shook her head, wearily. "Look, jerk. Harvey had become a problem, okay? He'd gone absolutely gooney for that Nordic ice princess of yours. Out of his mind in love with her. Giving her all sorts of shit and pouring money into her company. The Machados and I decided it was time to re-form the partnership, with me taking Harvey's place. We were in the process of arranging that when you happened along. But I didn't put that bullet in Harvey's brain. That wasn't how we were going to do it.

I had in mind something involving Harvey, your princess, Miss Suntanned Crumpet here and her airplane—all ending up somewhere at the bottom of the Gulf of Mexico. If things had really gone my way, you might have been there, too. But they didn't go my way. So I'm improvising."

She tossed the open briefcase and the loose papers into the back of the Cadillac, some of the bank records fluttering over the seat. Andy wondered what this was about. Surely Ramona Fitch wasn't going to drive out of there in his rusty old crate.

She came up to him now, very close. "You know, Andy darling, I did for the briefest of moments even consider letting you wander off after we got these records back. I do care what people say about me. I'm not happy about the idea of you sending those very intimate pictures of me and my lover boy to all my favorite magazines. I'm not big on being gossiped about by all those fucking snoots and snots in Mortimer's. In fact, the idea really pisses me off." She took a step even closer. He found himself looking for surgical scars at the edge of her face. "But I've got my new man, don't I? And Fabio's worth a hell of a lot more than Harvey was. There are other cities. Rio ain't bad, Andy. Fuck Le Cirque. And fuck you, too. You and your girlfriend get in the car."

He was confused. Were they letting him and Glory go after all? He opened the door and helped Glory ease painfully onto the seat. Then he went around to the driver's side. Fabio watched him intently. Andy could see three or four other men back in the shadows.

They weren't going to let them just drive away. There were no keys in the car.

He reached and held Glory's hand tightly. He hadn't seen her this scared before.

"We need to burn these papers, Fabio," Ramona said. "All of them. Every word and number. Now. Quick."

She stepped back from the car. Fabio, to Andy's immense discomfort, came toward it, a fiendishly mirthful grin spreading across his wounded face.

Andy's discomfort increased. Fabio was going to the rear of the Cadillac, taking out a handkerchief. Andy heard the spring-loaded license plate holder creak down, and then the sound of the gas cap being unscrewed. He remembered the car Fabio had blown up with its own gasoline at that little airfield near Lafayette. In the rearview mirror, he saw Fabio light a cigarette. The lighter in his hand was still flaming.

Glory's eyes were shut tight. Andy pulled her closer.

"We've bought the bloody farm," she whispered.

"No. We've got a chance. Get a foot against your door. When I say 'Go,' we roll out of here. On my side."

"No. Can't make it."

"Yes."

"They'll just shoot us."

"Maybe. It's better than this. And Crayfish . . ."

Fabio was bending down, gone from the rearview mirror. It would take a second or two more for the handkerchief to catch fire. Andy reached and slowly pulled back on his door handle.

The mirror showed a flicker of orange light—and Fabio dancing quickly away from the car. Andy made a calculation, listening, counting.

"Go!" he said.

He swung the door open with a screeching crack. Glory shoved with her foot, while he yanked hard on her arm, and they both came tumbling out in a backward lunge, falling shoulder first onto the ground. Glory rolled over him, landing on her back just as the rear of the car gave forth an enormous *thwump*.

The air seared with heat, but it swept up above them, roaring and twisting. A great curling ball of orange and yellow flame, laced with oily black, belched into the sky, as fire engulfed the entire passenger compartment. Whatever had been in the backseat, including Andy's camera, wasn't anymore.

Andy and Glory kept rolling. There was another sound now, like firecrackers. Andy wondered if Glory's gun had fallen out into the car and these were its bullets going off. But the shooting continued in staccato waves. He could see bullets striking the ground. He reached to Glory's waistband. The Glock was still there.

They kept moving, crawling, running at a crouch, then falling flat to earth again as bullets came near. It was cooler now. They were in a damp, shallow depression. He pulled Glory close again, then lifted his head slightly.

His burning Cadillac illuminated the entire yard and all the buildings brightly, its hellish light extending beyond the house and shacks. Two of Fabio's men were down. Others were running for shelter. One of those fell. Then another. A third caught a round in the lower back and screamed as though he'd been impaled. Off by the ruin of Hercule's old truck, another of Fabio's thugs started shooting in the direction of the causeway, then he went tumbling back. Coquin's people were very good—professionals.

A dark figure was running off to the other side, toward the swamp. Dark clothes. Gold hair. Bullets cut into the trees around her, dropping showers of leaves, but she kept going unhindered and abruptly vanished into the dark.

More shots scattered around the area, some in bursts from a low-caliber automatic weapon. Andy pressed his face back against the dirt, waiting.

Finally, there was blessed silence. He very carefully raised his head again. There, in the center of the carnage and devastation, a cigarette still in his lips, stood Fabio. Not a single bullet had touched him. It took Andy a while before he realized that astonishing result had been deliberate.

Fabio's eyes were wide, a little like a trapped beast's, but, ever the macho man—even though he knew something very, very bad was going to happen to him—he held on to his self-control. He turned about slowly, as Coquin's street crew converged upon him, as if daring them to come near. One of the bigger of the bunch, holding an Uzi or Mac 10 slung casually over his shoulder, accepted the challenge. He came up and kicked Fabio with great violence in the crotch, much, much worse than what Fabio had done to Glory.

Machado fell forward, screaming. Andy guessed he'd been damaged permanently. Even if granted a reprieve now, life would never be the same for him—especially nightlife.

The face of Bleusette appeared dimly at the periphery of the lighted area. She stared hard at Fabio, then turned away, knowing what was coming. For all her tough talk, Bleusette didn't like violence. It had been one of the downsides of her previous career.

Andy did not want to see what was about to happen, either, but he steeled himself to do so, holding firm to the remembered image of Beth Hampshire's dead face.

Coquin came and stood over his enemy, who lay contorted on his side, clutching his groin with both hands, mouthing what must be Portuguese obscenities. Finally, he returned to English.

"Do it, you fuck! Go on!"

Crayfish Joe laughed, a jolly sound. His belly shook as in the children's verse about St. Nicholas.

"You whacked my boy Philippe, yes? It was you who kill him? You tell me straight and then I think about what happen to you."

"Yes! The prick steal my Felicie."

"So what? He never keep anybody long. You should have taken it up with her later—leave Philippe out of it."

"Fuck Philippe."

"You are *très stupide*."

"You gonna shoot me or not?"

"We are gonna shoot you, *bien sûr*."

"Then do it!" Fabio screamed again, as though in punctuation.

"Not fast," said Coquin, who commenced to waddle around Fabio's writhing form, looking at it from various angles. "We shoot you more *doucement*. You know how many rounds go into that poor Felicie? Police say twenty-seven. You shoot her twenty-seven times. Imagine that. *Incroyable.* She probably dead by the time you get half those bullets into her."

Fabio was quiet now, staring.

"Well, my boys very good with guns. *Des fusiliers splendides.* You see how quickly they cut down your boys? But now you will see them at their very best. We are going to put twenty-seven shots into you, maybe more, but not to kill you, *compris?* To hurt you very much, but very careful, *très précis,* so you stay alive, so we know how much you are enjoying it. *Bien? Et moi, je le commence.*"

Like an operating-room nurse, an assistant handed him a big automatic pistol. Coquin, resting his firing arm on his immense belly, aimed carefully and pulled the trigger, hitting Fabio in what remained of his testicles, effectively obliterating them. Andy wondered where Fabio found the energy for his continuing yowls.

Now each of Coquin's men came forward, taking a shot in turn, like sporting gentlemen in a tournament. Fabio twitched, yelped, bellowed, jerked, began shaking, then screamed some more, subsiding finally into a grotesque primal moan. The next gunshots provided percussion to the mournful monotone of this bleating song—a bullet in the knee, in the foot, in the shoulder, in the hip, and on and on. At length, Fabio stopped moving. The echoes fell away. There was quiet, except for the intermittent crackle of the burning car. But then came a loud gurgle, and a pleading scatter of words in Portuguese.

"How many you count, boys?" Coquin said.

"Twenty-one, Monsieur Coquin. Six to go."

"But he don't look so good. Hit him too many more times, maybe he go into shock. What you think, Machado? Are you a macho man, or are you going to go under?"

Fabio mewed something. Coquin laughed. "Bring me a twenty-two. *Quelque chose petit.*"

A minion did as instructed. Coquin took the small automatic he was given and leaned over Fabio. Like someone using a stapling machine, he began firing into Fabio's curled up body, moving the gun swiftly but carefully from point to point, making certain to hit nothing vital.

"You are bleeding *beaucoup, cochon,*" he said, pausing. "You die soon if I don't hurry."

He got off three more rounds, then stood leaning over Fabio's head. "Twenty-eight, Machado. That's one more than Felicie. And you're still alive. *Merveilleux.*"

Coquin leaned closer now, putting the pistol to Fabio's face. "*Et maintenant, le coup de grâce, oui?* Put you out of your misery."

Fabio's eyes looked like those of a landed fish.

"*Mais, non,*" said Coquin. "You should have thought much more careful when you decide it okay to whack the son of Joe Coquin, you *stupide.*" He motioned to several of his fellows. "You boys, come pick up this piece of shit. We are going to give him a last ride. In a Cadillac! Very nice."

Amazingly, Fabio found it within him to bubble forth some unintelligible word. Then Coquin's men heaved the bleeding, burbling form into Andy's still-burning car. Fabio landed in the flames facedown, hanging over the seatback in much the same position as Felicie Balbo had been found. He blackened almost in an instant, like a Cajun dish.

Glory was hugging Andy. "They're going to kill us now."

"No. These are all local gentlemen. Friends of friends, and all that. I think. I hope." He sat up, his arm bringing Glory close to him.

Coquin's men brought Bleusette into the circle of light.

"You see what you do for me, Cousin Bleusette?" said Co-quin. "What can I say? I am so grateful. Without you, I never avenge my Philippe. I owe you very big." He paused to belch and hand the .22 automatic back to one of his men.

"*Mais, malheureusement,*" Crayfish continued, "you were all witnesses to this hit, which, in this country, *tant pis*, is still a crime—punishable by the death penalty in the state of Louisiana, even when you whack a piece of scummy alligator shit like this no good Machado cocksucker."

"Nobody here going to snitch on you, Joe," Bleusette said. "I was in the life, yes? I know what goes and don't on the street. And Jean-Robert, he from here. One hundred percent Cajun. As long as you don't do nothing to our family, he won't be telling anyone a fucking thing."

"*Vous avez raison, Bleusette,*" said Coquin, patting her on the head. "But your *amour* here." He looked to Andy. "And this woman. I know nothing about her. She even work for the Macha-dos, no? How am I to trust such a woman? And your Andy, he sell those pictures of Philippe. I cannot forgive this, Bleusette. I am sorry. Very sorry. But we will have to kill them."

Bleusette's dark eyes were reflecting the burning car, but much of their fiery look was coming strictly from within.

"You do that, Joe, and whole French Quarter turn against you, I swear."

"*Mais non, ma petite.* They will think this nothing to do with me. It will look like big trouble between these two and the Brazil-ian drug pricks. I will leave that bag full of money here as proof that's what it is and nobody think otherwise."

"I will think otherwise, Joe. Me and my family. You will be *beaucoup* sorry you ever do this to me, goddamn you, fat Joe, you shit-eating pig."

Crayfish sighed. "I understand. *Je suis triste, Bleusette.* That's why I'm gonna have to kill you—and Jean-Robert, too. It's just a bad night, you know?"

"But you promised you will help me with my new business!"

"If I didn't have to kill you, I would help you, Bleusette. *C'est vrai.*"

Bleusette appeared confounded by this and fell silent. For a moment, no one spoke. There was only the hideous crackle of freshly and fleshly fueled fire coming from the remains of Andy's car.

No, there was something else. Not insects, not swamp noises. Something more powerful and man made. Glory hadn't noticed it. She was in so much shock over what had happened, she seemed incapable of noticing anything. But it was there, a sound worth waiting for—if Andy could somehow provide the time.

He stepped forward. "What business are you talking about, Bleusette?"

"What the fuck do you care, Andy? You never come around the old one."

"We're supposed to be family. Yet there you were cutting deals with a mafioso, asking his help, and you don't tell me?"

"I say it again. What the fuck do you care? You been off with that Princess Astrid and this airplane woman down in the islands, and you don't say a goddamn thing to me. Why are you starting this big fight with me now? This son of a bitch is going to shoot us."

Andy kept talking. "How can you open a new business? You've sunk every penny you and Long Tom took off that woman you killed into your restaurant."

"You kill somebody, Bleusette?" Coquin asked. "Who you kill?"

"Same hoodoo woman who burn out Andy's studio and cause all that big trouble in the Quarter last summer. And I didn't kill her personal, *entendu?* Long Tom and I arrange to have her go away, but the way it works out, it's for good. *Quel dommage.* She left some money. Caused a lot of trouble, that witch. Burn my property. We had expenses. So we take what's fair, and I open my restaurant."

"That's why I never wanted to go in that place," Andy said. "It was blood money."

"Why did you not tell me that?" said Bleusette. "If you worried about dead woman's curse, I understand. Shit, that one was *très mauvaise.* Always wearing black. Maybe she curse that money *très fort.* Maybe that's why the restaurant make me so unhappy, cause so much trouble between us."

"So what's this new business? And why do you need this fat bastard's so-called help?"

"Hey, Derain," said Coquin. "You insult me like that again and you gonna go slow like the *Portagee frite* over there. Slow fry, *comprenez-vous ça?*"

"Oh, shut up," said Glory.

"What?"

"I said shut up. *Fermez la bouche.* Listen."

They all were. Everyone could hear the sound now.

And then they could see its source—not one but a whole flock of helicopters appearing suddenly over the trees to the south and ripping along toward them over the water, lights blazing and twirling. Andy counted four of them. When they were nearly overhead, he clearly saw the stenciled lettering on the underside of one: U.S. Government.

Crayfish Joe was staring upward in stupefied amazement, as were all his crew. A number of Coquin's men had their weapons raised but held back from firing, so confused were they about what was happening to them. Andy took a step toward Glory, pulled the automatic from her waistband, and bounded to the mobster's side while the man was still gaping skyward, jamming the barrel of the weapon to Coquin's head in movie-desperado fashion.

"Tell your men to drop their guns!" Andy said, shouting over the helicopter roar. "You don't want a gunfight with these guys!"

Crayfish Joe gave Andy the sort of look he usually reserved for people who interrupted him during a meal.

"Tell them!" Andy ordered again. "These are feds! They'll wipe you out *tout de suite!*"

Actually, the government men didn't seem in much of a hurry to do anything. There weren't a lot of safe landing spots left to them in the clearing. One of the choppers began drifting back over the entrance road, looking to set down there. Another began to follow.

Coquin's men decided to seize the moment. One by one, they turned and began running for the surrounding dark—not caring that it was all swamp and bog and mangroves.

Crayfish Joe stepped away from the gun—only a few inches but enough to turn and face Andy, which he did contemptuously. There were certain qualities that marked the difference between mobster chieftains and burned-out fashion photographers. Joe knew precisely what they were.

He peered at the pistol barrel, then looked back into Andy's face, a superior smile twisting itself into the greasy folds of his face. Shaking his head as though with amusement—and perhaps a philosopher's appreciation of the irony of the situation—he waddled away after his men into the night, a hippopotamus attempting to play swamp fox. Andy imagined it would take the feds all of ten minutes to bring him back in, once they got their machines onto solid ground. But it was taking them such a long while to do that.

Finally, the last of the choppers settled into place. The men aboard each—some in quasi-military garb and a few in suits—converged together in a huddle for a quick quarterbacking, then spread out rapidly along both sides of the clearing.

Andy recognized the man in the lead. As soon as he'd seen the helicopters, he'd wondered if Agent Kelleher might be with them, though Andy couldn't understand how or why they'd been drawn to this place. If they'd been shadowing Fabio and Ramona, they were arriving far too late.

He was about to ask Kelleher about this, but before he could, the agent did something Andy hadn't expected at all. Walking right by Andy, he went up to Glory and took her in his arms.

Chapter
·29·

"You can't fly," Andy said. "You haven't had any sleep."

"I don't intend to. There's another pilot taking the Pilatus back to Key West. The rest of us get to ride."

It was now past dawn, and pink sunlight was creeping in sideways between the stacked clouds to the east. He and Glory were sitting on the embankment outside the terminal building of Lake Front Airport, where she had left Kelleher and his mob of agents to work things out with the state and local police. Andy was surprised he hadn't been called in to make some sort of statement, but Glory said that would come later, in the form of a federal court subpoena.

"Your fellow passengers will include our friendly neighborhood Agent Kelleher?"

"Yes. Of course."

"How long has he been tagging after us?"

"Since we got back to New Orleans. I called him from our hotel room. He and his colleagues were all set to snatch Fabio in Jackson Square, but we made a botch of it."

They were on a ledge, looking out over the still gray waters of Lake Pontchartrain. To their right, a long freight was rattling along the Great Southern Railroad tracks that hugged the New Orleans shore. To their left, past the end of the runway, they could see a few twinkling lights on the northern edge of the lake, barely visible in the mountainous dark that still lingered in that part of the sky.

The air was very calm, and cool. The water shrugged a few inches up and down the pilings of the impoundment before them but otherwise barely seemed to move.

"Glory, you told me you weren't a cop."

"I'm not a cop."

"Then what are you?"

"I'm a naturalized U.S. citizen by marriage in the employ of the United States government—but I work as a pilot. Just a pilot. Now let's not go into it again."

"That should be no problem. You're about to fly off with friendly Agent Kelleher."

She pulled up her bare legs and wrapped her arms around them, resting her chin on her knees. Her gray eyes narrowed as they fixed on what looked to be building into a glorious sunburst. The slanting light, turning yellow now, made her tan seem to glow.

"Jim and I had a bit of a thing once, when I first hired on— after my husband was gone. We're still close friends. But he's married. And that means everything it's supposed to as far as I'm concerned."

"Oh."

"And none of it has anything to do with us and the man-groves. Or us and anything."

"Okay."

A vague bit of breeze stirred from somewhere, fluttering some strands of her hair.

"I had this odd idea you might stay on," he said.

"What, here?"

"Yes."

"That is an odd idea."

"Fabulous town."

"You'd have me give up my lovely job and hang about with you in the French Quarter? Spend all my nights in scuzz joints like the Razzy Dazzy and my days keeping house while you're off shooting pictures of gruesome corpses and nude women? And all of them far more beautiful than I? No thank you, thank you very much."

"It wouldn't be like that."

"Andy, you already have someone keeping your house."

He picked up a small chip of concrete and threw it into the water. He lost sight of it but heard the plop.

She turned her head to face him, pressing her cheek to her knee. Her hair was all over her eyes. He could recall just such a photograph of Amelia Earhart, only in coveralls—no bare knees.

"It's goodbye, Andy," she said.

She'd said it so gently and warmly and plaintively, he almost thought she'd said, "I love you." But that was wishing, not listening.

She looked away again. "It won't work, Andy. It can't."

"You're absolutely sure?"

"We're not the kind of people to make it work."

He sighed. "I guess not."

"I'm sorry, Andy. I truly am." She stood up. "I've got to think about going."

"I've been thinking about your doing that all night."

"Well, there it is, isn't it?"

He rose as well.

"It looks fairly decent weather. Perhaps I'll do some of the flying after all."

"How soon do you leave?"

"The minute I get on the plane. Jim's just waiting on me. Gave me time to say goodbye. I imagine I've taken a lot longer than he thought."

She began walking.

"Nice guy," Andy said, moving to keep up with her, trying to imagine Glory and Kelleher ever having a "thing." Maybe the man was nutty about airplanes.

"Quite nice, actually," she said. "He's a bit peeved at the moment. He doesn't have much to show for all the time and money that was spent on this larkabout."

"What do you mean? A dozen New Orleans gangsters. A million or so in cash. Plus Fabio and Harvey Fitch dead. Who could ask for more?"

"I haven't told him about the money yet. Bloody forgot all about it, if you can believe that. I don't think there's quite a million here, but maybe it will cheer him up. He was hoping so to get his hands on Andao Machado and Ramona Fitch, too, and he really, really wanted those bank records."

"I wonder where Ramona is."

"Probably doing vile things to some truck driver in payment for a ride out of Louisiana. I expect she'll rejoin Andao presently. Unlike Fabio, I think he appreciates her mind."

"No sign of Crayfish Joe. That's a little strange. There's much too much of him to disappear."

"Perhaps he's in the bayou. He didn't strike me as much of a swimmer."

"What a feast for the fish and the alligators. The crayfish are probably cleaning up the leftovers. Revenge."

"You're being ghoulish."

"Sorry. That kind of night."

They were nearing the terminal building. She stopped and brought her canvas bag around to the front.

"This is all supposed to go into the United States Treasury," she said. "Perhaps they'll use it as down payment on a new federal office building named for some dead congressman, or maybe the Corps of Engineers can build some more jetties with it to keep the shore safe for beach houses. But we've been through a lot here, haven't we, you and I? There were accidents, expenses. Things got lost." She put two bound stacks of currency in his hand. "So here. I really insist, Andy. I want you to have it."

"I already have . . ."

"Have some more. They won't know."

"I can't do this. It's drug money. Machado drug money."

"It's just money, Andy. God only knows where it's been. It was bound for New York. Perhaps some would have ended up in those fancy restaurants you used to frequent."

She shoved the money into his pocket. "There. Should be about twenty thousand in that lot. Your car was burned up. Your camera. They owe you for that. Not another word. Just take it."

"My car wasn't worth twenty thousand dollars—more like twenty, period."

She patted his pocket. "You loved that car. Enough said."

There was a wire trash basket nearby—a plastic convenience-store bag near the top of its contents.

He turned back toward the lake. The cloud-framed sunrise

had reminded him of a painting, and now he realized what it was—a Childe Hassam seascape he'd seen with Beth Hampshire once in a museum in Boston when they'd been up there on a fashion shoot.

"May I kiss you?"

"Of course, Andy. Why would you ask?"

They stared into each other's eyes, then closed them as their lips came together. Even their knees touched. They swayed like that, then she pulled back a little, her cheek gently touching his, her hair teasing his brow.

"In an odd way, I didn't want to kiss you," he said, "because it means goodbye."

Glory kissed his cheek and hugged him tightly.

"Yes," she said, taking a deep breath. "Goodbye."

"Goodbye."

Andy took the small pistol out of his pocket and stepped back.

"What are you doing, Andy?"

"I . . . I want you to take this back. I don't need it anymore."

She accepted it. "Right."

Neither moved further.

"I want the rest of the money, Glory. The rest of the million or whatever."

Her eyes widened, then turned hard. "What's wrong with you?"

"Nothing. Absolutely nothing. It's not for me. I ran away from this kind of money when I left New York, and I'm still running from it. It's just that I don't want this money that we've dragged around all over hell to go for some federal office building or beach resort seawall. I want to do something good with it, something important—something maybe to atone."

"Like what?"

"I can't tell you. I . . ."

She was walking away. She stopped. They had reached the corner of the terminal building. The tail section of her Pilatus was visible just beyond.

"I'm crazy," she said.

He said nothing.

"You have nothing to carry it in," she said. "I need this bag."

"Wait." He hurried over to the trash basket and retrieved the plastic sack, shaking out the empty paper cup and sandwich wrapper it contained.

She hadn't moved an inch. There were many different emotions showing in her eyes. Some of them he could have done without.

"We can put it in this," he said.

She filled it quickly.

"Glory . . ."

He got one more look from her, utterly impassive, and that was all. Swinging around, she started toward the airplane.

The cab let him off at the curb outside the Garden District house. There was an old-model Jeep Cherokee in the driveway, so banged up, rusted and covered with caked mud and dust it was hard to tell its original color, although Andy guessed at blue. He glanced in the back and saw tangled fishing line, a bait bucket, and a soiled flyer advertising Randol's Seafood Restaurant et Salle de Danse. Doubtless one of Bleusette's relatives from the bayous had come to call.

But the house seemed empty—at least altogether quiet. Not even music.

He put the plastic bag full of money in the front closet behind a couple of broken tennis racquets that hadn't been moved in months. Zinnie was in the kitchen, working with string beans.

"You a long time gettin' back home, boy."

"But here I am."

"Miz Bleusette's upstairs. You best be talkin' to her right now, 'cause she's fixin' to be gone real soon. You got some phone calls, but I think them can maybe wait."

"'Fixin' to be gone'?"

"Gone, boy. Just like you been."

He found Bleusette in their bedroom. There were two open suitcases on the floor, two more on the bed, and a closed one standing by the door. Bleusette adored nice clothes. Since she had come into her money from the dead lady arsonist, she had acquired quite a few.

"What's this?" he asked.

"Those fucking feds will be wanting us to testify against those Crayfish Joe boys they arrested out there. That is not something a smart New Orleans girl should be wanting to do. I think I go away for a while."

"Where?"

"I don't know. I hear my mother is in St. Martin or Trinidad. Maybe I go there."

"You won't need all these clothes."

"*Bien sûr,* I will, Andy. It could be weeks before they do that trial."

"Bleusette, you seem to be packing every stitch you own."

She stopped, putting her hands on her hips and surveying the room.

"*Oui.* I am."

"Why?"

She turned around, glancing over everything, then sat back on the bed. She was barefoot and wearing another flower-print dress, very low cut.

"We are not going to be married," she said quietly, staring down at her neat little feet. "This is something we have both decide, *n'est-ce pas?*"

"I suppose."

"'Suppose'? *C'est évident.*"

"If you want, I can . . ."

"Look at me, Andy. There has never been no bullshit with us. It is always *tout droit, tout vrai.* Yes?"

"With a few minor exceptions."

"You mean those arrangements I make with Crayfish Joe? *C'est n'importe.* I'm talking about what really counts with us. We are always square with the big shit, right?"

"Right."

"So listen to me. I have never said to you, Andy, that I love you, and you have never said that to me. It's the truth. I don't even know what love is, maybe. What is love and what is fucking. Maybe it's just something in a *mauvaise* song, *une chanson mauvaise et triste,* something to make you blue. What I do know is that, you and me, Andy, we are not like that little man and woman on the wedding cake."

"You'd make a lovely bride."

"No joke, Andy. Look, I like you a lot, okay? *Très beaucoup. Très fort.* I have known you it seems like all my fucking life, and you are the nicest guy I ever know. But when we talk last summer—about getting married and me moving here with you in the Garden District . . . I was *très heureuse*. But it was arrangement, Andy. Only arrangement. *Seulement*. Not love. It was a way to put the life behind me for good, *compris*? Become *Madame* Derain. Live in the Garden District. Do you know what I am saying?"

He realized he had known it from the very beginning.

"I want you to have what you want, Bleusette."

"I don't want no bullshit marriage—no fine, big, fancy wedding in St. Louis Cathedral. I don't want any of that, not now. Not yet. *Vraiment*. So I'm gonna go. I still got that house on Burgundy Street. I'm going back."

"But you like this one better."

"*N'importe*."

"It is important. It makes you happy. So why go?"

"What are you saying to me, Andy?"

"I'm saying I think you should stay. This house suits you. It needs a fashionable lady as chatelaine. You are the most fashionable lady in New Orleans, *bien sûr*. More fashionable even than my mother. You belong here. My Auntie Claire dotes on you. Zinnie adores you. I don't know how I could face a morning without you sitting naked at the kitchen table drinking Pernod. So please. Make us both happy. Stay."

"You really sure about this, Andy?"

"Yes."

"But what about your airplane lady?"

"That's not in the cards. I just said goodbye."

"That's why you look so blue?"

"Yes."

"What if she come back? She might. Women do these things."

"She won't."

"She sure as shit is not the only other woman you know."

"Look. It's a very big house. You're family. That's that."

Bleusette just kept staring at the floor.

"It's settled, then," said Andy. "You stay."

"All right. It make no sense, but I stay."

He kissed the top of her head.

"That car in the driveway," she said. "That's for you, Andy. Gift from my family in the bayous. You save my life and Jean-

Robert's and you lose your Cadillac. It's only fair. You will always have friends in Houma."

He smiled. "Okay. *Je les remercie.*" He stood up. "Bleusette, just what kind of business is it you're going to go into?"

"No more restaurant, Andy. Too much work, too long hours, too risky. I want something more easy, more reliable. Something that will maybe give me time to live like a lady here, help Auntie Claire in the garden. Learn about roses."

"And what's that?"

"I'm going to open a strip joint."

He smiled. How long had it been since he'd done that.

"One more thing, Andy. You got a telephone call. From that Princess Astrid."

His jaw fell. "What?"

"Princess Astrid. She called. She wants to talk to you."

He searched Bleusette's dark eyes, wondering if she was playing some more fun Cajun bayou games. But he found nothing there but honesty—and perhaps a little irritation over the hardness of his stare.

"When did she call?"

"This morning. Just a little while ago. She's in New York. She said she been trying to reach you."

"You're sure? This morning? You're absolutely sure?"

"*Absolument. Bien sûr.* You think I bullshit you about something like that?"

He'd resigned himself to Astrid's being now forever dead, as dead as Beth Hampshire and the others, as dead as his own parents. Bleusette's telling him that Astrid had called sounded as bizarre to him as if she'd said that his father was waiting for him downstairs.

He'd put Astrid in a grave in his mind—burying with her as much as he could of his aching guilt over what had happened and his terrible imaginings of how she might have gone to her death. He did so knowing she'd eventually come back to him again, come crawling into his thoughts some sodden tormented night at the Razzy Dazzy, or in the dark sleeplessness of his bed, for nights to come, for the rest of his life. He'd remember her long blond hair as he'd glimpsed it through the windows of the Machados' yacht. He'd remember it as he would Beth's hair, billowing in the currents of the deep water, and Beth's staring face.

She'd called? From New York? Like, how was your trip?

"Did she say she'd call back?"

"She left a number. I put it somewhere."

"That's all right. I know it."

Astrid was in her Greenwich Village atelier but closeted with someone
her assistant said was, like, enormously important. Andy said
he'd wait, which prompted the woman finally to go and inform
the princess he was on the line. Astrid picked up quickly, but he
sensed she'd gone to a room where she could talk privately.

"Andy, Andy! You're all right? You're back home and safe?"

"I'm fine. Everyone's fine, except . . ."

"My poor girls. And Ernst Konig. Good God, Andy, I never
knew there could be people that evil in the world. Those men,
that damned Ramona. There can't be anyone on the streets of
New York as horrible as them."

"Most of them are dead now, for whatever it's worth. Including Fabio Machado."

"Really? It's true? He was alive when Harvey Fitch took me
off the boat."

"He's very dead."

"Did you do that?"

He paused. "No. But I was there to see it. I sort of hooked up
with some federal agents when I was looking for you. We all
ended up back in Louisiana, and there was a shoot-out down in
the bayous."

"My friend. Look what you did for me, once again. I want to
give you a great big kiss."

"I didn't . . ."

"I can always depend on you, Andy. You are my true friend. Is
Ramona dead?"

"Don't know. Probably not. Her husband Harvey is, but you
probably know that."

"I do! But I didn't find out till I got back here."

"Really?"

"Yes. I left Harvey at the condominium."

"How did you get back to New York?"

"I called a cab and caught the morning plane to Miami. Harvey wanted me to go. He was going to meet me in New York."

It was a simple matter of deciding whether Astrid or Ramona was telling the truth. That shouldn't have been a difficult choice.

"I'm fine now," she continued. "Everything's fine."

"Happy to hear."

"Andy, Harvey wasn't a bad man."

He was about to bring up the bank records that established dear, sweet Harvey as general partner to two of the most murderous scumbags in the hemisphere, but there was no point. The records had turned to wisps of smoke drifting into nothingness over the bayous.

"Harvey did something amazing," Astrid said. "I knew he was fond of me—well, really fond of me—but I didn't realize . . . Andy, Harvey made me his heir, his principal heir. There are some relatives, a sister or something, in New Jersey. But mostly it's me. He had his lawyers rewrite his will just before he came down to Grand Cayman. He disinherited Ramona completely. That horrible woman. Do you suppose she'll contest this?"

"I think she's a fugitive from justice, Princess. She was last time I saw her."

"Fugitive? Do they think she killed Harvey?"

He thought of the photograph he'd slipped into Harvey's pocket. What more could Inspector Whittles want?

"It's what I'd like to think," he said.

"She was responsible for what happened to the girls. That's what Harvey told me. Ramona and that Fabio. They came looking for me that night, but I wasn't there so they grabbed Konig and the girls. Then they came back for me the next night."

"Fun couple."

"Andy, do you know how much it is?"

"What?"

"The bequest. They called to tell me yesterday. I've been trying to reach you. One of Harvey's lawyers is here now, in my office. Andy, it's just unbelievable. It's something like a hundred million dollars at the least—I think a lot more, when all is said and done."

Andy could imagine Astrid's icy blue eyes, sparkling like northern waters in the noonday sun.

"I guess that's what they call serious money."

"Well, his sister does get some, and his mother. And there's a long list of charities—a lot of money set aside for a Harvey Fitch Wing or something at one of the art museums. And he did have some debts and there's taxes and something about some disputed land trusts, though Harvey's lawyer doesn't think it amounts to anything. Anyway, Andy, there it is. A hundred million dollars. It's just unbelievable! I've never had more than two hundred thousand dollars to my name."

"Well, Astrid, I'm really happy for you."

"For us, Andy. I want you to share in this."

"No thanks, Astrid. I have everything I need."

"Listen to me, Andy. I want you to have some of this inheritance. You went all the way down there to help me. You risked your life. It's only right. But I need your help. I don't know what to do about all this, how to handle it. I don't really trust Harvey's lawyers. I'm not sure I trust any lawyers. And I know I'm going to have all kinds of creepy men come on to me now. Not to speak of all the greedy swine in the fashion business. It's just going to be very, very hard coping with all this, and . . ."

Everything he once imagined was all he wanted—the fabled Astrid, extraordinary wealth, the freedom to wander the world in search of perfect pictures.

Maybe he was getting old.

"Can't do it, Astrid."

"It would just be for a year or so, until everything goes through probate and the investments are taken care of and—"

"Astrid, I'm not coming up there."

"You could go back to New Orleans for visits whenever you wanted. I'd go with you, sometimes. Go to some of those restaurants you've always talked about."

"I'll be happy to take you to Mr. B's and Brennan's anytime you want, Astrid, but I'm not coming to New York."

"I don't have anybody else, Andy. I mean, I don't trust anyone else. You've always helped me before, whenever I needed you. Always."

"A hundred million'll buy you all the help you need, Astrid. Trust, too. You can buy a lot of trust with a hundred million."

"Please, Andy."

"Can't. Promised someone I'd do something for her. Never go back on my word. You know that."

"Andy?" She spoke softly now.

"Yes?"

"Poor bears."

"No, love. Rich bears."

He gently hung up the phone.

Chapter

·30·

It was several weeks before Andy stopped listening for late-night knocks at his door and looking for following cars in the rearview mirror of the old Cherokee, which he happily decided to keep, though the lingering odor of old fish and vegetables proved intractable, and the vehicle creaked loudly making turns.

Glory, he gathered, had never told Kelleher about the money, or had lied to him about its true disposition. Otherwise, there were doubtless a fascinating array of charges Andy could be in jail on now, but he'd never heard a word about it, not in all the weeks that had passed.

The total had come to nine hundred twenty-seven thousand, eight hundred fifty-three dollars, and he'd done precisely what he'd wished with it. The money was now in someone else's hands. For good. He'd soon be able to forget all about it.

But not about Glory. She seemed a little stuck in his mind—as much as Astrid had been once. He'd heard nothing at all from her—not even a postcard.

Andao had been sighted, as had Ramona, a short time after the shoot-'em-up in the bayous—on a new, less tubby, and much faster motor yacht. Machado had pulled out of the Caymans and reportedly was working out of islands closer to the coast of South America.

Bleusette had remained in New Orleans. As it turned out, Crayfish Joe's surviving sons were so pleased with their unexpected inheritance and the new leadership responsibilities that went with it that they refrained completely from any churlishness toward those who'd been involved in the sudden change in their circumstance.

Martin Coquin, the elder of the two—sometimes called "Marty Gras" because of a girth that measured up to his father's—went out of his way to be amicable and reassuring to Bleusette, and to make certain she had everything she needed to open her exotic dance salon, including the swift approval of all her Bourbon Street competitors and assorted municipal licensing authorities.

As for the judicial inquiry into the unpleasantness out at her late Uncle Hercule's, there never was one. The men from Coquin's street crew who'd been arrested for their part in the affair all made bail and then vanished.

Crayfish Joe finally ceased to be vanished. His remains were found by a fisherman. There was little left but bones. He was identified by dental records and the gold cross found on his body.

Andy stayed in the Garden District house but moved his studio from the basement to a place in the French Quarter, renting a little four-room wooden-frame house on Dauphine Street, not far from the Razzy Dazzy.

He begun work again on his long-planned book of nudes, but it was going slowly. Though he'd lost his film of Glory posing by the bayou near Houma, the roll he'd shot of her naked in their hotel room had survived. He had several frames from it enlarged and framed and hung on his studio wall. They were perfect for the book, but he'd need shots of other women, and he found he couldn't work up much interest in pursuing those.

But his book of New Orleans street scenes was progressing surprisingly well. He came back with at least one good picture for it every day. To earn money, he got a couple of advertising jobs, plus a very grand and highly profitable society wedding. He supposed he should be happy. Bleusette was happy—as happy as Mrs. Boulanger next door was not.

One afternoon, unable to concentrate on work, he stopped in

as usual at the Razzy Dazzy, finding Long Tom working at a back table and Freddy Roybal behind the bar.

Freddy went immediately to the tape machine. Pat Metheny was well into the first cut of *Off Ramp* before Andy got his drink.

"We gonna hear that goddamn mournful music every time you come in here now?" Tom asked, leaning back in his chair.

The only other customer in the place was slumped over the bar, snoring, and raised no objection.

"We don't need to," said Andy. "Doesn't do any good."

"Sure it does," said Freddy. "When my Angélique got killed that time in Thibodaux, I listened to Nat King Cole's 'I Love You for Sentimental Reasons' for a whole fuckin' year."

Angélique, Freddy's favorite girlfriend, had been shot to death accidentally in a barroom fight Freddy had started.

"It's all right," Andy said. "Put on something else. A little Preservation Hall, maybe."

But Freddy let the tape play. Long Tom leaned back in his chair, stretched, yawned, then got to his feet and wandered back behind the bar.

"Just remembered," he said. "You got some mail last night."

Andy took a comfortable swallow of his whiskey, then turned to see what Tom brought him.

There wasn't much. A letter in a soiled envelope.

"Thanks. How come I get mail here?"

"This ain't exactly regular U.S. Postal Service delivery," Tom said, pouring himself some bourbon. "Friend of a friend brought it in. From out of the country."

The envelope had his name crudely printed on it, and the words "Razzy Dazz Cafe"—the misspelling and the odd penmanship indicating a correspondent perhaps not too comfortable in English.

Inside was a small folded note and a photograph.

The note was brief—a couple of lines—in what seemed to be Spanish. Andy handed it to Freddy.

"Can you translate this? My Spanish isn't that good."

Freddy studied it. "This ain't fuckin' Spanish, Andy. This Portuguese."

Andy stared at him. "Portuguese? Can you read it?"

"Enough. I think it says, 'We're even. Stay away from me.' Something like that."

Portuguese. Even. Even?

He snatched up the photograph, a Polaroid. He looked at it until he couldn't anymore. Then finished his drink.

"Is Greasy Griswold back to work?"

"That's what they say."

"Good."

"Andy," said Freddy. "I fuckin' forgot. Your Cousin Vincent is looking for you. Called a couple hours ago. Couldn't find you anywhere."

"I wasn't in the studio. I was over uptown, looking for a shot. I didn't get my street picture today."

"Your Cousin Vincent said he's found what you're looking for. It just came in."

Andy finished his drink and stood up. "Then I've got to go."

Chapter
·31·

The Smithsonian's National Museum of American Art wasn't the most imposing institution, sharing quarters as it did with the National Portrait Gallery in one of Washington's old neoclassical office buildings, formerly occupied by the U.S. Patent Office. Nothing so grand as the National Gallery of Art down the hill, or New York's Metropolitan. But that didn't matter. It would do splendidly. The museum was owned by the people of the United States. It would be around for a long time.

Andy had forgotten how miserable the weather could be in the nation's capital in late November. He'd worn his best clothes—white duck trousers, white bucks, dress shirt, striped tie, and old navy blazer—an ensemble hardly suitable for the windy cold even when augmented by a plastic raincoat he'd bought at the airport. He hurried shivering up the steps of the museum, pausing only briefly at the top to glance behind. There had been times in New Orleans he'd thought someone might be following him, but there'd been no sign of such here.

The warmth inside the antique marbled building gladdened him, as did the very nice people he found waiting for him in the museum's foyer.

All were women—the museum director, the curator, the public affairs person, even the staff photographer. They were chatty, making jokes about the clammy Washington climate as they led him to an elevator that took them all to the third floor.

The place chosen for the receipt of his gift was a large, well-lit gallery off to the right of the main corridor, its entrance blocked off just now with a velvet rope hanging across between two brass stanchions.

A guard pulled the rope aside for them. Inside the gallery, a woman introduced as one of the museum's restorers greeted him cheerily. The painting, covered with a soft cloth, was leaning against the wall beneath an empty space between two century-old American Impressionist works.

There wasn't much of a ceremony. The cloth was removed. The curator and the restorer lifted the painting and, with extraordinary care, set it in place on the wall. The museum director made a very short speech thanking him. Then they all posed for pictures.

He lingered afterwards. "I'd like to just look at it a while," he said. "If you don't mind."

"Not at all," said the director. "I'll have the guard leave the rope up so you won't be disturbed."

They thanked him again, shook hands again, then departed. The museum was not a crowded place, and when they had gone the quiet was absolute.

Vincent hadn't been able to find a Childe Hassam—at least not one available for the money Andy had had to spend. But he did locate a George Bellows. Bellows had also been one of her favorites. It was one of his early works—a Southern summer scene, a lawn gathering outside a great white-pillared house beneath enormous trees. The women were all in long white summer dresses and the men in white pants and dark jackets, a couple of them wearing straw boaters. The pretty woman in the foreground, leaning against one of the big leafy trees, even resembled her a little. Andy counted that as serendipity.

He stood there, gazing at the work, then closed his eyes, remembering her.

The velvet rope had failed. All but mesmerized, he suddenly heard someone moving very near him and opened his eyes. What he saw was the back of a raincoat and honey-colored hair, then tan legs and brown penny loafers.

The intruder bent down to look at the shiny new bronze plaque just below the painting.

"'Given anonymously,'" she read, "'in memory of Elizabeth R. Hampshire.'"

Glory stood up straight again, eyes moving back to the picture.

"I must say, I'm impressed, Andy. I hadn't figured you for anything so tasteful. You don't find much art like this in the Razzy Dazzy."

He waited until she turned to face him. She wore a white blouse and a pale blue sweater beneath her raincoat, along with a beige skirt. She was still so tan she might have stepped directly from Grand Cayman.

"Thank you."

She came a bit closer, but not much. "It's a bit expensive for a noble gesture," she said. "But I certainly can't find any fault with it. And this museum does belong to the American taxpayers."

"You were afraid I'd gone off to the Riviera?"

"Something like that. Couldn't be sure."

"How did you know I was here?"

"Let's just say that my colleague Mr. Kelleher has been very attentive to your comings and goings since I saw you last. He's been quite convinced you might lead him to Ramona Fitch—or that she might come searching for you to settle accounts. At all events, when he got wind of your coming to Washington on this interesting museum business, he passed that information on to me. And here I am."

"Why not before?"

She shrugged.

"It's been a couple of months, Glory."

"Didn't see the point."

"Why's that?"

"We've discussed all this, haven't we done? Very early one morning on Lake Pontchartrain?"

"Wouldn't work, you said."

"We said. The both of us."

"So why are you here now?"

"Mostly curiosity. How he spends a million dollars tells you a lot about a man. I wanted to make sure I hadn't made a mistake. Made enough of those in my life, haven't I?"

"Does Kelleher know about this?" said Andy, nodding toward the Bellows.

"The money was burned up in that fire in the bayous, wasn't it? I don't think Jim's been much concerned with your spending habits. He just wants his hands on Ramona and holds out the hope she might try to get back in the country and come after you. He was terribly crushed to discover that Fitch took her out of his will—that all that ill-gotten wealth slipped through the government's fingers."

"The government has enough ill-gotten wealth."

"Jim doesn't think so. He's got a court order for the confiscation of all of Ramona's remaining assets—if he can serve the paper on her."

"Won't do any good. She won't be coming back."

"How do you know that?"

"Let's go somewhere. Not here."

He took one more look at the painting, then turned away. If Beth's spirit was in the room—and he was strangely coming to believe in such things, after a fashion—he didn't want to trouble it any longer.

They took the elevator to the first floor, then followed a corridor past several paintings of American Indians to a small cafeteria, where he bought them both coffee. They took their cups to a small table overlooking the building's interior garden courtyard.

The leaves were gone and nothing was in blossom, but the sun was shouldering its way out of the overcast, dappling the tabletop with its light. Glory sipped, then held her steaming cup with both hands, resting her elbows on the table. She seemed more relaxed, and very, very pretty. Cheeks a little flushed beneath the tan. Rather like a schoolgirl's. Everything he had felt about her was with him now, very strong.

He had to get the Ramona business behind them.

Andy took the soiled envelope from his pocket and looked at

the Polaroid again himself. He supposed Glory had seen worse, though not by much.

"It's not a pretty picture," he said.

It was taken at night. Ramona's naked body and golden hair stood out brightly in the camera flash against an almost black background. She was lying on her belly on what looked to be a flagstone terrace, her surgically-adjusted and liposuctioned bottom to the fore. Her severed head was placed next to it, propped up against her right shoulder, the eyes open and staring but looking very dead.

"I suppose you could call it 'Ramona's last face lift.'" He handed it to her gingerly.

"Good God!"

"I think she and Andao had a falling out."

"How did you get this horrible thing?" Glory said, studying it but holding it somewhat away. After a moment, she set the photo aside, facedown. Her expression hadn't changed but her complexion was a little paler. "You didn't take that, did you?"

"No. Never seen anything like that before despite all my years in New Orleans. Andao sent it to me. His way of settling accounts, I guess. Maybe she just drove him nuts. Anyway, her case is closed. Give the picture to Mr. Kelleher."

"He won't be thrilled. For myself, I don't want to look at it ever again."

"Her case isn't completely closed, as I think upon it. Not quite yet. I made a very good copy of that thing and gave it to a photo dealer I know in New Orleans. Fellow named Griswold. Crayfish Joe had him put in the hospital for selling *Crime Scene* magazine some pictures I took of Joe's dead son. This dealer's not the most savory character in the business but I figure I owe him for it. If he can't sell the copy of Ramona to one of the news magazines, *Crime Scene* will pay him big for it."

"Appalling."

"She never once said no to having her picture in print."

Glory put the photo in her purse, then sipped her coffee slowly, then looked at him, a bit more happiness creeping into her expression. "What?"

"I'm just compulsively and obsessively staring at you. It's been a while."

Her eyes lowered. "As you said. A couple of months."

"I didn't think there'd be another time. I'm a little stunned."

"I didn't know how I'd feel myself. I suppose that's one of the reasons why I came. To find out."

"And how do you feel?"

She looked at him very directly. "To be perfectly honest, rather good, except for when I was looking at that picture."

"How long will you be staying?"

"In Washington?" She toyed with her spoon. "As it happens, as things stand, that's entirely up to me now. I've a bit of leave due. I can take it whenever I want."

"Why not come to New Orleans? It's in the sixties down there today. Clear skies."

"Too bloody chilly for me even at that. I've been thinking about someplace warmer. I was going to send you a postcard from there. Sort of a joke. Sign it, 'Poor bears.' "

"Not Grand Cayman and the lovely town of Hell?"

"No. The Bahamas. Paradise Island."

They didn't move or speak for a long moment.

"Would you have waited for me to respond to your invitation?" he asked.

"I probably would have done. What I really thought is that you'd be off somewhere with that Astrid—and all her good fortune."

"No chance."

"Someone else then."

"No one else."

"Two whole months."

"Do you still want to go?"

"Yes, I rather think I do. But I've thought of a better place. The Turks and Caicos Islands, not so many tourists. Not so many people, period. Quite lonely, actually, most of it. Unless you're with someone."

"Then . . ."

Glory's hand moved into his, and a smile came slowly to her lips. "Then perhaps you should come with me."

He smiled, holding her hand tightly. "Did that once. Hell to pay."

"Can't say there won't be again."

"And it won't work."

"Not at all."

"Can't last."

"Nothing does."

He stood up, still holding her hand. She hesitated, then did the same.

"So what are we doing?" she asked.

"We're leaving this place."

They started for the main museum corridor. Their arms went around each other, and they walked slowly.

"What's our destination?" she asked.

"A word comes to mind," he said.

"Not 'Paradise.'"

"No, a better one. 'Love.'"

"Love? And where do we find that?"

"I didn't know for the longest time, but now I do."

They were passing by a large painting hung in the museum's entrance foyer: the original of Abbott Thayer's *Angel*.

He abruptly turned and took her in his arms and kissed her, oblivious to the museumgoers around them. The sun was now quite bright outside. He imagined it shining down on the Turks and Caicos Islands, wherever those were.

"It's a long way to the airport," she said, finally.

"Maybe we can stop somewhere along the way."

"No mangroves."

"Not today."

She looked up at him. He wanted a picture of that, too.

"There are no happy endings, Andy. You learn that."

"Glory. This isn't the ending."

Acknowledgments

I should like to thank Ambassador Robin Renwick and Peter Bean of the British Embassy in Washington, the governor's office of the Cayman Islands, the very splendid crew of *The Spirit of Ppalu*, and Diana of Divers Supply in West Shore Center, Grand Cayman, for their help in adding to my knowledge for this book. I am also indebted to New Orleans and Washington newspaperman Chris Drew, to national aerobatic champion Patty Wagstaff, and to Kelly Cibulas of the Federal Bureau of Investigation. I am grateful to my wife, Pamela, and sons Eric and Colin, as only they can know.

About the Author

REX DANCER is a veteran newspaper reporter, columnist, and photographer who has lived, traveled, and worked in the American South for many years. The author of ten other novels, he currently resides in Virginia and West Virginia.